'A colourful story with a richly-drawn backdrop
of London in the grip of the plague.
A wonderful debut novel'
Carole Matthews

'Romantic, engaging and hugely satisfying.
This is one of those novels that make you feel
like you've travelled back in time'
Katie Fforde

'A vivid tale of love in a time of plague and prejudice'
Katherine Webb

'If you are looking for a cracking good story and to be
transported to another age, you really can't beat this'
Deborah Swift

'A thoroughly enjoyable read which will keep
you enthralled until the very last page'
Jean Fullerton

Charlotte Betts began her working life as a fashion designer in London. A career followed in interior design, property management and lettings. Always a bookworm, Charlotte discovered her passion for writing after her three children and two stepchildren had grown up.

Her debut novel, *The Apothecary's Daughter*, won the YouWriteOn Book of the Year Award in 2010 and the Joan Hessayon Award for New Writers. It was shortlisted for the Best Historical Read at the Festival of Romance in 2011 and won the coveted Romantic Novelists' Association's Historical Romantic Novel RoNA award in 2013. Her second novel, *The Painter's Apprentice*, was also shortlisted for Best Historical Read at the Festival of Romance in 2012 and the RoNA award in 2014. *The Spice Merchant's Wife* won the Festival of Romance's Best Historical Read award in 2013 and was shortlisted for the Romantic Novelists' Association's Historical Romantic Novel RoNA award in 2015.

Charlotte lives with her husband in a cottage in the woods on the Hampshire/Berkshire border.

Visit her website at www.charlottebetts.com and follow her on Twitter @CharlotteBetts1

Also by Charlotte Betts:

The Apothecary's Daughter
The Painter's Apprentice
The Spice Merchant's Wife
The Milliner's Daughter (e only)
The Chateau by the Lake
Christmas at Quill Court (e only)
The House in Quill Court

The Dressmaker's Secret

Charlotte Betts

piatkus

PIATKUS

First published in Great Britain in 2017 by Piatkus
This paperback edition published in 2017 by Piatkus

1 3 5 7 9 10 8 6 4 2

A CIP catalogue record for this book
is available from the British Library.

PB ISBN 978-0-349-41416-4

Typeset in Caslon by M Rules
Printed and bound by CPI Group (UK) Ltd, Croydon, CR0 4YY

Papers used by Piatkus are from well-managed forests
and other responsible sources.

Piatkus
An imprint of
Little, Brown Book Group
Carmelite House
50 Victoria Embankment
London EC4Y 0DZ

An Hachette UK Company
www.hachette.co.uk

www.littlebrown.co.uk

For Oliver

Acknowledgements

It is often said that it takes a whole village to raise a child and it's the same with publishing a book. I may have given birth to *The Dressmaker's Secret* but I was assisted by many others.

The story was conceived whilst on a writing retreat with Carol McGrath, Deborah Swift and Jenny Barden, all historical novelist friends. I was searching for inspiration when I read about the extraordinary life of Princess Caroline of Brunswick. Full of excitement, we discussed my initial ideas, over a glass of wine or two, in the simmering heat of a Greek summer.

My agent, Heather Holden-Brown, was endlessly supportive as I wrestled to refine the story into something resembling an outline fit to present to my publishers.

Research into Caroline's story and the Villa Vittoria in Pesaro continued over many months. Local architect Roberta Martufi, who had some years before been involved in renovation works at the villa, patiently answered my email enquiries.

My wonderful writing group, WordWatchers, made time to read the whole manuscript of *The Dressmaker's Secret* and offered constructive criticism. As always, their suggestions were sweetened with copious supplies of tea and cake.

Once the manuscript was delivered to Piatkus, my lovely editor, Dominic Wakeford, made helpful suggestions for revisions and then Lynn Curtis copy-edited the revised manuscript with a light and careful hand.

My very grateful thanks to all of the above and, not least, to my husband and family who listened with only slightly glazed eyes when I banged on about Caroline of Brunswick, yet again.

Chapter 1

January 1819

Pesaro, Italy

As Ma and I approached Pesaro for the first time I was still simmering with resentment and the atmosphere between us was as frosty as the January afternoon. For days now the coach had lurched along the rutted road up one side of the snow-dusted mountains, only to plunge perilously down the other while we clung, white-knuckled, to the travelling straps. Despite the trials of the journey we'd barely exchanged a word since Arezzo.

Ma huddled into the seat opposite me with a blanket wrapped around her diminutive form. I stared out of the window, mulling over our quarrel as the mountains gave way to undulating hills and farmland. Finally, we reached the sea at the town of Fano, where the other passengers alighted. Ma and I remained shrouded in uneasy silence as the coach continued along the coast road. How many times had the wind blown us into a strange town to make a new start? Perhaps this time, *please* this time, we'd stay for good. My mother and I had always drifted like thistledown on the breeze, landing for

1

a few precious months in a village or town until a panicky squall of her perpetual unease whisked us away again.

Despite my annoyance with Ma for insisting we move on yet again, my spirits lifted as I studied the coastline. A bracing wind buffeted the coach as we bowled along. I had never lived near the sea before and a prickle of unexpected excitement made me fidget. White horses danced along the tips of the waves rolling in from the sea and I itched to run down to the water's edge and feel the salty spray on my face. Dragging down the window, I leaned out.

'Emilia, it's too cold!' protested Ma.

An icy gust of wind snatched my breath away and I laughed and clutched at my hat as my hair whipped across my cheeks.

A warning shout, almost drowned by the pounding of the sea, made me glance at the road behind. Ears back and necks out-stretched, two piebald ponies galloped towards us at breakneck speed. Behind the runaways was a high-perch phaeton, careering from side to side while its passengers shrieked in terror. Within seconds the ponies had bolted past and the little carriage crashed against our coach, scraping along one side with an ear-splitting screech. As the impact threw me backwards I caught a glimpse of the driver, his features set in a rictus of fear as he struggled to bring the ponies under control.

Ma screamed as we veered off the road and, with a bone-shaking crash, thumped into a tree. I was thrown violently to the floor and pain exploded in my shoulder. Outside, there was a yell and a clatter. A horse whinnied in terror. Then there was silence except for the creak of leather as our swaying coach settled.

I exhaled slowly.

Ma, her round face bleached with shock, looked at me mutely with a question in her grey eyes.

Rubbing my shoulder, I pulled myself to my feet and opened the door. My French and Italian were fluent since we'd spent my lifetime travelling but Ma still had a noticeable English accent. She always

2

preferred me to communicate with others since she was frightened of drawing unwanted attention.

Our coachman was already calming his horses as they tossed their manes in fright.

I ran ahead to where the phaeton lay upside-down with its wheels still spinning. The piebald ponies lay tangled in the traces, pawing the grass, eyes rolling and flanks heaving.

The driver, a little younger than myself, lay sprawled on the ground fingering a trail of blood that trickled from beneath his sandy hair.

'Are you all right?' I called.

He nodded. 'Idiot ponies!' His eyes were pale blue and since his Italian was as heavily accented as Ma's, I surmised he was English.

I caught sight of what appeared to be a bundle of clothing tossed on the ground but then it moved. I hurried to investigate and discovered it was a little girl. Black ringlets lay across her face and I smoothed them away to reveal a lump the size of a pigeon's egg on her forehead. Her eyelashes fluttered as I gathered her up in my arms.

A faint cry came from behind the phaeton and then a foot encased in a scarlet boot waved in the air.

I sat the little girl on the ground and ran to help.

A stout middle-aged lady lay on her back, her skirts rucked up above her stockings to expose plump thighs. 'Victorine! Willy!' she called. She had a guttural accent, German perhaps.

I helped her into a sitting position and pulled down her skirts to restore her modesty. She appeared to be unharmed, though her outrageously high-crowned hat, adorned with enormous ostrich plumes, had slipped sideways over her eyes. Disconcertingly, the black wig she wore under the hat had slipped, too.

'Where is my son Willy?' she asked. Her lips were painted a garish vermilion, her eyebrows blackened and cheeks heavily rouged.

I brushed a clump of mud off her shoulder. 'The driver? He has a cut to the head but is otherwise unhurt.'

She looked wildly around. 'And Victorine ... Is she safe? Where is my little treasure?'

'Don't worry, I have her.' I returned to the child and lifted her up.

The woman held out plump, beringed hands. 'Come to Mamma, my darling!'

Surprised, I placed the whimpering child in her arms. No amount of white lead or rouge could make her look like the girl's mother rather than her grandmother.

Victorine howled, burying her head in the woman's pillowy bosom.

Our coachman ran his hands over the piebald ponies' fetlocks and then released them from their traces. 'You won't be driving that rig home,' he said to Willy. 'The wheel is buckled.'

The young man stuck out his bottom lip and kicked at the offending wheel. 'Useless thing!'

'Help me up!' called the woman.

I took the wailing child while Willy pulled his mother to her feet. She was short, even smaller than Ma, but rotund, with a bosom that formed a pronounced shelf under an embarrassment of chins.

Handing the reins to Willy, the coachman rocked the phaeton and heaved it the right way up. It was a most extraordinary vehicle, shaped like a conch shell, heavily gilded and decorated with mother-of-pearl. The inside was padded with blue velvet and embellished with silver fringing.

We stood watching in a shivering huddle, while Willy and the coachman dragged it back onto the road.

Victorine clung to me, hot tears soaking my shoulder as I attempted to soothe her. 'Would you all like to come in the coach with us to Pesaro?' I said over the child's noisy sobs. 'I expect you'll find a wheelwright there to repair the phaeton.'

'Someone will have to pay for the damage to my rig, too,' said the coachman, looking pointedly at Willy. 'The front's all stoved in and the paintwork's ruined. I shouldn't wonder if it's off the road for days.'

The woman waved her hand. 'It shall all be taken care of. Take us to Villa Vittoria and you will be reimbursed for your trouble.'

'I'll tie your horses to mine and they can trot along beside us.'

We trooped back to the coach and climbed inside. 'I am Emilia Barton,' I introduced myself, 'and this is my mother, Sarah. We're going to settle in Pesaro.'

'Come to dinner tomorrow,' said the woman, rocking the coach as she plumped her not inconsiderable weight down onto the seat beside Ma. 'I wish to make amends for inconveniencing you.'

Ma glanced at me in alarm but I refused to meet her gaze. I knew she wouldn't want to go; she preferred us to keep ourselves to ourselves. 'We'd like that,' I said.

'Villa Vittoria is at the foot of Monte San Bartolo above the town. Anyone will give you directions.'

I'd have a battle with Ma but I was determined to grasp this opportunity of making acquaintances in the town that was to become our new home. Victorine curled up on my lap; her sobs had subsided into the occasional hiccough by the time the coach rolled away. Willy sat beside me staring sulkily at his feet.

I looked out of the window, eager for my first glimpse of Pesaro. We passed a cluster of terracotta-tiled houses amongst vineyards and olive groves, and it wasn't long before we drove through the gateway of the walled town, clattered across a colonnaded piazza with a granite fountain set in its centre and then passed along a narrow street before turning into the courtyard of an inn. I sat Victorine beside her mother and Ma and I descended from the coach.

The woman leaned out of the window, her hat and wig still askew. 'Don't forget! Villa Vittoria tomorrow.'

Victorine waved at us as the coach trundled back out of the courtyard.

Ma glanced up at me, a muscle flickering at the corner of one eye, and a wave of pity washed over me for her constant state of anxiety. We had always been so very different, despite being travelling companions and so dependent upon each other.

The aroma of fried onions drifted from the inn and the exhaustion, unhappiness and frustration I'd felt over the previous days suddenly melted away. We had arrived and this was to be our new beginning.

I held out my hand to her. 'Shall we go in, Ma?' I said.

The next day we braved the bitter north wind to walk up the steep hill to Villa Vittoria. Vineyards, olive groves and mature oaks lined the country road. Our host at the inn had told us to look out for the other elegant villas, the *casini di delizia*, which had been built by the wealthy on the Colle San Bartolo in the seventeenth century. In those days the Della Rovere family had held a flourishing court in Pesaro.

Ma had put on her best dress of bronze wool, but her shoulders drooped and worry creased her brow. 'We should be out finding work,' she said, 'not paying social calls.'

As itinerant dressmakers we lived from hand to mouth and were permanently concerned about where we'd next find gainful employment.

'We'd be in a better financial position if you hadn't made us spend most of what we earned from the Conti bride's wedding dress on the coach fare from Florence,' I said. 'Still, the lady we helped after the carriage accident may be persuaded to give us introductions.'

'Perhaps. But ...' Ma caught my sleeve. 'Don't walk so fast, Emilia!'

'But what?'

Frowning, she said, 'There was something odd about the lady in the phaeton, wasn't there? Her rings indicated she has a wealthy husband and her velvet pelisse was of excellent quality. But then there was that peculiar hat and those scarlet boots . . . Not at all suitable for a lady of her age.' Ma pursed her lips. 'And she wears paint.'

'Many women wear paint.'

'But it's sorely out of fashion now and women of consequence and breeding don't wear it applied in such a haphazard way. I can't think how her maid allowed her to go out looking like that.'

Ma, always discreetly dressed, never resorted to even a dusting of rice flour on her nose. She frequently said it was important to impress on our clients that we had impeccable taste. Once upon a time, before I was born, she'd been personal maid to a lady of the aristocracy and had learned how to conduct herself in a genteel fashion. Occasionally, she spoke wistfully of the natural elegance of her kind mistress and the grand houses they'd lived in.

Ma glanced up at the winter sky. 'We must leave in good time. It would be very disagreeable to have to find our way down this hill after dark.'

The wind was bitingly cold and I was relieved when we came to the avenue of cypress trees, which the innkeeper had informed us led to Villa Vittoria. We walked briskly through an orchard until we arrived at a substantial stone house whose new roof was embellished with a large cupola. The grounds were littered with piles of sand and stacks of timber, and workmen climbed the scaffolding heaving blocks of stone on their shoulders. A colonnaded gallery to one side of the building was in the process of being infilled, while a matching wing was being added to the other.

A pair of soldiers stood either side of the front door, dressed in the gaudily striped uniform of the Papal Guard complete with helmets and halberds. Since Napoleon's defeat, the Congress of Vienna had returned the Marche to Papal rule but I couldn't imagine why soldiers were on watch at Villa Vittoria. Our steps faltered but, since we were not challenged, I lifted the iron doorknocker and let it fall.

Two great dogs loped towards us, barking loud enough to wake the dead. Ma and I froze to the spot.

A man hurried after them. 'Titus! Bruna! Come here, you brutes!'

'We're here to visit your mistress,' I said, once he had the dogs under control.

A maid opened the door, took our pelisses and indicated we were to follow her. I heard the clatter of pans and of women's voices raised in argument from behind one of the doors leading off the hall. In the air hung the mouth-watering scents of fried garlic and baking bread.

A child's high-pitched laughter rang out as the maid opened the door to the *salone* and announced us. 'Ma'am, Signora and Signorina Barton.'

Ma and I paused on the threshold. The woman we'd rescued from the phaeton was on her hands and knees on the floor, skirts tucked up, pretending to be a horse. Victorine sat on her back, shrieking with delight as her mount bucked and whinnied. A bruise stained the little girl's forehead but otherwise she seemed none the worse for her tumble of yesterday.

Ma glanced at me, clearly shocked by such unladylike behaviour.

'Come in, come in!' Victorine's mother rolled over so that the little girl slid off her back and dropped onto the floor in a fit of giggles.

We stepped into the *salone*, a generously proportioned room with a high, beamed ceiling and arched windows. It was richly decorated in the Turkish style. A log fire blazed in the great stone fireplace and portraits in gilt frames adorned the walls. Our hostess could clearly afford to live in comfort.

'I hope you have recovered from the unfortunate accident, Signora?' I said.

She shrugged, her fat little legs encased in sagging silk stockings stretched out on the floor in front of her. 'It was only a tumble, though Willy was very naughty to give us such a fright. I had to scold him severely.' She held out her hands. 'Pull me up! We've been playing horses for the last half-hour,' she said, 'and I'm quite done in.'

8

'I'm not surprised,' I answered, grasping her hands. Victorine giggled and came to add her efforts to mine as I heaved her mother to her feet.

She sat down heavily on an overstuffed chair and waved us towards a sofa laden with tasselled pillows. There was a spider's web in her hair and her skirt was smudged with dust. 'Angelica, my dear, come and meet my saviours, Signora and Signorina Barton.'

A small cough came from behind me and I saw a dark-haired lady sitting in the corner of the room.

'This is the Countess Oldi, my lady-in-waiting,' said our hostess.

Ma glanced at me, her eyes wide.

Countess Oldi, a handsome woman of about thirty, came forward as we made our curtseys. 'Do you have family and friends in Pesaro?' she asked.

'None at all.' We had no friends or family anywhere. Just for a moment I pictured my friend Giulia's happy smile and anger with Ma for making us move on yet again rose up like bile.

'Come to Mamma,' our hostess said, pulling Victorine onto her lap. 'I have been here only two years but the climate is good and the scenery delightful. In the summer I bathe in the sea ... so good for the health.' She leaned forward and said in a theatrical whisper, 'And it is very cheap to live in Pesaro.'

The room was overheated and, as my fingers began to thaw, I wondered how to broach the subject of introductions. I glanced at Ma, who sat with her eyes lowered and hands folded. Clearly, she wasn't going to assist me so I took a deep breath, driven on by our urgent need. 'My mother and I are both talented dressmakers,' I said. This was no time for false modesty since we might never again find a wealthy lady so clearly under an obligation to us. 'We've recently completed an extensive trousseau for Signorina Lucrezia Conti in Florence. She's marrying the Duke of Mantova's brother and only the most skilled work was acceptable. We have references and will be happy to show these to any interested parties. Perhaps some of your friends ...'

The Signora clapped her hands together and her face lit up like a child's. 'I was forced to dismiss my lady's maid a while ago and my wardrobe is sadly out of order. I have a fancy for a new ballgown. Emerald, perhaps, in the Russian style with gold lacing. You might make it for me?'

Ma, her expression a model of controlled restraint at the very thought of such a garment, said, 'We'll call on you at your convenience with our pattern books.'

I let out my breath, relieved that I'd succeeded in my mission. I realised then I didn't know our hostess's name. Our unconventional reception had distracted me and it was awkward to ask her now.

Victorine began to fidget, winding her fingers through her mother's hair and pressing kisses on her cheeks to gain her full attention.

Ma whispered to me, 'You see, I knew she couldn't have a lady's maid to dress her properly.'

'I'm hungry!' said Victorine. 'When is Papà coming home?'

'Soon, my treasure. Why don't you go to the kitchen and wheedle a piece of bread?'

The little girl slid off the sofa and skipped from the room.

The savoury aroma of roasting meat wafted in from the kitchen. I was hungry, too, and wondered when we might eat. I didn't have long to wait.

The front door slammed and there was the sound of hearty male laughter and footsteps clattering across the hall.

'Ah, the Baron has returned from his hunting!' Our nameless hostess smoothed the wiry curls bunched over her ears and turned expectantly to the door.

It burst open and two men entered. The taller of the pair, aged about thirty-five with thick black hair and an extravagantly curled moustache, came to lift her hand to his full lips.

The pungent scent of horseflesh rising from the men's mud-splashed clothing made Ma's nose wrinkle.

Victorine ran back into the room and clasped the Baron around his knees. 'I was waiting for you, Papà!'

The Baron bent to kiss her. 'And who have we here?' He turned to look at Ma and me. At well over six feet tall, his splendid physique and confident presence seemed to fill the room.

'This is Signora and Signorina Barton,' said Countess Oldi. She turned to us. 'My brothers, Baron Bartolomeo Pergami and Luigi Pergami.'

'Ah, yes!' said the Baron. 'The two Good Samaritans. I believe we owe you our gratitude and apologies after Willy drove you off the road?'

'Not at all,' I mumbled, overawed to find him looming over us. I couldn't help thinking that he was the most unlikely husband for the little dumpling of a woman we had helped. He must have been at least fifteen years younger.

'Let's eat!' he said.

We trooped into the dining room where we found Willy, an elderly woman dressed in black, and a soberly dressed young man with a mop of unruly dark curls all awaiting our arrival. No one introduced us and Willy ignored us.

Menservants in gold waistcoats under embroidered black coats lined with scarlet silk pulled out our chairs. A variety of soups, pies, roasted game birds, fricassées and puddings were laid before us.

Covertly, I eyed the young man who sat beside me. A little older than I, he had an aquiline nose that would have graced a Roman soldier. Although not conventionally handsome, it was the hint of suppressed laughter in his eyes and his wide smile that caught my attention.

'I am Alessandro Fiorelli,' he said, 'Victorine's tutor.' His voice was warm and mellow.

For two heartbeats I gazed into his amber eyes. 'Emilia Barton,' I said, heat suffusing my cheeks.

The Baron and his brother began to relate the tale of their morning's hunting, verbally sparring with each other, and their laughter

11

reverberated around the room. The old woman silently watched them as she chewed her dinner. Willy drank a great deal of wine.

'Signorina Barton, Victorine told me how you saved her,' said Signor Fiorelli. 'Where do you come from?' he asked. 'Your mother is English, I believe?'

'Where do I come from?' I said. 'Everywhere. And nowhere.' I couldn't begin to remember, never mind name, all the places where we'd lived since we rarely stayed anywhere for more than a few months. 'We're both English,' I said, 'though I've never been to England.'

He looked at me with a puzzled expression on his face but must have sensed I didn't care to discuss the matter for he changed the subject.

I drank sparingly of the thin red wine, anxious that I might say something foolish under its influence. I watched Signor Fiorelli's well-shaped mouth as he spoke and admired his dark hair and smooth olive skin. It was so very different from my pallid English complexion and strawberry-blonde tresses.

Time seemed to have no meaning while I was talking to Signor Fiorelli and when Ma attempted to catch my attention, I'm ashamed to say I ignored her.

Once we'd finished our dinner I glanced out of the window at the darkening sky. 'We must leave at once, before it's too dark to see our way back,' I said, alarmed.

Ma bit her lip with anxiety.

'Don't worry,' said Signor Fiorelli. He smiled at our hostess. 'With your permission, Ma'am, I shall escort these ladies back to the inn.'

A short while later we were outside in the cold. We walked quickly and when Ma stumbled in her haste to match our longer strides, Signor Fiorelli took her arm.

'I hope we're not taking you out of your way?' I said.

'Not at all. We pass my family house on the edge of the town.'

'Since we are strangers,' I said, 'I wonder if you know of anyone here who has a cottage available to rent?'

'I shall ask my mother,' he said. 'She always knows what is going on in the town.'

Signor Fiorelli pointed out his home as we passed by, a sizeable house with a neat garden.

Soon we arrived at the inn. 'I shall call on you in a few days,' he said, 'if I have any news.'

'There's one other thing,' I said. 'I'm embarrassed to admit this but I don't know the name of your employer. The maid didn't introduce us and then it was too late to ask.'

Signor Fiorelli laughed. 'I expect the maid assumed you knew of the Princess.'

'Princess?' Ma said.

'Indeed,' said Signor Fiorelli. 'Your hostess is Her Royal Highness, the Princess of Wales, daughter-in-law of your English King.'

Ma clutched his wrist. 'Not Princess Caroline of Brunswick?'

'The very same!'

'*Well*,' said Ma, 'that explains a very great deal!'

Chapter 2

The following day we took our dinner in the restaurant in the Piazza del Popolo.

'My hands are frozen,' Ma complained as we settled ourselves at a table by the fire. I looked longingly at the next table where two men were enjoying roast veal. As usual, Ma and I ordered *ribollita*, bean soup, the least expensive item on the menu. I wondered how long it would be before we found ourselves a commission to replenish our dwindling resources.

'Tell me about the Princess of Wales,' I said as we waited for our soup. 'Why is she in Pesaro? I know little of what happens in England.'

Ma sighed. 'I haven't been home for so very long.'

How curious that although she rarely mentioned England, she still called it 'home'.

'It's a strange story,' she continued. 'The Prince Regent is often called "the First Gentleman of England", although, if you ask me, he's anything but!' She leaned towards me and spoke in an undertone. 'Still, having met his wife, perhaps that's easier to understand. Surprisingly, Princess Caroline was popular with the people.'

'What is easier to understand?'

Ma raised her eyebrows. 'Does she behave like a princess?'

I laughed. 'Not at all. She's …' I was lost for words. 'Unconventional,' I said at last.

'Quite. She has no sense of her proper position in life and is always happy to mix with the common people, despite being the Prince of Wales's cousin.'

'I thought she might be German.'

'It was a political marriage. She was past the first bloom of youth when she arrived in England and only met the Prince three days before they were married.'

'I shouldn't have cared for that!'

'As it turned out, neither did he. The gossip at the time was that when he first greeted her, he reeled back and called for brandy.'

I frowned. 'Why?'

'Apparently she was not fastidious about her person,' was my mother's prim response. 'Anyway,' she continued, with a gleam in her eyes, 'he drank for the whole three days before the wedding, had to be held up during the ceremony and then collapsed, dead drunk, into the grate on his wedding night.'

I tried not to laugh at the picture of events she presented. 'Hardly the behaviour of a gentleman! But why is the Princess in Pesaro?'

'The couple wrangled for years. They had a daughter, Princess Charlotte, nine months after the wedding.'

I smiled inwardly. The Prince of Wales wasn't totally incapable on his wedding night then.

'Within months they were living apart,' said Ma. 'The Princess of Wales behaved disgracefully, flirting with all and sundry. The Prince Regent wanted to divorce her and investigated her for alleged infidelity, despite certain …' Ma glanced at me from under her eyelashes '… irregularities in his own private life. Nothing was ever proved against her but she left the country. I didn't know she'd settled here.'

Our *ribollita* arrived and I ate mine slowly. If Princess Caroline was married to the Prince of Wales, what was Baron Bartolomeo Pergami to her, if not her husband? He was Victorine's father and the Princess was her mother so the child must have been born out of wedlock. And then there was the Princess's son ...

I put down my spoon. 'So, Willy is the future King of England?'

Ma spluttered into her soup. 'Oh dear me, no! That sullen boy isn't her son at all. The Princess adopted him when he was a baby. As for Victorine ... ' She broke off, her cheeks blazing. 'Oh dear, it's all most irregular. And now this woman of highly questionable morals is our best chance of immediate employment.'

'Ma,' I said, 'do you never want to go home to England?' She only ever spoke of the past reluctantly and if I pressed her.

She stared at her soup plate, suddenly very still. 'I can't,' she said, after a brief pause.

'Why not?'

'It holds nothing but unhappy memories for me.'

'But we must have family there ... '

'No!' She took a steadying breath. 'I grew up in an orphanage.'

'I thought you said your family lived in Essex?'

Her cheeks turned scarlet. 'Before I was orphaned.'

'What about my father's family?'

'I never met them. There was a quarrel and if they're anything like him, we're better off without them.'

I loved Italy and had no desire to leave. It was only that, sometimes, I felt there was a part of me I couldn't quite make out. My recollections of my father were vague since he'd abandoned us sixteen years ago when I was five. If I closed my eyes I could still hear echoes of Ma's cries when he hit her. I remembered the sour smell of his breath, acrid with tobacco and red wine. I used to hide on the floor between my bed and the wall but sometimes he'd drag me out by my hair and shout at me, his face scarlet with rage. I shuddered. It did no good to think about those terrible times. I did wonder,

16

though, if the lack of closeness between Ma and myself was because she saw his likeness in me. I certainly didn't look like her so I suspected I must take after him.

Once we'd finished our *ribollita* we whiled away an hour visiting the cathedral, admired the exterior of the grand Ducal Palace and the red granite fountain in the cobbled piazza, and then there was still enough daylight for a wind-blown stroll down by the sea. It was dark when we returned to the inn and a serving maid handed Ma a note as we came in.

'It's from Signor Fiorelli,' she said. 'There's a cottage he'll take us to see at ten o'clock tomorrow morning.'

I held out my hands to the fire so she wouldn't see the spark of pleasure in my eyes. She didn't like me to have friends, but I wanted to know Signor Fiorelli better and was determined Ma wouldn't prevent it.

I dressed with care in my violet wool walking dress with the embroidered collar. The sun shone and I was full of anticipation at the thought of seeing Signor Fiorelli again. After smoothing my curls, I put on my bonnet, pinched colour into my cheeks and went down to the public room.

Ma waited for me there, her fingers plucking anxiously at her skirt. 'There you are, Emilia! I've been having second thoughts about staying in Pesaro,' she began.

My heart descended into my calfskin boots. Not again! 'Ma . . .'

'We cannot work for the Princess of Wales.' She spoke breathlessly, the words tumbling out of her.

'We need the money!'

'Listen to me, Emilia.' She gripped my hands. 'Think what it might do to our reputation if we become involved with that unsuitable household. No lady of quality would wish to use our services then.'

'The Princess is a member of the Royal Family. How could anyone find fault with that?' I sighed, exasperated.

Ma lowered her gaze. 'It may be indelicate to mention it but she and the Baron have a daughter and the Princess is married to someone else. How can we countenance such flagrant behaviour without being considered immoral ourselves? Besides, it's not just that.'

'What then?'

She glanced over her shoulder at the deserted room. 'We may have been followed here from Florence.'

'Ma, please don't make us move on again! You *promised* we'd settle this time.'

'But we had to make such a fuss to secure ourselves places on the first coach to leave ... someone may remember us. And your red hair is so noticeable. If your father asks after us, he'll find out where we went. We must move on, more discreetly this time.'

'No! Why must you *always* do this, Ma?' I could hardly breathe for the fury that gripped me. 'I'm tired of roaming like a gypsy and I'm sick of being poor because we constantly spend our savings on travelling. And all because you have some misguided notion that my father wants to harm us.'

'He does, I'm sure of it!'

'He left us *sixteen* years ago, Ma! He can't hurt you anymore and your fears are utterly nonsensical.'

'You know we had to leave Florence because a man had been asking about us.'

'It was probably an enquiry for our dressmaking services.'

Her lips folded together in a stubborn line. 'I'm sure it was your father.'

I paced across the room. 'What possible reason could he have for wanting to harm us, after all this time?'

She opened her mouth to speak and then closed it again.

'You didn't let me say goodbye to Giulia in Florence.' Resentment coloured my voice. 'She was the best friend I've ever had and you insisted we left overnight without even giving me the chance to explain to her. I'd promised to make her wedding dress.' I fought

18

back sudden tears. 'She'll be broken-hearted and think I didn't care about her.'

The door creaked open and I wiped my eyes as Signor Fiorelli entered.

'Good morning, ladies!' He came to greet us with outstretched hands and a wide smile on his handsome face. 'We have a cottage to see.' His voice faltered as he saw my tears and Ma's flushed cheeks.

'It's kind of you to arrange it,' I said, forcing a smile. Ma opened her mouth to protest and quickly I said, 'Shall we go?' I allowed Signor Fiorelli to escort me from the room, hoping Ma wouldn't balk.

A moment later her footsteps pattered after us and I let out a sigh of relief.

We crossed the piazza and reached the point where the River Foglia flowed into the Adriatic. I listened intently while Signor Fiorelli pointed out places of interest and all the while I prayed Ma wouldn't be difficult. Her groundless fears always came to nothing and, this time especially, I wanted to stay.

After a while we came to the harbour, bustling with boats and stalls selling mackerel and sardines. Fishermen called out to each other as they unloaded their catches and the air was full of the bracing scent of the sea.

'It's here,' said Signor Fiorelli, pointing to a higgledy-piggledy row of houses beside the harbour, all colour-washed in different shades of terracotta, ochre and cream. I was delighted when he stopped outside a primrose yellow cottage with a tiled roof.

'It belongs to my cousin's great-aunt, Prozia Polidori,' he said. 'She's too old now to manage on her own and she's gone to live with her daughter. The family want to keep the cottage and its furniture so are happy for it to be rented.'

The front door led into a sunny parlour furnished with a bookcase and rocking chairs to either side of the fireplace. A door opened into a dining room with an old-fashioned kitchen behind, leading to a walled yard with a pump and a privy. Up the winding staircase from the dining room were two bedrooms, not large but perfectly adequate.

'It's perfect!' I said as we descended into the dining room again. 'And this table is large enough to use for our sewing. The light in the parlour is excellent, isn't it, Ma?' I held my breath.

She looked hesitant. 'Is it available on a short lease?' she asked. 'If we don't find work here we shall have to move on.'

'I'm sure Prozia Polidori will find that acceptable,' said Signor Fiorelli. 'She lived in this house from the day she was married and frets about it remaining empty.'

'Then, if the rent is not too high ...' I said.

Signor Fiorelli mentioned a sum that seemed perfectly reasonable.

Impulsively, I hugged Ma. 'We'll take it!' My spirits soared as Signor Fiorelli shook my hand.

He beamed at me. 'I knew, if anyone could help, it would be my *mamma*.'

'When can we move in?'

'As soon as you like,' he said.

My new bedroom overlooked the harbour. I stood by the window looking out at the forest of masts and watching the fishermen mending their nets. Seagulls wheeled overhead. Humming, I opened one of my travelling bags. It never took long to unpack since we always travelled light.

Peggy, the calico rag doll I'd carried everywhere with me for as long as I could remember, smiled up at me. Her woollen hair, tied into two pigtails, was far redder than mine and she wore a spotted muslin dress, replaced from time to time according to what leftover scraps remained after completing a commission. Of course, I was far too old for dolls, but Peggy had always been there to comfort me when I was lonely and was the eternally faithful companion of my childhood. I lifted her out of the bag, kissed her freckled nose and set her on the pillow.

The remainder of my possessions was soon stowed away. I carried my sewing box downstairs and found Ma unsuccessfully trying to light the fire in the kitchen.

'The paper's damp,' she said. There was a smudge of soot on her cheek.

I kneeled in front of the grate, rearranged the kindling and blew on it until the paper caught.

'It's burning well now,' I said a while later as I held out my palms to the dancing flames. 'I'll light the fire in the parlour, too, and then everything will be comfortable.'

'I'll boil some water and start the cleaning.'

I didn't say that everything looked perfectly clean already; it would have been pointless. Ma always scrubbed everything from top to bottom when we moved into a new place.

'I'll buy something for supper.' I buttoned my pelisse and collected the shopping basket.

'Tuck your hair into your bonnet,' said Ma. 'Anyone looking for a redheaded girl will soon be on our trail if you go out like that.'

Sighing, I pushed a stray curl behind my ear. 'My hair is less likely to lead anyone to us than your English accent,' I said tartly.

'That's why I ask you to do the talking.' Ma turned away to lift a pan of water onto the fire.

Signor Fiorelli had told us that the market was held on Tuesdays and Saturdays but I was pleased to find shops nearby. I bought bread, olive oil, beans and polenta then counted out the remaining coins carefully. Just enough. I bought a small chicken. It was an extravagance but I wanted to celebrate our new home. And perhaps Signor Fiorelli might be persuaded to join us for dinner.

Ma scolded me when I returned. 'We can't afford meat until we have work.'

'Then we must hope the Princess sends for us soon.'

21

'I told you, we can't work for her.' She swept the floor vigorously, thumping the furniture with the broom as she muttered under her breath.

'The grocer was happy to display our card,' I said. We were often successful in finding clients that way when we moved to a new town.

'You didn't put our address on it?' Ma's expression was tense.

I sighed. 'You know I never do. I paid the grocer to make a note if anyone showed interest and said we'd call by to check. Then I introduced myself to the baker's wife. I'm to go back tomorrow because she might have some plain sewing for us, chemises and petticoats.'

'That won't bring in enough to pay the rent,' said Ma.

Somehow she always managed to spoil the small triumphs in life. It was too exhausting to keep wrangling with her.

Later that afternoon Ma was sitting in a rocking chair beside the kitchen fire, a pair of spectacles perched on the end of her nose while she darned her stockings. I was making polenta for dinner, wondering how to approach Signor Fiorelli with an invitation to share our chicken the following day.

There was a knock on the front door and Ma dropped her scissors in alarm. 'Who can that be?'

I wiped my hands and hurried to find out.

'Don't answer it, Emilia!' called Ma. 'We don't know anyone here.'

A lady stood on the doorstep with a covered basket in her hands. She wore plain but well-cut clothes and a smart bonnet over her greying hair. 'Signorina Barton?' She smiled at me with warm brown eyes.

I nodded.

'I am Signora Fiorelli. My son Alessandro told me that you were moving in today.'

I opened the door wide. 'Please, come in out of the cold! I understand we have you to thank for finding us this pretty cottage?'

Signora Fiorelli's eyes twinkled. 'And I see my son was correct when he said you have the face and hair of a Botticelli angel.'

'He said that?' I flushed with pleasure.

'Indeed he did. Several times, in fact, so I thought I'd better come and see for myself.'

I heard Ma's footsteps behind me and pulled her forward to greet our visitor. 'Signora Fiorelli, may I introduce my mother, Signora Barton?'

Ma bobbed a curtsey.

'I hope you are settling in?' said our visitor.

'Yes, thank you,' Ma replied.

Signora Fiorelli cast her gaze rapidly around the room and I was relieved we'd lit the parlour fire and made everything tidy.

'May we offer you some refreshment?' I asked.

'Another time, perhaps? The family is waiting for their dinner but I've brought you something for tonight in case you've been too busy to cook.' She uncovered her basket and held out a dish to Ma. 'Rabbit stew. It only needs heating.'

'How kind!' said Ma.

After Signora Fiorelli had gone I carried the stew into the kitchen. My pulse raced and I couldn't stop smiling. Alessandro Fiorelli thought I had the face of a Botticelli angel.

Chapter 3

The following morning, I was returning to the cottage with a parcel of cotton lawn together with several items of the baker's wife's undergarments to use as a pattern when I saw Signor Fiorelli hurrying towards me. I couldn't prevent a smile from spreading across my face.

'A note for you from the Princess,' he said. 'I was on my way to deliver it.'

I unfolded it and sighed. 'She asks us to call tomorrow.'

Signor Fiorelli frowned. 'I thought you'd be pleased.'

'It would be an excellent commission but ...'

'What is it?'

I decided to tell the truth. 'Ma is very cautious,' I said. I was too embarrassed to mention the extent of her irrational fears. 'She's worried it might affect our reputation if we work for the Princess since her household is somewhat ...' I hesitated, not sure how to put it. 'Irregular,' I said at last.

'The Princess is very hospitable,' said Signor Fiorelli. He shrugged. 'Perhaps some of her parties are a little high-spirited. She takes a lively interest in whoever she meets, whatever their station in life, and is generally well liked. What is it that Signora Barton objects to?'

'The Princess isn't married to the Baron, is she?'

He shook his head. 'Bartolomeo Pergami is her steward.'

'But Victorine is the Baron's daughter?'

'Yes, indeed.' He looked puzzled but then his expression cleared. 'Ah!' He grinned. 'I understand now! Victorine is not the Princess's child.'

'But . . .'

'Victorine has been encouraged to call the Princess "Mamma" because her real mother lives elsewhere. Since the tragic death of her own daughter eighteen months ago, the Princess has taken the little girl to her heart. She even named the Villa Vittoria after her.'

'I remember I read in the newspaper about the heir to the British throne dying in childbirth.'

'Princess Charlotte's death was a terrible shock,' he agreed. 'The Princess is only now beginning to recover her usual good spirits.'

'So Ma can have no justifiable objection to our working for her.' Relief made me bold. 'I wonder . . .'

'Yes?'

'Would you care to join us for dinner? We're having roast chicken.'

Signor Fiorelli beamed. 'I should be delighted! But now it's time for Victorine's geography lesson.' He pulled a serious expression but there was laughter in his eyes. 'Today I shall teach her about England and its strange inhabitants with their peculiar customs.'

'You had better teach me, too,' I said, 'since I am far more Italian than English.'

Signor Fiorelli laughed as he walked away.

I returned home in high spirits to break the good news to Ma.

'I'm still not sure,' she said, doubt written on her face.

I dropped my parcel on the dining-room table. 'Why not?' I asked, irritated.

'If you ask me, the Baron runs a pretty rackety household.'

'We need the work.'

'I know but . . .' She gnawed at her fingernails.

'Ma, we can't stay here if we don't pay the rent next month and we certainly haven't enough saved for another coach fare. Besides,' I said, 'you promised me we'd settle this time.'

Ma sighed heavily and opened the baker's wife's parcel. She examined the chemises and petticoats we were to copy. 'Go and see the Princess then!' she said. 'You can take her measurements and advise her on styles . . . but for goodness' sake, make sure she chooses something tasteful or she'll frighten off any other potential clients. Meanwhile, I'll make a start on these.'

'I'll do that,' I said. 'By the way, I invited Signor Fiorelli to share our chicken later on.'

Ma looked at me through narrowed eyes. 'I hope you aren't growing too fond of that young man?'

'I hardly know him,' I said, turning my attention to the baker's wife's petticoat.

The sun shone as I knocked on Villa Vittoria's front door, sewing bag in my hand. I was hoping to see Signor Fiorelli again. We'd had a very pleasant dinner the previous evening and he'd even managed to make Ma smile with his light-hearted conversation. He'd told us his father was a doctor and that he had an elder sister and seven younger brothers and sisters.

The maid showed me into the salon, where Countess Oldi sat in her usual place.

The Princess lay on a day bed with a handkerchief clutched in her hand. She presented a sadly changed appearance from our previous meetings.

I curtseyed and she sat up, her eyes red and her rouged cheeks smudged with tears.

'My dear, I'm so pleased you've come,' she said. 'You're just in time to divert me from sinking into another depression of the spirits.'

26

'Your Royal Highness, I do hope you are quite well?' I said.

'We are not at court here in my little cottage in the country. You may call me Ma'am.' She sighed. 'My dearest child passed away a little while ago and not a day goes by without my shedding tears of sorrow.'

I was at a loss to know what to reply to this. I hesitated. 'Would it help to talk about her?'

The Princess swung her legs over the side of the day bed. 'Sit with me.'

I perched on the seat beside her and couldn't help noticing that her dress was stained. Ma would have been shocked.

'My Charlotte was the flower and the hope of the nation,' she said, 'and the only good thing to come out of the union with that wretched husband of mine.' She shuddered. 'If you knew the slights and insults that the Prince of Wales has thrown at both my person and my position, you would never believe it.'

'Although I'm English my knowledge of these matters is negligible,' I said. 'I've never visited the country.'

'Then you will not have been poisoned against me by wicked lies.'

'Indeed not!'

'Charlotte was only twenty-one when she died.' The Princess dabbed at her eyes. 'I waited and waited for news of my first grandchild's arrival but no letter came. Then a courier from England was passing through on his way to Rome to present a letter to the Pope. No one interesting travels through Pesaro without my being informed and the courier was brought to me in the hope that I might gain some information about my grandchild.' She twisted her handkerchief in her hands, unable to go on.

'If it's too painful to speak of . . .'

The Princess shook her head. 'My angel had died in childbirth and my grandson with her. And that venomous brute, the Prince of Wales, didn't even have the courtesy to write and tell me of our daughter's passing.' She bowed her head as a fresh paroxysm of sobs overwhelmed her.

I was deeply shocked. Almost without thinking, I put my arms about her and she rested her head on my shoulder. Her shoulders shook as I patted her back. What kind of a husband was the Prince to fail in such a duty? Surely the two parties should have been united in grief at the loss of their child, whatever else had happened between them?

'And now,' sobbed the Princess, 'not only have I lost my daughter but also any means of regaining my rightful position. Once she'd become Queen, my Charlotte would have welcomed me back to England and I would have taken my proper place at Court. If not for my dearest Baron and his family, I don't know what I should do now.'

A rustle of skirts came from the corner of the room. Countess Oldi was watching us intently and I became aware that it was impertinent of me to touch the Princess. Gently, I released her.

'You are a kind girl,' she said, lifting her sodden handkerchief to her eyes. 'You must be much the same age as my own sweet child was?'

I nodded and handed her my clean handkerchief.

'She was pretty, like you, with blue eyes and fair hair. Everybody loved her.' The Princess sighed heavily and made a visible effort to smile. 'But you have not come here to see me weep.'

'Would you prefer me to return another day?'

Shaking her head, she said, 'I must go on with my life and I still have much to be grateful for.'

I took my sketchbook from my sewing bag, hoping to distract her from her unhappiness. 'Shall we talk about your new ballgown?' I said. 'I've sketched some designs for you to look at.'

We spent the next hour discussing styles, looking at swatches of silks and samples of trimmings. I used all my skills in diplomacy to guide her away from unsuitably low necklines, transparent fabrics

and garish gold braid and fringing, finally fixing on a style in ame-
thyst and mustard silk that was elegant, if a trifle more flamboyant
than I would have advised.

'We require an initial payment to cover the cost of materials,' I
said as I took her measurements. 'Then, this afternoon, I'll write to
our stockists in Florence for the silk and the trimmings. As soon as
they arrive I'll prepare the gown for your first fitting.'

'Very good,' said the Princess. She turned to Countess Oldi.
'Angelica dear, will you find the Baron and tell him I need funds for
the new gown to give to Signorina Barton?'

Countess Oldi nodded and left the room, leaving the door ajar.

'My wardrobe is in grave disorder,' said the Princess. 'I haven't
been in any state of mind to care. I believe I mentioned that I had
to dismiss my maid, Louise Demont?'

'You did, Ma'am.'

'Cruelly, it happened at the same time as Charlotte was taken
from me and I was brought so low. I thought Louise, so elegant and
respectful, was my friend. I haven't been able to bear the thought of
taking on another maid since.' Tears glittered in her eyes again. 'I
trusted her and she betrayed me.'

'How very dreadful that must have been for you.'

'One of my couriers, Giuseppe Sacchini, stole gold Napoleons
from my box. I dismissed him, of course, but discovered that Louise
was his lover and accomplice, so she had to go too. She retaliated by
spreading untruths about me and Sacchini. I've never been so taken
in by anybody.' The Princess shook her head dolefully.

'I'm sorry to hear that.'

'Louise wrote all my letters since I have such a poor hand. Now
the Baron looks after my financial affairs and no one will cheat me
again.' Her face brightened. 'He is a splendid figure of a man, isn't
he? So tall and handsome!'

'Why, yes,' I said, hardly knowing how to answer such a question.
This was one part of our discussion I decided not to relay to Ma.

29

High-pitched laughter came from the hall. The door was thrown back and Victorine came skipping in, her black curls flying. 'Mamma, Mamma!' she called. 'Look what I have made for you!' She climbed onto the Princess's knee and thrust a sheet of paper at her.

'Well, what a very fine dog you have drawn,' said the Princess.

'Silly Mamma! It's a cat, can't you see?'

I was studying the way the Princess's eyes had lit up and how tenderly she kissed the little girl's cheek so that I didn't notice, at first, Signor Fiorelli standing in the doorway.

'Good morning,' he said. 'I hope my charge does not disturb you, Ma'am?'

'How could she, the little darling?' The Princess smothered Victorine in noisy kisses until she was helpless with giggles.

'I am going to take her on her daily walk,' said Signor Fiorelli. 'Perhaps we may escort Signorina Barton back to the town when you have finished your consultation?'

'By all means,' said the Princess. 'We are waiting for the Baron first. Will you see what keeps him? Victorine may remain with me.'

Signor Fiorelli gave a small bow and returned to the hall.

'Such a charming young man, don't you think, Signorina Barton? If only I were ten years younger ...' The Princess sighed and gave me a sly glance.

Covered in confusion, I picked up the child's drawing from where it had fallen to the floor. 'Does your cat have a name, Victorine?' I asked.

'Beppo,' she said, twisting one of her curls around her finger. 'He lives in the kitchen because Mamma doesn't like cats.'

We chatted about her drawing for a while and it was easy to see why the Princess loved this little girl with her sparkling eyes and happy nature.

Signor Fiorelli returned with the Baron, who handed me a purse full of coins before I took my leave.

I curtseyed to the Princess. 'I'll send a note as soon as your ball-gown is ready for its first fitting,' I promised.

'Come and see me before then,' she said. 'We'll take a drive into the countryside or make toast by the fire.' She gave me a wavering smile.

As I walked out of Villa Vittoria I reflected that the life of a princess was not always an enviable one.

Chapter 4

Two weeks later Ma had gone to the market and I was alone in the cottage. I sat on a rocking chair, sewing by the light of the parlour window and looking out for her while I listened to the keening cry of the seagulls.

Since we'd finished the chemises and petticoats for the baker's wife we'd received two more commissions. I had cut a pattern ready for the Princess's ballgown and was in daily expectation of receiving the silk from Florence. We were earning enough money for the occasional sweet confection from the *pasticceria* or some sausage for our dinner. Ma seemed less anxious than usual and I was happier than I'd been for weeks.

Signor Fiorelli regularly called on us. Frequently he brought Victorine with him and we'd walk along the beach searching for shells. I'd grown fond of the child and sometimes I let her play with Peggy. She laughed at the rag doll's carroty plaits and chattered to her, just as I had once upon a time.

A movement outside the window made me put down my needle. Ma was hurtling towards the cottage, her mouth ajar and gasping for air.

I hurried to open the door for her as she scrabbled at the lock from outside.

She stumbled into the room, banging the door shut behind her. Her basket was empty.

'Whatever happened?' I asked. 'Were you robbed?'

Supporting herself against the door, she looked up at me with terrified eyes. 'He was following me!'

'Who was?'

'I don't know.'

I felt as if a lead weight had suddenly settled on my chest. 'If you didn't recognise him, then it can't have been my father.'

She slammed the shutters over the parlour window and bolted them with trembling fingers. 'I called in to the grocer's shop,' she said, still panting, 'to see if there had been any interest in our card.'

'And was there?'

'The grocer said a gentleman, a *foreigner*, had asked about a dress for his wife. His name was John Smith and he was staying at the Albergo Duomo.'

'Did you go to the hotel?'

She nodded. 'But there's no John Smith staying there. And when I left the hotel there was a man watching me from the other side of the street. He was much too tall for an Italian. I set off for the market but then I heard footsteps behind me. I turned to look but there was no one there.'

'I expect he'd turned up a side street.'

She twisted her hands together. 'I started to run and I heard him coming after me.' Her breath caught on a sob. 'Emilia, I was so frightened.'

'Ma, you must be mistaken.' I made an effort to curb my impatience. 'If a man had wanted to catch you, he would have done so.'

'It wasn't like that,' she said, her mouth set in a mulish line. 'I hid behind a market stall.'

33

'There was no one following you when you ran down the street just now.'

'I told you, I lost him in the market. But we're wasting time.' She ran into the dining room and wrenched open the door to the staircase. 'We must pack immediately,' she said.

'No!' Furious, I caught hold of her shoulders. 'Ma, you have to stop this! You live in a perpetual state of fear. It's ruining our lives.'

'But I saw him!'

'You may have seen a man and thought he was following you but it wasn't my father. Why would anyone else have cause to follow us?'

'Emilia, come upstairs and help me pack.'

Something inside me turned to iron. 'I will not,' I said, my hands balled into fists.

She looked at me uncertainly, one foot on the stairs. 'You have to.'

'I'm tired of roaming from place to place because of your strange fancies,' I said. 'You go if you want but I'm staying here in Pesaro.' I watched her begin to tremble and sink down onto the stairs.

Tears welled up in her eyes. 'You know I can't speak Italian properly. I need you.' Her chin quivered and she began to weep.

'Ma,' I said, gently this time, 'you're perpetually caught up in a web of fear of your own making. Please, help me to understand.'

She sniffed, staring at her feet. The silence stretched almost to breaking point and then she lifted her tear-stained face. 'It isn't only your father who wants to find us.'

I stared at her.

She closed her eyes.

'Who else does? Tell me the truth, Ma. I'm not a child any longer.'

'No,' she said. 'Perhaps it is time. God knows, it's a hard burden to bear on my own.'

A frisson of excitement mixed with disquiet ran down my spine. I went to the cupboard and took out a bottle of wine and two glasses. 'Sit down,' I said. I poured the wine and pushed a glass towards her. 'Drink that to steady your nerves.'

34

She grasped the glass in trembling hands and drank the wine straight down.

'Tell me,' I said.

She heaved a deep sigh. 'You already know I was a lady's maid to a Lady Langdon in Grosvenor Street in London. One morning her baby son was found dead in his cradle. My mistress was distraught. Sir Frederick seemed to blame his wife for their son's death and their marriage became very troubled. Sometimes he hit her.'

I shuddered, remembering my father's violent nature.

'One day they had a terrible quarrel and Sir Frederick locked my mistress in her bedroom for weeks.'

'How dreadful!'

Ma nodded. 'Lady Langdon decided to run away to friends in Paris and asked me to help her escape. She promised me a year's salary if I'd accompany her and, fool that I was, I agreed. You see, the money meant that your father and I could afford to marry at last.'

'How did you help her to escape?'

'I took her bedroom door key from the cupboard in the kitchen and had a copy made. Sir Frederick was at his club that night. We tip-toed downstairs with our baggage. We were in the hall when we heard Sir Frederick coming up the front steps.'

'He'd returned earlier than expected?'

Ma shivered at the memory. 'I knew he'd turn me off without a reference. Lady Langdon told me to take her travelling bags and run out of the kitchen door while she returned to her room, in case he looked in on her. She said not to wait in case she couldn't leave until later but to take the coach to Dover. I was to stay at the inn there until she arrived.'

'What happened?' I asked.

'I waited five days,' said Ma. 'I was nearly mad with worry. I sent a note to Joe, my intended, asking him to make enquiries.'

'And did he?' I asked.

Ma burst into tears again. 'Sir Frederick had found his wife's clothes on the riverbank. My mistress drowned herself.'

'But she wanted to go to her friends,' I said.

'Sir Frederick had told everyone she'd drowned herself because she was grieving for her baby and he'd posted notices offering a reward for my capture, accusing me of absconding with my mistress's clothes and jewellery.'

'That wasn't true!' Ma was always honest.

'But it was!' Her face crumpled. 'Joe said the only thing to do was for us to marry and go to France as it wasn't safe to stay in England. Later on, we hadn't enough money so we had to sell Lady Langdon's possessions.'

'It was so very long ago,' I said, taking her in my arms. 'We've travelled extensively since then. I promise you, Sir Frederick couldn't find us even if he did come looking. Now dry your tears. This is a special day, the first day you stop being scared of your own shadow and begin to live without fear.'

Some of the lines on her forehead eased a little. 'I suppose you're right.'

I hugged her. 'Now give me a smile!'

It was a poor effort but it gave me a glimmer of hope for better understanding between us in the future.

I was hemming Widow Mancuso's mourning dress while daydreaming about Signor Fiorelli's mischievous smile when hooves clattered past. A shadow fell over the parlour window as a horse and its rider passed by and a moment later there was a pounding on the front door.

Ma looked up from her sewing, wide-eyed and motionless.

Even though we'd agreed her fears were groundless, old habits died hard. 'It's all right,' I said. 'I'll go.' Hastily, I plucked some loose threads off my skirt.

The Baron, dressed in a scarlet uniform and plumed hat, stood on the doorstep, holding the reins of his black stallion. He bowed. 'The

Princess's compliments. She requests that you accompany her for a ride in her carriage.'

'The Princess?' I said, astonished.

'She awaits you.' The Baron waved his hand up the street and I saw a barouche and four. Victorine was standing on the seat and waving at the boats in the harbour. The Princess, sitting opposite Countess Oldi, waved at me.

'How delightful,' I said. 'I'll fetch my pelisse.'

The Baron nodded. 'Victorine says will you bring Peggy?' He mounted his horse and set off towards the barouche.

I closed the door behind him. 'Well!' I said. 'When I last saw the Princess she suggested I might take a drive with her, though I didn't imagine it was really her intention. But I can hardly refuse, can I, Ma?'

'I suppose not,' she said.

I put on my bonnet and pelisse and tucked Peggy under my arm.

'Don't be long,' said Ma. 'You must finish Widow Mancuso's dress tonight.'

I hurried down the street to where the Baron waited beside the barouche, his stallion dancing from side to side.

The coachman closed the carriage door behind me and returned to his perch at the front.

'I received bad news this morning and needed fresh air and good company,' said the Princess as we rolled away. She spoke in English. 'Victorine told me where you live and I thought I should like to enjoy the sympathetic company of my little dressmaker friend.'

Victorine slid off the seat beside the Princess and climbed onto my knee.

'Signorina Barton,' she said, 'may I hold Peggy?'

The Princess smiled indulgently, watching the little girl as she whispered into Peggy's ear. 'It does my heart good to see her happy when the world is so full of troubles.'

'Did you say you had bad news this morning, Ma'am?' I ventured.

'The Prince of Wales continues to send his spies to Milan to conjure up evidence against me,' she said. Her hands were clasped together so tightly in her lap that her knuckles were white.

I glanced at Countess Oldi who stared ahead with her customary bland smile. 'I'm not sure I understand, Ma'am,' I said.

'Have you heard of the Milan Commission?'

I shook my head.

'The British government will not allow the Prince of Wales to divorce me,' said the Princess. The corners of her mouth twisted in a bitter smile. 'How could they, when there are no grounds for it except for his personal dislike of me? So my husband, conniving hypocrite that he is, has set out to *find* grounds for divorce. He has set up the "secret" Commission in Milan to interview anyone who might provide proof of my so-called adultery.'

I caught my breath, astonished that the Princess discussed such matters with me.

Her mouth trembled. 'Dismissed servants, like Louise Demont, who have a grudge against me, men who provided my household with candles, an innkeeper, a sea captain whose boat I sailed on ... all these people are being questioned.' Her voice rose in indignation. 'They are asked to suggest others who will malign me and some grow so fat on the Prince's bribes they will never need to work again.'

'That's outrageous!'

'My husband has always been outrageous,' she said. Her jaw clenched. 'He's profligate, squandering his fortune on that seaside pavilion in Brighton or the latest fashions. He rarely pays his debts and would prefer to spend a morning buying paintings rather than discussing affairs of state. And then there are his many mistresses, though what they see in him now he has grown so very fat, I cannot imagine!' She glanced at the elegant figure of the Baron, riding his stallion alongside us, and gave him a fond smile.

The way the Princess described the Prince of Wales led me to believe he would be the worst kind of king, when the time came. But then, perhaps the Princess was hardly an ideal queen, either.

We drove through the gate in the massive walls to the old town. I enjoyed being in such a smart barouche as we threaded our way through the cobbled streets. Pedestrians stood back and touched their foreheads when we passed and I wondered what it would be like to have people notice you everywhere you went.

'How long is it since you were in England?' I asked.

'Five years now,' she said. 'And since my Charlotte has been taken from me, I've no desire to return. I am happy here.' She sighed. 'Or I would be, if my husband and his spies would leave me alone. Now there is no heir, I suppose he's more anxious than ever to rid himself of me.'

We stopped in the Piazza del Popolo so Victorine could look at the marble horses prancing in the fountain.

The Baron was attentive to the Princess, handing her down from the carriage and kissing her fingers.

'Thank you, *amore*,' she said.

I tried not to smile but he was so tall and elegant in his scarlet uniform and the Princess so dumpy that they made an ill-assorted pair.

Victorine ran to the red granite pool with its splashing fountain, her footsteps echoing across the piazza. She laughed in delight at the stone seahorses, frozen in motion as they frolicked at the edge of the pool. Spouting dolphins and mermen supporting a giant shell blew jets of water from their pipes.

The Baron lifted Victorine onto the low wall surrounding the pool and held her hand as she walked.

The Princess shivered. 'It's pretty in the summer but the water looks cold today.' She glanced at three or four ragged street children crouched in the square playing five-stones, and beckoned to the Baron. 'Will you buy bread for those children?' she said. 'They look hungry.'

Five minutes later, the ragamuffins, clutching crusts of bread in their grimy fists, waved as we set off again in the barouche. We drove through the gate on the opposite side of the walled town and down to the sea.

I breathed in deeply the invigoratingly salty air and watched the waves as they frothed onto the golden sand.

The Baron thundered off along the beach, his horse kicking up clumps of wet sand behind them.

'Catch him!' shouted the Princess to the coachman.

'Hold tight, Victorine!' I said, as the coachman cracked his whip. The barouche lurched forward and I clung to the side as we rattled along.

Victorine squealed, her eyes sparkling. 'Look at Papà! Go faster or we won't catch him!'

The Princess laughed, snatched off her hat and waved it in the air, hooting with delight.

The Baron was only a tiny figure in the distance now.

Countess Oldi, a terrified smile frozen on her face, gripped the door.

I was filled with exhilaration as we bounced over the sand at breakneck speed. The wind was in my hair and my pulse raced. I'd never travelled so fast in my life. A dog ran towards us and snapped at the horses, making them canter even faster and the Princess laugh louder.

At last, the Baron galloped back towards us.

The coachman pulled on the reins, turned the barouche in a wide circle so we faced the San Bartolo hills again and we settled down to a more sedate pace.

'That's put the roses in our cheeks,' said the Baron as he came to ride beside us.

'Can we do it again, Papà?' asked Victorine.

'Another time, perhaps.'

We trotted back towards the harbour and stopped near the cottage.

'Thank you for the outing, Ma'am,' I said. 'The fresh air has certainly blown the cobwebs away.'

'I am refreshed, too,' she said. 'You remind me so much of my dear Charlotte, I knew I should like your company.' She patted my hand.

Victorine hugged the rag doll tightly in her arms. 'Can I keep Peggy for tonight?' she asked as I descended from the coach.

'If you promise to keep her safe for me,' I said.

The barouche's wheels began to turn.

Victorine waved Peggy's calico arm vigorously at me. Smiling, I turned towards the cottage. The Princess might, at first glance, appear a figure of fun, but it seemed to me that she had been poorly treated. I admired her for dismissing her troubles and bravely making the best of things. And, unlikely as it seemed, I felt there was a tentative friendship blossoming between us.

Chapter 5

'If only you hadn't gone gallivanting off with the Princess yesterday you'd have finished Widow Mancuso's dress earlier,' scolded Ma.

'Well, it's done now,' I said. I finished folding the garment, wrapped it in tissue paper and tied it with a black satin ribbon.

'Come straight home afterwards,' said Ma. 'I need you to help me to finish these shirts before the light goes.'

I went to the post office and collected the parcel of silk for the Princess's ballgown before making my way to Widow Mancuso's. She lived just within the town walls in a once-fine house, now sadly neglected. She received me with old-fashioned courtesy in the gloom of her *salone*, where an almond cake and glasses of wine had been laid out in readiness. I couldn't hurt her feelings by refusing her hospitality.

It was nearly half past five and growing dark when I made my escape back to Harbour Cottage. The full moon was reflected on the water over the harbour wall and the fishing boats were moored in neat rows. Lights were already glowing from behind the shutters in the houses but Ma hadn't yet lit our candles.

I tapped on the front door and hopped from foot to foot, shivering, while I waited for her to let me in. The wind from the sea had sprung up again and I drew my shawl tightly around my shoulders. Perhaps she'd fallen asleep over her sewing. 'Ma,' I called, 'open the door!'

There was no sound from inside. The shutters were folded across the window though not secured, but I couldn't see into the parlour through the tiny gap. I rapped on the casement but still there was no response. I peered at the upstairs windows. Did I imagine it or did the lace curtain move?

Annoyed now, I hurried down the street and into the alley behind the cottages, feeling my way by moonlight. Footsteps came running down the alley. A man blundered towards me out of the shadows. I froze when he loomed over me but I needn't have worried. He didn't say a word but rudely pushed past, thrusting me back against the wall in his haste.

I counted the gates along the wall until I came to the one that gave access to our yard. I found a toehold in the crumbling brick and stretched up to fumble blindly over the top of the wall until cold metal touched my finger. Triumphant, I withdrew the key we'd secreted there. But when I went to unlock the gate, it swung inwards when I touched it. Nonplussed, I ran my hand over the wood and drew in my breath as splinters drove into my palm.

The unease within me flowered into dread when I discovered the kitchen door was wide open. Standing very still, I listened. There was no sound from within.

'Ma?' I whispered.

Nothing.

I fumbled my way to the dresser and lit a candle from the embers of the fire, expecting her to call out at any moment. As candlelight illuminated the room I gasped when I saw the pretty majolicaware had been swept off the dresser and smashed into shards on the tiled floor.

Shielding the candle flame, I tip-toed into the dining room. Fear prickled at the back of my neck. Our sewing boxes were upside-down and the floorboards littered with spools of thread, pins, scissors, thimbles and tailor's chalk. An intruder must have run out of the kitchen door and smashed the lock on the yard gate.

'Ma?' I called.

In the parlour the cushion covers were slashed to ribbons and feathers lay on the rug like a carpet of snow. The bookcase was overturned and volumes lay strewn over the floor.

Frightened now, I sprinted up the stairs, coming to a sudden stop in Ma's bedroom doorway. My stomach lurched. She lay in a crumpled heap on the floor. I fell to my knees, heedless of the wax that seared my wrist in my haste to put the candle down. Blood ran from Ma's temple and her cheek was swollen and turning purple. Her eyes were closed but my own heartbeat steadied a little when I felt her breath against my cheek.

'Ma, wake up!' I shook her gently and she murmured and stirred. 'Thank God!' I lifted her up in my arms and gasped when I saw her wrists and ankles were tied together with coarse twine. Carefully, I placed her on the bed, shocked by the vicious bruising on her arms and throat. I stroked her hair until her eyes opened.

She looked around wildly and tried to sit up. 'He had a stick and he hit me!' She began to shriek with terror and I held her firmly.

'He's gone and you're quite safe.' I rocked her until her cries gave way to hiccoughing sobs. 'I'm going to fetch the scissors and free your hands and feet,' I said.

'Don't leave me!'

'I'll only be a moment.' I ran downstairs, bolted the back door and snatched up my embroidery scissors from the floor.

Ma's wrists and ankles were so swollen and chafed it was hard to sever the twine without slicing her skin. Anger boiled up inside me. 'What happened, Ma?'

'I *told* you they were looking for us,' she said, hysteria rising in her voice again.

My heart sank. This was the worst possible thing that could have happened, when I had so recently persuaded her that her fears were ungrounded.

'Did you see him?' I asked.

She nodded.

'And did you recognise him?'

Her teeth were chattering and I wrapped a blanket around her shoulders. 'No.' She cupped her hands over her eyes. 'It wasn't your father or . . .'

'Sir Frederick?' I asked.

'Who?' Her face was ashen.

'Your mistress's husband.'

She looked perplexed. The head wound must have made her forget temporarily. 'You thought he might be looking for you,' I said.

'Why would he be here?'

'No reason at all. I'm sure your attacker was simply a chance thief,' I said. But, just for a moment, I'd wondered.

'A thief?' She wrinkled her brow and touched the lump on her temple. When she saw the blood on her trembling fingers she frowned.

'A thief,' I said, firmly. 'He ransacked the cottage.'

Ma leaned back against the pillows. 'I didn't tell him about them,' she said.

'About what?'

She closed her eyes and I took water from the ewer and poured it into the basin to wash the blood from her face. She winced as I cleaned the cut on her head. It wasn't deep but, despite my gentle pressure, she groaned as my fingertips explored the swelling around the wound.

'What didn't you tell him?' I asked.

Puzzled, she looked at me with a blank stare. 'Who?'

She was still shaking and confused and I decided any further questions could wait until later. It was too late to report the assault and, besides, I couldn't leave her alone. 'I'll fetch some salve to soothe your wrists and a cold cloth for your head.'

I returned to the kitchen to boil water for tea and sweep up the broken earthenware. Once Ma was asleep I'd tidy up the remaining ravages wrought by the intruder, to spare her further distress in the morning.

We sat together to drink our tea but as soon as I'd taken the empty cup from her she began to retch. I snatched up the slops basin and held it while she vomited.

Afterwards I wiped her face and laid her down against the pillows. 'Go to sleep now, Ma. In the morning everything will be better.'

I sat beside her and waited until she drifted into a doze before going downstairs to tidy up the rest of our jumbled possessions.

My silver thimble glinted on the dining-room floor amongst the scattered contents of my sewing box. I wept when I saw it had been crushed flat. Ma had bought it for me when I was only a little girl and she first taught me to sew. Tears of sadness gave way to rage at the wretch who'd barged into our cottage, frightened my mother nearly to death and despoiled our possessions.

Fuelled by fury, I rushed about like a whirling dervish, righting the furniture, putting away the crumpled books and sweeping up the feathers. I flung the shredded cushion covers into the fire, where they flared and spat as they twisted in the flames.

Once my ire was spent, I was overcome with exhaustion and wearily climbed the stairs to see Ma again. She muttered in her sleep. I lay on the bed beside her and, after a while, I dozed.

Ma was restless for much of the night, her face and limbs twitching while she dreamed. She murmured the name 'Harriet' several times and, once, spoke distinctly. 'Joe,' she said, 'I won't leave Harriet!'

Later, she lay so silent and motionless I touched her in sudden panic. She sighed deeply and opened her eyes, looking at me without recognition, as if she still dreamed.

'Go back to sleep,' I whispered.

She closed her eyes again.

I lay beside her thinking about what she'd said. Harriet . . . There was something about the name that tugged at my memory. I sighed, too tired and upset to think about it anymore.

It was nearly dawn when Ma's sobs awoke me.

She sat beside me, rocking and holding her head in her hands.

'Ma?'

'My head hurts so,' she whimpered.

I got up and dipped a cloth in the ewer.

The cool compress seemed to ease her pain a little. I placed a few drops of lavender oil onto a handkerchief for her to sniff and it was then that I saw the blood trickling from her ear. I wiped it away but Ma looked at the bloodied cloth with horror.

'I'm going to die, aren't I?' she whispered.

'Of course not!' I said, forcing my voice to sound calm, 'but Signor Fiorelli's father is a doctor. I'll fetch him to examine you.'

'Don't go!' She clutched my arm so hard that I knew I'd have bruises later. 'I don't want to die alone!'

I couldn't leave her when she was so upset. 'We'll see how you are later, then.' I changed the subject to calm her. 'You were dreaming last night,' I said. 'Ma, who is Harriet?'

She turned her poor swollen face towards me, her mouth slack with shock. 'Harriet?' she said at last.

'You were mumbling and said, "Joe, I won't leave Harriet."'

She burst into tears. 'God forgive me! I can't take this to my grave.'

'You're *not* going to die!' My curiosity was piqued now. 'Tell me about it and perhaps you'll feel easier?'

Ma's mouth quivered and tears rolled down her cheeks. 'I've kept the secret for so long . . .'

'Then tell me,' I said as persuasively as I could. There was so much she hadn't told me about herself and, sometimes, what she did say conflicted with an earlier story. She'd always been secretive and sometimes that made me feel I didn't know her at all. 'Tell me, Ma!'

Her mouth worked and she brushed tears away. 'I told you about my mistress?'

I nodded encouragingly.

'When Lady Langdon begged me to help her,' said Ma, 'she planned to take her four-year-old daughter Harriet with her.'

'I remember you said she had a baby that died but you didn't mention a daughter.'

'When Sir Frederick came home early that evening, my mistress ordered me to hurry on ahead to the inn with Harriet.'

'You took the child with you?'

'She cried desperately for her mother for days,' said Ma. 'Later, when Joe came to the inn and told me my mistress was dead, I didn't know what to do.' She closed her eyes, tears seeping from under her eyelashes. 'Sir Frederick had already sent out a handbill offering a reward for news of my whereabouts and I'd have been accused of kidnapping as well as theft if I'd gone back. I'd have been hanged.'

'So what did you do?'

'When Joe said we must run to France, I refused to abandon Harriet. I didn't trust Sir Frederick – he had no real affection for his daughter. I couldn't bear for the poor motherless scrap to have no one to love her.'

I stared at her. 'You took Harriet away from her father? To France? How could you do such a terrible thing?'

'Joe wanted to leave her at an orphanage and that's when our troubles began. We quarrelled constantly. He made me sell Lady Langdon's jewels and, when he couldn't find work, spent the money on drink.' She began to rock backwards and forwards. 'I was so alone and I didn't speak French. I was too frightened to take Harriet back to London and leave her on her father's doorstep.'

'So you took her to an orphanage?'

Ma winced as she rubbed her head. 'I couldn't do it.' She began to weep again. 'The little girl's name was Harriet Emilia Langdon,' she sobbed. 'For her safety, I called her Emilia Barton.'

Dry-mouthed, I stared at her. There was a rushing sound in my ears and a sudden heaviness in the pit of my stomach, as if I'd swallowed an iceberg. Black flecks flickered at the edge of my vision and I gripped my hands together to dispel the sudden dizziness. Ma was not my mother. Not only that, but I was not the person I'd always thought I was, either.

'Emilia?'

I opened my mouth but I couldn't speak.

'Marrying Joe was a disaster,' she said. 'He'd imagined we'd be rich if we sold...' She paused and her gaze slid away from me. 'If we sold the contents of Lady Langdon's baggage. He was disappointed by how little her goods fetched, and then he grew angry. He resented being saddled with a child and was so harsh with you I was frightened for your life. So, for your sake, I fled from him to the South of France.'

'How *could* you?' I said. 'You stole me away from my family!' Listening to her story, I didn't know who I really was and nothing would ever be the same again.

Her eyes pleaded with me. 'I did it to protect you.' Tentatively, she reached out to touch my wrist. 'Now you are all that I have in the world.'

I shook my head in disbelief. It felt as if the very ground had crumbled away from under me. I surged to my feet. I had to get away. I rushed down the stairs and out of the front door.

Lifting my skirts, I ran through the echoing streets, not caring where I went. It was raining and I ran and ran until a stitch in my side forced me to lean over with my hands on my knees. Afterwards I sprinted on again until my feet crunched over sand and then splashed into the foaming sea. When the icy water reached my thighs I gasped and stood still.

Tipping up my face to the rain, I wailed and sobbed. A wave surged past me, soaking me up to my waist. The shock of it caused a modicum of sense to return. I couldn't remain standing in the sea.

I would catch my death. Or walk to it. Slowly, I turned towards the shore and ploughed my way through the water, the sand sucking at my shoes. What was I going to do?

I stood on the beach in the grey dawn, dripping wet and shivering in the wind. There really was nothing else to do but to go back to Ma.

Fishing boats were returning to the harbour with their catch by the time I reached the cottage. Gulls screamed overhead as fishwives gutted the catch, tossing the entrails over the harbour wall. Women were already gathering with their baskets, inspecting the mackerel and sardines on display. One or two glanced at me as I passed, my wet dress almost transparent and moulded to my body.

In my mad rush to escape I'd left the front door ajar. Inside, I slipped off my shoes, sand rubbing grittily between my toes. The stairs felt like a mountain to climb and I paused at the top, gathering the strength to face the woman who wasn't my mother after all.

She lay on her side, the pillow stained with fresh blood. There was something about her motionless form that made me pause in the doorway. Then I ran forward, my heart hammering like a black-smith's anvil. Her sightless eyes were half-open and not a breath stirred the air.

Sarah Barton, the woman I used to call Ma, was dead.

Chapter 6

Panic-stricken, I ran to the Fiorelli house and hammered on the door, shouting for Dottore Fiorelli. The family were at breakfast and a sea of faces turned to look at me. Tutting and shaking her head, Signora Fiorelli wrapped a blanket around my shoulders while her husband patiently questioned me. I can't remember what I told him but his assured manner was calming.

Alessandro watched anxiously while I told the story, barely able to speak for sobs. Afterwards he and his father left for the cottage and his mother took me upstairs to peel off my sodden clothes. The eldest daughter, Cosima, found me one of her dresses to wear.

Signora Fiorelli sat me by the kitchen fire and wrapped my shaking hands around a cup of soup. 'Drink it quickly, you're chilled to the bone.'

Obediently, I sipped the chicken broth, my teeth chattering against the china rim. I finished the soup and stared into the flames while the sounds of the Fiorelli family talking in hushed tones washed over me. My head spun as I went over and over what Ma had said until a deathly exhaustion overcame me. All I wanted was to climb into bed and pull the covers over my head.

Alessandro and his father returned and Dottore Fiorelli touched me on my shoulder. 'It is with great regret, Signorina Barton,' he said gently, 'that I confirm your mother has passed away.'

'If only I'd come for you last night,' I wept, 'perhaps you might have saved her.'

'Do not reproach yourself,' he said. 'The blow to her head caused an injury to the brain, causing it to bleed. Nothing could have saved her. It was better for her that you stayed close to her during her final hours.'

I couldn't look into his kind brown eyes. 'But I didn't,' I said with a sob. 'We argued and I ran down to the beach. I wasn't there long but when I returned . . . ' I hung my head, recalling her last words to me. '*I did it to protect you.*' I remembered her fingers on my wrist for the very last time. '*Now you are all that I have in the world.*' I buried my face in my hands.

'Hush! She is at peace now,' said Signora Fiorelli. 'And I am going to put you into Cosima's bed and you shall sleep.'

'Swallow this draught,' said the doctor, handing me a small glass. 'When you wake you will feel better.'

I had no energy to protest and allowed myself to be led upstairs. Signora Fiorelli shooed me into bed and closed the shutters. I pulled the covers over my shoulders and, within a few minutes, sank into oblivion.

I stretched and yawned. Peggy lay on the pillow next to me and I stared into her unblinking blue eyes. I clasped her against my chest with my chin on the top of her head as I had done every morning for most of my life. But this wasn't my bed.

I heard a giggle and turned to see Cosima sitting beside me.

'Two redheaded sleeping beauties,' said a voice. Alessandro Fiorelli stood in the doorway, smiling at me. 'How are you?'

Slowly I pushed myself into a sitting position. 'Muzzy,' I said, rubbing my eyes. My mouth was dry. Suddenly the memories of the recent events crowded in. 'I must go home,' I said, throwing back the bedclothes in a panic.

'Not yet,' he said. 'Mamma says dinner is ready. Are you hungry?'

I shook my head but my stomach growled.

Downstairs it was daunting to see so many faces around the table, unused as I was to large families. For as long as I could remember it had only ever been Ma and myself.

Cosima took my hand and urged me forwards. 'You shall sit by Alessandro, who is the eldest of us left at home. Delfina is two years older than Alessandro and lives with her husband and baby Enzo in Fano.' She pointed at two young men who bore a remarkable likeness to their older brother. 'Salvatore and Jacopo are next. I'm the second eldest girl. Then Fabrizio is fourteen and Luca is twelve. Gina is my younger sister and last of all is Alfio.'

'I'm five!' piped up the little boy.

'A late and unexpected gift from God,' said Signora Fiorelli, ruffling his dark curls.

Despite everything, I ate my supper. I spoke only enough to be polite but was comforted by the cheerful chatter of the family. Afterwards, while the women cleared the table, Dottore Fiorelli requested that Alessandro and I join him in his study.

'Signorina Barton,' he said, pushing back the gold-framed spectacles that rested on the end of his imposing nose, 'I have been obliged to report to the police chief, Capitano Bischi, that a thief broke into your cottage and the resulting death of your mother. Alessandro also told them that he saw a man looking in through the downstairs window yesterday afternoon.'

'A man?' I frowned.

'Victorine and I came to see you,' said Alessandro. 'You remember we'd promised to return your doll? Victorine was walking along the top of the harbour wall when I saw a man peering in through your parlour window.'

'When was this?' I said.

'About half past three or four, perhaps. As I approached the cottage I thought he looked ... ' Alessandro shrugged and turned up his palms. 'He looked furtive. So I called out, "Are you looking for someone?"'

'What did he say?'

'That was the strange thing. He glanced at me and ran off. Great long legs, he had. And a white face.'

'I doubt he'd have run away if he hadn't been up to mischief,' said the doctor.

'I couldn't run after him,' said Alessandro. 'Victorine was in my care. So I knocked on the door and spoke to your mother.'

I opened my mouth to say that she wasn't my mother but the wound was still too raw to talk about that.

'She said you'd gone to deliver a dress not five minutes before but you were expected back within the hour. So Victorine and I walked in that direction, hoping we might meet you and restore Peggy to you.'

'You didn't tell Signora Barton about the man, Alessandro?' queried the doctor.

He shook his head. 'He'd gone so I only said to her that I'd call back.'

The doctor raised one eyebrow. 'It was so urgent to return the doll?'

Signor Fiorelli shrugged but I saw spots of pink flare on his high cheekbones. 'We returned an hour later but the shutters were closed. I presumed Signora Barton was out.'

'Her attacker must have been in the cottage by then,' I said, my stomach churning. 'It was almost dark when I arrived at half past five. It would have taken him some time to search the cottage and then to intimidate ... ' I pressed my fingers to my mouth.

'What is it?' asked Alessandro.

'When I knocked at the front door I saw the bedroom curtain move. As my mother didn't come, I went into the alley behind

54

the cottage to enter by the kitchen. By then it was dark and a man ran towards me out of the shadows. He nearly knocked me flying.'

'You think your mother's assailant ran out of the back of the cottage when he heard you at the front?' said the doctor.

I nodded and swallowed. If I'd had my door key with me and had let myself in, would he have killed me too?

'Signorina Barton,' said the doctor, 'you must speak to Capitano Bischi and tell him what you saw. There is time enough for that tomorrow. Also there is the matter of . . .' He hesitated. 'I took the liberty of informing the priest of your mother's death and making arrangements for her burial. Do you have any family or friends I can contact for you?'

'No,' I said. The look of pity on the doctor's face was almost my undoing. I breathed deeply and swallowed back my tears. 'I have no friends or family,' I said. 'None at all.'

The Fiorelli family were extraordinarily kind to me over the following days. Signora Fiorelli insisted I stay with them and Cosima and ten-year-old Gina shared their bed with me. Although I'd often shared a bed with Ma, it was strange to be tumbled together with two friendly girls I barely knew, like a basketful of puppies. At night I listened to their giggles and whispered confidences and wished I had been blessed with sisters.

Dottore Fiorelli escorted me into town to talk to Capitano Bischi. Dark-eyed and dapper, the police chief bade me sit down and I told him my story, omitting Ma's confession. Capitano Bischi shrugged his narrow shoulders and said that her attacker must have been an opportunist thief. Signora Barton's subsequent death had been most regrettable but appeared to be without motive other than theft. He assured me every effort would be made to find the thief but held out little hope of apprehending him. Dottore Fiorelli and I returned to the house in silence.

I owned no mourning clothes but Signora Fiorelli opened the cedarwood chest in her bedroom and took out a crepe mourning gown. 'It was my mother's she said. 'The style is outdated but you may have it if you care to alter it. Sewing will keep you occupied at this difficult time.'

There was a great deal of material in the full skirts and, with careful cutting, I was able to make two dresses and a spencer. It was ironic that I'd only recently finished Widow Mancuso's mourning dress without the slightest inkling that I should be making a mourning wardrobe for myself a few days later.

Ma's body was brought to the Fiorellis' house on the night before the funeral and her coffin laid on trestles in the *salone*. Unable to sleep, I dressed and crept downstairs in the small hours. I peeped into the open coffin, half afraid of what I would see but, despite her bruised cheek, Ma's waxen face was serene with all worry lines erased away. She, at least, was at peace.

I kept vigil beside her body for the rest of the night. I was still angry with her for stealing me away but also nagged by guilt. If I'd taken her fears seriously we'd have moved on and she'd still be alive. Everything about my life had changed and I felt as if I stood on the edge of an abyss, not knowing what terrors awaited me below.

It was still dark when Signora Fiorelli came downstairs. 'I wondered if you might be here, all alone,' she whispered. Leaning over Ma's body, she sighed. 'Too young to die,' she said. She took my hand and I was grateful for her warm touch. We sat quietly together until dawn broke.

Alfio trotted downstairs and Signora Fiorelli firmly led me out of the *salone* and made me sit with the little boy at the kitchen table. I sipped hot coffee and crumbled a piece of bread while I responded to Alfio's childish chatter. One by one the rest of the family joined us.

Alessandro, looking unusually sombre, sat beside me and watched me from under his dark eyelashes. 'You're very brave,' he said. 'But you mustn't be embarrassed to cry. You are amongst friends here.'

At once my eyes began to prickle and I looked down at my folded hands. Ashamed that my feelings towards Ma were so confused, my throat closed up.

Alessandro passed me his handkerchief and patted my arm with great tenderness.

'It is time,' said his father.

Signora Fiorelli led me into the parlour again and gently pushed me towards the coffin. 'You must kiss your mother, Signorina.'

I looked down at Ma's face. She was the only mother I remembered and I was sorry that her life had been so troubled because of me. Leaning over, I touched my lips to her cold forehead for the last time.

Since Ma's coffin was small, Alessandro, his father, Salvatore and Jacopo were all the pallbearers needed.

As they carried the coffin into the church there was a clatter of hooves and I glanced up to see the barouche come to a smart stop outside. The Princess, accompanied by Countess Oldi, descended and hurried after us.

After the burial we returned to the Fiorellis' house for wine, *biscotti* and *panforte*. Cosima and Salvatore were charged with offering the refreshments to the party and Signora Fiorelli whispered to me that it was fortunate she'd set out the best glasses since she hadn't expected to entertain royalty.

The Princess, however, stood on no ceremony and hugged me to her ample bosom. 'My dear little friend,' she said, 'I grieve for you in your loss.' She sighed heavily. 'We are companions in our sorrow.'

'I'm honoured that you came today,' I said.

'I couldn't bear to think you might be alone,' said the Princess, 'but I see your friends are caring for you.'

'The Fiorelli family have been so kind,' I said, imagining how unbearable it would have been if I'd had to arrange everything on my own.

Signora Fiorelli enfolded me in a lavender-scented embrace. 'But now we must decide what you will do next.'

'I've presumed upon your hospitality too long,' I said. 'I'll return to the cottage this afternoon.'

A chorus of protests broke out from her children and only died down once Signora Fiorelli had flapped her hands at them as if they were squawking chickens.

'Whatever would people think?' she said, her expression shocked. 'A young, unmarried lady living alone?'

'Your honour must be protected,' said Alessandro in a firm voice.

I knew they were right. There had been security, or so I'd thought, in two women living together, but my reputation would be at risk if I lived alone. In any case, I doubted I could earn enough by myself to be able to afford the cottage.

'Perhaps I'll find a room to rent,' I said.

Countess Oldi brushed *biscotti* crumbs from her lips. 'Not at all suitable,' she said.

'I doubt you would find one,' said Dottore Fiorelli, shaking his head. 'Not many people would care to be responsible for a young lady on her own.'

'What he means, Signorina Barton,' said Signora Fiorelli, 'is that you are far too pretty for any woman to risk her husband's attention straying if you lived in her household.'

Anxiety fluttered in my breast. Where could I go? Then I had an idea and decided to speak before my courage failed me.

'Ma'am,' I said to the Princess, trying to keep my voice even, 'if you were to find me a place in your household I could undertake any household sewing tasks or alterations to your wardrobe. I speak Italian, French and English fluently and write a clear hand in all three. Perhaps I might be entrusted with your correspondence?' I gripped my hands together while a pulse fluttered in my neck.

The Princess thought for a moment. 'Since I have dismissed my maid, my wardrobe undeniably needs attention. Most of my household are living off the premises, at least until the building works are completed, but there's a little room on the ground floor, if that will suffice?'

I let out my breath in a sigh of relief. 'Indeed it will!'

Later that afternoon I was grateful for the company of Cosima and Signor Fiorelli when I returned to the cottage. I'd dreaded facing the memories of Ma's death on my own.

Alessandro unlocked the door and we followed him inside.

'Oh, no!' said Cosima.

It was immediately apparent that the intruder had returned. Again, the parlour furniture was overturned and even the rug had been rolled up to expose the floorboards.

'Go outside,' ordered Alessandro. 'Hurry now! I shall make sure there's nobody here.'

Wordlessly, Cosima slipped her hand into mine. Her brown eyes were full of pity for me. I allowed her to draw me outside.

The harbour wall was so cold when we sat upon it that it seemed to drain all the warmth out of my body. I shivered and rose to my feet in a panic. What if the intruder were still inside and had harmed Signor Fiorelli? But at that moment he beckoned us back into the house.

'What can he have been looking for to risk coming back?' I said. 'We had nothing of value.'

'Shall I help you to tidy up?' asked Cosima.

I left Signor Fiorelli righting the overturned furniture and Cosima picking up the contents of the sewing boxes while I went upstairs. The mattresses had been sliced open and our clothes tipped out of the chest. My heart sank. I would have to replace the landlady's mattresses, further depleting my purse. One by one I lifted up the scattered clothes and placed them neatly in my travelling bag.

Ma's quilted winter petticoat swung against my ankles as I picked it up and I was surprised by how heavy it was. It was then that I made my discovery. All around the hem, on the inside, was a double row of little cambric pockets. Each one contained a gold coin.

I sank down on the edge of the slashed mattress, my legs suddenly weak. I remembered then that, on her deathbed, Ma had said, '*I didn't tell him about them.*' Perhaps these coins were what the thief had been searching for? I had no idea how Ma could have come by such riches. We'd often gone so short it was hard to believe she'd saved anything much from our meagre earnings.

Agitated, I paced across to the window. However she'd acquired the coins, I needed them now and they'd be a godsend.

Without hesitating I pulled on the petticoat under my skirt and tied the tapes firmly around my waist.

Chapter 7

Victorine was sitting on the front steps watching the builders when Signor Fiorelli and I arrived at Villa Vittoria. I caught my breath as the guard dogs came bounding up to investigate.

'Down, Titus!' commanded Signor Fiorelli. 'Down, Bruna! Don't worry, Signorina Barton, they're more bark than bite.'

'Nevertheless, I'm pleased you're here to control them,' I said, gripping my bag tightly.

'They'll soon get to know you.' His eyes were full of sympathy for me. 'After all that has happened, coming here must feel very strange. Remember, I am your friend and you may call on me whenever you wish.'

I forced a smile. 'I am a little nervous.'

'Don't be. And come and have dinner with my family again.' He smiled, his teeth white against his olive skin. 'If you can stand the noise and the squabbling.'

Two members of the Papal Guard were standing by the front door, as usual.

'You are coming to live with me, Signorina Barton?' Victorine hopped from foot to foot.

'For a while,' I said.

'Will you play with me?'

I ruffled her dark curls. 'I shall be working for the Princess but when she doesn't need me, then I'll play with you.'

Signor Fiorelli lifted my bags down from the barouche. 'We'll go round to the servants' door,' he said.

Victorine skipped along ahead of us, jumping over heaps of sand and stacked timber boarding.

'I've no experience of the correct etiquette in a royal household,' I admitted.

'Don't be concerned. The Princess is moderate in her demands. She asks only that you are loyal and efficient in your duties.'

'How could I not be loyal to her?' I said. 'I don't know what I should have done if she hadn't offered me a place.'

'Mamma would never have turned you out into the streets,' he assured me.

'I don't intend to be a burden to anyone,' I said.

At the side of the house we paused to look at the stable yard with its rows of horseboxes. The yard echoed to the clang of the farrier's hammer and the acrid scent of burning hooves hung in the air. Lads were busy grooming the horses and mucking out the boxes. Victorine climbed up on the gate and waved at one of the grooms.

'There are forty-eight horses,' said Signor Fiorelli, 'from the smallest piebald ponies to the finest Arabian stallions. And several carriages are housed here for the Princess's use.'

I gazed at him in surprise. 'But this is hardly a palace.'

He laughed. 'No, not yet. The Princess hasn't lived here very long, remember. Before she bought Villa Vittoria she rented the Villa Caprile nearby. That was much grander. Although the Princess and her architect have plans to enlarge Villa Vittoria, she likes to call it her country cottage.'

'So the household is smaller than it was before?'

'Mostly it's the Pergami family who live here,' he said, 'together with Willy Austin, Victorine's nursemaid, two equerries and a few servants. There'll be more space for live-in servants once the building works are finished.'

'And the Baron's family live here also?'

Signor Fiorelli nodded. 'The Baron oversees everything. He hires the staff, which includes his mother, his cousins, brothers and sisters, and controls the household accounts.'

'Victorine's mother doesn't live here then?'

'No,' said Signor Fiorelli. He inclined his head towards me. 'And a word of advice, if I may? You would do well to remember the Baron has almost complete authority over everything at Villa Vittoria.'

Behind the house I glimpsed another avenue of cypresses and a half-completed Italian garden. Soldiers of the Papal Guard patrolled the grounds and two more stood by the back door.

'Are the soldiers always here?' I asked.

'Night and day. Fourteen of them. The Princess is anxious that her husband's spies might infiltrate the villa and poison her,' he added in an undertone. 'The Pope allows her the guard to ensure her safety.'

I glanced at Victorine, who was watching us with bright eyes, and resolved to find out more another time. She grasped hold of her tutor's hand and led the way indoors, past the kitchens.

'I'll take you to Mother Pergami,' he murmured.

I followed him into the servants' dining room. The old lady in black I'd seen when I first visited Villa Vittoria sat at the long table with a younger woman, counting piles of sheets.

'I bring you Signorina Barton,' said Signor Fiorelli.

Signora Pergami's face was deeply wrinkled, like an apple that has sat on a windowsill for too long. Her almost toothless jaw moved from side to side as she looked me up and down. Finally, she nodded in greeting and I dropped a small curtsey.

'Faustina,' she said to the younger woman, 'take her to her room. And then the Baron will see her.'

'I must say goodbye for now, Signorina Barton,' said Signor Fiorelli. 'It's time for your lessons, Victorine.' He held out his hand to the little girl.

Loneliness gripped me for a moment until I saw him glance back at me through the doorway with a grin on his handsome face.

Faustina, who would have been pretty if her features weren't quite so coarse, pushed herself to her feet and picked up my bags.

I followed her along the passage, watching her hips roll from side to side as she sauntered along as if she had all the time in the world. A few locks of black hair had slipped from her hairpins and lay in greasy tresses on her shoulders. She opened a door and dropped my bags on the tiled floor inside. When she unlatched the shutters, light poured in to illuminate a bed covered in a striped cotton coverlet. There was a rag rug on the floor and a washstand with a rough white towel folded on the top. There was no fire in the empty grate.

'There's hooks behind the door for your clothes,' she said. 'A maid'll bring you water in the morning and the privy's out the back beside the stables.'

'Thank you,' I said. The room was whitewashed, with dark timber beams above and terracotta tiles on the floor, simple but adequate.

She gave me the glimmer of a smile. 'Unpack later. My brother's waiting for you now.'

I realised with some surprise that Faustina must be one of the Baron's siblings and therefore Countess Oldi's sister too. Her position at Villa Vittoria was far less elevated than that of the Princess's lady-in-waiting.

We returned along the passage and Faustina knocked on another door. A male voice bade us enter.

The Baron sat at his desk, pen poised to write in the ledger before him. 'Ah, yes, Signorina Barton. You may go, Faustina.'

The Baron beckoned me forward.

A fire crackled in the hearth and the room was very warm. I was close enough to smell his hair oil.

He didn't ask me to sit down. 'The Princess has instructed me to arrange the details of your employment as her sewing woman and, when required, secretary,' he said. 'You shall have your board and lodging and an appropriate salary will be paid half-yearly. You may have an afternoon off each fortnight to visit your mother's grave.'

'Thank you, Baron.' I wasn't brave enough to ask what an appropriate salary might be. In any case, I was in no position to haggle.

He stood up and I was reminded again of how his physical presence dominated a room.

'Your discretion must be absolute,' he said. 'You will not discuss anything you see or hear in the Villa Vittoria with any person outside these walls. Do I make myself clear?' His gaze bored into me.

'Absolutely, Baron.'

'There are those who may wish the Princess ill and it is the duty of every member of this household to protect her. Should you discover any unknown person entering the grounds or the villa, you will inform either myself or one of the guards immediately. Furthermore, the corridors are patrolled all night. You will not leave your room after retiring until the following morning.' He fixed me with an unsmiling gaze that made me faintly uneasy.

I nodded in acquiescence but was startled to learn that the risks to the Princess's well-being were considered so high.

'You will take your dinner now in the servants' hall and the Princess will see you afterwards in her dressing room to outline your duties. Do you have any questions?'

'Not at present,' I said.

The Baron turned his attention back to his ledger and I took it that I was dismissed.

I returned to my room and hung up my other mourning dress and placed my undergarments in the chest. I pushed Ma's travelling bag beneath the bed, along with the package of silk for the Princess's ballgown.

I took Peggy out of my bag and hugged her tightly, trying to dispel the hollow feeling inside me. It distressed me that I had no memories of the time before Ma, or Sarah as I must learn to call her, had stolen me. She'd said I'd cried bitterly for my mother so I must have loved her. And then there was my real father, who was not Sarah's husband Joe as I'd always supposed. I wondered if he could really have been as unkind as Sarah said. She had been fond of her mistress, my real mother, and her judgement of the situation could have been clouded.

I sat on the bed and closed my eyes, letting my mind drift to see if I could remember anything about my long-ago family. My very earliest memories were of hiding behind the furniture with my hands over my ears, listening to a hectoring male voice, but that must have belonged to Joe. The recollection made me feel as forlorn as I had then.

Sighing, I stood up. Sarah's petticoat was heavy but I daren't take it off until I'd found a suitable hiding place for the gold coins. I straightened the bedcover and left the room.

I followed the buzz of conversation to the servants' hall and slipped into a vacant place at the refectory table. The girl beside me pulled her skirt aside to make room.

I smiled. 'I'm Emilia Barton.'

'Mariette,' she said, before continuing her lively banter with another maid. It would take time before I was accepted, I supposed.

Dinner was plain but plentiful, a thick vegetable and bean soup with chunks of crusty bread, but I had little appetite. I glanced at the others, mostly maids but also a number of male servants. Signora Pergami sat at the head of the table beside her daughter Faustina and son Luigi.

There was no formality and one by one the servants began to drift away to resume their duties. Signora Pergami was picking at what were left of her teeth with a knife when I went to ask her how to find the Princess's dressing room.

'The Princess has guests for dinner,' she said. 'You must wait in the hall until she's finished.'

I returned to my room to collect my sewing box and the parcel of silk before sitting down on the hall chair. Gales of laughter emanated from the dining room and a footman went in and out with dishes from the kitchen.

Eventually the door burst open and the Baron and three other men strode across the hall and stood in a noisy group. A maid appeared from the back of the house with coats and hats in her arms and waited by the front door. Willy Austin sloped out of the dining room with his hands in his pockets. Then came the Princess, laughing uproariously at something her companions, a middle-aged couple, had said. Countess Oldi stood silently beside them, nodding and smiling.

The maid helped the couple into their coats and saw all the visitors out of the front door.

The Baron spoke to the Princess in a low voice while she looked up at him with an adoring smile. He rested his hand on her shoulder for a moment before walking away.

I was uncomfortable at witnessing what appeared to have been a private moment. The Princess turned towards the drawing room and I stood up and cleared my throat. She caught sight of me and clapped a hand to her forehead. 'My dear Signorina Barton! I forgot I asked you to attend me. How are you?'

'I'm well, thank you, Ma'am.'

'Still sad, I expect.' She smiled sympathetically. 'But we shall share some rides in the carriage together to take your mind off your wretchedness.'

'You are very kind. If it's not convenient for you to see me now, shall I return later?' I noticed she'd spilled gravy down the front of her bodice.

'Not at all.' She waved at Countess Oldi. 'Come with us, Angelica.'

I followed them upstairs to the Princess's dressing room. It was all I could do not to shudder at the sight that met my eyes. The room was crammed with chests and wardrobes. Garments hung from hooks on the walls and lay in towering piles on the floor. Shoes were tumbled into a corner. Grubby shifts spilled out of drawers and over everything hung the musty odour of unwashed clothing.

'I can never find anything to wear,' complained the Princess. 'Since that traitorous girl left me, I've had a succession of maids to dress me but none has properly managed my wardrobe.'

'I do not profess to be a lady's maid,' I said faintly, 'but perhaps I may see what needs mending, altering or cleaning? I'll arrange everything neatly, though it may be necessary to put some out-of-season items into storage. I fear we must be ruthless and discard items you no longer wear.' I picked up a crumpled dress from the floor. 'Does this fit well?'

The Princess nodded.

'Then I'll sew on this loose button and mend the tear in the hem before sending it to the laundry.'

'Faustina oversees the laundry maids,' said the Princess.

I set to work while she and Countess Oldi sat by the window discussing the Princess's scheme to turn one of the upstairs rooms into a music room.

Some time later I had a pile of clothes ready for mending, a larger one for the laundry, and several items that needed letting out.

'Where would you like me to work, Ma'am?' I asked. 'I shall need a table by a window so that I have sufficient daylight to keep my stitches neat.'

'I'll have a table brought in here for you.'

I glanced at the half-open door that led to the Princess's bedroom and was conscious that it might not always be convenient for me to have free access to the dressing room. I glimpsed a child's bed set at the foot of the large bed, draped with muslin curtains, and a large portrait of the Baron hanging on one wall. 'Are there times you would prefer me not to be working in here?' I asked.

The Princess shrugged. 'If so I shall tell you.'

'Very good.' I unwrapped the bundle of silk I'd brought with me. 'I have brought the material for your new ballgown for you to approve.'

The Princess fell upon the silk with cries of delight. I draped it around her shoulders so that she could see the effect in the looking glass. 'I shall wear this to the Perticaris' ball next month,' she announced.

'Then I will make sure it is ready.'

The Princess smiled. 'I can see I am going to be very happy with my new Mistress of the Wardrobe.'

'Thank you, Ma'am.' I curtseyed, pleased that she had awarded me such a title.

'I have plans for a bathroom with a sunken bath and frescoes on the ceiling,' said the Princess, 'and I have an appointment with my architect now. I'll send for you later, Signorina Barton. I need you to write the invitations for a dinner here on Friday.'

I curtseyed again and the Princess and Countess Oldi returned downstairs.

Gathering up an armful of dirty clothes, I sighed. The organisation of the Princess's wardrobe was going to be more onerous than I had imagined.

Chapter 8

March 1819

I sat by the window with a purple crepe dress spread out before me.
The seams had been let out before and there was barely enough
material remaining to do so again in order to accommodate the
Princess's expanding hips. I made my stitches small and reinforced
them at the point of strain, hoping there wouldn't be an embarrassing accident if she bent over suddenly.

The past month had flown by as I settled into the Princess's
household. Gradually, I was bringing order to her wardrobe. The
fusty smell had gone from the dressing room and, since I'd packed
away any items that weren't suitable for the time of year, there was
sufficient space to house everything neatly.

Sewing was a quiet pursuit, providing time to reflect, and my
thoughts frequently turned to Signor Fiorelli. I smiled to myself at
the memory of the way his face lit up whenever we met. Despite
that I was still unsettled and confused, plagued by guilt that I had
abandoned Sarah to die alone and yet remaining angry with her also
for her deception.

A patter of footsteps could be heard along the landing, the door opened and Victorine appeared. 'Haven't you finished?' she demanded.

'Almost,' I said, looking over her shoulder to see her tutor smiling at me.

I added the last stitches to the seam and snipped the thread. 'It's done.'

'It's a beautiful day for a walk,' he said.

Ten minutes later we set off along the avenue of cypresses and into the lane leading down to the town. Victorine walked between her tutor and myself, swinging our hands.

As we reached his home, Signor Fiorelli said, 'I promised Mamma I'd take Alfio with us.' He smiled. 'Victorine likes the company and Mamma enjoys the peace.'

'And how are you, Signorina Barton?' asked Signora Fiorelli when she opened the door with Alfio at her side. 'The Princess is keeping you occupied?'

'She certainly is,' I said. 'She often likes me to sit with her in the *salone* while I'm sewing or writing her letters and she talks to me about Princess Charlotte.'

Cosima came to greet me with a shy smile, while Alfio and Vittoria tugged at Signor Fiorelli's coat, anxious to go out.

'Come and eat with us when you can, Signorina Barton,' said Signora Fiorelli. 'Any friend of Alessandro's is always welcome at my table.' She smiled at me and then gave her son a searching look. I wasn't sure which of us blushed the deepest.

'Can we see the boats now?' asked Alfio.

Signor Fiorelli tickled his little brother's chin. 'Of course we can.'

We said goodbye to Cosima and Signora Fiorelli.

I stopped to buy thread in various colours at the draper's in the town and then, as we passed the grocer's shop, I paused.

'I'd like to call in here for a moment,' I said.

Inside the shadowy shop, the grocer leaned over the counter between a pyramid of cheeses and a bowl of eggs. A row of dried sausages hung from a rack above, their pungent aroma enveloping us.

'I am Signorina Barton,' I said. 'A few weeks ago you displayed a notice in your window regarding our dressmaking services.'

'Indeed I did.' The grocer shook his head sorrowfully. 'My condolences. I was sorry to hear your poor mother has passed on since then.'

'Thank you. Perhaps you remember she came to ask you if there had been any enquiries for us?'

He smoothed down the front of his apron. 'I told her a man had asked me about you. I remember it well because he was a foreigner. And he seemed very curious about you and your mother.'

'Do you remember what nationality he was?'

The grocer shrugged. 'German perhaps. Or English. I thought at first he might have come to ask more questions about the Princess of Wales.' He pulled at his moustache. 'There have been many enquiries of that sort but the Princess is a good customer of mine, with so many mouths to feed up at Villa Vittoria, and I'll not say a word against her.'

Victorine tugged at my skirt. 'I'm hungry,' she whispered.

'Just a moment, sweetheart.' I took her hand. 'What did he look like, Signor?'

He turned up his palms and shrugged. 'Foreigners all look the same, don't they?'

I glanced at Signor Fiorelli, who was trying not to laugh. 'Please try to remember.'

The grocer narrowed his eyes while he thought. 'Pale. And very tall. Thin.'

'Then he might be the man I saw outside the cottage,' said Signor Fiorelli.

The grocer took a notepad from under the counter and flipped through the pages. 'This is him,' he said, peering at his notes. 'His name was John Smith and he was staying at the Albergo Duomo. His wife wanted a new dress.'

'My mother enquired but no such persons stayed there,' I said. 'If you see him again, would you be kind enough to let me know? I'm staying at the Villa Vittoria.'

'Ah, working for the Princess?'

'I am.' I glanced down at Victorine. 'And in the meantime we'll have a few slices of your best salami.'

We left the shop, nibbling upon the salami as we walked. When we reached the harbour the children ran ahead of us, squealing with laughter as they chased seagulls.

We passed the cottage where Sarah and I had lived and the door opened. A young woman carrying a baby came out and crossed the street.

'I'm relieved that a new tenant was found so quickly since I had to leave without notice,' I said. 'I loved the cottage and had hoped so much that we'd settle there.'

'Don't look so sad!' said Signor Fiorelli. 'I can't bear you to be unhappy.' He took my hand and lifted it to his lips. 'You must miss your mother very much.'

I didn't answer for a moment. His amber eyes were filled with compassion and I decided to tell him the truth. 'She wasn't ...' I closed my eyes, feeling the dull ache of her loss. 'She wasn't my mother,' I confessed.

'Not your mother?'

I shook my head, unable to speak for the sudden constriction in my throat. I'd had no one to talk to about it and I longed to tell him the whole story.

He glanced at the children but they were happy watching the boats. 'She adopted you?' he asked.

'No. She stole me.'

His mouth fell open.

'I didn't know that until the night she died.' All at once the great well of my grief overflowed.

Signor Fiorelli made a small sound of distress and took out his

73

handkerchief. Gently, he blotted my tears. 'Don't cry, Signorina Barton!'

His tenderness made me weep all the more and he put his arm around me. I didn't care what any passer-by might think and buried my face in the comfort of his shoulder, breathing in the scent of clean skin and feeling the rough texture of his coat against my cheek. He rubbed my back and kissed my fingers and at last my tears were spent.

'What did you mean when you said Signora Barton stole you?' he said.

'When I was four years old she took me away from my home and family in London.'

He shook his head as if he didn't believe me. 'But why?'

I related the story Sarah had told me on her deathbed and when I'd finished he sat with his head bowed. At last, he said, 'Family is everything. I cannot imagine what it might be like not to have my family. Of course we fight sometimes but it would be inconceivable for me not to have my parents and siblings beside me, giving their love and support.' He looked up at me. 'They are my life.'

'Sarah and I were never very close,' I said. 'I've been lonely for as long as I can remember. Yes, we travelled together and we relied upon each other, but there was always something missing. We thought so differently about everything.' I shrugged. 'If my real mother hadn't died, then Sarah would have returned me to my father. For most of my life I thought her fears were irrational and it made me angry. I'm still angry.' I swallowed the lump that had risen in my throat. 'She said she took me away because she wanted to keep me safe but all I wanted was a normal life, with a proper family. Like yours.'

'It wasn't her fault your real mother died, though. Did you never wonder why you looked so different from Signora Barton?' he asked. 'I noticed that the first time we met. She was so small, plump and dark while you are tall and slender with hair the colour of a Botticelli angel's.'

74

I couldn't help smiling, despite my misery. 'Your mother told me you thought I looked like a Botticelli angel. I'm flattered. He's one of my favourite artists.'

He shook his head, his mouth curving into a wry smile. 'Mamma allows me no private thoughts.'

'If I considered it at all, I presumed I looked like Sarah's husband, Joe, the man I thought was my father.' I squinted at the horizon while I tried to picture him. 'His face was always red,' I said. 'Usually he was drunk or angry and his breath smelled rank. Sometimes, in my dreams, I hear his shouts echoing in my head. The memory of him still makes me afraid, even though he left when I was younger than Victorine is now.'

'The children!' Signor Fiorelli reared up and looked around him, one hand clasped to his breast. 'I forgot the children!'

'It's all right,' I said. 'They're over there.' I pointed to where they sat on the wall further down the harbour, playing with a collection of seagull feathers.

'Come,' he said, taking my hand again.

I looked down at his strong brown fingers enfolding my pale ones and felt a flicker of hope or happiness, I wasn't quite sure which.

He rubbed his thumb over my wrist. 'Signorina Barton, will you call me Alessandro?' he said. 'In private, at least. I cannot bear to think of you so very alone.' He glanced up at me, his expression tense. 'I want you to know I am your very good friend.'

A comforting warmth, tinged with elation, blossomed inside my chest. I gripped his hand. 'That means a great deal to me, Alessandro.'

He laughed and kissed my hand. 'Emilia,' he said. 'Such a pretty name, like its owner.'

Upstairs, the banging and hammering reached a crescendo as carpenters constructed bookshelves for the new library, while the Princess paced up and down the *salone* muttering under her breath. Countess Oldi and I bent our heads over our sewing.

At last I could stand it no longer. 'Is there something I can do for you, Ma'am?' I enquired.

The Princess's face was flushed with anger. 'My husband continues to plot against me!' She threw herself down on the sofa beside me.

I put down my needle.

'My lawyer came from Milan to see me this morning,' she said. 'Avvocato Codazzi tells me that snake in the grass Louise Demont was called to testify to the Milan Commission last month. They have employed an architect to make a plan of the Villa d'Este, where I used to live in Como. He went there with Louise and bribed the doorkeeper to let them in. The architect made sketches while Louise informed him of the former occupants of each of the bedrooms.'

'I'm not sure I understand,' I said.

The Princess sighed. 'The Commission hope to provide proof that my relationship with the Baron is adulterous because our rooms were near to one another's.'

'But that doesn't prove anything,' I said. The Baron and the Princess had adjacent rooms at Villa Vittoria but, despite their apparent affection for each other, I'd never seen any evidence of wrongdoing between them.

'The Prince of Wales goes too far!' hissed the Princess. 'He wants to be rid of me but it is impossible for him to prove any adultery, no matter how many lies they tell about me.' Her chin quivered. 'In the beginning, I tried to be a good wife, despite the continuous humiliations and his lack of consideration for my feelings.' She dabbed her eyes, smudging the charcoal on her darkened eyebrows. 'The first time I saw him I was disappointed. He was so fat and not at all like his portrait, but still I smiled and tried to be jolly.' She gave me a wan smile. 'Did you know I was forced to have my husband's mistress, Lady Jersey, as my waiting woman? It was . . . ' She swallowed. 'Intolerable.'

'How humiliating for you.'

'Princesses rarely marry for love,' she said, 'but both parties must make the best of the situation.' The expression in her eyes was inexpressibly sad. 'George never even tried.'

'Is there no way,' I said, treading carefully, 'that you can agree to part amicably?'

'If we divorce it is I who will come out badly, far worse than he will, and my allowance would be cut yet again. I'm already in debt. As a divorced woman I would never be able to return to England.'

'But, forgive me, Ma'am, do you want to return there?'

Countess Oldi put down her sewing and watched the Princess intently with her unfathomable dark gaze.

The Princess stared down at her hands. After a long pause, she sighed. 'Now that my Charlotte is dead there is little reason to return, I admit. I have never been so happy in my life as I am here with my Italian family.'

Countess Oldi dropped her scrutiny of the Princess and lifted up her sewing again, a smile curving her lips.

'Perhaps,' I said, 'you might agree to a divorce if he made you one large payment, enough to live on for the rest of your life? Once you had the funds, there need be no further concern that your allowance might be cut.'

The Princess paced the floor. 'I wish my old adviser, Henry Brougham, were here to discuss this with me.' Her face brightened. 'But my trustees are sending his brother James to see me about my accounts. I will ask him to pass a message to Henry when he returns to England.' She sat down on the arm of the sofa and patted my hand. 'I'm very happy you came to live here, Signora Barton,' she said. 'Not only are we sisters in our sorrow but you always speak such good sense.'

Chapter 9

The Fiorelli family, including Alessandro's sister Delfina, her husband Franco and their baby Enzo, was gathered around the table. Signora Fiorelli presided over the vast dish of oxtail stew while Dottore Fiorelli poured red wine. Even little Alfio had a splash of it in his water.

'Is your family always as noisy as this?' I said to Alessandro.

He laughed. 'You should hear it when we argue! Since there are so many of us we always have to shout to make ourselves heard.'

The baby began to cry, his wails rising above the hubbub, and Signora Fiorelli lifted him to her shoulder and sang to him, nuzzling into his little neck.

Watching the baby's head nodding against his grandmother's cheek as he fell asleep, I wondered for a moment if my real mother had cared for me so tenderly. The pain of not remembering her was sharp.

I looked around at Alessandro's family and saw how they touched each other all the time: Jacopo playfully punching Fabrizio on his shoulder, Delfina tucking a loose curl into Gina's hairband, Dottore Fiorelli trailing his fingers over his wife's arm as he passed by and tickling Alfio's neck.

'Will you hold him a moment?' Signora Fiorelli handed the baby to me while she fetched cheese and fruit to the table.

The infant was warm and milk-scented, heavy in my arms as he slept.

'Beautiful, isn't he?' said Alessandro, dropping a kiss on his nephew's forehead. 'It doesn't seem five minutes since Alfio was this small.'

'Am I holding him properly?' I asked. 'I've had so little to do with babies.'

Alessandro laughed. 'Don't be nervous. Babies are tough little creatures.'

Did I imagine that Signora Fiorelli had a speculative gleam in her eyes as she looked at us? I bent my head to study Enzo's tiny fingernails and hide my blushes.

After supper, we retired to the *salone* and Cosima played the piano while the rest of us sang.

Later, I glanced at the clock on the mantelpiece and touched Alessandro's sleeve. 'I must go,' I said. 'The Baron locks the doors after dark.'

I said my goodbyes to each member of the family and left with a chorus of good wishes resounding in my ears. Flushed with wine, song and good company, Alessandro and I went out into the darkening evening.

'What a lovely family you have,' I said to him.

'I thank God for them every day.'

Hand in hand, we walked along the tree-lined lane and climbed the hill.

As we walked, I imagined what it would be like to be part of such a family. The safety and security of it would be wonderful but there would be little privacy or space to think your own thoughts.

'You're very quiet,' said Alessandro later, when we reached the avenue of cypress trees leading to Villa Vittoria.

'I was wondering about my lost family,' I said.

He squeezed my hand. 'You'll make a family of your own one day.'

'I hope so.'

He took me by my shoulders. 'You *will*,' he said. And then he kissed me.

His lips were warm and he held me as lightly as thistledown.

A tremor ran through my limbs and I closed my eyes, enjoying the strange sensation.

Then he released me. 'Goodnight, Emilia,' he murmured.

'Goodnight, Alessandro,' I said. I wanted him to kiss me again but he set off home.

Reluctantly, I set off down the avenue. Halfway along, I turned and saw him wave to me before fading into the gloaming.

The servants' dining room was full of gossip about the Princess's visitor.

'Faustina took wine and olives to him while he was talking to the Baron,' Mariette said as we ate our soup. 'James Brougham, he's called,' she said, struggling with the unfamiliar pronunciation. 'He's come to look at the Princess's accounts.'

'The Princess mentioned he was expected,' I said.

Mariette whispered, 'Everyone knows the Princess has big debts in England as well as here. She had to sell the Villa d'Este to pay some of them off and came to Pesaro because she can live more cheaply here.'

'Was the Villa d'Este very grand, then?' I asked.

'Oh, yes!' Mariette opened her brown eyes wide.

'What a pity she had to sell it! Still, Villa Vittoria is being renovated.'

'It's hardly a palace, though, is it?' said Mariette. 'But then, she doesn't live like a princess.' She mopped up the last of her soup with a piece of bread. 'Oh, well, best get on. There's to be a party tonight to welcome Mr Brougham.'

'I wrote the invitation cards,' I said. 'Cardinal Albani will be here, along with the cream of Pesaro society.'

Mariette made a face. 'More work for us mere servants, then.'

I returned to the Princess's dressing room to sew a piece of lace onto the frill of her shift.

Later that afternoon, the Baron pushed open the dressing-room door. 'Signorina Barton,' he said, 'the Princess wants you in the *salone*. You're to write a letter for her.'

Downstairs, a man with a large nose and a determined chin was sitting with the Princess.

The Baron strode over to lean his elbow on the mantelpiece and rest one booted foot on the fender. As usual, he appeared entirely at ease.

The Princess gestured me towards the writing desk. I took out a piece of paper, a pen and the inkwell.

The visitor, James Brougham, glanced at me and then at the Princess with one eyebrow raised.

'Signorina Barton is my Mistress of the Wardrobe and my secretary,' she said. 'You may speak freely before her.'

'I see,' said Mr Brougham, looking me up and down.

I decided I didn't like him.

'I wish to attempt negotiations again with the Prince of Wales,' said the Princess. 'My previous allowance of thirty-five thousand pounds a year is insufficient for my responsibilities now. It cannot be less than fifty thousand.'

I hoped my gasp hadn't been audible and hurriedly dipped the pen in the inkwell.

'The Prince of Wales may not agree,' said Mr Brougham. 'Perhaps a lump sum and a smaller income to follow?'

'I doubt I'd ever receive it,' said the Princess.

I held the pen ready. 'Will you dictate, Ma'am?'

'I never find the right words,' said the Princess, 'especially in English. No, you write it, Signorina Barton, and pass it to Mr Brougham to look at. Address it to Mr Henry Brougham.'

I frowned and the Princess smiled at my confusion. 'Mr Henry Brougham, my adviser, is Mr James Brougham's elder brother.'

'I see,' I said.

'And don't forget to tell the Prince of Wales that if he agrees to my terms, I will promise never to return to England.'

'Yes, Ma'am.' I bent my head over the paper. My previous duties as the Princess's secretary had consisted of writing invitations to dinners or the occasional letter to an acquaintance but this was far more challenging. I took care to write neatly and to set out the proposal as discussed.

As my pen scratched across the paper the Princess and James Brougham continued their conversation while the Baron silently watched them.

'Perhaps it is a good time to finalise a divorce now,' said Mr Brougham, 'before the Milan Commission report their findings to the Prince of Wales. It would be better for all parties if there was a dissolution of the marriage by Parliamentary Bill rather than in open court.'

The Princess shuddered. 'I agree.'

Mr Brougham turned to the Baron. 'I must see the account books to make my report to the trustees. Will you be on hand if required?'

'Most certainly,' said the Baron. 'I shall bring them to you in the morning room.'

'Really, I don't know why my trustees are so anxious about a few trifling debts,' said the Princess. 'If I were to die tomorrow they could all be paid off at once. There are the horses and my jewels, for a start.'

'Unfortunately,' said Mr Brougham, 'your creditors require to be paid now, not at some distant date in the future.'

'I doubt I'd have debts,' grumbled the Princess, 'if my gentlemen and servants before I came to Pesaro hadn't been so incompetent or so determined to cheat me. Thankfully, the Baron is managing my affairs now.' She smiled at him, busy cleaning his nails with a pen-knife as he leaned against the mantelpiece.

'And you are content to live in Pesaro?' asked Mr Brougham doubtfully. 'It's very provincial and this house does not befit someone of your position.'

'I have rarely felt as settled as I do here amongst the Italians,' said the Princess, 'except for my fear that the Prince of Wales will send his spies to poison or kill me.'

I put down my pen and blotted the ink dry.

'Finished?' asked the Princess.

'Yes, Ma'am.' I handed the letter to Mr Brougham and returned upstairs.

The dressing-room window was left open while I sewed, letting in a gentle spring breeze and the sound of the builders, hammering and sawing. My thoughts began to drift, reliving the warmth and gentleness of Alessandro's kiss. He made my heart beat faster and I hoped, how very much I hoped, that he felt the same about me.

Through the half-open door to the Princess's bedroom, I heard a floorboard creak. The maid had cleaned the room earlier so perhaps the Princess was preparing to take a nap. I tip-toed towards the door, intending to close it, and was surprised to glimpse Mr Brougham's reflection in the mirror, examining the items on the dressing table.

'May I help you?' I asked.

He jumped and dropped a silver-backed hairbrush onto the dressing table with a clatter. 'You startled me!' he said.

I waited, aware that my position in the household did not empower me to accuse him of trespass.

Under my questioning gaze, Mr Brougham turned slightly pink. He cleared his throat. 'You may wonder why I'm here . . .'

I waited.

He coughed again and examined his fingernails. His expression cleared. 'The Princess's trustees have charged me with the responsibility of determining how she lives.'

'How she lives?' I echoed.

'Indeed,' he said. 'My purpose is to discuss ways and means for the Princess to make economies and structure a method of paying her creditors.'

'And that relates to your presence here in the Princess's private quarters?'

'I am required to satisfy the trustees that she is not overly extravagant.' Mr Brougham glanced around the bedroom until his eyes rested on Victorine's bed and he frowned. 'Does the child sleep here, with the Princess?'

'I believe so.'

'Every night?'

'My quarters are downstairs so I couldn't say.'

'And the Baron's bedchamber is adjacent to this room?'

'The Princess must be protected,' I said. 'There have been threats to her life.'

'I've finished here,' said Mr Brougham. He sounded disappointed.

'Do let me show you out, then.'

He followed me through the dressing-room door and paused to study the neatly arranged shelves and piles of hatboxes. He ran a finger over a pile of folded nightshifts and lifted the lid of the ottoman to peep inside. 'Does the Baron keep his clothes in here, too?'

'Certainly not,' I said, in as reproachful a tone as I could.

Mr Brougham sighed. 'Would you say the Princess's wardrobe is extravagant, Signorina Barton?'

'Not at all,' I said, 'especially for a woman of her rank. Many of the Princess's clothes have seen better days and I'm in the process of mending and refurbishing them.'

He nodded approvingly. 'It's essential to curb any excessive spending.'

I opened the door to the landing. 'Good day, Mr Brougham.' I watched him until he had descended the stairs before returning to my sewing.

The encounter left me unsettled. My hackles had risen when I saw him creeping about the Princess's quarters and handling her private possessions. He may have been the Princess's guest but there was something very unsavoury about his line of questioning.

Closing the dressing-room door behind me, I went downstairs and tapped on the door of the Baron's study.

He bade me enter and I found him standing before the window with his back to me, apparently lost in thought. I waited in silence until he turned to face me.

'Was there something, Signorina Barton?'

'Yes, Baron.' I found it awkward to put into words what had to be said. 'When I came to Villa Vittoria you asked me to keep you appraised of any irregularities.'

His eyes narrowed. 'An intruder?'

'No,' I said. 'A guest.'

'Brougham?'

'I found him in the Princess's bedroom looking at her personal items,' I said, finding it impossible to meet his eyes. 'He asked me if you shared her dressing room and about the sleeping arrangements on that floor.'

'And what did you tell him?'

'As little as possible except that Victorine's bed is in the Princess's room and, as far as I was aware, that is where she sleeps every night.'

The Baron nodded his head. 'Which is all perfectly correct. You have done well, Signorina Barton.'

He smiled at me with unusual warmth in his eyes, which made me uncomfortable.

'Then I shall return to my duties,' I said.

He opened the door for me with a flourish. 'I shall tell the Princess you are a good and faithful servant, Signorina Barton. It's good to know you have her welfare at heart.'

'I trust there was never any doubt of that, Baron.' I held my head high and swept from the room.

Chapter 10

June 1819

The sails billowed and cracked above our heads as the Princess's yacht turned into the wind. The breeze teased my hair from the front of my bonnet and I lifted my face to the sun, breathing in the briny air. I had shed my mourning clothes a few days before and was revelling in the cool comfort of lightweight muslin after months of unrelieved black.

'You look happy,' said Alessandro, his eyes bright with enjoyment.

The sunshine touched his hair with bronze lights and I longed to run my fingers through it, as I had the night before when we'd lingered in the avenue of cypresses to kiss each other goodnight. We'd been entranced by the lights of a myriad fireflies illuminating the darkness: a romantic display seemingly provided just for us.

'Emilia?'

I came back to the present, a half-smile playing on my lips. 'It's so exhilarating!' I said. 'We're travelling much faster than we could in any coach.'

A short distance from us the Princess, dressed as an admiral in a naval-style coat and tricorn hat, sat with Willy and the Baron.

She stared out to sea, her tense expression at odds with the jaunty feather in her hat. Countess Oldi, a poor sailor, had retired to the cabin. Victorine peered over the side of the yacht, squealing whenever sea spray splashed her face. Her father kept a tight grip on her skirt.

'It was kind of the Princess to invite us today,' I said to Alessandro. I didn't mention she'd said she liked to see young people enjoying each other's company and that I ought to give handsome Signor Fiorelli more encouragement. Perhaps she'd noticed more than I thought but, unlike most employers, she hadn't forbidden me to have a suitor.

'She looks anxious,' said Alessandro.

I nodded. 'Lord Brougham has written to tell her divorce proceedings against her may start in November.'

'Even if there is a divorce, she can't marry the Baron,' said Alessandro. 'Not while his wife is alive, anyway.'

'They act as if they're a married couple, don't they?' I murmured, watching the Princess lean forwards and touch the Baron's arm. 'However unlikely their relationship, there's a genuine affection between them.'

Alessandro shrugged. 'The Baron knows who butters his bread.'

Victorine prattled to the Princess, making her laugh. Willy was watching the little girl, too. His mouth was twisted in its usual sneer but I remembered Marietta telling me that he'd slept in the Princess's bedroom until the Baron came into her life four years before. Although I didn't much care for Willy, I felt sorry for him if Victorine had displaced him in his adoptive mother's affections.

'What do you mean by "he knows who butters his bread"?' I asked.

'Bartolomeo Pergami wasn't a baron until the Princess bought the title for him,' said Alessandro.

'No!'

'The Princess is surrounded by the Pergami family. They're all living off her wealth. Besides . . .'

'Besides, what, Alessandro?'

'It's gossip,' he said, 'told to me by one of the footmen who was with the Princess before I came to work at Villa Vittoria. I don't know if there's any truth in it but stealing wasn't the only reason Louise Demont was turned off.'

'What then?'

'The Princess discovered the Baron had been, shall we say, rather too *close* to Signorina Demont.'

I caught my breath. 'But if that were the case,' I said, 'wouldn't the Princess have turned off the Baron, too?'

'She's in thrall to him,' said Alessandro. 'He runs every aspect of her household. All her English attendants have gone, the Baron made sure of that, and she can't do without him. I suspect the Princess simply pretends it never happened so all can go on as before. And I wouldn't be surprised if he is making a tidy profit out of managing the household.'

'I don't like to think of her being cheated,' I said. 'She's shown me nothing but kindness.'

'You remind her of her daughter.'

Covertly, I watched the Princess playing a clapping game with Victorine. It wasn't so strange if she looked for a substitute child. 'This morning she said she may go to London to settle the matter of a divorce,' I said.

'London?' Alessandro frowned. 'Surely she wouldn't take the Baron there?'

'That would annoy the Prince of Wales, wouldn't it?' I said, turning my face into the wind.

The jagged coastline slid past as the yacht sliced through the water and I wondered if the Princess really would visit London. I'd never thought much about England but now I was intensely curious. My real father lived there and I'd begun to lie awake at night wondering about him.

Half an hour later the Captain anchored the boat off a small bay.

The crew lashed a sail into a sunshade and placed a table underneath. They spread it with a linen cloth and served a picnic of poached fish and cold meats, crusty bread and bowls of olives with rosemary and lemon. Bottles of white wine cooled in buckets in the shade.

'Sailing always makes me ravenous,' said the Princess, picking up a chicken drumstick and eating it from her fingers. She pulled off a small piece of meat and fed it to Victorine.

Willy piled his plate high and ate without speaking, occasionally throwing a piece of bread to the seagulls who cried overhead.

The Princess, her face flushed by the sun, smiled at the Baron. 'Isn't this perfect, my love?'

I was pleased that the excursion had lifted her spirits. My wine glass was refilled as soon as I finished drinking it and, after we'd eaten the picnic, I grew drowsy in the warmth of the sun. The Princess retired inside the yacht and the Baron sat in the prow with a bottle of wine. Willy stared morosely at the coastline.

Victorine climbed onto my knee and pushed her thumb in her mouth. A few minutes later her eyelashes fluttered and she became warm and heavy in my arms. I yawned and glanced up to see Alessandro was smothering a yawn, too.

He blew me a kiss and smiled lazily at me as I rested my chin on the sleeping child's head. Happiness flowed through my veins. I tipped back my face to watch powder puffs of cloud drift across the cerulean sky. The yacht rocked gently on the swell of the sea while waves slapped rhythmically against the side of the boat.

Unable to resist any longer, I slept.

I put down the pen and waited for the Princess to decide what she wanted me to write in her letter to Lady Charlotte Lindsay. The air in the *salone* was stifling and I looked longingly out of the window. The long, languorous days of summer in Pesaro were so hot that sometimes it was difficult to find the energy to do more than seek out a new patch of shade.

The Princess lay on the sofa, wriggling her bare toes and fanning herself. 'You can write that the report of the Milan Commission is evidence that the Prince Regent is maliciously at work against me,' she said. She poked a finger under her wig and scratched her scalp. 'I desperately want to be rid of him but perhaps separation by agreement has the advantage of avoiding taking the matter to Parliament.' She nodded decisively. 'Tell Lady Charlotte to chivvy Henry Brougham to hurry up and respond to my proposal.'

I dipped the pen in the inkwell and began to write.

The Princess rubbed the heels of her hands in her eyes. 'I must be quit of this blackguard of a husband before I go mad with worry.' She stood up and slipped on her shoes. 'I'm going to sit in the garden. I shan't need you this afternoon if you want to take Victorine swimming. It's too hot for her to walk so take one of the carriages.' She smiled. 'And ask Signor Fiorelli to accompany you.'

'Thank you, Ma'am, I'd like that.' Even the thought of a dip in the sea made me feel cooler.

I found Alessandro sitting in the shade of an oak tree with Victorine. He leaned against the trunk with his sleeves rolled up, listening to her read.

'The Princess has given me the afternoon off to go swimming,' I said.

Alessandro's face broke into a wide smile and the little girl clapped her hands. 'Can we go now?'

'Finish that page first,' he said.

She scowled but picked up her book again, her finger moving beneath each word as she read.

'Very good,' said Alessandro, when she finished. 'There's nothing more fulfilling than seeing a child's mind blossoming,' he said as we walked towards the stables. 'Every child should have the opportunity of an education. I dream of owning my own school one day. One where I can educate poor boys . . . '

'And girls?' I asked.

He smiled. 'And girls.'

'That's a worthy ambition, Alessandro.'

'I've spoken about it to the Princess, since she's so fond of children. Willy, of course, she took into her household but she also adopted several poor orphans in England, fostered them in suitable families and educated them.'

I heard the zeal in his voice. 'You should ask her to support you in such a venture,' I said.

Fifteen minutes later we were in the shell-shaped phaeton jogging along a lane perfumed with the honeyed scent of wild broom. We collected Alfio from the Fiorelli house and soon after we arrived at the wide stretch of golden sand that was the Baia Flaminia. The sea was as calm as a millpond and melded at the horizon with the great dome of blue sky.

Others had come down from their villas and horse-drawn bathing machines were lined up in the surf. I hired one and Victorine and I went inside to change into our swimming shifts.

'Hold on to the bench, Victorine,' I said, tucking her hair into a muslin cap. I rapped on the wall and a moment later the bathing machine began to roll into the sea. Once it came to a standstill I helped her down the steps into the water. I gasped as a wave broke over my thighs.

Victorine squealed. 'It's cold!'

Silver fish swam around our feet as we wriggled our toes on the sandy seabed, avoiding fronds of drifting seaweed. My cotton swimming shift billowed out around me and there was a delicious freedom in the feeling of the water against my naked skin beneath. The sun was hot on my shoulders but the rest of me was blessedly cool.

I heard a shout and saw Alessandro wading towards us with Alfio on his shoulders.

'How are my little mermaids?' he called.

Victorine splashed him and screamed when he splashed her back.

'Isn't it glorious to be cool?' I said, bobbing up and down in the undulating waves.

We stood in a circle holding hands and I sang 'Ring a Ring o' Roses' in English, and told the children the tale of the Plague in London a hundred and fifty years before. 'And then there was a Great Fire,' I said, 'and all the rats and the fleas were burned and the Plague went away.'

We sang the song again and the children shrieked with laughter when we fell down, dipping our heads under the water. My mob cap floated away and my hair tumbled around my shoulders.

'My beautiful Botticelli Venus,' said Alessandro. He picked up one of my curls and lifted it to his lips, never taking his eyes off me. His wet shirt was moulded to his muscular chest and there was a hint of dark hair on the sun-kissed skin exposed by the open-necked collar.

A quiver ran down my spine as I imagined him without his shirt.

'Cold?' he whispered.

I shook my head and he laughed. 'Come on, I'm going to teach you to swim.'

An hour later the children were shivering and their lips turning blue. 'Time to come out of the water,' I said, ignoring their cries of protest.

Victorine and I returned to the bathing machine to change. Afterwards, Alessandro and Alfio were waiting for us, their shirts and breeches already drying in the sun. I rubbed Victorine's hair with a towel and she and Alfio set off along the tideline to collect the mother-of-pearl shells that shimmered in the sand.

Alessandro lay with his arms behind his head and regarded me through heavy-lidded eyes.

I let sand trickle through my fingers whilst my head was bowed so he wouldn't see my blushes. I wanted so much to lie down beside him but propriety forbade it.

'I wonder if your mother was as lovely as you?' he said.

'I wish I could remember her.' I gazed out to sea, listening to the gentle hiss of the waves as they foamed on the shore.

Alessandro touched my mouth with the tip of his finger to still its trembling. 'Your home is here in Italy now.' He turned on his side to face me. 'Emilia, you do know that I love you, don't you?' A muscle flickered in his jaw.

I lifted his hand to my cheek. 'I hoped so,' I said, kissing his palm, 'because I love you, too.'

The tension faded from his face. 'As soon as I saw you,' he said, 'I knew we were destined for each other.'

Joy blossomed in my heart. 'I felt the same. I could hardly look at you in case you guessed.'

Alessandro laughed, his eyes shining. 'Was that why you blushed?'

I leaned towards him to drop a kiss on his salty lips. 'Now you know my innermost feelings,' I said.

'Don't let us keep secrets from each other, Emilia.' His fingers gripped mine. 'Promise me?'

'I promise,' I said, looking into his eyes.

Chapter 11

October 1819

Lyons, France

I slid the claret silk gown over the Princess's head, careful not to open the loosely tacked seams. We'd purchased the silk from one of the Lyonnais weavers shortly after we arrived here, since the Princess was determined to make an elegant appearance on her arrival in England.

The past weeks had been exhausting. It was ironic that I'd arrived in Pesaro with the firm idea of escaping my nomadic life but no sooner had I found a place to settle than the Princess's restlessness moved us on. Almost overnight her household had been packed into three post-chaises and we'd set off, incognito, for Parma.

The Baron hired Villa San Bono for us in the Piacentini Hills. The Princess received visitors late at night and her emissaries, including her Milanese lawyer, came and went. In the middle of September, a courier arrived with a letter from Henry Brougham warning her not to go to London but to Lyons, where he would meet her. That same night the household left Villa San Bono.

We spent a month in a dilapidated castle in the province of Alessandria, in the King of Sardinia's lands. The Baron and Willy Austin went backwards and forwards to Milan and Como, seeking witnesses to testify for the Princess against the Milan Commission. A month later we departed in a flurry for Lyons. Then we waited for Lord Brougham.

'Be careful of the pins, Ma'am,' I warned as I helped the Princess to remove the emerald gown.

'I cannot bear not knowing what is happening in London,' she said, fretfully. 'I need to know the mood of the people so I'm prepared for the kind of reception I'll receive.' She sighed. 'Write to Lady Hamilton and ask her to travel back to London with me after Henry Brougham's visit. Always assuming, of course, that he does eventually grace me with his presence.'

'There's still no confirmation of his arrival, Ma'am?'

She shook her head. 'It angers me that I came to Lyons at his request instead of going straight to London. Soon the winter will come. I don't care to travel long distances in the cold.'

I sat down at the Princess's writing desk. Once I'd finished her letter I returned to the parlour, where Alessandro was reading with Victorine. Peggy was propped up beside them.

'I see you have two attentive pupils today, Signor Fiorelli,' I said.

'They're working very hard.' Alessandro's smile was warm. 'Perhaps a walk in the garden as a reward?'

Outside, we ambled along the gravel paths while Victorine skipped ahead, clutching Peggy under her arm. Russet leaves twirled down from an oak tree and I smiled as the little girl jumped up to catch them.

'The poor Princess,' I said, shivering in the autumnal breeze. 'Her spies have informed her Louise Demont is in London, ready to provide evidence against her. The sooner Lord Brougham arrives, the better. She'll not regain her equilibrium until she's faced her antagonists in London.'

'Once she's sailed for England, we can return to Pesaro,' said Alessandro. 'I want so much to go home to my family.' A gust of wind loosed one of my curls and he tucked it behind my ear. 'You look strained,' he said. 'What is it?'

I hesitated then said, 'But where is *my* home? Isn't home wherever your family is?'

Alessandro studied my face, his expression suddenly watchful. 'Has all this talk of London unsettled you?'

I shrugged. 'I keep wondering about my father . . .'

'You can't change the past,' he said, kissing the tip of my nose. 'You must look forward to the future.'

I sat up late stitching the Princess's gown and then lay awake while I went over and over in my head what Sarah had told me about my parents. I tried desperately to recall my father but could only hear Joe's cruel voice in my mind. For nearly as long as I could remember there had been just Sarah and me. Alessandro's friendship and love had eased my loneliness but still I wept from a painful yearning to belong, to know that I was connected by blood with another.

In the morning I took out the quilted petticoat and counted the gold coins sewn into the hem. I sat on the edge of the bed for an age deciding what to do.

After breakfast I asked the Baron if it was convenient for the Princess to have a further fitting.

Half an hour later she admitted me to her bedroom and I helped her into the gown. 'It suits you,' I said.

'I shall look very fine once the pearls are sewn onto the skirt,' she said, studying her reflection in the mirror.

I busied myself adjusting a shoulder seam while I plucked up courage. 'Ma'am?' I said. 'There's something I should like to ask you, if I may.'

She waved a hand. 'Ask!'

'Since Henry Brougham has still not arrived,' I said, 'I wondered if it might be helpful if I travelled to England? You wished to know what kind of reception you might receive in London. I could gauge that and write to you. Also, I could visit Lady Hamilton and request she comes to attend you.'

The Princess raised her eyebrows. 'Why would you do this?'

'I have a particular reason for wishing to visit London.'

'Explain yourself!'

My mouth was dry. 'A little while ago I discovered Signora Barton was not my mother.'

The Princess pressed a hand to her mouth, her eyes gleaming. 'How intriguing!'

'When she was dying, she confessed that, after my real mother died when I was four, she stole me from my family,' I said. 'It came as a great shock.'

'I can see that it must have.'

'She was fond of me and worried about my father bringing me up without my mother to guide him and so she took me away. Now that I know I have a father in London, I want to find him.'

'You might not like him,' said the Princess. 'Families can be very strange.' She sighed. 'This I know for a fact.'

I waited, my fists clenched so hard my nails bit into my palms.

'You must finish my gown quickly, Signorina Barton,' the Princess said. 'You will want to travel before the winter storms arrive.'

I was anxious to speak privately with Alessandro but there were ears behind every door in the cramped rented villa where we stayed with the Princess. Later that afternoon, I asked him to accompany me to the remains of the Roman amphitheatre. Hand in hand, we strolled through the cobbled streets of Lyons, my apprehension growing with each step I took.

At last we stood at the brow of the hill looking down to where archaeologists were excavating the outer perimeter of the arena. I could delay no longer and, stomach churning, told Alessandro that I had decided to go to London.

'No!' he said, the colour draining from his cheeks.

'I leave in a few days and the Princess has written to Lady Hamilton telling her to expect me,' I said, trying to keep my voice calm.

'You could be gone for months and you didn't think to discuss this with me?'

The last thing I wanted was to hurt him. 'Alessandro, it was a decision I had to make by myself.' I clenched my fists. 'I cannot be at peace until I find my father.'

'But you don't even remember him.' Alessandro's chin quivered. 'He's nothing to you.'

I looked away from him, unable to face his misery. 'It's true that, even if I find him, it's possible I may feel no sense of connection. But don't you see, I must be sure?'

He gripped my shoulders. 'Please don't go.' His jaw clenched. 'I forbid it!'

One of the archaeologists glanced up from his digging and stared curiously at us.

'I have to know where I come from and you have no right to forbid me to find out,' I said.

He stepped back as if I'd slapped him. 'But I want that right,' he said, quietly. 'I love you and I thought you loved me?'

I couldn't bear seeing pain in his eyes and knowing I was the cause of it. 'You know I do!' I reached out to him. 'But surely you understand how important this is to me? I've spent most of my life wandering with no place to call home. Since Ma died it's as if the ground has been swept from under my feet.'

He grasped my hand. 'If you loved me, you wouldn't leave me.'

I stared at him, wounded he was thinking only of himself and didn't understand my feelings. 'If *you* loved *me*, you'd let me go with your blessing,' I said. I swallowed a wave of nausea and spoke in a more conciliatory fashion. 'I won't be away more than a few months. Don't you want me to be happy, Alessandro?'

He ran his hands through his curls, leaving them standing up like a halo. 'I shall make you happy. I will! I love you, Emilia.' Imprisoning me so tightly in his arms that I could barely breathe, he pressed desperate kisses on my face. 'I can't bear to lose you. Stay here and marry me!'

I struggled free from his clinging embrace. This wasn't how a proposal of marriage should be. Where were the sweet words, the consideration for my needs and the gentle caresses? 'You know I love you,' I said, 'but I could never marry a man who would deprive me of the chance of finding my family.'

Alessandro shook his head. 'Too much time has passed to build the years of memories that bind you into a proper family.' He cupped my chin in his hands and made me look at him. 'My family love you already. Mamma even unwrapped her wedding veil the other day to show me. We'll have children and make a family of our own. Emilia, tell me you'll marry me?'

I shivered with the icy realisation that we had reached an impasse. I'd hoped so much that Alessandro would propose, but not like this.

'Emilia?' he said.

If he truly loved me, he'd wait for me. 'Alessandro . . .' I said, my voice breaking. 'I *have* to go to England but I'll come back.'

His face crumpled. 'You won't,' he said, his voice leaden with despair. 'You'll find your father and want to stay with him.'

'I will come back!' I said. 'Meanwhile, we can write to each other.' I took a deep breath and gripped his hand. 'Look at me! I love you, Alessandro, and I do want to marry you, but I must come to you with a willing heart. If we marry now I may never have the chance again to look for my father,' I said, 'especially if we have children. I'd always have regrets and that would place an intolerable strain on our love.'

'How long must I wait? I need you here, with me.' He pulled his hand away.

I caught hold of his sleeve. 'Write to me!' I pleaded.

He didn't look at me but after a long moment he gave a brief nod and slipped out of my grasp.

Shaking, I stared after him as he hurried down the hill, unable to believe that Alessandro didn't love me enough to let me leave with his blessing.

Chapter 12

November 1819

London

It was growing dark when the Lidcomes' carriage drew up outside Lady Hamilton's family home in Portman Street. I glanced through the window at a street of narrow townhouses built of grimy yellow brick and couldn't help thinking how dreary the scene looked by comparison with Italy's golden stone and colour-washed façades.

Mrs Lidcome patted my wrist. 'Are you sure you wouldn't like me to come in with you, Miss Barton?'

I resisted the impulse to accept. I'd set this train of events in motion and must see it through. 'I've trespassed enough on your goodwill,' I said, 'but perhaps you'd wait until I've gone inside?' I'd been worrying ever since we left Dover about what I would do if Lady Hamilton hadn't received the Princess's letter or if she wasn't prepared to allow a complete stranger to stay with her.

'My dear, I wouldn't dream of driving away until I knew you were safe!' said Mrs Lidcome.

The carriage door opened and I sighed to see the rain hissing down and bouncing up off the pavement. It had rained without ceasing ever since I'd gone on deck as the packet approached the white cliffs of Dover. A penetrating wind and sullen sky had done nothing to lift my sadly sunken spirits.

The coachman held an umbrella over my head as I scurried from the carriage. I shivered, contemplating my sodden shoes and damp hem until he returned with my travelling bags, then knocked on the door. I glanced back at Mrs Lidcome, her face ghost-like at the streaming carriage window. She nodded encouragingly.

I'd been lucky to find such a pleasant travelling companion for the sea crossing. Willy Austin had escorted me on the long journey from Lyons to Calais and left me at an inn while he searched for a suitable chaperone. Mr and Mrs Lidcome had been prepared to undertake the task and I'd kept their children amused while their mother suffered the effects of a rough crossing.

The door opened. I swallowed my trepidation and went inside.

Lady Hamilton, dressed in deepest mourning, received me in her elegant drawing room. Unsmiling and dark-haired, she looked me up and down with sharply inquisitive eyes. I dropped a curtsey and she languidly waved her long fingers at a chair.

'I do hope my arrival is not too much of an inconvenience, Lady Hamilton?' The chair was plumply upholstered and I arranged my damp skirt so as not to sully the pristine cream satin.

'The Princess still requires me to join her?' Still she didn't smile or make me feel any less uncomfortable.

'She would be pleased to have your company,' I said. I glanced at the fire crackling in the marble chimneypiece and longed to sit closer to it.

Lady Hamilton sighed as she smoothed her impeccably cut skirt. 'I suppose I must uproot myself to carry out her bidding.' She pursed her lips. 'How does she like her Italian lady-in-waiting?' She leaned her angular body forward and studied me intently.

'The Countess Oldi? I believe the Princess finds her agreeable.'

Lady Hamilton sniffed. 'Pergami's sister, with a failed marriage behind her. And is the Princess still racketing about seeking diversions here, there and everywhere?'

'She's too apprehensive of what the Prince Regent will do next to take a great deal of enjoyment from anything at present,' I said.

'Perhaps that is as well. This would not be a good time to make herself look undignified or foolish. The Prince Regent wouldn't hesitate to use it against her.'

'The Princess would welcome your support. She doesn't care to return to England attended by her Italian household.'

Lady Hamilton fixed me with a gimlet stare. 'And what is your role in her employ, Miss Barton?'

'I suspect you will find it very irregular, Lady Hamilton.' I was absolutely sure that she would. 'The Princess's home in Pesaro is not as imposing as the Villa Caprile and certainly not as magnificent as the Villa d'Este. In fact . . . '

'Yes, yes,' said Lady Hamilton. 'I understand Villa Vittoria is little more than a farmhouse.'

'The Princess calls it a cottage.' I hesitated. 'I'm sure you're aware how informal she can be . . . '

'That may be an extremely polite way of describing her actions, Miss Barton,' said Lady Hamilton with a dry smile. 'Apparently you came to her rescue after she was involved in a carriage accident?'

I nodded. 'Subsequently, she offered me a position as her Mistress of the Wardrobe. And I write her letters for her.'

'How did you come to be in Italy, Miss Barton? What of your family? Surely you were not travelling alone?'

'I was not,' I said. 'But I have come to England to find my father.'

Lady Hamilton's nostrils flared as if she had scented something unpleasant. 'You do not *know* your father, then?'

I shook my head, realising that she probably imagined I was illegitimate. 'My father is Sir Frederick Langdon. He used to live in Grosvenor Street. Perhaps you might have heard of him?'

'Indeed I have.'

Despite my curiosity and excitement, Lady Hamilton's expression discouraged me from asking her about him. 'A little while ago I discovered that I was stolen away from my family by my mother's maid when I was four years old.'

Lady Hamilton drew in her breath. 'I remember the scandal. Sir Frederick's wife drowned herself . . .'

'My mother,' I said.

'Do you have proof that you are who you say you are?'

I shook my head. 'I want nothing from my father, except to meet him.'

'Are you telling the truth? Are you really the lost Langdon girl?' Her tone was sharp.

'Yes.' I looked her firmly in the eye.

'Then at least I may console myself that the Princess has been waited on by the daughter of a member of the landed gentry and not simply another of her waifs and strays.'

'Landed gentry?'

Lady Hamilton gave me a wintry smile. 'Your father owns the Langdon Hall estate in Hampshire.'

'So he isn't still living in Grosvenor Street?' I rubbed my eyes. 'I'd hoped to meet him and then travel back to Italy with you,' I said. 'But if I have to go to Hampshire . . .'

'His London house is still in Grosvenor Street, as far as I am aware,' said Lady Hamilton. 'I daresay he stays there while Parliament is sitting.'

'If he'll receive me, I shall call on him tomorrow.' I sighed. 'All I want is to meet him but I expect, like you, he'll think I'm a fortune hunter.' Suddenly I was so tired I could cry.

Surprisingly, Lady Hamilton's expression softened. 'We shall see what tomorrow brings.' She rang the bell on the side table and a moment later the maid arrived.

'Take Miss Barton to her room and send up some supper on a tray,' said Lady Hamilton.

Relieved that I was to avoid a formal dinner, I dropped a curtsey and followed the maid upstairs.

The guest room was comfortably furnished but chilly, even though a meagre fire burned in the grate. I kicked off my wet shoes and sat by the fire to warm my toes. I must have dozed because the next thing I heard was the maid placing a supper tray on the table beside me.

After I'd eaten the soup and apple pie I began to unpack. Drooping with fatigue, I released the pins from my hair and searched the bag for my hairbrush. It was then I realised with a jolt that Peggy wasn't there. I snatched up the second bag, delved under the folded clothes and then tipped everything out onto the bedroom chair. Nothing. In my haste to pack I must have left the doll behind. I remembered then that I'd last seen her in Victorine's arms.

I missed Alessandro so much and there was a horrible aching void in my chest. My life would be unimaginably bleak if my father wouldn't see me and if Alessandro didn't still want to marry me when I returned to Pesaro. Shivering, I undressed and climbed into the cold bed, close to tears. In Peggy's absence, I hugged one of the pillows, attempting to draw comfort from its downy softness.

The following morning, I awoke when the maid lit the fire. It took me a moment to realise where I was. Grey light filtered in through the curtains and I sat up in bed. The bedroom chair was strewn with possessions and my stomach lurched as I remembered the desperate search for Peggy.

'Did I wake you, miss?' asked the young maid. She wiped her hands on her apron and pulled back the curtains. 'I'll bring you hot chocolate directly.'

'What time is breakfast?' I asked.

'Ten o'clock, miss. Lady Hamilton is always prompt. You'll hear the hall clock chime the hour.'

I'd counted the quarter-hours as the hall clock chimed all through the night while I fretted about Alessandro and imagined how my father might receive me.

After I'd drunk the chocolate I contemplated my tumbled clothes and shook out the blue silk dress I intended to wear while making my visit to Grosvenor Street. I wished I'd laid it flat the night before but natural optimism encouraged me to hope that the creases would fall out from the warmth of my body. The dress had been one of the Princess's cast-offs and, although too short for me, I'd taken it in and added a band of contrasting blue damask to the hem, using the same material to trim the sleeves and bodice.

I took extra trouble with my hair, coiling it up with a ribbon but allowing a few curls to frame my face. As I regarded my reflection in the mirror I remembered how Sarah had stood behind me when I'd looked in another mirror many years ago. She'd shown me how to style my hair to flatter my pointed chin and high cheekbones and taught me the tricks of her trade as a lady's maid. Even though we'd had our differences, she'd always tried to do her best for me. We'd done everything together and I missed her.

I stood by the window looking dejectedly at the rain as it pelted down on the pavement. The sky remained gloweringly grey. The day I'd left Italy there had been blue skies and golden autumn sunshine. I almost wished I'd never come to London.

A carriage rolled along the street, sending up a spray of water and drenching a pedestrian. Turning away from the depressing view I paced up and down, planning, without a great deal of success, what I would say to Sir Frederick. I was uncomfortably aware that he might very well have me thrown out as an imposter.

At last, the hall clock chimed and I slipped on my shoes, still damp, before going downstairs.

Lady Hamilton acknowledged me with a nod as we went into the dining room.

'Good morning,' I said. I hadn't seen her standing up the day before and was surprised to see she was at least six feet tall and certainly six inches taller than myself.

'I trust you were comfortable?'

'Very, thank you.' The pleasantries over, we sat down.

Anxiety at the prospect of meeting my father made my stomach churn but I drank coffee and nibbled a piece of pound cake.

'Your father never remarried,' said Lady Hamilton. 'The death of your mother affected him greatly, I believe. You may not be aware,' continued my hostess, 'that the Prince Regent is a staunch Tory and that Sir Frederick supports him. The Whigs, on the other hand, support the Princess.'

'I know little of English politics,' I said.

'Perhaps you do not take my meaning?' said Lady Hamilton. 'Sir Frederick may not take kindly to discovering that his long-lost daughter has been residing in the enemy camp. Feelings run very high against the Princess in those quarters.'

I placed my coffee cup carefully on the saucer. 'I see. Nevertheless,' I said, 'since I've travelled so far, I shall still visit him, even if he turns me away. I'm very grateful to the Princess for offering me a position in her household when I needed it and my association with her is nothing to be ashamed of.'

Lady Hamilton smiled for the first time. She pushed back her chair. 'If you are ready, I shall send for the carriage.'

I peered out of the carriage window as it progressed along Grosvenor Street. Everything in London was grey and damp. The street was wide and lined with substantial townhouses with slate roofs, not the warm-coloured terracotta tiles I was used to. The brickwork was dusted with soot deposited from the coal-fire smog that loured like a funeral pall over the town. It was all very different from Pesaro. Still, there was a general air of prosperity and elegance in the façades of these buildings, even though I had no memory of ever living in this illustrious area. Lady Hamilton had gone to the trouble of asking her brother, Lord Archibald Hamilton, to find out the exact location of my father's residence and very soon we drew up outside.

I was too nervous to notice more than that the house had a wide frontage with a pillared portico and a freshly painted front door and railings. My knees trembled as the coachman handed me down but I made a show of holding my head high and walking confidently up the stone steps. The lion's head doorknocker was brightly polished and I knocked twice.

A footman opened the door almost immediately.

'I am Miss Barton,' I said. 'I should like to speak to Sir Frederick.'

'Sir Frederick isn't at home.'

I was in such a state of nervous anticipation and false bravado that I could only stare at him. Of course, there was no reason to assume that Sir Frederick would be there.

'I've travelled from Italy,' I said.

'Perhaps you'd care to wait?' said the footman. 'He's expected shortly.'

'I arrived in London only yesterday.'

The footman glanced sideways at me and I knew nervousness was making me talk too much.

The hall was decorated with a bold, almost masculine, paper hanging of purple and gold stripes and the floor was black and white marble. A great number of gilt-framed paintings were displayed on the wall beside the mahogany staircase and a pier glass over a matching console table reflected a magnificent arrangement of hothouse flowers. There was an air of opulence that I had only encountered in the homes of some of our richest clients in Italy and it made me even more nervous.

The footman showed me into a morning room painted in faded pea green and I sat down to wait. The room spoke of ease and comfort, although here the upholstery was sadly worn and the curtains had faded where the sun caught them. All was in such contrast to the sumptuousness of the hall that I suspected the room might not have been redecorated for many years. I indulged a fancy for a moment that my mother had sat by the window at the satinwood desk to write her letters. I wondered if she might have chosen the flower paintings and the china figures in the glazed corner cupboard. I sat quietly, my hands gripped together while I tried, without success, to remember if I had played with my toys at her feet.

I don't know how long I sat there but, when I heard the front door open, my fingers were stiff as I unclenched my hands. There was a murmur of voices and then footsteps echoed across the marble. My heart began to gallop as the footsteps approached. Hurriedly, I pinched colour into my cheeks.

The door opened and a man stood on the threshold. Slightly above average height and a little fleshy around the jowls and stomach, his iron-grey hair was combed back from a noble brow. From the top of his pomaded hair to the tips of his gleaming boots, he looked as sleek and well fed as a pigeon. 'Miss Barton?' he said.

'Yes,' I croaked. 'Sir Frederick, I presume?'

He moved quietly for such a solid man and was inside the room with the door closed behind him in one catlike movement that barely stirred the air. 'My footman said you've travelled from Italy?'

I nodded. Now I was face to face with him I couldn't seem to make my mouth form the words to tell him who I was.

He strode across the room and came to a stop in front of me. His face was impassive but his slate-coloured eyes were watchful.

'I've lived in France and Italy for nearly all my life,' I said. 'But recently I discovered that I was born in England.' It unnerved me to have him study me so intently. 'I've come to London to find my family.'

'Your family?'

My mouth was as dry as sandpaper. 'Before she died, the woman I thought was my mother told me that she was, in fact, my natural mother's maid. She said she'd stolen me and that my name was really Harriet...' I swallowed, unable to look at him. 'Sir, I have reason to believe I am your daughter.'

'Harriet Emilia Langdon.' His voice was low and expressionless.

'I realise this must be a shock to you.'

White-faced, he clenched his jaw. 'Did you really think I wouldn't know my own daughter?'

'It's the truth! I know you may not believe me but...'

He lifted a trembling hand to smooth his already smooth hair.

'I'm not a fortune hunter,' I said, lifting my chin. 'I want nothing from you...'

'I didn't say I didn't believe you.' Suddenly, he snatched off my hat and tossed it on the carpet.

I gasped and shrank back.

He plucked the ribbon from my hair, allowing it to tumble to my shoulders. Grasping me by my upper arms, he pulled me out of the chair. 'I could never have forgotten the colour of your hair. I'd have picked you out in a crowd.'

His eyes welled with tears and I felt the dawning of hope.

'My dearest child,' he said, 'I searched for you for years all over France and Italy. I advertised a reward for you. And now,' he held me at arm's length to study my face, 'after all these years, you've simply walked back into my life.'

'So you do believe me?'

'Isn't that what I've been telling you, silly girl?' He hugged me to his broad chest again and I felt a sob catch in my throat.

I had found my father.

Chapter 13

'I never stopped looking for you, Harriet,' said my father, 'even though I thought you might have drowned with your mother. I can't tell you how many false trails I've followed.'

'Perhaps Sarah was right after all,' I mused. 'I always thought she was imagining that people followed us.'

He scowled. 'Don't talk to me of that woman. She's caused me more agony than you can possibly imagine. To lose both my children and my wife so close together was a living hell.' He took my hands. 'You must tell me everything, all the smallest details of your life. We have seventeen missing years to talk about. How did you live? Was it very terrible?' Drawing a chair close to my own, he sat down beside me.

I remembered what Alessandro had said. *'Too much time has passed to build the years of memories that bind you into a proper family.'* But was it really too late for us? Father hadn't rejected me as I'd expected. On the contrary, he'd welcomed me. I began to tell my story.

Some considerable time later I sighed and leaned back in the chair.

'I don't understand how you managed,' said Father, frowning. 'Surely the income earned as travelling dressmakers cannot have been enough?'

'We survived,' I said. 'Sometimes we went hungry but that served to sharpen our appetites to work harder.'

'Did you not have anything to sell that might have brought in some money?'

I saw how his hands gripped the arms of his chair. 'My mother's jewellery, you mean?'

He shrugged. 'Or any other little treasures Sarah might have brought with her?'

'Anything of value was sold while I was still small,' I said. 'Sarah's husband Joe was a drunkard and he drank the proceeds.'

'Nothing remained?' asked my father. A muscle twitched in his cheek.

'Was there something special you're thinking of?' I asked.

'Well,' he said slowly, 'there was a sapphire brooch that had belonged to my mother.' His eyes met mine. 'It was valuable and I should have liked you to have it.'

I shook my head. 'I don't remember ever seeing it. After Sarah died I found gold coins sewn into her petticoat. She'd never mentioned them. When I think of all the times we went hungry ...'

'She was a wicked thief,' said Father, fists clenched. 'But I'm glad you told me about the coins.'

'Why shouldn't I?' I said.

'I don't want there to be secrets between us.'

'Then will you tell me about my mother now?' I said.

Father stood up and riddled the fire with a poker. When he turned to look at me his face was etched with lines of pain. 'She was beautiful,' he said, 'like you. But when our son Piers died then something in her died, too.'

I hesitated but I had to ask. 'Sarah said you quarrelled with my mother and confined her to her room. She said that's why Mother tried to run away.'

'Of course I confined her!' Father's eyebrows drew together. 'After Piers died she lost her reason and threatened to harm herself.' He looked directly at me. 'And you, too.' He rubbed a hand over his face. 'I tried to keep her safe until she was well again but that interfering maid got her a key. And so Rose ran off and threw herself in the Thames.'

'I wish I could remember her.' I spoke in a low tone, my voice full of regret.

Father curved his hand around mine. 'I cannot give you your mother back and, God knows, I still miss her. But there is someone else you must see. Wait!' He hurried from the room.

I leaned back in the chair and closed my eyes, utterly drained. I'm not sure, perhaps I dozed, but then Father entered the room, steering an elderly lady by the elbow.

'This is Miss Weston, your great-aunt Maude,' he said. 'My mother's sister.'

I bobbed her a curtsey, looking at her with curiosity.

Thin and frail, she leaned upon an ebony stick and blinked watery blue eyes at me. 'Harriet?' she said, her voice quavering. 'You really have returned to us?' Her face was bone-white against her black shawl and a few silvery wisps of hair had escaped from her cap.

'I answer to Emilia,' I said. 'I'm too accustomed to it now to revert to Harriet.'

Father smiled. 'It will take me a little time to become used to that.'

'Frederick told me that your mother's maid stole you away,' said Aunt Maude. 'And you have been abroad with her all this time?'

'She died,' said Father, 'and poor Emilia was forced to live in Caroline of Brunswick's peculiar household. Can you imagine? Still, there's no reason to mention that to anyone. None at all.'

I remembered Lady Hamilton's comments about his support of the Prince Regent.

'I daresay Emilia will have returned abroad before any of your cronies hear where she's been living,' said Aunt Maude.

'Return to Italy? Certainly not!' Father patted my cheek. 'My little girl has come home again and I'm not letting her out of my sight.'

'But I must return ...' I began, thinking of Alessandro.

'Emilia, listen to me!' said Father. 'I cannot allow my daughter to return to a life of penury, working as a travelling dressmaker, of all things. Or, even worse, as a servant to that appalling madwoman.' The distaste in his voice made it sound as if I'd been earning my living on the streets.

'The Princess took me in when I was left alone,' I protested. 'Besides, I have friends in Italy.'

'It's perfectly natural for Emilia to wish to return to the life she knows, Frederick,' said Aunt Maude.

'You have *family* in England,' said Father, ignoring his aunt. 'Where are you staying, Emilia?'

'Portman Street,' I said, 'with Lady Hamilton. I shall accompany her back to Italy in a few days' time since she'll be taking up her position as the Princess's lady-in-waiting again.'

'It gets worse!' he said, striding across the room. 'You absolutely cannot stay there. Lady Hamilton's brother is the Radical MP Archibald Hamilton. I'd never hear the end of it! I'll have your luggage collected immediately.'

'Perhaps you should ask Emilia what she wants, Frederick?' Aunt Maud glanced enquiringly at me.

Father came to stand before me. 'My dearest girl, won't you come home? Even if it's only for a few days. I've just found you. Please don't deprive me of that pleasure.'

His expression was so imploring I couldn't have denied him, even if I'd wanted to. 'I'd be very happy to stay with you until I return to Italy,' I said, 'but first I must thank Lady Hamilton for her hospitality.'

'We shall go together,' said Father, picking up my hat from the carpet.

Over his shoulder I saw Aunt Maude watching us. Just for a moment I thought I glimpsed an expression of distress, or was it annoyance, on her face?

'Aunt Maude,' said my father, 'will you instruct the housekeeper to make up the best guest room?'

She bowed her head.

As I left on my father's arm, I glanced back at her. There was no doubt in my mind then that she was looking at me with animosity.

Later, when my father and I returned to Grosvenor Street, the servants were lined up in the hall, waiting for us. The butler, the housekeeper, the cook, two footmen, two housemaids and a scullery maid all bowed or curtseyed as I walked past them. Hot with embarrassment under their curious glances, I was relieved when the housekeeper stepped forward.

'Welcome home, Miss Langdon,' she said.

I glanced behind me and then realised she was talking to me.

'Shall I take Miss Langdon upstairs to the guest room, sir?' Her voice was quietly modulated and her narrow figure as rigidly upright as if she had a steel rod sewn into her stays.

'By all means, Mrs Hope.' Father smiled at me. 'Come down to the drawing room when you're ready, my dear.'

A footman, carrying my travelling bags, followed us upstairs but I couldn't help pausing to look at the paintings that lined the staircase wall.

On the first floor the housekeeper opened one of the panelled mahogany doors. 'The drawing room, Miss Langdon.'

I glimpsed an ornate gilt mirror over a chimneypiece of white marble before she closed the door again. We ascended to the next floor and Mrs Hope led me into the guest room.

It was luxuriously appointed with blue velvet curtains and a silk bedspread heaped with cushions. My feet sank noiselessly into the carpet.

The footman placed my bags on the chest at the end of the bed and silently withdrew.

'If you wish to refresh yourself there's hot water in the ewer,' said Mrs Hope. 'I apologise that we do not have a lady's maid to attend you but I shall send up one of the housemaids to unpack for you.'

'Please don't trouble,' I said. 'I have so little luggage I shall put it away in a trice.'

'It's no trouble at all,' said the housekeeper, bristling. 'We shall make the proper arrangements by tomorrow but we weren't aware of your impending arrival. Is there anything else you require?'

I ran my fingers over the soft towel on the washstand and bent to sniff the hothouse flowers perfuming the air by the dressing table. 'No, thank you,' I said. 'I have everything I need.'

'Very good, Miss Langdon.' Mrs Hope inclined her stately head and silently left the room.

Once the door had closed I toed off my shoes and bounced on the bed. I doubted I'd ever slept on a mattress so soft or in a room so lavishly appointed. Lying on my back and looking at the ceiling, I let out my breath in a sigh of contentment. This would do me very well for the few days before I returned to Italy. Best of all, my father really wanted me to stay. Lady Hamilton, however, had appeared relieved I'd no longer be a burden to her and agreed to send me a note when she was ready to travel. Meanwhile, I had to discover what kind of reception might face the Princess when she arrived on these shores.

There was a soft knock on the door and a housemaid entered. Small and slight, she stopped dead when she saw me on the bed. 'Sorry, miss! Shall I come back later?'

'No, come in, though really there's no need for you to unpack for me.'

Her grey eyes widened and she appeared genuinely shocked. 'You can't do it yourself, miss!'

I opened my mouth to say I'd unpacked my travelling bags more times than she'd had a hot dinner but thought better of it. She'd probably tell Mrs Hope, who would then inform my father that I didn't show proper consideration for my position. 'What is your name?' I asked instead.

'Daisy, miss.'

'Then please unpack my bags for me, Daisy.'

She hurried to oblige before I changed my mind.

After she'd placed the last of my shifts in the drawer and arranged my hairbrush on the dressing table, she said, 'Will that be all, Miss Langdon?'

'I wonder, where is the nursery?' I asked. 'I should like to see the room where I slept as a child.'

Daisy gave me a curious look. 'If you'll follow me, miss?'

I hurried behind her up to the third floor. The stair carpet was of coarse drugget, worn in places, and the walls were painted rather than papered.

Daisy opened a door. 'This was the nursery, miss. It's not been used since . . . ' She looked away.

'Since I left,' I finished. 'Thank you, Daisy. You may go now.'

She hurried away down the stairs.

The nursery was in semi-darkness. I pulled up the blind, exposing safety bars fixed to the windowframe. The walls were painted a faded primrose colour and there was a multicoloured rag rug on the floorboards. I sat in one of the armchairs placed to either side of the mantelpiece. Something hard pressed into my thigh and I put down my hand and retrieved a silver rattle. I shook it gently and wondered if it had belonged to my little brother. It saddened me to have no memory of him. If he'd lived he would have been seventeen or eighteen now.

A brass fireguard was fitted securely over the grate and it was then that I had a fleeting recollection of a stout woman leaning over the flames and remembered the smoky aroma of toasting bread. In my mind I heard the faint echo of a child's voice, my voice, saying, 'Corky, it's burning!' I sat very still, listening, but the memory had gone.

I stood up to spin a globe standing on a nearby cupboard. Opening the cupboard doors, I saw jigsaw puzzles, chalks and a slate, gaily painted wooden bricks and a spinning top. I didn't remember any of them.

There was another door and I pushed it open to find the night nursery. I pulled up the blind and hesitated before opening a chest of drawers and peeping inside. It was filled with neatly folded small items of clothing, from flannel petticoats and a tissue-wrapped christening gown to frilled and tucked cotton dresses. I imagined for a moment how Victorine would squeal with delight at the sight of such treasures. Perhaps my father would allow me to take them back to Italy for her.

My eye was caught by a beautiful doll with a delicately painted wooden face, lying on the white counterpane on the bed. I examined the doll's tiny kid slippers and her old-fashioned dress with panniered skirts. Her blonde hair smelled dusty and was slightly rough under my fingers. Something tugged at my memory. Crying. An all-consuming misery and a tearing sense of loss as I sat in a coach jolting through the dark. Suddenly I was four years old again and sobbing, desolate at having left my beloved Annabelle behind. Now, after all this time, I had found her again and she was a precious link to the life I'd once had.

I kissed the doll's painted face and, still clutching her in my hand, investigated the rest of the night nursery. A curtained alcove contained another bed, a row of wall hooks and a chest of drawers. I wondered if that was where the nanny had slept. There was no sign of a cradle. I pulled down the blinds before returning to the guest room. Carefully, I laid Annabelle on the pillow. Perhaps, one day, Alessandro and I would have a little girl who would love Annabelle as much as I had.

On my way downstairs I stopped on the staircase to take a closer look at the paintings I'd noticed earlier. There were several pastoral landscapes and a number of portraits, some very old, judging by the ruffs, doublets and hose the subjects were wearing.

Father stood at the foot of the stairs. 'There you are!'

'I was admiring the paintings,' I said.

'You like art?'

'I'm not very good at drawing,' I said, 'but I like to look at good paintings.'

Father beamed. 'There! Blood will out. As a young man I had pretensions of becoming a famous artist but, try as I might, the beautiful pictures I saw in my head never materialised on the canvas when I applied my brush to it.'

I laughed. 'Sad, isn't it?'

Father looked up at me, shaking his head sorrowfully but with a smile in his eyes.

'Many of the churches in Italy have wonderful frescoes,' I said. 'It's easy to lose yourself for an afternoon looking at them. One very hot day, when I was no more than ten or twelve, we reached the Scrovegni Chapel in Padua. We went inside to escape the heat and I was entranced by Giotto's fresco cycle of the Life of the Virgin Mary.' I paused. 'That day was the first time I truly believed that God existed.'

'Because no earthly hand could paint anything so glorious without God's guidance?'

'That's it exactly.' I smiled, a warm feeling growing inside me because we'd found common ground. 'Ever since, whenever I had the opportunity, I'd find out if there were any treasures in the town we were visiting and make a point of going to see them.'

'I'll show you my art collection later but we can't stand on the stairs all day talking about Art and God,' said Father. 'Come into the drawing room.'

I'd failed to appreciate the full magnificence of the room I'd glimpsed earlier. Three tall windows flooded it with light, even on such a grey and miserable day. The high ceiling was richly decorated with intricate plasterwork, and softly coloured carpets floated like jewelled islands on a sea of golden parquet flooring.

Aunt Maude sat straight-backed in an armchair. She glanced up at me from her embroidery but didn't return my tentative smile.

Cream damask drapes with muslin under-curtains framed the windows, concealing us from the inquisitive stares of pedestrians in the street below. It was all so sumptuous that I felt completely out of place.

I sat down carefully against the plump cushions on the sofa and Father offered both Aunt Maude and myself a glass of ratafia from a silver tray.

I took a sip and then said, 'Father, who is Corky?'

He started and spilled a few drops of ratafia. Wiping them off the side of his glass with the tip of his finger, he said, 'I thought you remembered nothing from your time here?'

'I don't. Not really. I glanced into the nursery a moment ago and recalled an old lady called Corky burning toast on the fire.' Aunt Maude, I noticed, had put down her embroidery and was watching me with narrowed eyes.

'Miss McCorquordale was your nanny,' said Father, his lips tightening. 'She was an utter disgrace to her profession!'

'How so?'

'On the morning you were discovered to be missing, she was fast asleep in a cloud of gin fumes.'

'What happened to her?'

'Turned off without a reference, of course.'

'Did she usually drink?' I asked. 'Or was she given the gin so that she wouldn't notice when I was taken?'

'Whichever it was,' said Father dismissively, 'she failed in her duties with the most terrible result.'

I sipped my ratafia reflectively. Either my mother or Sarah must have led the poor woman down the path to oblivion.

'Tell me, Emilia,' said Father, 'did you receive any kind of education at all whilst on your travels?'

I bristled at the implication. 'Sarah taught me to read and write ...'

'I suppose we must be grateful to her for that, at least,' he said.

'I went to school sometimes,' I said, 'but we always moved on just as I began to make friends. We were never in one place for more than a few months. I loved to read and often, when we had work where we lived temporarily on the premises, I'd be allowed to borrow books from the owner's library.'

'What did you read?'

'Poetry, art and philosophy. Botany. Anything I could find on art, architecture and antiquities. I even picked up a little Latin.' I was pleased to note that Father's eyebrows had risen. It appeared that travelling about the continent with a mere maid had allowed me to acquire a surprisingly respectable education.

He nodded. 'What about mathematics?'

'Well, there was the practical side of dressmaking. I learned to estimate quantities of dress material required and do the bookkeeping and place orders. And I can sew, of course, and speak French and Italian fluently.' I didn't mention that I could swear as well as any stable lad in both languages, too. 'I was the one who arranged our lodgings and booked our coach tickets since Sarah found anything other than her native tongue very difficult.'

'Astonishing,' said Father. 'Most girls cannot claim to have learned as much at their schools. Can you dance?'

I shrugged. 'There were village fiestas sometimes.'

'Hmm.' He looked thoughtful. 'There will be deficiencies in your education but nothing, I believe, that we can't remedy. What do you think, Aunt Maude?'

The old lady put down her embroidery. 'It sounds to me as if Harriet, I beg your pardon, *Emilia*, has as much education as she needs for her position in Princess Caroline's household.'

'Ah, well, that's something to discuss in the future,' said Father. He stood up and offered me his arm. 'Shall we look at my paintings, my dear?'

'I should be delighted.'

'Of course, only a part of my collection is here,' he said, as we went into the hall. 'I shall take you to Langdon Hall to see the rest. Now that *is* something I look forward to.'

What a pity, I thought, that there wouldn't be time to visit the family seat in Hampshire before I returned to Lyons and thence to Italy.

Chapter 14

The candles guttered in the draught as the footmen, James and Edward, brought more dishes to the dining table. Soames the butler watched as the domed covers were lifted with a flourish to reveal a dozen spatchcocked game birds, a great rib of beef and a haunch of venison. My mouth watered at the delicious aroma of roasted meat. After a fortnight in my father's house in Grosvenor Street I was already becoming accustomed to the rich food, which was far more plentiful and of higher quality than in the Princess's household in Pesaro.

'Tell me more about your travels, Emilia,' said my father. 'Where did you go after Florence?' he asked, proffering me a slice of beef.

Every day he asked me to tell him all the places Sarah and I had visited, encouraging me to reminisce about even the smallest villages and towns.

'Once we stayed in a hill-top monastery near Castellina in Tuscany,' I said. 'We mended the altar cloths and turned all the monks' sheets sides-to-middle.'

'A monastery near Castellina?' said Father, putting down his knife and fork. 'And what did you see there?'

I smiled. 'It was more a case of what we didn't see.'

'What do you mean?'

'There was a painting of the Last Supper on a wall in the refectory,' I said. 'It wasn't very good and I asked if one of the monks had painted it. Brother Anselm told us the original had been stolen some years before and the thief had left the poor copy hanging on the wall instead.'

'An audacious thief, indeed,' said Father with a snort of laughter.

'After that we stopped in Siena for a few weeks,' I said as the footman refilled my glass with claret. 'Long enough to find and complete two commissions.'

'Did you see any antiquities or frescoes there?' asked Father. 'And did you by any chance visit an art dealer who has premises just off the square? He writes to me sometimes if he buys a particular treasure he thinks might interest me.'

'You seem to have art dealer acquaintances all over Italy,' I said.

'I buy and sell art and antiquities to my friends and acquaintances. It's my passion,' he said. 'And why not, when I've had no wife or child to spend my fortune on?' He smiled at me. 'Until now, that is. That reminds me . . . I saw a pretty shawl in the window of a shop in Cheapside. We'll go and look at it tomorrow and, if you like it, you shall have it.'

'Father, you spoil me! It was a fan last time, even though I don't have any occasion to use it.'

'Just a few trifles, my dear. And, pretty though it is, you cannot go on wearing that same dress every day. I shall take you shopping.'

Sometimes I awoke in the night, wondering if the last two weeks had all been a dream, but then I touched the finely woven sheets and the silk bed curtains and remembered that I was in my father's house. Such luxury was unimaginable after the penny-pinching life I'd lived with Sarah. I hadn't imagined I'd be so readily welcomed into Father's life. I could only wish that Aunt Maude would accept me more readily.

Sitting opposite me at the table, she ate in silence and rarely engaged me in conversation. She had rejected my tentative advances of friendship ever since I'd arrived. I sighed. Still, she wouldn't be troubled by my presence for a great deal longer. Every day I expected Lady Hamilton to send me a note to say she was travelling to France. And soon after that I'd be back with Alessandro. My thoughts drifted to that summer evening when we'd watched the fireflies dancing in the avenue of cypresses. In the circle of his arms I'd known with absolute certainty that we were meant for each other. But now ...

'Emilia?'

'Sorry, Father,' I said. 'I was daydreaming.' Alessandro and I *would* make it all right between us again. We had to.

He smiled indulgently and patted my hand. 'And what were you thinking?'

'That I haven't heard from Lady Hamilton.'

'You don't still have it in mind to return to Lyons with her, do you?' The smile had gone from his face. 'I cannot like the thought of you returning to Caroline of Brunswick's household. There's so much still for us to talk about and I haven't yet taken you to see the London sights. And there's a play on at the Adelphi I thought might amuse you.'

I didn't answer him directly. 'Father, have you heard whether Mr Brougham has left for Lyons?' I asked. 'He promised to meet the Princess there before she travelled to England.'

He looked at me sharply. 'Is she definitely coming then?'

I shrugged. 'Mr Brougham led her to believe the divorce case would come to trial this month but soon it will be Christmas. The Princess wants the whole business settled so that she can return to live a quiet life in Pesaro.'

'She wouldn't bring that raggle-taggle band of Italians with her, surely?' Father's expression was incredulous. 'She'd be hounded back across the sea. Especially if she was accompanied by that blackguard Pergami.'

'That's why she wants Lady Hamilton to join her, so that she has an English courtier with her when she arrives.'

'Brougham was in the House of Commons the other day,' said Father, sipping his claret. 'Emilia, if Caroline of Brunswick intends to come to London soon, why the rush for you to return to her side? Will you then return to London with her?'

I shook my head and made a show of cutting up my meat to avoid looking at him. 'I'm no courtier and I have friends in Pesaro,' I said, assailed by a sharp longing for Alessandro. It hurt to remember how we'd parted.

'A special friend?' said Father. When I didn't answer, he said, 'Emilia, we said we wouldn't have secrets from each other. Is there a young man I should know about?'

Reluctantly, I nodded.

'Tell me about him.' He spoke gently.

'His name is Alessandro Fiorelli,' I said, needing little encouragement. 'He's a tutor to the Baron's daughter, Victorine.'

'Tutor?' Father sighed. 'I suppose I shouldn't be surprised ... you've been working as a dressmaker. It won't have been easy for you to meet suitors appropriate to your birth. What of his family?'

'Alessandro's father is a doctor.' I bristled at the implication that his family wasn't good enough for me.

'Alessandro? Is there a formal understanding between you that you refer to him in such familiar terms?'

'He proposed to me,' I said, 'but we had a disagreement about my coming to London to look for you. Now I don't know ... ' Reliving the hard words between us before I left Lyons, I knew I couldn't say any more without breaking down.

'Dearest girl, all I want is your happiness,' said Father. 'If this Alessandro Fiorelli is the right husband for you, he'll wait a while and then you can spend the rest of your lives together. But you've only just returned to me and I hope you won't think me selfish if I say how terribly sad I would be to lose you again so soon. Why, I haven't even had time to show you Langdon Hall yet.' He stroked my hand, which was curled into a fist on the tablecloth. 'Are you not happy here?' His tone was imploring.

'How could I not be happy, when you have taken me in and welcomed me?' I said, my thoughts confused. I wanted to return to Alessandro.

'Could you not write to this young man,' said Father, 'and tell him you wish to stay with your newfound family for a few months? Is that too much to ask?'

I rubbed my temples, the quandary making my head ache.

'You'll have to decide soon,' said Father, 'if Lady Hamilton is leaving shortly.'

'I know,' I said, pushing my unfinished food away.

'Shall we take our tea in the drawing room?' said Aunt Maude. She stood up and I had no choice but to follow her lead.

'I shall join you ladies as soon as I've finished my brandy,' said Father.

Aunt Maude and I retired to the drawing room, where the tea tray awaited us. As usual she poured the tea and handed me a cup.

We sat in uneasy silence while I wondered if Alessandro would wait for me if I delayed my return.

'Emilia,' said Aunt Maude, putting down her cup.

I looked at her, surprised. She barely spoke to me except out of necessity.

'Your father can be very persuasive,' she continued. 'But, if you love this young man of yours, you mustn't allow Frederick to keep you apart.'

Her comment surprised me even more. 'I do want to return to Alessandro,' I said, 'but I've longed for a family of my own for so long ...'

'If you delay your return it may be too late.' She looked intently at me. 'Go to your young man while you can, Emilia.' There was such

127

passion in her voice that I wondered if, in her distant youth perhaps, she'd been parted from a man she loved.

The drawing-room door opened then and Father entered. 'Emilia, shall we play a hand of cards?'

I glanced at Aunt Maude but she was staring at the flickering flames in the hearth, giving no indication that she had spoken to me at all.

The following afternoon, I set off in Father's carriage. He'd refused to let me walk by myself, though I'd protested that I often walked alone through the streets in Italy. Aunt Maude, her lips pursed, commented that no young lady of breeding ever ventured abroad without a companion. So it was that my great-aunt sat opposite me in Father's carriage.

It was bitterly cold and she sat with the collar of her pelisse turned up and her gloved hands folded in her lap. Her face was resolutely turned away from me so she could look out of the window.

The noise in the streets was even worse than in Florence and I caught my breath as a curricle raced past with only a couple of inches to spare. The young blood driving the equipage flicked his whip and surged forward, scattering the pedestrians crossing the road. I was happy to look out of the window as we rattled past an endless array of smart shops. The fashions worn by the stylish London ladies were subtly different from those worn in the Italian cities. I made mental notes as to the cut of a pelisse or the drape of a skirt to take back to Italy for my clients, in due course.

Despite the freezing weather, streams of shoppers ambled along the pavements, girls sold scraps of lace and trinkets from handcarts, here a man juggled oranges and there a beggar in military uniform propped himself up on his wooden leg and proffered his hat for coins. Everything was unfamiliar and therefore interesting to me.

The carriage came to a halt outside the Hamilton house in Portman Street and Aunt Maude didn't object when I took her arm to guide her over the cobbles, which were slippery with ice.

'Are you quite sure you're making the right decision?' she asked as we waited for the door to open.

I wasn't at all sure I was doing the right thing and I'd worried about it most of the previous night, wondering what to do. 'You and Father are the only relatives I have left,' I said.

'That's all very well,' said Aunt Maude, 'but you don't know us at all.'

'But now I have the chance to remedy that,' I said. And it grieved me to realise that if Alessandro didn't understand that I needed time to get to know my father properly, then perhaps he wasn't the right man for me after all.

A footman opened the door and we followed him across the hall to the drawing room.

'Miss Weston and Miss Langdon, ma'am.'

'So, you're not Miss Barton any longer,' said Lady Hamilton, gesturing to us to sit down.

I wasn't sure if I liked being called Miss Langdon. It wasn't who I was. But then, I admitted, sighing, I wasn't Miss Barton either. 'It feels strange,' I said, with a wry smile. 'My father, however, is prepared to compromise and my Christian name remains Emilia.'

'How complicated!'

I didn't say that it was far more complicated for me than it was for her. 'I've brought a letter for the Princess,' I said, 'and should tell you that I've decided not to return to her at present. Now that I'm reunited with my family after so long, I intend to stay here for a while.'

'I daresay the Princess can spare you,' said Lady Hamilton.

'Before I left her, she asked me to ascertain what is happening in London with regard to Mr Brougham's visit to her,' I said. 'It appears he was in the House the other day and not on his way to Lyons as the Princess expected. She believed the matter of a divorce was to come to court this month.'

'I haven't heard any indications of that,' said Lady Hamilton. 'The politicians are far too preoccupied with the massacre at Peterloo.'

'Massacre?' I said.

'Don't you read the papers?' asked Lady Hamilton. 'There was an assembly of sixty thousand Radicals and Whigs in St Peter's Field, near Manchester, to demand the reform of parliamentary representation.'

'I don't see how that influences Mr Brougham's movements,' I said, puzzled.

'The Tory government sent in the cavalry with sabres drawn to dispel the assembly,' said Lady Hamilton. Her expression was grim. 'Fifteen died and seven hundred were injured. The people call it the Peterloo Massacre, after the Battle of Waterloo.'

I resolved to read the newspaper every day after Father had finished with it. Perhaps it would help me to glean some information that could be of use to the Princess. 'That's appalling,' I said, 'but I still don't understand ...'

'Brougham hasn't time to go gallivanting off to France,' said Lady Hamilton impatiently, 'not while emergency legislation is being debated in Parliament. He's marshalling the rest of the Opposition, Whig and Radical, to argue against the proposed measures.'

'The poor Princess,' I said, 'waiting in vain all this time.'

'She needs careful guidance since she's so prone to impetuousness,' said Lady Hamilton. 'Now is not a good time for her to arrive in London. Much better to wait until next year.'

'I see.' I opened my reticule and took out the letters I'd written that morning. 'This is for the Princess.'

She took the missive from me.

'And then there is another letter for a member of her household,' I said. 'I would be extremely grateful if you would arrange for this to be handed to Signor Fiorelli.'

Lady Hamilton took my letter for Alessandro between the tips of her fingers as if it were something distasteful. 'I am not in the habit of acting as a postman to servants,' she said, 'but I will take your communication this time. Or, if I decide not to travel now, I'll send them on to her.'

My cheeks burned. 'Thank you, Lady Hamilton,' I said. I'd toiled over the letter to Alessandro, writing and rewriting it three times, explaining that I'd decided to stay in England longer than I'd expected. I'd told him I loved him and begged him again to understand and to write to me.

The clock in the hall struck a quarter past three and Lady Hamilton rang the bell on the side table. Our visit was at an end.

'I suppose,' she said, 'since your father is acquainted with the Prince Regent, you may hear of developments the Princess should know about. In such a case you may write to me. Deliver any such letters here and my servants will forward them in my absence.'

I hesitated. 'Would you send a brief note to me now and again when you do return to the Princess? I have no way of knowing how she fares or if there is any small service I can render to her.'

I glanced at Aunt Maude but she sat straight-backed, her gaze fixed on her hands folded in her lap.

Lady Hamilton sighed. 'I will communicate to you any news of particular note. I shall send such letters here to Portman Street and one of my servants will deliver them to you at Grosvenor Street.'

'Then there is nothing for me to say except to wish you a safe journey, Lady Hamilton,' I said.

In the carriage on the way back to Grosvenor Street Aunt Maude sighed. 'Well, you've burned your bridges now, haven't you?'

'I know you don't want me to stay in your home ...'

'Believe me, it isn't *my* home,' she retorted.

I clasped my hands tightly together. It upset me that she had taken against me. 'I shan't let you stop me forging bonds with my father.'

'I can see that.' She glanced at me, an odd half-smile on her mouth.

I capitulated and asked the question that had troubled me since the first day we met. 'Why do you dislike me so?'

Aunt Maude shook her head. 'I don't dislike you,' she said. 'You were an adorable child. 'You used to call me Auntie Maudie and bring all your little treasures to show me.' She looked out of the carriage window and sighed. 'But that was so long ago. We cannot go back to the past and do things differently with the benefit of hindsight.'

'No,' I said.

Aunt Maude shrugged. 'I didn't want you to have regrets about not returning to your young man, that's all.' She faced me, her pale eyes glittering. 'Once I was considered pretty. I never imagined I'd end up as a spinster, living on my nephew's reluctant charity.'

I studied her fine bone structure and could see that she might have been lovely once. 'I hope I haven't lost my chance with Alessandro,' I said. 'But I need time with my father or I'll always wonder what it would have been like to know him properly.'

'Sometimes the things we want aren't the things that finally bring us happiness,' said Aunt Maude. 'Very well then, since despite my best efforts I haven't managed to frighten you away, we shall make the best of it, my dear. And I sincerely hope we shall regain our earlier friendship.'

Then, to my utmost astonishment, she patted my hand.

Chapter 15

Christmas 1819

Langdon Hall

I started awake as Father touched my knee.

'We're here,' he said.

He, Aunt Maude and I had set off early. We'd sought refreshment at the Feathers Inn in Hartley Wintney and afterwards the heavy pastry of the chicken pie had rested uneasily on my stomach. I'd watched the endless countryside roll past the carriage windows until my head began to nod. Aunt Maude dozed and before long I'd succumbed to sleep, too.

'Emilia?' said Father. 'Come and look!' He took my hand as I clambered down, stiff-legged, from the carriage.

We'd come to a halt at the end of a long carriage drive that led through parkland studded with ancient oaks. In the distance was a substantial house built of mellow red brick, with pointed gables and twisted chimneys.

'Langdon Hall,' said Father, unable to keep the note of pride from his voice.

I caught my breath in shocked surprise. 'It's beautiful!' Welcoming lights glimmered behind some of the stone-mullioned windows.

'It was built in the early sixteenth century,' Father said, 'by a Roger Fforbes. It's been in the Langdons' possession for the last two hundred years.'

Although I'd realised Father was wealthy, I'd had no idea that his country house would be so impressive.

Father looked at me intently. 'You have no memories of the Hall?'

I shook my head.

'I can't give you back those years,' he said, echoing my own thoughts. 'If that wretched maid hadn't stolen you away you wouldn't have been deprived of the life you should have had; all the fine dresses, music and dancing lessons, a pony . . . ' He sighed. 'I'll make it up to you.'

'You've spoiled me enough already!' It was true: he'd bought me new clothes, taken me to the theatre and given me books, paints and a gold bracelet.

'Nothing that wasn't due to you.' He reached for my hand. 'Let's go in.'

We returned to the carriage and set off again, the wheels crunching over the gravel. I glimpsed a church tower and a village in the distance through the gathering dusk.

'If the King in his chambers at Windsor Castle is as cold as I am, I doubt he'll live to see the year out,' said Aunt Maude, her teeth chattering.

'I've given orders for fires to be lit in all rooms,' said Father. 'And we must pray for King George to recover from his afflictions.'

If he didn't recover, I reflected, the odious Prince Regent would become King. What would happen then to Princess Caroline?

As we approached Langdon Hall I noticed the glint of light on water immediately in front of the house. 'Is that a lake?' I asked.

Father shook his head. 'A moat. It's no longer used for defensive purposes and the drawbridge is fixed down.'

The carriage rolled onto the bridge, the horses' hooves clattering across the timber. The great gates were open and we proceeded under the gatehouse arch and into a sizeable quadrangle, coming to a halt before the entrance to the Hall. The oak door, framed by carved stone, was flanked by flaming torches to light our way.

Simmering with anticipation, I took Aunt Maude's arm and Father ushered us into the entrance hall. The servants were lined up to greet us and, although I recognised those who had travelled from the London house, there were many more I'd never seen before.

The housekeeper, an imposing figure in black bombazine, curtseyed to us. 'Welcome home to Langdon Hall, Sir Frederick,' she said. 'I trust you had a good journey?'

'Thank you, Mrs Bannister,' said Father. 'Miss Weston and Miss Langdon will wish to refresh themselves but we'll have tea in the library in half an hour.' He turned to the butler. 'Bannister, come with me to discuss the wines for dinner.'

'Very good, sir.'

Aunt Maude's maid, Jane, stepped forward and led her away upstairs.

Mrs Bannister nodded at Daisy.

'This way, if you please, Miss Langdon,' said the girl.

I followed her into the rear hall, up the wide oak staircase and into a long picture gallery overlooking the quadrangle. Marble busts on granite columns were displayed in niches. Halfway along the gallery, Daisy opened a door.

My room was dominated by a carved four-poster bed hung with embroidered claret velvet. Tapestries of hunting scenes adorned the oak-panelled walls and the tall windows were magnificently decorated with leaded lights in a lozenge-shaped pattern. A fire crackled in the hearth and I held out my hands to warm them. Briefly, I remembered the simple whitewashed walls and tiled floor in my little room in Villa Vittoria and marvelled at the contrast.

'Will you change out of your travelling clothes, miss?' said Daisy. 'I wondered if you'd like to wear your new blue gown.'

I nodded. 'And the silk shawl, too, please.' Mrs Hope had protested when I said I wanted Daisy for my maid but I'd been adamant I could train her myself. I liked the girl and she seemed sensible enough. Besides, I wouldn't be in England for more than a few months.

'Shall I fetch your hot water, miss?'

I nodded, luxuriating in the softness of the richly patterned carpet beneath my feet and stroking the silky velvet curtains. There was a window seat heaped with cushions and I couldn't resist sitting in that cosy nest to look out of the window at the garden.

It was almost dark now but I could make out a stone-flagged terrace below with steps leading down to a parterre. To either side of the gardens were rows of substantial yew trees, clipped alternately into balls and cones. Beyond that was the moat.

Excitement made me want to laugh aloud. I could never have imagined that my family owned such a glorious house and I couldn't wait to write and tell Alessandro about it. As usual when I thought of him, a pang of longing lodged somewhere under my breastbone. It was painful to remember how we'd parted and I hoped desperately that, by now, he'd accepted and understood my decision.

When Daisy returned with the hot water, she lit the candles and drew the curtains while I washed and changed.

'I'm impatient to see the rest of the house,' I said.

'It's like going back in time,' said Daisy, 'after the modern conveniences of Grosvenor Street.' She pulled a face. 'There's no indoor necessary house here, for a start.' She giggled and pressed her fingers to her mouth. 'Except for your father's garderobe. His valet showed it to me. It overhangs the moat.'

'It's certainly an ancient house,' I said, standing up. 'Can you tell me where to find the library?'

'Shall I show you?'

I picked up the candlestick. 'I have a suspicion I might lose myself and never be seen again if I roam the galleries alone.'

'You'd have a ghost to keep you company.' There was a hint of laughter in Daisy's grey eyes as we set off down the gallery again.

'I don't believe in ghosts,' I said.

'Perhaps not, miss,' said Daisy, 'but if you wander about in the middle of the night and hear Sir Godfrey Mylton wailing and bemoaning his fate, you might change your mind.'

'And who might Sir Godfrey Mylton be?'

'Roger Fforbes, who built the Hall, was a Catholic and Godfrey Mylton was his priest. After King Henry broke with Rome, the Fforbes family pretended not to be Catholic anymore.'

My candle flickered in a draught as we reached the head of the stairs.

'But Mylton carried on holding services in the secret chapel that Fforbes built,' said Daisy. 'One day the priest was reading the Bible in the library when an unexpected visitor looked through the window and saw him. Mylton ran to warn Roger Fforbes, who shut him in the secret chapel when he saw the soldiers coming over the drawbridge. There was a terrible fight. Roger Fforbes and his sons were killed.'

'What happened to the priest?' I asked.

'After Roger Fforbes died no one knew the priest was in the secret chapel.'

'He starved to death?'

Daisy nodded, her eyes like saucers. 'So his ghost roams Langdon Hall at night.' She came to a stop. 'Here's the library, miss.' She bobbed a curtsey and hurried away.

Father and Aunt Maude were waiting for me, seated on sofas by the blazing fire.

'What a welcoming room!' I said. A candelabra cast a warm glow and the long walls were lined with mahogany bookshelves. The mellow tones of the leather bindings added to the rich appearance of the room quite as much as the Persian carpets, tapestry curtains and comfortable furnishings. Dutch still lifes and interiors were displayed on the two end walls.

'This is our winter drawing room,' said Father. 'In the summer we use the parlour since it has doors to the garden. Do read any of the books that you wish. Some are old and valuable but others are recent and may be more to your taste.'

'Most of my reading has been in Italian and French with some Latin,' I said, 'so I shall enjoy reading in English for a change.'

A footman carried in a laden tea tray and disappeared as silently as he had arrived.

Aunt Maude poured the tea and I handed it around. 'I understand this library caused the downfall of the Fforbes family,' I said.

'Whatever do you mean?' asked Father.

'Wasn't this where Godfrey Mylton was reading the Bible when a chance visitor saw him through the window?'

Father paused in the act of dropping a lump of sugar into his cup of tea. 'I suppose the servants have been gossiping?'

'You can't deny it makes an interesting story.'

'And a story is all it is,' said Father. 'There is no secret chapel. The priest probably escaped through a window. He was never heard of again but, you're right, that was the end for the Fforbeses.'

'Will you take me on a tour of the Hall?' I asked.

'Tomorrow,' said Father. 'You can't see my paintings properly until it's daylight. We'll have some supper in the little parlour this evening and a hand or two of cards before an early night.'

'Travelling is so fatiguing,' said Aunt Maude, smothering a yawn, 'especially over winter roads.'

'Christmas is only a few days away,' said Father. 'We shall have guests. My heir, Adolphus Pemberton, will join us, too.'

'Your heir?' I said.

'My cousin's boy.' Father made an expression of distaste. 'I never cared for my late cousin. I was his fag at Eton and he was a vicious bully. Unfortunately, the Langdon Hall estate is entailed and, since my son died, Adolphus is my closest living male relative. It's a bitter pill to swallow that I cannot leave the house to you, Emilia.'

'I shan't lose any sleep over that,' I said, 'since I wouldn't have the slightest idea how to manage it. Besides, I shall be in Italy.'

Father raised his eyebrows. 'You don't mind?'

'I never expected to inherit anything so I shan't miss it.' This was true but I had to admit to myself how much I was enjoying my new, if temporary, elevated lifestyle.

'I shan't forget you,' said Father. 'You shall have a dowry, if you make a suitable match.'

'I don't expect ...'

'I know you don't,' he said. 'A dowry, and a trust set up in your name, on condition that I approve of your future husband.'

'I see,' I murmured, hoping he would like Alessandro. There was no doubt a dowry would be welcome but, assuming Alessandro still wanted to marry me, I'd give up any financial expectations to be with the man I loved.

'Still,' said Father, 'I suppose Adolphus Pemberton is marginally better than John Harvey, the next in line to inherit.'

'You don't care for him, either?'

'He's another cousin. His father cut him off without a shilling after he eloped with the daughter of a butcher and ended up going into the trade.' Father shuddered. 'A butcher, imagine that!'

'At least he should have a decent piece of beef for his Sunday dinner,' I said.

'It's no joking matter, Emilia,' said Father. 'It grieves me deeply that I have no son to inherit the estate. I wish I could leave it to you, the only child of my blood.' He sighed heavily.

'I've found you and Aunt Maude,' I said. 'That's all that matters to me.'

'Dear child!' she said.

'Aunt Maude has agreed to bring you out,' said Father.

'What do you mean?' I asked.

'She will prepare you for your presentation at Court in the spring. Afterwards I shall give a ball in your honour and in turn you will be invited to other balls and supper parties, with the opportunities of making friends and meeting a suitable husband.'

'Oh, but . . .'

Father held up his hand. 'You're going to mention Alessandro Fiorelli. Are you engaged to him?'

'Not exactly, though he did propose to me.'

'Then there is no impediment to your having a season. If at the end you haven't met a man you wish to marry, then you shall return to Italy. You will be accomplished and elegant and a suitable bride for anyone.'

'Alessandro is quite happy with me as I am,' I said, bristling.

'And so he should be,' said Father. 'But, as a tutor, he cannot hope to keep you in the comfort you deserve. If you indulge me by spending this time with me first and taking the opportunities that I can give you, then you may return to this young man with a dowry. Once I have approved him, of course.' He reached for my hand. 'Now tell me that you think I'm being fair.'

'More than fair,' I said. 'May I think about it before I agree?'

'We're all tired,' said Father. 'Let's have our supper and we'll talk about it tomorrow.'

After breakfast the next morning, he took me on a tour of the house. We began in the Great Hall, the most impressive room. Six wrought-iron light fittings, each a yard in diameter, hung over the massive refectory table. The beamed ceiling from which they were suspended soared above us. Between the beams the plaster was painted dark blue and embellished with gold stars, like a night sky. It was a great deal more magnificent than the farmhouse dining room at the Villa Vittoria.

'As children,' said Father, 'if it was raining too hard for us to go outside, we used to gallop up and down in here on our hobby horses.'

'Did you have brothers and sisters then?' I asked. It hadn't occurred to me that I might have more relatives.

'There was Cecilia, who was a year older than I, and Margaret, who was two years younger,' said Father. 'Cecilia died of the measles when she was eight and poor Margaret died in childbirth.'

'And my grandparents?'

Father sighed. 'My father died when I was a young man and Mother soon after you were born.'

'So you and I and Aunt Maude are the only remaining members of the family?' I said, sorry not to have known about these other relatives before.

He put his arm around me. 'We have each other now,' he said, kissing the top of my head.

I smiled at him, sad I hadn't grown up secure in the knowledge of his love. It pained me that, despite all his kind attentions, I didn't as yet feel love for him. Alessandro was right, a family was glued together by years of memories and although Father and I were bound by blood, we were not yet bound by love. But if I spent more time with him, as long as Alessandro would wait for me, perhaps we could build those precious memories.

'And here,' said Father, pointing above a heavily carved screen across one end of the room, 'is the minstrels' gallery. We used to hide in there and peep down through the screen when my parents held a party.'

'How wonderful to grow up with this history all around you,' I said. I ran my finger along the polished surface of the table and my footsteps echoed up from the flagstone floor as I went to study the stags' heads adorning the oak-panelled walls.

'Your grandfather was a great huntsman,' said Father, 'but these are of more interest to me.' He showed me a number of gilt-framed landscapes and spent the next twenty minutes teaching me about perspective.

'Forgive me,' he said, at last. 'Once I start talking about my beloved paintings I forget to stop. I've grouped them by type and period in different locations so I'll show them to you as we go from room to room.'

'I've already noticed the Dutch paintings in the library and the Roman busts in the niches in the gallery upstairs,' I said.

'Ah, yes, the Long Gallery,' said Father. 'It's the perfect place to display my treasures and was added by one of our ancestors in the late sixteenth century. Before that there were no corridors and you entered each room through another.' He linked his arm with mine again. 'Shall we see the rest of the house?'

We went all over it, looking into the half-timbered attics where the servants slept, poking our noses into nine bedrooms and several dressing rooms. One door was locked and Father told me it had been my mother's room. His forbidding expression prevented me from asking if I might look inside. We wandered through the hall again, discussed the paintings in Father's study, the morning room and the small parlour. I'd lost count of the various staircases, closets and anterooms.

Father showed me numerous beautiful works of art: Italian Renaissance drawings, Russian icons, English portraits, medieval religious paintings and collections of Roman and Egyptian sculptures and artefacts.

'It's like living in an art gallery,' I said. 'Aren't you ever afraid such a wonderful collection might be stolen?'

Father smiled, as if I'd said something particularly amusing. 'A number of pictures have been stolen from some of my acquaintances over the years but I've taken steps to ensure it won't happen to me. The paintings are very carefully fitted to the walls with a framework of my own devising at the back. A thief can't lift anything down without using a special tool.'

'Perhaps you should raise the drawbridge at night?' I said, only half joking.

Laughing, he said, 'That's not a bad idea but the servants have strict instructions to double lock the doors and to patrol the grounds at regular intervals.'

'Wise precautions,' I said.

'Shall we return to the library now?'

'I thought you must be lost,' said Aunt Maude as we joined her by the fire.

'I might never have been seen again, if Father hadn't been there to guide me.'

'What did you think of your father's art collection?'

'I'm amazed by it,' I said, 'but there's too much to take in all at once. I shall enjoy revisiting the paintings one by one.'

'When the weather improves I'll show you the statues in the garden, Emilia,' said Father. 'You've seen enough for today and now I have estate business to attend to.'

After he had left us I leaned back on the sofa.

'You look exhausted, dear,' said Aunt Maude. 'I'm afraid your father always forgets the time when he's talking about art.'

'But it's good to feel so passionate about something, isn't it?'

Aunt Maude pursed her lips. 'Sometimes you can have too much of a good thing.'

Chapter 16

On Christmas Eve I awoke to find the inside of my bedroom windows etched with frost flowers. I rubbed the glass with a fingertip to reveal that it had snowed during the night and caught my breath at the beauty of the scene. The sun shone in a blue sky and the skeletons of the leafless trees were crusted as if with glittering diamonds.

When Daisy brought me my morning chocolate she found me curled up on the window seat, watching the birds hopping about in the snow.

'Isn't it lovely?' I said.

'You'll catch your death by the window, miss.'

'I'll have my chocolate in bed,' I said, retreating to the warmth of the four-poster.

Later, dressed in my warmest clothes, I let myself out of the garden door. The terrace was slippery with snow and I trod carefully down the steps to the parterre. Marble statues were placed at intervals around the garden and gravel paths followed the curving patterns of the flowerbeds, all edged with clipped box. In the centre was a pool with a fountain, where icicles clung to the rim of the bowl, as if the water had suddenly been turned to ice by magic. There was something very beautiful about an entirely white garden.

I walked down to the moat and stood on the bank, careful not to slip on the snowy grass. Bulrushes, sparkling with frost, crowded against the bank and a pair of ducks paddled by. I looked back at Langdon Hall, blinking in the bright light reflected off the snow. There were stables to one side of the house and a walled garden to the other with the whole surrounded by the moat. My heart swelled with pride because this lovely place belonged to my father and I was able to claim borrowed ownership of it, even if only for a while. If I'd had a letter from Alessandro the day would have been perfect.

I heard a shout and saw Father hurrying through the parterre.

'You're up early,' he said. His cheeks were ruddy from the cold.

'I couldn't resist coming out to look at the snow,' I said. 'It's a shame our footsteps have spoiled its perfection.'

'There'll be fresh snow tomorrow.' He tucked my arm through the crook of his. 'The servants are bringing in the Yule log and the Christmas greenery this morning. I wondered if you'd like to direct them with decorating the hall?'

'I'd be glad to,' I said.

'Then shall we have an early breakfast before you set to work?'

The Yule log, all wrapped in hazel twigs, was dragged indoors by the gardener and his boys and deposited in the huge stone hearth in the hall. Mrs Bannister clapped her hands for the housemaids to clear up the pieces of brushwood and clumps of mud and moss that lay scattered in its wake. Another maid was sent to fetch the small piece of charred wood retained from the previous year's log and the household watched while the ancient tradition was followed of using it to light the new one. Once the fire was crackling, the servants returned to their duties.

'That should burn for a few days,' said Mrs Bannister. 'Sir Frederick said you're happy to oversee the decorating, Miss Emilia?'

'I look forward to it,' I said.

She bustled away to organise someone else.

The gardener's boys had deposited a large heap of holly and other greenery on the floor and stood by with knives and twine awaiting my instructions. There was much good-natured chatter as I had them running up and down ladders to hang the garlands of greenery.

Two hours later Aunt Maude came to find me. 'It's looking very festive, dear,' she said. 'And the Yule log is blazing well now.'

I wound another piece of ivy around one of the iron light fittings that had been lowered onto the vast refectory table and turned to study the fruits of my labour. The stags' heads had all been given ivy wreaths and a crown of holly. A mistletoe kissing ball decorated with red ribbons hung at each end of the hall and wreaths made from bay, rosemary and holly hung at intervals along the panelling, joined by thick swags of ivy. Scented pomanders were piled in silver bowls and their fragrant perfume mingled with the resinous scent of the Yuletide greenery.

'It's a magnificent room, isn't it?' I said. 'I can imagine the minstrels of a couple of hundred years ago singing in the gallery while the lord of the manor feasted below, throwing chicken bones over his shoulder to the dogs.'

'I'm not sure what Mrs Bannister would have had to say about that,' said Aunt Maude.

I called to one of the gardener's boys and set him to winching the branched light fittings, as large as a waggon wheel, back up to the ceiling before collecting the remaining scraps of greenery into a heap. 'I'll tell Mrs Bannister I've finished.'

'Send a message by one of the servants,' said Aunt Maude. 'Then you must go and change before Adolphus Pemberton arrives. I shall wait for you in the library.'

I added a final sprig of holly to one of the wreaths and then went to find the housekeeper. The buttery was behind the carved wooden screen at the end of the hall and a passage led to the domestic quarters. I glanced through an open door to see a footman polishing an array of silver dishes. A clatter of pans came from the kitchen, together with the sound of frantic chopping and the aroma of boiling ham. I called out to a passing scullery maid.

'Where will I find the housekeeper?'

'Mrs Bannister's room is at the end of the passage, past the still-room,' she said. 'Shall I fetch her for you?'

'That's all right,' I said, 'I'm sure I'll find her.'

The girl gave me an uncertain look and scurried away, the bucket banging against her skinny legs.

I tapped on the housekeeper's door.

She sat at a table and rose to her feet when she saw me. 'Miss Emilia! Is everything all right?'

'I've finished decorating the hall,' I said, 'but a maid will need to sweep up the trimmings.'

Her mouth was set in a disapproving line. 'Will that be all?'

Unsure what I'd done to make her cross, I nodded.

'Robert will escort you back to the hall.'

'I'm sure I shall find the way.'

'Nevertheless,' she said, 'please come with me.'

The footman was called away from the silver cleaning and hastily removed his protective cambric cuffs and apron before leading me back to the hall.

'Thank you, Robert,' I said. 'Will you ask Daisy to attend me?'

He bowed his head and returned to the domestic quarters.

Aunt Maude was walking upstairs as I hurried up to change.

'I found the housekeeper in her parlour and she'll send a maid to sweep up,' I said.

Aunt Maude came to a sudden stop. 'You went to Mrs Bannister's parlour?' Her tone of voice was scandalised.

'Why shouldn't I?' I asked.

'My dear, you have a great deal to learn. *Always* send for the housekeeper and *never* wander about below stairs. The servants will think you're spying on them.'

'I didn't mean any harm.'

'I'm sure you didn't,' said Aunt Maude, 'but you have a position to maintain in your father's house.' She sighed. 'There are so many things I must teach you, to make you fit for society.'

'What kind of things?'

'Not to shrug and wave your hands about when you are speaking, for example.'

'I don't!' I frowned. 'Do I?'

Aunt Maude inclined her head. 'It's an unbecomingly continental habit and will not be well received in an English drawing room. You must never appear excessively animated, Emilia, as you are wont to do.' She patted my cheek. 'Don't look so forlorn, my dear. Your intentions are good and you have natural grace. We'll soon turn you into an English lady.'

We stopped outside her bedroom door. 'I'll see you downstairs in a little while,' I said.

As I walked along the gallery, I heard a horse trot into the quadrangle below. I peered out of the window to see a man in a caped travelling coat dismounting from a grey. I wondered if this was my father's heir. Curious, I watched as a groom came to take the horse but then the man disappeared into the house.

Washed and changed into my blue dress, with my hair brushed and beribboned, I went downstairs to the library. My father was seated by the fire reading a newspaper and Aunt Maude was sorting her embroidery silks.

'You look delightful, my dear,' said Father, standing up as I came in. 'That dress brings out the blue of your eyes.'

'Emilia is so like her mother, isn't she?' said Aunt Maude. 'Have you shown her Rose's portrait, Frederick?'

'There's a picture of my mother?' My heart began to race. 'And you didn't show it to me yesterday?'

Father sighed. 'I thought it might distress you.'

'Why should it?' I asked. 'May I see it?'

'Another time since Adolphus is expected imminently.'

'I saw a man arriving a little while ago. What is he like, this heir of yours?' I asked.

Father steepled his fingers while he thought. 'A well-educated gentleman of fashion,' he said, 'though not interested in art.'

'He's a dandy,' said Aunt Maude, succinctly.

'I can see, then,' I said, 'that he falls far short of being your ideal heir, Father.'

He laughed. 'You're beginning to understand me very well, Emilia.'

Before I could reply the door opened and Robert announced, 'Mr Adolphus Pemberton.'

My father's heir paused in the doorway with a slight smile on his handsome face. His elaborately tied cravat gave him no option but to look down his nose at us. He was taller than average, his long legs encased in buff trousers and his cut-away coat impeccably tailored. His skin was very light against his dark hair, which was carefully arranged in Grecian-style curls.

'Adolphus,' said Father, standing up. 'I trust you had a good journey?'

'Tolerable.' The vision of elegance advanced into the room. 'Aunt Maude,' he said, bowing low before her. 'Always a pleasure.'

'Emilia,' said Father, 'may I present your second cousin, Adolphus Pemberton.'

Adolphus bowed and I inclined my head.

'So,' he drawled, 'it's to be Emilia and not Harriet, is it? And, please, all my friends call me Dolly. Adolphus is terribly formal, don't you think?'

I glanced at Father, who gave me the briefest of nods. 'I'm delighted to meet another member of my family,' I murmured, slightly discomfited by Dolly's gimlet gaze.

'Indeed. Your return to the family fold is the talk of the *ton*, dear coz.' He cleared his throat and sat down on the sofa beside me.

'It was a most' – I paused momentarily – 'unexpected turn of events and I'm only now becoming used to the idea of belonging to a family.'

'Your father called me to meet him at his club,' said Dolly, 'and explained that you'd returned from the dead and how you'd been living.' He shook his head sorrowfully. 'Too dreadful to contemplate.'

'I didn't remember any other life,' I said, 'so I was quite happy.'

'But, in retrospect,' said Dolly, 'you must be very angry with the maid who stole you?'

A momentary picture of Sarah's anxious face formed in my mind and I felt a pang of loss. 'It's exhausting to be angry all the time about something you can't change,' I said. 'Now I must look to the future.'

'And what *does* the future hold for you?' His dark blue eyes were fixed upon me again.

'As to that,' I said, 'it's too early to say.' I knew what he was really asking was if I was going to run off with some of his expected inheritance. 'I'm happy to accept my father's invitation to return to the family home for a while. After that,' I gave him a bright smile, 'who knows?'

'Who knows, indeed?' he murmured.

On Christmas morning it snowed again and, in deference to Aunt Maude's age, we decided not to risk slipping on the ice and took the carriage to St Bartholomew's in the village.

I was uncomfortably aware of the curious gaze of several members of the congregation and of the whispering going on behind gloved hands as we sat in the Langdon pew. I supposed if I had been in their shoes I'd have been curious, too, about the girl who'd returned from the dead. I stared straight ahead, my cheeks burning.

150

Father squeezed my hand. 'They'll soon lose interest,' he murmured. 'You must admit, it's an extraordinary story.'

Dolly gave me a sideways glance of amusement as he sang the hymns in a light tenor. 'Hold your head up high, coz,' he whispered.

The sermon was interminable and my thoughts drifted to Alessandro, wishing he were beside me. An impatient rustling mounted amongst the worshippers who wanted their Christmas dinner. Prayers were said for the King's recovery from the chill to his lungs.

At last it was over and we milled about with the rest of the congregation to wish the vicar a Merry Christmas. Several churchgoers jostled us, to pass on their festive greetings to Father and to take a good look at me, and I was relieved when we climbed into the carriage and returned to Langdon Hall.

Father's guests, mostly local landowners, a few couples from London, the vicar and several worthy spinsters, began to arrive at five o'clock and were shown into the library. The story of my return had spread like wildfire through the county, and by the time Dolly led me into dinner, I felt like an exhibit in a circus freak show.

In the hall the Yule log crackled and spat in the hearth as the thirty guests found their places. Once we were assembled the vicar said grace and there was a scraping of chairs until everyone was seated.

I looked at the expectant faces as the guests chattered to their neighbours. I sat on Father's right at the head of the table. 'This room was made for feasting,' I said. 'It's wonderful to know that Christmas has been celebrated here for generations and the tradition will continue far into the future.'

'I do hope so,' said Father. 'Although, unfortunately, not with a Langdon at the head of the table.' He turned to Dolly. 'Emilia has made an elegant job of decorating the hall, don't you think?'

'Admirable,' he replied. 'Your daughter has good taste.'

I glanced up at the ivy wreaths wound around the light fittings, the candle flames flickering in the warm rising air. The hall was perfumed with the scent of evergreens, cinnamon, oranges and mulled wine, and I was pleased with my efforts.

Bannister the butler poured the wine and the footmen brought in course after course of dishes. Father explained this was the latest fashion, introduced by the Prince Regent, of serving dinner *à la russe*, instead of having all the dishes placed on the table in two or three removes.

A trio of musicians played in the gallery but the music could barely be heard over the hubbub of conversation.

'Your father keeps a fine table,' said Dolly, as we ate white soup, followed by stuffed pike with oysters and fried sole. 'I believe even the Prince Regent, well known for his extravagant tastes, would find no fault if he were here.'

'Do you know the Prince Regent?' I asked.

'A passing acquaintance,' said Dolly. 'Your father knows him better than I do.' He smiled. 'Prinny admired my cravat.'

'What is he like?' I asked, curious about the Princess's husband.

Dolly cleared his throat and leaned closer. 'Between the two of us, he's rather fat. Although known for his modish style and wit, his extravagant lifestyle has done his figure no favours. When he bends, he creaks.'

'Creaks?'

Dolly's eyes gleamed with malice. 'Whalebone corset,' he said, succinctly.

I stared at my plate and bit the inside of my cheeks in an attempt to stop myself from laughing.

'Did you ever attend any dinners as elegant as this on your travels in Italy?' said Dolly, just as if he hadn't noticed.

'I stayed in some very grand houses.'

'But how unfortunate for you that you were there in your capacity of dressmaker rather than as a guest.'

I sipped my wine and smiled blandly at him. Dolly was amusing and outwardly friendly, but I would take care never to turn my back on him, I decided.

'Your father told me you were living with the Princess of Wales,' he continued.

'I'm surprised he mentioned that,' I said, 'since he forbade me to talk of it.'

Dolly smiled guilelessly. 'But this is all in the family, isn't it? Tell me, how did you find her? Is she as frightful as the Prince Regent says?'

'Not at all!' I said, indignant that he should think so. 'She has her foibles, of course ...'

'You mean she never washes, flirts outrageously, and lives as man and wife with a so-called Italian noble fifteen years younger than herself, who is no more than her servant?'

'If you'd been to Pesaro,' I said, 'you'd know it isn't like that.'

'Ah, but I haven't been to Pesaro,' said Dolly. 'Can't abide foreign travel.' He shuddered. 'Bugs in the bed, garlic in the food, and all that sort of nonsense.'

I paused while I decided how to describe her. 'The Princess of Wales dresses inappropriately sometimes but there's no meanness or pretence about her. Perhaps she grows restless too easily, like a child. I was surprised by how much she dislikes formality, to the extent that she confided in me her distress when she discovered, quite by accident, that her daughter had died. Can you believe the Prince Regent didn't trouble himself to send her the news?'

'I believe he vowed some years ago never again to communicate with his wife.'

'In my opinion, he's behaved badly towards her.'

'In Sir Frederick's household,' said Dolly, 'I'd advise you to keep that opinion to yourself. Your father is vociferous in his condemnation of the Princess, if only to demonstrate his support of the Prince of Wales.'

'Residing in the Princess of Wales's household for several months has brought me to an entirely different, and possibly more informed, judgement of her character,' I said.

'Your father, however, has no patience with any view that doesn't support his own,' said Dolly. 'I heard that the Princess has taken her entourage to Marseilles to overwinter incognito in a small hotel.'

'Marseilles?' This was news to me. 'I expected her to arrive in London soon.'

'The talk in the coffee houses is that she's merely waiting for better weather to sail back to Pesaro.'

I sipped my wine while I reflected on this. So Alessandro was probably in Marseilles. I wondered if Lady Hamilton had travelled to Marseilles, too, and if he had received my letter yet.

The footmen carried in a succession of dishes: roasted goose, venison, a baron of beef, innumerable capons and pheasants decoratively dressed with their tail feathers, and several beautifully ornate Christmas pies.

'I can't eat another thing!' declared Aunt Maude some while later.

The guests raised a cheer as two footmen circled the table, holding aloft a flaming Christmas pudding, while the musicians played a lively march. I recalled Sarah had made an English Christmas pudding one year but I'd found it too rich and preferred *panettone*.

After we'd finished the pudding, bowls of grapes, slices of fresh pineapple, candied apricots and marchpane sweets were placed at intervals along the table. Glasses of dessert wine were poured and then Father rose to his feet and tapped his glass with a spoon.

'Ladies and gentlemen,' he said, 'I wish you all a Merry Christmas and I'm delighted you could be here to share our festive feast today. As you know, this is a very special Christmas since my beloved daughter has been returned to me.' Father looked straight at me. 'Please raise your glasses with me in a toast to Emilia.'

'Hear, hear!' said Dolly.

I blushed as the entire company toasted me, chorusing my name. I pictured Alessandro's face for a moment and heartache and longing washed over me.

Chapter 17

After breakfast on Boxing Day, a dozen ancient widows and several of the deserving poor of Upper Langdon village shuffled into the hall to collect their annual parcels of surplus food and clothing. Once they had given their grateful thanks, Father and I distributed the Christmas boxes to the servants, who were then granted the rest of the day as a holiday.

Father, Dolly and two other male house guests went off to join the local hunt, leaving Aunt Maude and myself to entertain the wives. We took a turn around the garden and exclaimed how invigorating the fresh air was after the rich food of the previous day, before returning to the comfort of the library fire.

'I remember your mother,' said Mrs Digby, the wife of Father's solicitor. 'You are very like her with the same pale skin, fine features and red hair.'

'I can't picture her at all,' I said. 'I'd hoped coming to Langdon Hall might bring back the memories.'

'And it didn't?' Her hazel eyes were sympathetic.

I shook my head. I only remembered Sarah, who had defended

me from her husband's cruelty and been my companion for most of my life.

'Grief over the loss of a baby sometimes makes a woman lose her reason,' said Mrs Digby. 'I was greatly shocked by the news of your mother's death, though.' She shook her head. 'Rose Langdon always had her feet so firmly on the ground.'

Later, the men returned, full of loud bonhomie and boastful stories of how they'd outwitted the fox. Hunting had sharpened their appetites and they fell on the cold collation laid out for us in the Great Hall.

After dinner, the house guests sent for their carriages and Dolly came to say goodbye, too.

'I understand from your father,' he said, 'that Aunt Maude will be grooming you for your presentation at Court.'

'Mmm,' I said. 'Father believes it's necessary.'

Dolly raised his finely arched eyebrows. 'Why so gloomy? I thought all girls liked to have new clothes and go to balls?'

'He's hoping to find me a suitable husband.'

'Don't you want a husband?'

'Eventually,' I said, 'but I'm not sure about balls and routs.'

He smiled at me down his long nose. 'I shall be on hand to escort you.' He brushed an imaginary speck of dust off his beautifully tailored sleeve. 'I anticipate your return to Grosvenor Street with great pleasure,' he said, bowing.

Once the guests had left, I wasted no time in cornering Father. 'Will you show me my mother's portrait now?' I asked.

He sighed. 'It's upstairs.'

Lighting a candle, he led me up a back staircase to the attics and opened a small door. 'Wait here,' he said.

I peered over his shoulder into a windowless storage room tucked under the eaves. By the wavering light of his candle I caught sight of various discarded pieces of furniture, a broken lamp and assorted trunks. 'Is that a cradle just behind you?' I asked.

'It was yours and then your brother's,' he said. 'I put it away after Piers died, so it wouldn't further distress your mother.' He lifted his candle and pulled back the corner of a dust sheet. 'Here,' he said. Tucking the picture under his arm, he came out of the store, brushing dust off his hands. He carried the portrait to the landing window.

My heart thudded and my mouth was dry as I gazed upon my mother's likeness. Her blue eyes seemed to be looking at me and I couldn't look away. There was a hint of a smile around her full mouth and I touched her painted cheek as if I could bring her to life again.

Father watched me without smiling.

After a moment I sighed. 'Mrs Digby was right. I see a likeness, except that Mother's hair is redder than mine.' There was a hollow ache in my breast, as if I'd been crying for so long that, even when the tears stopped, intense sadness remained. 'I do so wish I could remember her,' I said.

Father looked at the portrait, his face expressionless. 'Some things are best forgotten,' he said.

'May I have the portrait in my room?' Mother's painted face was so lifelike it made me shiver with longing to feel the warmth of her flesh. 'She has such a gentle expression, doesn't she?' I whispered.

Father passed one hand across his face and shielded his eyes for a moment . 'Emilia,' he said, 'it's time I told you what really happened.'

Something in his tone broke the spell cast by the portrait and I stared at him. 'What do you mean?'

'Not here,' he said. 'Come to my study.' He set off down the stairs and I followed him, carrying the portrait carefully in my arms.

In the study he closed the door behind us and lit the candles. Then he took the portrait from me and turned it to face the wall. 'I don't want to look at it,' he said. He sat at his desk, pulled a bottle of brandy out of the drawer and slopped a generous measure into two glasses. He drank deeply from one and then pushed the other towards me.

Tentatively, I sipped it.

'Over the ten or fifteen years before Piers died, there had been a series of notable thefts,' Father began, staring into the candle flame. 'Priceless paintings had been stolen from the homes of the rich and famous and it was assumed the thief was either a member of the aristocracy or had a well-connected accomplice who fed him information.'

'Were those the art thefts you mentioned before?'

He nodded.

'What have they to do with my brother's death?' I asked.

'His birth was difficult,' said Father, 'and Rose was slow to recover. Piers cried a great deal, colic the nurse said, and your mother couldn't love the baby as she should. She spent a great deal of time lying in a darkened room, weeping. Aunt Maude will tell you that. And then one day, Rose found Piers dead in his cradle.' Father drained his brandy glass. 'It may have been a sad but natural event. Or perhaps she saw an opportunity to release herself from her guilt for not loving her son enough.'

I gasped. 'Surely not?'

He shrugged. 'In the light of what happened later I've wondered about that, but we'll never know. Anyway, Rose grieved terribly but then, over the following year, she began to improve. She started to meet her friends again. Sometimes I even heard her laugh. But she became cold towards me.' He sipped his brandy. 'So cold, in fact, that I suspected she was having an affair.'

Shock and distaste rippled through me. That wasn't at all what I'd expected, or wanted, to hear.

'And then one night in Grosvenor Street, I was woken by a noise in the hall. I crept out of my dressing room and went downstairs. The front door was ajar and there was a light in the drawing room. A man was lifting one of my paintings down from the wall.'

'What a shock!'

'It all happened so quickly. He dropped the painting and came at me with a cudgel. I thought my head had split in two when he

159

hit me. I saw him run out of the front door and then I passed out. When I regained consciousness your mother was leaning over me. She'd come out of her room and seen the thief attack me. He had the painting tucked under his arm. She said he barely broke stride, struck me then ran outside.'

'Was he ever caught?'

'No,' said Father. 'The thing was,' he poured himself another brandy, 'when the thief attacked me, the painting was still on the drawing-room carpet, not under the thief's arm.'

'I don't understand,' I said.

'Neither did I, at first,' he said. 'It was the next day that I realised something wasn't right about your mother's story. I went to her room and questioned her. She laughed and said I was imagining things but she kept glancing towards her wardrobe. I threw open the door and rummaged through the contents but there was nothing there. When I climbed onto her dressing-table chair to reach the top of the wardrobe, she stopped laughing.'

My stomach turned over as I realised what he was going to say. 'The picture?' I said.

'Wrapped in one of her shawls.' Father looked at me, his face taut. 'She was defiant. She said she despised me and the thief was her lover. She'd intended to take the painting and run away to Paris with him. I didn't know what to do. The scandal would have been terrible. So I locked her in her room.'

Suddenly I felt like crying. My mother looked so lovely in her portrait and it hurt to know that her sweet smile was merely assumed. I remembered Sarah had told me Mother intended to go to Paris to stay with friends. 'Sarah never mentioned the theft,' I said.

'Of course she didn't!' said Father. 'It was a small but valuable painting and easy to transport. I hung it back on the wall so no one ever realised it had been removed. I begged Rose to tell me who the thief, her lover, was but she set her mouth in a mulish line and refused. It angered me and I told her she'd stay locked up until she did tell me.'

'Was it was someone you knew?'

Father rested his head in his hands for a moment. 'I've tormented myself with that thought for years. But he never tried to contact Rose and she never revealed his identity. She grew pale and thin but remained obstinate.'

'Were there more thefts after that?'

'Not for a couple of years but then they began again so I assumed he'd returned to London and perhaps found another accomplice.' Father looked directly at me. 'I still lie awake at night sometimes, wondering if it's someone I know, one of my friends. It's unnerving to imagine he's been laughing at me all this time.'

'And he used Mother and then abandoned her.'

'If you'd heard the things she said to me,' said Father, his voice bleak, 'things a daughter should never hear, you'd know she was no innocent party.'

I swallowed, sick with the thought of what he had suffered. Mother had used Sarah, too, and it had ruined her life.

'And then,' said Father, 'I came home early from my club one night and I heard Rose's bedroom door close as I came up the stairs. I checked my pocket but I still had my key. I assumed the housekeeper had been careless but, when I tried the handle, the door was still locked. When I unlocked it with my key, I found Rose in her travelling clothes. I realised then that she'd been attempting to escape when she heard me come in and had returned to her room.'

'Sarah made a copy of the housekeeper's key,' I said.

'I was so angry,' Father told me. 'I shouted at Rose and she screamed back at me and then began to laugh so hard she couldn't stop. I had to slap her.' He sat with his head bowed and his fists clenching and unclenching on the desktop.

'What happened then?' I asked.

He heaved a sigh. 'She mocked me and said I couldn't keep her locked up forever. Her lover was waiting for her at Dover. I asked her how she thought she'd survive without money. She taunted me, saying her lover had given her Lord Beaufort's miniatures for safe keeping and they were in her travelling bags, along with her jewels.' He looked up at me. 'Sarah had already gone on ahead with the luggage, you see. Rose and her lover intended to sell the miniatures and live off the proceeds.'

'Miniatures?'

Father opened his desk drawer and took out a wooden box. He lifted out a number of newspaper clippings, yellowed with age. 'These relate to some of the paintings stolen over the past thirty years, mostly in England but also in France and Italy. The press called the culprit the Picture Frame Thief because he usually left a sketch of an empty picture frame in place of the item he stole.'

'How cruel to mock the owner of the painting so!' I said.

'Indeed.' Father picked out one of the clippings. 'This set of three miniatures had been stolen from Lord Beaufort, an acquaintance of mine. We'd been his house guests a couple of weeks before they were stolen and your mother must have fed information back to the thief. As you see, they were extremely valuable.'

I took the clipping from him and read that the three miniatures were of the Infanta Isabella Clara Eugenia, the daughter of King Philip II of Spain and his wife, Elisabeth of Valois. They were painted in 1598 by Sofonisba Anguissola, one of the first female court painters, on the occasion of the Infanta's betrothal to her cousin, Archduke Albert of Austria VII. Shocked, I placed the clipping back on Father's desk.

'Emilia,' he said, leaning forward to look closely into my eyes, 'did you ever see those miniatures?'

'Never!' I said.

He sighed and leaned back. 'They were in the baggage Sarah took away. I hoped you might know what became of them. It's been a terrible burden, knowing that Rose was involved in their theft. I want to return them to Beaufort.'

'Is that why you quizzed me so hard about where Sarah and I had travelled?'

His smile was fleeting. 'You noticed that? I've written to all the art dealers in the towns you mentioned, asking if they might have bought such an item.'

'I wish you'd confided in me before, Father. I'll make a list of the towns we travelled through as far back as I can remember.' I thought of something and pressed my fingers to my lips. 'Those gold coins I found in Sarah's petticoat, do you think they might be the proceeds of such a sale?'

'Almost certainly,' he said. 'I don't believe dressmakers' earnings are high enough to save very much.'

'Indeed not,' I said. If Sarah had sold the miniatures, perhaps we'd been living off the proceeds for years? 'What shall I do with the remaining coins?' I said, in a sudden panic. 'I've already used some of them for my crossing to England.'

'They ought to go to Beaufort,' said Father unhappily. 'But I don't care to explain to him how we came by them. Shall I put them in the bank and use them towards buying back the miniatures, if I can find them?'

I nodded and watched him as he went to stir the embers of the fire. He was still a handsome man. 'Did you never think of marrying again?' I asked.

'I had no heart for another marriage,' he said. 'Anyway, it wasn't possible.'

'Why not?'

He replaced the poker on the hearth. 'I stayed at Rose's side all that night after she tried to escape. By morning she was in despair because she knew her lover would already have sailed to France. She threatened to throw herself in the river off Westminster Bridge. I had an important meeting that morning but I'll never forgive myself for leaving her unattended while she was in such a state.' He paced up and down, running his hands through his hair.

'What happened?' I asked, my stomach churning.

'She escaped and then it was discovered you were missing, too. The servants and I searched for you. After her earlier threat I went to Westminster Bridge.' He covered his eyes with his hand.

'Tell me!' I said, feeling sick.

'We discovered Rose's shoes and shawl but her body was never found.' He swallowed convulsively. 'And that's why I was unable to marry again and lost any chance of a son of mine inheriting Langdon Hall.' He took my hands. 'I thought that you must have drowned with her and everyone I'd loved had left me.' His shoulders began to shake and he clung to me. 'The only good thing to happen out of the whole dreadful business,' he sobbed, 'is that you have come back.'

Chapter 18

London

Aunt Maude was a hard taskmaster. I walked the length of the Grosvenor Street drawing room with Samuel Johnson's *Lives of the Most Eminent English Poets* balanced on my head. As I made my turn at the end of the room, the book slipped and struck my shoulder before bouncing, painfully, off my foot.

Aunt Maude sighed. 'Really, Emilia, when I think how graceful your mother was ...'

'I don't want to talk about her,' I said, a tight knot of unhappiness under my breastbone. I had kept her portrait in my room at Langdon Hall but with its face turned to the wall, unable to look into her adulterous eyes.

'That's as may be,' said Aunt Maude, 'but if you will clump about as if you were a stable lad carrying a bale of straw ...'

'I'm not!' I said, deeply insulted.

'Don't argue with me – it's unbecoming. Glide! You must glide forward like a swan.' She took a few steps to demonstrate. 'Now put

165

the book back and try again. All the other girls will have learned in the schoolroom how to walk gracefully and you don't want to be the only ungainly one.'

Grimacing, I picked up the book.

We'd returned to Grosvenor Street a fortnight before and Aunt Maude had drilled me for several humiliating hours every day on how to walk, to greet new acquaintances, and on which subjects were suitable for conversation. A dancing master had been engaged twice a week to teach me English country dances, Scottish reels, the quadrille and, daringly, the waltz. To my surprise, I discovered I enjoyed dancing.

'That's it!' encouraged Aunt Maude. 'Head up, shoulders down, back straight. Smaller steps, please, Emilia, you are not an elephant.'

As I walked towards the window, I decided Aunt Maude would have been excellent at drilling army recruits. I glanced down at the street and saw a man hurrying away from the house. There was something uncomfortably familiar about his gait that made me pause and stare. I shivered but then the drawing-room door opened. I turned, allowing the book to slide off my head again, and saw Dolly and a young man standing in the doorway.

'Hard at work, Emilia?' said Dolly. 'Aunt Maude, allow me to present Mr Francis Gregory. Francis, Miss Weston.'

Mr Gregory bowed to Aunt Maude as low as his starched neck cloth and tightly fitting coat allowed.

'Emilia, this is Mr Gregory,' said Dolly. 'Francis, Miss Langdon.'

Mr Gregory bowed and brushed back one of the artlessly arranged blond curls that had fallen over his forehead. 'How delightful to meet you!' he said, his pale blue eyes looking me up and down. 'Dolly has told me all about you.' His teeth were rather small in his plump, pink-cheeked face and I was immediately put in mind of the painted cherubs I'd seen in Italian churches.

'I trust we do not interrupt?' said Dolly.

'Not at all,' I said. 'I'm glad to have an excuse to stop walking around with a book on my head.'

Dolly nodded, his mouth twitching. 'I should rather think you might be.' He and his companion sat down, deftly flicking their coat-tails aside in a practised motion.

Aunt Maude tutted under her breath. 'Emilia, please refrain! You must remember to talk only of subjects that will interest our guests.' She turned to Dolly. 'Will you drink tea with us?'

'Alas, I have an appointment with my tailor,' he said, 'but since we were passing I thought we'd drop in for a few moments.'

'I understand your father is holding a ball for you, Miss Langdon?' said Mr Gregory.

'In April,' I said.

'We shall send you an invitation,' said Aunt Maude. 'And I shall be asking your advice, Dolly, for the names of suitable young people to invite.'

The drawing-room door burst open then and Father hurried into the room. 'Have you heard the news?' His eyes gleamed with excitement. 'The King is dead!'

Aunt Maude gasped and pressed her hand to her mouth.

'Well, well,' said Dolly. 'Demented, blind and confined, it can only have been a happy release for Farmer George.'

'At long last,' said Father. He went to the side table, poured out glasses of sherry and handed them to us. 'A toast to King George IV!'

'Long live the King!' said Francis Gregory, rising to his feet.

'The King!' said Dolly.

I put the glass to my lips but did not drink. 'When did it happen?' I asked.

'Last night, at Windsor Castle,' said Father. He rubbed his hands together. 'At last Prinny will be free of the petty restrictions placed upon him by his father.'

It was then I realised that since the Prince Regent was now

the King, the beleaguered Princess of Wales was our Queen. Had anyone, I wondered, taken the trouble to inform her?

That night I awoke suddenly in the grip of a night terror. I sat up and clutched the sheet to my chest while my pulse thudded in my ears. I'd had the same old dream of hiding between the wall and the bed while a man's voice ranted and raved in the next room. I always woke up sweating and sick when I remembered the lash of a belt and a woman's terrified screams.

Of course, it couldn't have been him, but I knew what had sparked my nightmare. Earlier that day I'd seen a man walk away from the house. A man who looked just like Sarah's husband, Joe Barton.

Two weeks later Aunt Maude, Father and I were in the carriage returning to Grosvenor Street after attending church.

'Whatever the Queen may or may not have done,' said Aunt Maude, 'for the King to have taken such a step as to remove her name from the Liturgy is reprehensible. There is no proof of her adultery and therefore no reason to omit her from the customary prayers for the Royal Family.'

'Perhaps it wasn't a wise move on the King's part,' agreed Father, shrugging. 'It's certainly aroused the ire of the general public, thereby increasing her popularity, which, I should imagine, was not at all what he intended.'

'If he wishes to retain his own good standing,' I said, 'surely he must then discontinue his vindictive behaviour towards his wife?'

Father gave me a cold look. 'Emilia, your venturing such an opinion publicly may do us a great deal of harm. Aunt Maude, you clearly need to make greater efforts to teach Emilia what is and is not acceptable in polite society.'

I refused to be cowed. 'I shan't make such observations except in private, Father, but it's obvious to me that the opinion of many is that she's been sorely mistreated. When she arrives in London ...'

'God forbid!' said Father. 'If she comes to England now, the King will close up the Court, if only to prevent her from presiding over the royal Drawing-Rooms and disgracing the English throne.'

Despite his sharp comment, having been subjected to Aunt Maude's rigorous instruction on exactly what behaviour was suitable for a lady who wished to be accepted by society, I understood that Queen Caroline's conduct might not be considered merely eccentric, but completely unacceptable. I trusted that Lady Hamilton would have an edifying effect upon the Queen, restraining her from her worst excesses and saving her from public censure.

'If there are no Drawing-Rooms,' said Aunt Maude with a frown, 'then the young ladies will not have the opportunity of being presented.'

'I believe that may be the case.'

Aunt Maude sighed. 'Perhaps Emilia should come out at her ball? She may then be presented when the difficulties are resolved. Or even,' she glanced at me, 'upon her marriage.'

I frowned at her.

Father nodded. 'It's possible that the Duchess of Gloucester may hold a Drawing-Room after the Royal Family are out of the second change of mourning in April. I agree however that, in the circumstances, a later presentation is the best course of action. In any case, I can't imagine that Caroline of Brunswick will be Queen for much longer.'

'What do you mean?' I asked.

'The King is determined not to allow her at his Coronation,' said Father. 'She will remain uncrowned. Furthermore, he won't continue to pay her allowance should she come to London.' There was a spiteful gleam in his eyes as he said, 'I imagine that will encourage her to stay overseas.'

I looked thoughtfully out of the carriage window. The Queen would be fretting and, I guessed, no matter what the outcome, she'd still come to London to face her antagonists. The one positive thing she should know was that the ordinary people were on her side while the King's continuing excesses antagonised them. I resolved to write to her again. And, perhaps, I would brave Lady Hamilton's annoyance by including another note to Alessandro.

Mrs Webbe, a sought-after mantua-maker from Pall Mall, had been engaged to provide my new wardrobe for the coming season. It was strange to see her assistant kneeling at my feet as she pinned up the hem of my new spotted muslin dress. I'd lost count of the times I'd crouched at a client's feet performing the same action and, no doubt, I would be doing it again once I'd returned to Italy.

'Miss Langdon has pretty ankles and it would be a shame to hide them when she's ascending the stairs or climbing into a gig,' said Mrs Webbe.

'Not too short!' said Aunt Maude. 'It won't do to attract the wrong kind of attention.'

The assistant paused, unsure as to which instruction she should follow.

'Perhaps just half an inch?' I murmured.

Mrs Webbe nodded in assent and the assistant bent to her task again.

Sometimes I thought that the past few months were only a dream. Finding my father and Aunt Maude and being accepted into their lives was a wonderful thing and there was no doubt that it was very seductive, taking advantage of the many benefits that money brings. Father had even made me an allowance for such fripperies as ribbons and shoe rosettes and it would take some adjustment for me to return to my previous frugal way of life. On the other hand, I wouldn't have to obey the excessively irksome restrictions imposed upon me by propriety and take a chaperone with me everywhere. If all went well, I would have a substantial dowry by the time I was reunited with Alessandro. We might be able to buy a little cottage by the sea ...

The assistant dressmaker stood up. 'Shall you try on the ballgown next, Miss Langdon?'

We retreated behind the screen in the corner of the drawing room and the dressmaker pinned me into the dress of white satin overlaid with cream gauze. The puffed sleeves were trimmed with lace and I fingered the roses embroidered around the daringly low-cut neckline. I smiled. It was the most extravagant dress I'd ever worn and it made me look entirely different. There's a certain gloss that someone born into money carries with them and, in that dress, I looked like one of them. Remembering Aunt Maude's instructions, I held my head high as I came out from behind the screen and glided across the room.

She clasped her hands and smiled. 'Beautiful, my dear.'

Mrs Webbe tweaked the neckline and smoothed the bodice. 'You need a new pair of stays, Miss Langdon,' she murmured, 'to lift your *décolletage*.'

'No ornaments or feathers in her hair,' instructed Aunt Maude.

'I agree,' said Mrs Webbe. 'Fresh flowers, white of course, are the only acceptable choice for an unmarried girl.'

Feeling as if I were a prize pig being prepared for market, I stood still while the skirt was adjusted. I passed the time daydreaming about Alessandro, imagining him partnering me in the first dance at my ball.

Male voices sounded outside the door and then Father came in, accompanied by Dolly and Francis Gregory.

Father stopped short when he saw me. A muscle flickered in his jaw but then he smiled. 'So this is what I've been spending my money on?'

'Worth every guinea!' said Dolly.

Father took my hands and twirled me around. 'Fine clothes bring out your natural beauty, Emilia.'

'You're so slender,' Dolly observed, 'you could almost be a boy. Don't ever allow yourself to become matronly ... you're so very lovely just as you are.'

'Praise indeed from you,' I said, a faint flush warming my cheeks. Despite his fulsome compliment, it seemed to me that he studied me as if I were a work of art rather than a living, breathing being.

'I came to tell you I was talking to Lord Liverpool this morning,' said Father. 'I mentioned your miraculous return and he expressed an interest in meeting you. It appears he remembers being enchanted by your mother at a musical evening, long before he became Prime Minister. I said you'd invite him to your ball.'

'Aunt Maude and I collected the invitation cards from the printer this week,' I said. A great number of Father's friends were titled but it unnerved me to know that the Prime Minister wished to meet me, if only out of curiosity.

'Aunt Maude,' said Father, 'have you discussed the supper menu for the ball with Cook?'

'Yes, Frederick,' she said. 'And ices and ornamental confectioneries have been ordered from Gunter's. The florist will bring arrangements of white narcissi, early white azaleas and pink and blue hyacinths.'

Father nodded. 'Very good.' He turned to Dolly. 'May I have a word with you in my study?'

'Will it take long?' he asked, glancing at Francis.

'It's time I took my leave,' said his friend. 'I shall see you later, Dolly.'

Before long Father and he were closeted in the study. Mrs Webbe and her assistant soon followed Mr Gregory out of the front door and Aunt Maude and I were left in peace. She sat on the sofa and sighed deeply with her eyes closed.

'You look tired, Aunt Maude,' I said, suddenly guilt-smitten. 'You must let me do more to help with the arrangements.'

'As your father so often tells me, I need to earn my keep.'

'That's awful!' I was shocked that he might say such a thing.

'What is awful is being an elderly spinster with no home of her own,' said Aunt Maude. 'But your arrival here has given my life new meaning,' she said. 'I used to help your dear mother when she was organising a ball but I'm finding I'm too old for it now.' She sighed. 'I miss Rose. She was charming and I loved her quite as much as if she'd been my own flesh and blood.'

'Did you?' Perhaps she'd had two sides to her, the one Aunt Maude liked and then the deceitful side that had made Father suffer so. Still, if Aunt Maude hadn't known that aspect of my mother, I wouldn't spoil her happy memories.

'Your father gave me a home under sufferance,' said Aunt Maude, 'but Rose always made me feel like a valuable addition to the family.'

I felt sorry for her then and hugged her. 'Of course you are, Aunt Maude!' At least my mother had exhibited some human kindness. 'Why don't you go upstairs and rest,' I said, 'while I finish writing out the invitations?'

Chapter 19

London

I dreamed Alessandro was hurrying along an endless alleyway in the gathering dark while I scurried along behind, desperately trying to catch up with him. I called to him but either he didn't hear me or was pretending not to. I ran faster, shouting his name and reaching out for him, but he was always too far ahead.

Then he stopped suddenly and I ran into the back of him. He caught me by my elbows and held me at arm's length. The dream was so vivid I felt the heat of his hands through the thin muslin of my dress.

'Alessandro, I love you,' I cried. 'Why didn't you wait for me?' I took an involuntary step away when I saw no sign of the usual mischievous humour in his eyes.

'If you really loved me you wouldn't have left,' he said, and walked away without looking back.

I awoke with a hollow ache in my heart and my pillow damp with tears. I'd still received no response to the note I'd sent him, included with my letter to Queen Caroline. Sighing, I turned my thoughts to the ball.

The day had finally arrived. Aunt Maude had worked so hard instructing me on the right way to behave and I didn't want to make mistakes and let her, or Father, down. Dolly and his friend Mr Gregory had called on me regularly to see how I was progressing. Dolly was sometimes waspish but could be most amusing when he set his mind to it. We had spent many an afternoon playacting in the role of guests at the ball, engaging in the art of frivolously polite conversation. Angelic-looking Mr Gregory had made bold attempts at flirting with me while Dolly tried to keep a straight face and coached me on how to give a polite set-down. This had even raised a smile from Aunt Maude, my constant chaperone.

Daisy knocked on the door and came in. 'May I help you dress?' she said.

I swung my feet over the side of the bed, listening to her bright chatter.

'All the furniture's been taken out of the drawing room and it looks like a proper ballroom now,' she said. 'The hired chairs are here. Gilt they are and ever so pretty.'

Once I was dressed I hurried down to the morning room, where Aunt Maude was busy at the writing desk.

'Did you sleep well or were you too excited?' she said, looking up from her book of lists.

'My stomach is full of butterflies,' I said, 'from fear of saying the wrong thing or making a fool of myself.'

'Of course you won't!' said Aunt Maude. 'Your natural grace will carry you through and you don't need to exhibit too much town gloss. After all, you aren't out yet.'

'I have no friends in London. What if no one wishes to dance with me?'

'It's natural to be nervous,' said Aunt Maude, 'but no one would know you haven't had the advantages of being gently brought up.'

'Sarah was a lady's maid, not a scullery maid,' I said indignantly. 'I wasn't a complete hoyden.'

'Then perhaps we have some reason to be grateful to her.' Aunt Maude smiled. 'I'm certainly relieved you no longer wave your hands about when you are agitated.'

I sighed. 'What shall I do to help?'

'Will you check the latest invitation responses against the guest list, dear? And after breakfast you may inspect the ballroom and the supper room to see that the floral arrangements are in the correct positions. I saw the florist arriving half an hour ago.'

We worked together on the myriad lists, ticking off completed items.

An hour or so later I was crossing the hall to fetch Aunt Maude's shawl when one of the footmen came out of Father's study.

'A letter for you, Miss Langdon.'

I caught my breath. Was it from Alessandro? I recognised the wax seal on the folded paper as Queen Caroline's. I hurried upstairs to my room and closed the door behind me. I broke the seal with trembling fingers. It was a single, folded sheet of thick paper and I was bitterly disappointed to discover there was no enclosure from Alessandro. The note was written in Italian.

Dear Miss Langdon,

The Queen thanks you for informing her that she has the support of the public in her endeavours to obtain the rights and privileges due to her status.

Following the receipt of the news of her exclusion from the Liturgy, she wishes you to know that she will proceed with all haste to England with the intention of arriving on the thirtieth of April.

The Queen conveys her kind regards and will be pleased to receive you upon her arrival in London.

Caroline

I remembered so well the sprawling signature that the Princess, now the Queen, had added to the bottom of the letters I wrote on her behalf. I assumed that Baron Pergami now performed that task. Lady Hamilton, still in London, had forwarded my letters to the Queen.

Not only was she coming to England at last, but she was due to arrive in two days! I tucked the letter into the bottom drawer of the chest in my room and went to fetch Aunt Maude's shawl.

She and I were finishing our breakfast when Father came to ask me if he could have a private word. I gulped down the last of my coffee and followed him into his study.

'I have to go out,' he said, 'but I wanted to give you this.' He pulled open his desk drawer and handed me a small oblong box. 'They were your mother's,' he said. 'It seems appropriate you should wear them tonight.'

Curious, I opened the box. Inside nestled a double row of pearls. As I lifted them up I experienced a mixture of pleasure and pain. If my mother had cared more for my happiness than for her own misery, she'd have been here to give me the pearls herself. 'They're beautiful,' I said, 'but will it be distressing for you to see me wear them?'

He looked at me for a long moment and I wondered if it was my mother's face that he saw.

'She must have been wearing them when Sarah took away the rest of her jewellery. You're considerate to think of my feelings, Emilia, but I want you to have them. And the woman your mother was when I married her would have wished it too.' He glanced away from me to gaze out of the window. 'You remind me so much of the young Rose, when she was sweet and innocent, before everything changed.'

'I wish we could go back in time to stop those tragic events,' I said, looking down at the pearls coiled in my palm.

Father sighed heavily. 'We can't go back but I want to give you the best opportunities for a happy and secure future. My wish is that you'll meet a suitable man during the next few months . . .'

177

'Father, I've already told you that there's a man I love.'

He held up his hand. 'We agreed you would take this time to be sure you're making the right decision – one you must abide by for the rest of your life.' His eyes searched my face. 'And, as far as I'm aware, you've had no communication with Alessandro Fiorelli?'

'No, Father.'

'It's been five months since you saw him last. He'd have found a way to send you a letter if he still cared for you.'

I bowed my head so that Father wouldn't see my distress. Alessandro hadn't written to me in all this time and it worried me that he might not have forgiven me for coming to London. I ran my finger and thumb over every pearl in my mother's necklace as if it were a rosary, saying Alessandro's name in my head as I touched each one.

'I want you to be happy,' said Father gently, 'and I wouldn't want you to refuse a suitable offer of marriage because you're hankering after a man who doesn't love you.'

I stayed silent, afraid I'd cry if I spoke.

'Emilia, you must know Dolly is very fond of you?'

'Dolly?' I looked up, surprised out of my sadness.

'He admires you,' said Father. 'He's sophisticated and good-looking and only six years older than yourself. I've seen how he makes you laugh. It would be a good match.'

I was stunned. 'I thought you didn't like him?'

'Well . . . ' Father shrugged. 'Perhaps I was too hasty. The death of my only son was a devastating blow. I can't break the entail and it's natural I felt antagonistic towards Dolly but since you came home I've had the opportunity to get to know him better. And when he said he'd developed a fondness for you . . . '

I blurted out, 'I don't want to marry a man who is *fond* of me, I want to marry a man who *loves* me!'

'Believe me,' said Father, 'love flies out of the window all too easily. And what then? If you marry Fiorelli, assuming he still wants

178

you, how will you manage when a clutch of children arrive? A tutor's earnings are not large and there will be few servants to help you. You'll become a drudge. There won't be any fine clothes and you'll all be crammed into a small house, wondering where the next meal is coming from.'

'It wouldn't be like that!'

Father raked his fingers through his thick grey hair. 'Emilia, this is the most important decision of your life. You must choose a husband based on who can provide best for you. Dolly will inherit this house and Langdon Hall and the estate. As his wife you would live a life of ease.'

'I don't love Dolly.' The walls of the room felt as if they were closing in and I rose to my feet, my heart thudding.

'Many advantageous marriages begin without love,' said Father, 'but affection follows. And you will have children to love, including a new heir for the estate, carrying Langdon blood.'

'How long ago did you and Dolly cook up this plan between you?' My cheeks burned. 'It's a shame you didn't consult me. I'd have told you then you were wasting your time.'

'Emilia . . .'

'*No*, Father!' Dropping my mother's pearls onto his desk with a clatter, I ran from the room.

Later, Aunt Maude tapped on my bedroom door. She came and sat on the bed beside me.

'Did Father tell you to come and see me?' I asked.

'He didn't mean to upset you,' she said, 'especially today. I'm sure he has no intention of forcing you to marry Dolly.' She placed the box of pearls beside me.

I wiped my eyes with the damp handkerchief balled up in my fist. 'It's not only that I don't want to marry Dolly.' My chin quivered again. 'Alessandro promised to write but he hasn't. I can't bear it if he doesn't still want to marry me.' I leaned back against the pillows.

179

Aunt Maude stroked my hand. 'Perhaps a letter could have gone astray? Italy is a long way from here.'

'I suppose a letter from him might arrive with Queen Caroline's entourage,' I said. 'She wrote to me saying she expects to arrive at Dover in two days' time.'

'The Queen wrote to you?'

'I expect the Baron wrote it but she signed it. I had so hoped for a note from Alessandro.'

'Try not to worry about that today,' said Aunt Maude. 'I shall send up Daisy with a cool compress for you. We can't have you going to your ball with swollen eyes, can we?'

'The ball! I'd quite forgotten it.' Dread made my shoulders slump. 'How am I going to face Dolly?'

'With your usual good humour,' said Aunt Maude, her tone brisk. 'Remember that no one is compelling you to marry him. And you'll meet any number of suitable men over the coming months so you still have plenty of time to make your choice.' She saw my expression. 'Or not. At the end of the season you shall return to Italy if you wish. Most girls would give their eye teeth for these opportunities.'

I couldn't deny that Father had been very generous but he didn't know how deeply I felt about Alessandro. 'I suppose I ought to apologise,' I said.

'Frederick has gone to an auction to purchase a painting,' said Aunt Maude, 'and won't be back until later.'

I hugged her. 'I don't need a cold compress,' I said, 'and I'll come and help you with the final preparations.'

Aunt Maude patted my hand. 'That's the spirit! Let's go downstairs together.'

Chapter 20

Aunt Maude, resplendent in purple taffeta with a black lace over-skirt, smiled her approval from her seat by my bedroom window. 'You will dazzle them all tonight, Emilia.'

I touched a finger to the lustrous pearls Daisy had clasped around my neck, surprised that they weren't cold. It was almost as if they'd retained the warmth of my mother's skin after she'd last taken them off.

My silken skirts swished around my ankles as I drifted towards the mirror. I stared at my reflection, barely recognising myself. The glorious dress had worked its magic again and new stays had made a great deal more of my *décolletage*. My skin appeared as luminous as my mother's pearls against the cream silk. During the afternoon, the visiting *friseur* had dressed my hair into gleaming copper curls and then entwined them with silk ribbons and lilies. I looked confident and, even to my eyes, beautiful.

'Oh, Miss Langdon!' said Daisy. She clasped her hands to her breast. 'You look so lovely.'

'Thank you, Daisy.'

She handed me the bottle of lily-of-the-valley perfume Dolly had brought me as a gift a few days before. I rubbed a few drops onto my wrists and between my breasts, faltering a little as I wondered how I could face him after what Father had told me.

Aunt Maude stood up. 'Come, Emilia, we shall show your father how beautiful you are.'

'I hope he won't still be angry with me.'

Servants were bustling hither and thither as we went downstairs and the discordant sounds of musicians tuning their instruments drifted from the ballroom. Two men were carrying a harp up the stairs and magnificent arrangements of narcissi and hyacinths perfumed the air.

Aunt Maude tapped on the door of Father's study.

Dressed in formal evening dress of brocade coat, knee breeches and white stockings, he was studying a painting propped up on his desk.

I waited for him to turn around. Would he still be angry with me? Then I forgot my anxious thoughts as I looked at the painting. It was beautiful, a nativity scene showing a stable set against a backdrop of mountains. I peered at the serene face of the Madonna as she smiled down at her babe and took a step closer to scrutinise the brushwork of the flowing drapery of her gown. Frowning, I said, 'It looks like a work by Fra Angelico.'

'It does, doesn't it?' said Father, still gazing at the painting.

'But it can't be,' I said, 'it would be far too expensive.'

'Well done, Emilia,' said Father. 'It seems your travels have not been in vain. This is believed to have been painted by one of Fra Angelico's apprentices.' He laughed. 'And it was still very expensive. But worth it, don't you think?'

'I do,' I said.

'Have you completed that list of places you stayed yet? I want to make a final effort to write to all the dealers to enquire after the miniatures.'

'I'll give it to you tomorrow.'

'My art collection is not subject to the laws of entail,' he said, 'and I'm delighted that it interests you. Perhaps, if you stay in England, one day it will be yours.'

His suggestion astounded me but it wasn't enough to bribe me to marry a man I didn't love.

Aunt Maude coughed to gain Father's attention.

He turned then and stared at me.

Slowly, I twirled around so that he could inspect me from all angles.

He lifted my hand and kissed it. 'I knew you were beautiful,' he said, 'but tonight you are exquisite. I'm very proud to be your father, my dear.'

I looked down at his broad hand with its stubby fingers enclosing my slender white ones. 'Father, I apologise if I was rude earlier today. I'm sure you have the best of intentions in suggesting that I accept Dolly's suit.'

'Not another word!' he said. 'We mustn't spoil your first ball. All I ask is that you don't reject the idea without considering it carefully.'

I sighed, knowing he couldn't change my mind.

'The first guests will arrive soon,' said Aunt Maude.

The drawing room had been transformed into an elegant ball-room, where everything glittered and shimmered. All was brilliantly lit; the crystal chandeliers blazed, gilt torchères gleamed with the glow of beeswax candles, flickering candlelight was reflected into infinity by the faceted mirrors of the wall sconces.

The double doors had been opened wide to the adjacent sitting room, which was set up with card tables for those who did not care to dance. The musicians chatted quietly together while the harpist softly plucked the strings of her instrument and the air was perfumed with beeswax and flowers.

'It's very fine,' said Father, eyeing his reflection in the overmantel and smoothing back his hair.

I was immensely flattered that all this splendour was in my honour. 'A few months ago,' I said, 'I could never have imagined being invited to an event such as this.' I cast a glance around, checking there were sufficient chairs and noting the small tables set out for the chaperones to congregate around. The carpet had been rolled up and removed and the golden parquet floor beneath dusted with powdered chalk to prevent unfortunate slips during the more energetic dances.

'We shall sit down while we can,' said Aunt Maude, lowering herself onto one of the gilt chairs. 'Now, don't forget, Emilia,' she said, 'you may only accept one dance with each partner.'

'But two dances are acceptable with Dolly,' said Father, 'since he's family.'

Nerves fluttered in my stomach. What could I say to Dolly now I knew he wished to propose to me? It would be impossible to meet his eyes. I pulled aside the cream damask drapes to look at the street below. I couldn't see the torches that had been lit on either side of the front door but their welcoming light pooled over the pavement. Then a yellow carriage drew up.

My stomach gave a little lurch. 'The first guests!' I said.

Father nodded at the musicians and they started to play.

Aunt Maude led me to the door and Father joined us. A moment later one of the footmen announced our visitors as they came up the stairs. Then the next ones arrived and there wasn't time to feel nervous as I smiled and curtseyed to a seemingly endless procession.

I found myself looking up at Dolly, who was studying me with a proprietorial air. 'Good evening, Dolly,' I said. My voice was calm but a blush raced up my chest and neck.

'Well,' he drawled, 'the duckling has turned into a veritable swan. Congratulations, Emilia.'

'You look most elegant, too,' I said, regarding his immaculately starched neck cloth and understated but superbly cut coat.

'I shall claim you as my partner for the supper dance,' he said as he moved on.

'Almost all the guests are here now,' said Aunt Maude a while later, 'although we still await Lord Liverpool. Come with me and we'll make conversation until a young man asks you to dance.'

'Supposing nobody does?' I asked, anxious again.

'Of course they will!' said Aunt Maude.

It appeared she was right because in the following five minutes three young men and one elderly one crowded round to ask me to partner them. Father, however, appeared at my side and claimed me for the opening quadrille.

'After that,' he whispered, 'I must do my duty and partner the dowager duchess in the mauve silk.'

Mr Sandys, my dancing master, had agreed to act as Master of Ceremonies and made introductions between the young people. Soon there were enough couples for the first dance.

The strains of the violins, harp and flutes rose above the chatter of conversation. Mr Sandys clapped his hands and organised the dancers in facing rows.

I stood opposite Father at the top of the dance, waiting for it to begin.

My neighbour, a pretty girl with dark curls, smiled at me and said, 'At my last ball I danced until dawn and wore my shoes into holes.'

The violins played the introduction. Mr Sandys nodded and we began. At first I had to take care over the steps but before long my feet remembered what to do as we danced up and down the rows. Father proved to be a competent dancer and I began to enjoy myself. It took half an hour to move all down the set and then to repeat it. At the end I was flushed with enjoyment.

Father led me back to Aunt Maude before going to claim his dowager duchess. I had only a moment to sip a glass of lemonade before my next partner, a Mr Perry, came to find me. He had brown eyes and dark hair that kept falling over his forehead and made me think wistfully of Alessandro.

'I saw you talking to m'sister at the beginning of the first dance,' he said.

'The girl with the dark curls?'

'Araminta. She'll ask you to her ball next month.'

'I should like that,' I said. 'I've been living abroad and don't know many people here.'

'I heard about that,' said Mr Perry. 'M'father knows your father. Quite a mystery, when you disappeared.' He smiled. 'Still, you're home again.'

The music began and, as we readied ourselves, I noticed Dolly and Francis Gregory further up the set with their partners.

'I'd like to hear about your adventures abroad,' said Mr Perry as we began the dance. He wasn't a good dancer but remained cheerful throughout his mistakes. 'Always had two left feet,' he said as he stepped upon my toes again. 'Prefer to be out hunting than indoors practising my steps with some foppish dance teacher.'

Dolly, however, was an accomplished dancer, I noticed. He bowed and twirled with grace and elegance, his cool fingers touching mine briefly as we came together for a moment before we turned to our next partners.

Some two hours and five partners later I was looking forward to the end of a particularly energetic Scottish reel. I'd danced every dance and was hot, breathless and anticipating my supper. Father and a group of older men were watching me and I caught his eye as I spun around. He smiled encouragingly and then I was off again. At last the reel came to an end. I curtseyed to my partner and there was a touch on my arm.

'Come with me, Emilia,' Father said. 'Lord Liverpool is here and has brought a distinguished guest. He was dining with the King when he mentioned he was coming to your ball afterwards. The

King professed a desire to meet you and has accompanied him. It's a very great honour.'

I pressed my hands to my hot cheeks. 'The King! What do I say to him?' I was totally unprepared for such a meeting.

'Curtsey and, if he speaks to you, answer him as best you can.' Father tucked my hand into the crook of his elbow.

I recognised the King immediately from the illustrations I'd seen in the newspapers, except that he was a great deal fatter and much less handsome than his portraits. Flustered, I barely heard the introduction as Father presented me and simply murmured, 'Your Majesty.' I sank into a deep curtsey, my knees shaking, and stared at the King's highly polished shoes for a moment before rising.

'An uncommonly handsome girl, Langdon,' said the King, looking me up and down with protuberant blue eyes. 'You must be happy to have her returned to you after all this time.'

'I had given up hoping for it, sir,' said Father, 'so you may imagine my joy that she's at my side now.'

The King inclined himself slightly towards me. 'Enjoying the dancing, Miss Langdon?'

'I am indeed, sir,' I said. Dolly had been right, the King's corset did creak when he moved, and I suppressed a sudden desire to giggle.

'Used to like dancing myself,' said the King. 'People were astounded by my elegance when dancing the gavotte.'

'I am sure they were,' I murmured.

The King lifted a glass of punch to his small, pink mouth while I wondered what he would say if he knew I had been a member of his wife's household.

Father introduced me then to Lord Liverpool and I curtseyed again. My knees still trembled but I retained my outward composure.

'I knew your mother, Miss Langdon,' said Lord Liverpool. He shook his head sadly. 'A great loss to us all when she passed on. She was beautiful, too.'

'Thank you, sir.'

Over Lord Liverpool's shoulder, I saw Dolly watching us.

'Dancing always made me hungry,' said the King. 'Run along and have your supper.' He waved his hand in dismissal. The presentation was over.

I curtseyed and then Father took hold of my arm and we backed out of the royal presence.

I heard the King say, 'Attractive little thing with her cheeks all flushed and her curls coming loose, don't you think, Liverpool?'

'Very well done, Emilia,' whispered Father. 'What a feather in your cap to be presented to the King tonight!'

I let out my breath slowly and was fanning my hot cheeks when Dolly came to join us.

'The King has an eye for a pretty girl,' he said. 'His approval has sealed your success.'

'I'll warrant the invitations will come in thick and fast now,' said Father with satisfaction.

'It looks as though you've had enough excitement for the moment, Emilia,' said Dolly. 'Shall we take some refreshment?'

He went to fetch our supper and I was grateful to sit down for a while. It had been strange to meet the King; the man Queen Caroline had called a monster. He seemed a surprisingly ordinary, elderly man with broken veins on his nose and cheeks. I wouldn't have looked twice at him if I'd met him in the street. Despite that, knowing he *was* the King had made me nervous.

Dolly returned with supper plates laden with tempting delicacies. Mr Perry and Araminta came to sit beside us as we ate the poached chicken, jellies and sweetmeats.

'What is the King like at close quarters?' asked Araminta, her brown eyes wide.

'Very . . .' I tried not to picture the King's dissipated complexion. 'Very regal,' I said with as much diplomacy as I could muster.

'But he's terribly fat, isn't he?' she whispered.

'He called me an "uncommonly handsome girl",' I said, trying not to giggle as I avoided answering the question.

Mr Gregory and his supper partner came to sit with us, too, and after a while I felt less agitated and began to enjoy the lively conversation of my companions. By the time we returned to the ballroom the King and Lord Liverpool had left.

The dancing began again and young men were queuing up to partner me. I danced every dance but couldn't help noticing that Dolly's gaze was often upon me. Later, he arrived at my side to rescue me when one of my partners, spotty and sandy-haired Mr Fortescue, began to press moist kisses upon my hands.

'Miss Langdon is my partner for the next dance,' said Dolly. 'Let go of her immediately, if you please, and take a turn outside for some air.' He released the young man's limpet grip from my fingers. My rescuer's tone was light but there was an edge of steel to it. 'And I suggest you don't imbibe any more punch.'

'Thank you, Dolly,' I said, after Mr Fortescue had glowered and taken himself off.

'Irritating little cub!' He cleared his throat a couple of times and straightened his perfectly arranged necktie. 'Emilia,' he said.

I noticed his usually pale face was even paler than normal.

'Emilia, I'd hoped for the opportunity to have a quiet word with you tonight. I know that your father has mentioned to you that I spoke to him ... '

'He did.' I held myself ramrod straight, desperately wishing I were somewhere else and could avoid the forthcoming embarrassing exchange.

'Perhaps this is not the time to discuss the matter of my proposal.'

'You haven't proposed to me,' I said, 'only discussed the matter with Father, but I have no intention of marrying *anyone* in the immediate future.'

His lips curved slightly. 'Neither have I.'

'Oh!' I said, taken aback.

'Emilia, marriage is inevitable for both of us but there's no hurry. I do believe, however, that we might make an eminently suitable and convenient match in the fullness of time, should you wish it. My family are constantly pressing me to find a wife and your father wishes to see you settled. Perhaps there's some merit for both of us in suggesting that you are thinking about my proposal but require, say, six months or so to come to a firm decision. What do you say?'

I stared at him but his blue eyes were dark and unfathomable. My thoughts whirled so fast it made me dizzy. I intended to be reunited with Alessandro before six months had passed, unless, of course, he didn't love me anymore. I swallowed hard at the distressing thought. In that case, I might decide handsome, eligible Dolly was a good choice for a husband in the absence of the man I truly loved.

'This proposed mutual arrangement would allow us to make our own decisions in the fullness of time,' said Dolly, 'without familial pressure.'

I fingered the pearls at my neck while I thought. Aunt Maude had impressed upon me that if I passed this season by without accepting an offer, I could find myself on the shelf. I did very much want a family of my own so, however much I loved Alessandro, it would be foolish to slam the door on Dolly's offer.

'Emilia?' A muscle flickered slightly in his jaw.

'I shall consider your suggestion,' I replied.

He glanced at Mr Sandys, who was organising another dance. 'Shall we sit this one out?'

Relieved, I said, 'I must find Aunt Maude.'

She sat with the other chaperones and smiled up at me when we joined her. 'Well,' she said, 'the King's visit was a delightful and unexpected surprise!'

I nodded and smiled, not really listening to the conversations going on around me, and soon my next partner whisked me away. My shoes were pinching and I was relieved it was the final dance.

The guests began calling for their carriages and came to pay their respects before they left. I stood beside Father and Aunt Maude, bidding our guests goodbye. My face ached from constant smiling and trying not to yawn.

Dolly and Francis Gregory were the last to leave.

'The ball was a triumph,' said Dolly.

'An outstanding success!' declared Mr Gregory.

'May I call on you tomorrow, Emilia?' said Dolly.

'We shall expect you,' said Father, giving him a meaningful look.

After the last guest had gone, the musicians left with their instruments and at last the front door was bolted against the night. Yawning, the servants began to move the furniture back into the drawing room and remove the remains of supper to the kitchens.

Father put his arm around me. 'I'm proud of you, Emilia,' he said. 'Now go and get some sleep before the sun rises.'

'Goodnight, Father. And thank you. I shall never forget my first ball.'

He kissed my cheek and I watched him climb the stairs, wishing he'd shown Aunt Maude some sign of appreciation for all her efforts.

The poor lady drooped with exhaustion. 'Come to bed,' I said, gently. 'You've worked so hard to make everything perfect and must rest now.' She looked very frail and I helped her upstairs and handed her into the care of her maid.

Daisy was waiting for me in my room. I was grateful she was there to undress me and take the wilted flowers out of my hair. Afterwards, I lay in bed reliving the evening. I recalled the King's polished shoes and how my knees had trembled when I curtseyed before him; the heady perfume of narcissi and the aroma of beeswax candles. I remembered how Dolly had saved me from unpleasantness with Mr Fortescue and the subsequent extraordinary proposal. I recalled Father's proud smile and heard dear Aunt Maude's words of pleasure at my success.

And then, as dawn light began to creep through the curtains, I thought how I would have been pleased to forgo all of that, if only Alessandro could have been at my side.

Chapter 21

May 1820

London

The weeks since the ball had been a constant round of tea and supper parties, balls, routs and excursions, until I barely knew which day of the week it was. I soon discovered that more or less the same guests went to each event and, since I didn't much enjoy gossip, it was becoming tedious. Despite that, I'd made friends with Araminta Perry and her brother and was always pleased to see their cheerful faces.

Dolly and Francis Gregory, both eligible bachelors with prospects, were usually present at these occasions and so I hadn't been surprised to see Dolly at Violet Braithwaite's tea party.

Mr Perry made a point of sitting beside me, as he so often did. I suspected he was half in love with me and was hoping for a sign that I might encourage him. His chatter was generally of a frivolous nature but he aroused my interest when he mentioned the intense speculation in London on the date of the possible arrival in England of Queen Caroline.

'The Lord Chancellor,' said Mr Perry with a speculative gleam in his eye, 'says that bets are being laid, some as large as fifty guineas!'

'The Queen was going to come at the end of April,' I said, 'but then I read in the newspaper that she was indisposed and unable to travel.' I made a point of reading Father's copy of *The Times* every day after he'd finished with it, to keep myself up to date with the Queen's whereabouts and engagements.

'All hell will break loose when she does arrive!' said Mr Perry. 'The King will sue for divorce immediately she sets a foot on the shore at Dover.'

'She has a great deal of support from the people,' I said. 'Perhaps the King will change his mind?' I lowered my voice. 'He's already exceedingly unpopular with the press and if he's perceived to be persecuting her it won't help him rise in the public's esteem.'

'Ah, well!' Mr Perry's eyes gleamed. 'I have another titbit of gossip for you. Did you hear that John Chesterton's father was burgled?'

I shook my head.

'Chesterton told me about it last night,' said Mr Perry. 'One of his father's paintings, a Stubbs, has been stolen. An unusual subject, I'm told, because it wasn't one of Stubbs's usual equine portraits but that of a giraffe. The interesting thing is that it's not the first time.'

'What do you mean?'

'Another Stubbs, a painting of a lion that time, was stolen from the Chestertons five years ago. It seems the impudent rascal bided his time and came back for its companion piece!'

'My father mentioned there'd been a spate of art thefts in the past.'

'What clinched the fact it was the same thief,' said Mr Perry, 'was that he left a sketch of an empty picture frame in its place, glued to the wall.'

'The Picture Frame thief is a scoundrel with a sense of humour it seems!'

It was raining when Aunt Maude and I were ready to leave the party and I suggested that we drive Dolly to his lodgings. No sooner had we all set off than Aunt Maude fell asleep, lulled by the rocking of the carriage and the drumming of the rain on the roof.

'Poor lady,' I said, looking at her papery cheeks all crumpled with sleep. 'She's too old to have to suffer through the season with me. I think we must have a quiet day tomorrow.'

Dolly glanced at her. 'Emilia,' he said in an undertone, 'have you given any more thought to my suggestion?'

'That we tell Father I'm considering your proposal?'

He nodded. 'I've been trying to speak to you privately ever since your ball.'

'I've thought about it because Father keeps pressing me,' I said, unhappily. 'Every time I return from a social engagement he interrogates me about any young men I've met and then lists all your virtues again.'

Dolly smiled. 'I didn't know I had any! That's a marked change from his original opinion of me.'

'He's more than happy now to view you as his future son-in-law,' I admitted.

'I do believe,' said Dolly, studying me through narrowed eyes, 'we might make a good match. Certainly I'd rather marry you than any of those vacuous little misses at the tea party today.'

I thought of Mr Fortescue, who'd pestered me at my ball, and of Mr Chesterton, who was a trifle slow, and of Mr Perry, who was amiable but not blessed with common sense. If I hadn't loved Alessandro, I might have accepted Dolly's proposal. At least then my future would have been secure.

'Well,' he said, 'shall we stop your father from pressuring us by telling him that you will at least consider my offer?'

Aunt Maude stirred and I put a finger to my lips.

There were a great many carriages in the streets, due to the torrential rain, and I watched drops of water racing down the carriage windows. At least I'd been spared the sight of Dolly going down on bended knee to propose to me. I smiled to myself, imagining he'd take great care when kneeling so as not to sully his trousers. There had never been any hint of flirtation between him and myself and any arrangement we reached suggesting a possible attachment between us was purely for Father's benefit. I still hoped Alessandro would write to me and then I'd be certain of his feelings for me.

Soon we arrived at Dolly's lodgings. He thanked us for driving him home before dashing through the rain to his front door.

It was as the carriage splashed down Portman Street that I saw the stork-like figure of Lady Hamilton standing under her portico and directing her servants as they loaded a carriage with travelling valises. I rapped on the roof of our carriage and the coachman pulled up.

Aunt Maude sat bolt upright. 'Are we home?' she murmured.

'Not yet, Aunt Maude dear,' I said. 'I won't be a moment but I want to have a word with Lady Hamilton.' Before she could protest, I snatched up my umbrella and alighted into the street.

'Miss Langdon?' called Lady Hamilton as I hurried towards her.

'I was driving by and saw your servants stowing your travelling bags,' I explained.

'For goodness' sake, come out of the rain!'

I shook my umbrella and sheltered under the portico with her.

'You received the note I sent to you earlier today?' asked Lady Hamilton.

I shook my head. 'I left the house after breakfast.'

'I'm setting off at last to join the Queen.'

'I'd thought she was to arrive at the end of April,' I said, 'but I read in *The Times* that she was too unwell to travel.'

'She decided to return to the Villa Vittoria before coming to England. When she arrived there she had a severe attack of rheumatic fever, which confined her to bed.'

So Alessandro might have remained in Italy or could be part of the Queen's entourage travelling towards Calais.

'Once she'd recovered,' said Lady Hamilton, 'she packed up her jewels and personal possessions and set off for England again. She intends to present herself to the public as their Queen with all attendant ceremony. Unfortunately, she was taken ill with a stomach complaint on the journey and was forced to rest in Geneva. I'm to join her with all speed now and escort her to Calais.'

'You said you wrote me a note, Lady Hamilton?'

'I did,' she replied crisply. 'The Queen has commissioned several new items of clothing from Mrs Webbe in Pall Mall and has sent her favourite dresses to act as patterns. Her Majesty would be pleased if you would visit Mrs Webbe on her behalf to select the colours and materials that will suit her best.'

'Did she give any indication of her preferences?' I said, wondering how I'd be able to arrange this without making Father angry. I'd learned not to mention the Queen in his presence.

'They are all to be in a dignified English style,' said Lady Hamilton, 'since she's determined to present herself as a model Queen of England. She asked me particularly to say she will rely absolutely on your good judgement.'

'I am honoured,' I said.

Lady Hamilton looked up at the sky. 'I sincerely hope the weather doesn't worsen for the Channel crossing.'

I hesitated, unsure if I dared ask a favour, but decided I could lose nothing by it. 'If by any chance Signor Fiorelli is still with the Queen's entourage,' I said, 'would it be possible for you to ask him to write to me?'

Lady Hamilton surveyed me, stony-faced. Then she sighed. 'Love makes the young so reckless, doesn't it? I can't imagine Sir Frederick is happy to have his daughter chasing after a penniless tutor. Besides, I'd heard rumours that you are to marry his heir.'

I looked down at my feet to hide my blush of annoyance. 'Unfounded gossip,' I said.

'*If* I see Signor Fiorelli,' said Lady Hamilton after a moment, 'I will give him your message.'

I looked up at her, unable to disguise my gratitude. 'Thank you so much, ma'am.'

'Now hurry along, you're delaying me.'

And then I was back in the rain again, skipping through the puddles, heedless of my wet feet.

The following day Aunt Maude and I sat together in the morning room. I'd found *Belinda* by Maria Edgeworth in Father's library and offered to read it aloud. When I opened the first of the three volumes it gave me a little jolt to see that the flyleaf was inscribed with my mother's name in a firm and confident hand, all underlined with a flourish. Tracing the letters with my forefinger I wondered if she had been as self-assured as her signature.

'Rose loved books,' said Aunt Maude, watching me, 'though your father didn't approve of her reading novels. He thought they might inflame her imagination.'

'Perhaps they did,' I said, remembering what he'd told me about her adulterous affair. Maybe reading had encouraged her to seek romance outside her marriage?

'In the time I knew Rose, she was never given to flights of fancy,' said Aunt Maude. 'I always found her to be an eminently sensible young woman, much like yourself.'

The door opened and James the footman entered. 'Miss Langdon,' he said, 'your father requests you attend him in his study.'

I placed the book on the side table. 'I shan't be long, Aunt Maude,' I said.

A moment later James opened the study door and I saw that Dolly was with my father. Both men stood up as I entered.

Father, smiling widely, held out both his hands to me. 'Emilia, my dear child! Dolly has told me the wonderful news.'

I glanced at my *soi-disant* suitor, who looked even paler than usual. A slight tic twitched at the corner of one eye and I was afraid I knew what had happened. 'What wonderful news is that, Father?'

'Why, your engagement, of course!'

I disentangled my fingers from his warm grip. 'I assure you,' I said frostily, 'there is no engagement between us.'

Father waved a hand as if to dismiss my comment. 'As to that, I understand you wish to wait a while before any formal announcement ...'

'I have made it perfectly clear to Dolly that I have agreed only to *consider* his proposal,' I said. 'I'm in no hurry at all to engage myself to anyone at present.'

Dolly gave his usual nervous cough. 'And I am very happy to give Emilia all the time she needs to make up her mind. Months if necessary. Clearly, there must be no announcement until,' he caught my eye and had the grace to blush, '*unless* Emilia decides to make me the happiest of men.'

He didn't look very happy and it was then that I made up my mind to follow his suggestion. It seemed he wanted his freedom as much as I wanted mine so it was unlikely he'd pressure me into a hasty marriage.

My father breathed heavily and looked at both of us with something akin to anger in his eyes.

'Father,' I said in as conciliatory a tone of voice as I could, 'I am newly arrived in England and everything here is so different for me. I am still learning to know my own family. Allow me a few months more to make what is the most important decision of my life.'

He fixed his gaze on the painting by Fra Angelico's apprentice, which he had hung opposite his desk.

It was curious how calming an effect the sight of it seemed to have on him. His breathing slowed and the tension disappeared from his face as he studied the glowing colours and delicate details.

I caught Dolly's eye and he gave an apologetic grimace.

'Forgive me,' Father said, after a moment. 'It seems such a perfect choice for both of you and I do so want to see you settled. If Dolly is prepared to wait, I suppose I must be content to wait, too.'

'Then, if you will excuse me,' I said, 'I shall return to Aunt Maude.'

Father was spending an increasing amount of time in the House of Commons. At dinner he mentioned the endless speculation regarding the Queen's arrival and the disruption that might ensue. I drew him out on the subject since naturally Her Majesty's affairs were of great interest to me.

'Mr Brougham has suggested advantageous terms on which Caroline of Brunswick might consent to stay abroad,' said Father, 'but the wretched woman has a grossly inflated view of her rights. Furthermore,' he said indignantly, 'he's accused Parliament of being corrupt.'

'I daresay Parliaments over the ages have been accused of that many times,' I observed.

Father ignored my comment. 'The King has sent his old friend Lord Hutchinson off with Brougham to treat with her. His Majesty is determined to get rid of his wife but she'll have to renounce the title of Queen of England if she wants her fifty thousand a year for life.'

'Is the King so concerned about it because the Queen is more popular than he is?' I asked, trying to appear ingenuous.

'Don't ever suggest such a thing outside these four walls, Emilia,' said Father, his brow thunderous. 'I'm working hard to find a place on the King's advisory committee for the Coronation planning and it would destroy all my chances if he thought anyone in my family didn't support him completely.'

Over the next few days Father watched me covertly with a brooding expression on his face and I came to the conclusion that I'd surprised him, not only by my adamant refusal to be propelled into a hasty marriage but also by making that ill-judged reference to the Queen's growing popularity.

When I mentioned at breakfast one morning that I'd received several new invitations, he suggested that I might like some new dresses since the summer was upon us.

'Thank you, Father!' I kissed his cheek, wondering if the offer was a bribe for good behaviour.

I now had the perfect excuse for visiting Mrs Webbe, the Queen's mantua-maker. Aunt Maude, of course, would have to accompany me to Pall Mall and I realised it would be necessary to explain to her my errand on the Queen's behalf. I was relieved when she brooked no objection.

'You may count on me to be perfectly discreet,' she said. 'And really, I do think that the poor Queen has been very put upon by the King over the years. She may have misbehaved but His Majesty has hardly conducted himself like a gentleman. That she wishes to make a good impression during her visit here shows perfect sense, particularly now she's the Queen of England and not simply the estranged wife of the Prince Regent.'

'I have to admit she is a most eccentric lady,' I confided. 'Her conduct is not always dignified but, in my experience, she's good-hearted and very brave in the face of unhappiness.'

'Between us two,' whispered Aunt Maude, 'and whilst certainly not condoning it, I cannot blame her if she sought a little happiness with her Italian steward. After all, the King has had many mistresses.'

I was astonished by Aunt Maude's attitude. I hadn't expected it from someone of her age.

'Sometimes,' she continued, 'I'm extremely thankful that I never married. It seems to me that marriage is a risky business.' She shook her head regretfully. 'It certainly made your poor dear mother very unhappy.'

'So Father tells me,' I said. I didn't want to talk about my mother now I knew what kind of a person she had been and how much distress she had caused.

We left the mantua-maker after an appointment lasting nearly three hours. Two new dresses were to be made for me, one in pale green muslin with white sprigs and another in the palest primrose yellow with a flounced hem.

I had also made a careful choice of materials for the Queen's dresses, taking into account her florid colouring and rotund figure, and hoped that she would approve. The most useful thing I could do to help the poor woman at the moment was to make her feel elegant and self-assured. While she might be popular with the public, if it came to a confrontation in court, she would be dealing with some of the best legal minds in the kingdom, who all intended to win the King's favour by helping him to destroy her reputation forever.

Chapter 22

June 1820

London

Father threw down his copy of *The Times* on the breakfast table and sighed. 'The King will be in even more of a temper than yesterday when he reads this. Caroline of Brunswick – I really cannot refer to her as his Queen – set ashore in an open boat, would you believe, rather than wait a few hours until the tide had turned and the *Prince Leopold* could dock at Dover. That's just the kind of undignified and impetuous behaviour that will endear her to the lower orders.'

'It must have taken a great deal of courage to climb down from the *Prince Leopold* into a small boat on the open sea,' I observed.

'For heaven's sake, Emilia! That woman will do anything to play to the gallery,' said Father, scowling. 'The wretched common people had been waiting for her since dawn, milling about on the beach and the cliffs and getting drunk, dressed up as if they were going to a fête. And then the cannon at Dover Castle actually greeted her with the Royal Salute.' His lips twisted in a sneer. 'You can just imagine how cock-a-hoop that would have made her.'

'Who travels with her?' asked Aunt Maude.

'She's left the Italian rabble behind,' said Father, 'except, I believe, for her paramour's sister.'

Countess Oldi had come to England then but Alessandro had stayed behind. At least the Queen had one of her 'Italian family' to support her.

'Lady Charlotte Lindsay was asked to meet her at Dover,' said Father, 'and resume her position as lady-in-waiting, but the King warned her off. Alexander Hamilton, being such a staunch Whig of course, has allowed his sister to wait on her. Hoping to curry favour, no doubt. And that jackass Alderman Wood is with her, and the boy William Austin.'

'What will happen now?' I asked.

'Since Caroline refused to agree terms with the King's envoys, he'll sue her for divorce on grounds of her infidelity.'

'But what about the King's infidelities?'

'Emilia! It's not fitting for a young, unmarried woman to ask such questions.'

'But . . .'

'I will discuss this with you no further! As if there isn't enough to worry about with all that's going on in the House, now I have to contend with discord in my own home.'

Still grumbling, Father left for the House of Commons.

I picked up his discarded copy of *The Times* and took it into the garden. A pink rose, just coming into bloom, scrambled over the wall behind an ironwork bench. I sat down in the sunshine and spread the paper over my lap.

Neither at the landing of William the Conqueror nor that of William III had any arrival in England caused such a sensation, I read. I wondered what the Queen had felt when she'd landed on these shores after four years abroad. I suspected she'd have chattered away in a cheerful manner, however anxious she might have felt inside. I could picture her waving gaily to the crowds and hoped they'd cheered her on.

The Times described the Queen as she walked to the Ship Hotel: *Her blue eyes were shining with peculiar lustre but her cheeks had the appearance of a long intimacy with care and anxiety.*

The anxieties of her situation on top of her enforced parting from the Baron and little Victorine must have been terribly hard for her, especially since she couldn't know how long it would be until she was able to return to Pesaro.

I leaned back against the sun-warmed bench and watched a bee drift lazily past. The sun was hot on my shoulders. I closed my eyes for a moment, imagining I was back in Pesaro sitting on the cliffs of San Bartolo with Alessandro at my side, smelling the honey-scented wild broom and listening to the cries of the gulls over the turquoise sea. I'd had to come to England to find my family but, oh, I did so long to be with Alessandro!

Two nights later, angry shouts from down in the street awoke me. I heard shattering glass and leaped out of bed with my heart hammering. From out of the window I glimpsed a horde of men carrying flaming torches, chanting and waving sticks in the air as they passed by.

'No Queen, no King!' they yelled.

A man dressed in a nightgown leaned out of a second-floor window in the house opposite and a protestor called out, 'Put a candle in the window to show your support for Queen Caroline!'

The observer shook his fist for reply. 'Damned Queenites! Get away with you at once or I'll call the constable!'

The demonstrators roared their displeasure and a hail of stones flew through the air, smashing his window panes. Jagged shards of glass crashed to the pavement below and skittered across the street.

The man shrieked and clasped his head, while the front of his nightgown grew dark with blood.

I jumped at the sound of a thunderous knocking on our front door. Snatching up my wrap, I hurried down to the first-floor landing.

Leaning over the banister, I saw Father and James in the hall below. Their voices were raised in anger as they argued with several men standing on the doorstep.

'Put a light in your windows in support of Queen Caroline!' demanded one of the callers.

'Never!' Father replied vehemently.

'You'll be sorry if you don't!'

Father slammed the front door so hard it reverberated throughout the house. 'Ruffians!'

I hurried back upstairs, lit my candle and placed it on the window-sill. Father wouldn't like it if he knew, even if it did save our windows, but I wanted to support the Queen in whatever way I could.

Downstairs, Father was shouting orders at James and I went to see if any damage had been done.

'Unbelievable!' Father said when he saw me. 'Unruly rabble!' He paced across the hall. 'Queenites, indeed! They ought to be flogged ... along with that spiteful hoyden Caroline of Brunswick for encouraging them.' He shot the bolts home on the front door. 'Now you can see why any decent and reasonable person wants to be rid of her. God knows how you stood being part of her household, Emilia.'

A firecracker went off in the street and voices chanted, 'Long live Queen Caroline!' and 'No Queen, no King!'

Father turned to James, who was waiting for further orders. 'Don't just stand there, you dolt! Make sure the windows are fast. And bring me brandy!'

'You're not hurt, Father?' I asked.

'It takes more than a few troublemakers to rattle me.' He strode to the front door and checked the bolts again.

'Then I shall say goodnight,' I told him.

Upstairs, I moved the candle to one side of my bedroom window-sill and looked down at the street. Men carrying flaming torches still milled about, waving sticks and chanting their support of the Queen. Glancing along the street, I noticed several of the houses had placed lights in their windows, either out of fear or in genuine support for the Queen.

Eventually the disturbance faded away as the men marched off to break windows elsewhere. I returned to bed and pulled the covers up to my chin.

Somewhere a dog barked, the sound echoing down the deserted street, and, at last, I slept.

In the morning I found the front door open. Father was on the steps surveying the street and a number of servants were sweeping up shards of broken glass. At the house opposite a glazier in a brown apron was boarding up the downstairs windows.

'Disgraceful!' said Father. 'There's broken glass everywhere! The Queenite louts didn't dare damage my house, though.' He planted his hands on his hips and gave me a smug smile. 'They didn't like it when I stood up to them and slammed the door in their grubby faces.'

'We were lucky,' I said.

'No luck about it,' said Father. 'You have to stand firm and show the beggars you simply won't have it.'

'Yes, Father,' I said, reminding myself to take the candlestick off my bedroom windowsill.

'In any case, I heard yesterday the King is set on a divorce and he won't change his mind to please the mob. He's sent Lord Liverpool two Green Bags of evidence against his wife from the Milan Commission. A committee will have to be set up to examine it.'

Father took himself off to his study and I went to the morning room where Aunt Maude was waiting for me.

'Did you manage to sleep through the commotion last night?' I asked.

She smiled. 'I sleep very lightly these days. It was rather exciting, didn't you think? I worry for the horses, though, with broken glass in the street.'

'The Queen has some loyal supporters,' I said.

206

'It would appear so,' Aunt Maude observed, 'though a mob's good opinion can be fickle.'

'I doubt the so-called evidence against her from the Milan Commission will hold up in court.'

'Don't tell your father,' Aunt Maude whispered, 'but I put my candle in the window last night.'

I laughed. 'So did I!'

Aunt Maude smiled. 'A small victory for Womankind.'

'Father mentioned yesterday that the Queen is staying in Portman Street with Lady Hamilton,' I said. 'I'd like to call upon her. Her household was very informal in Pesaro but it could be very different here. She may not receive me.'

'I trust she will be pleased with the service you rendered to her in advising her mantua- maker.'

'I need to buy ribbons in Bond Street but, afterwards, will you accompany me to Portman Street?' I bit my lip. 'Of course, I haven't asked Father if I may go.'

'While I am not generally in favour of deceit,' said Aunt Maude, 'since Frederick hasn't expressly forbidden you to visit the Queen, I shall make no objection to your plan.' Her blue eyes twinkled. 'In fact, I shall be most interested to see this unusual lady.'

Later that morning, after I had purchased blue silk ribbons in Bond Street, we directed the coachman to drive us to 22 Portman Street. I placed one of my calling cards on a silver salver and a footman in scarlet livery bore it away. Aunt Maude and I waited on the hall chairs.

A short while later the footman returned and asked us to follow him upstairs to the drawing room where the Queen and her ladies sat. Queen Caroline wore a dress made from material I had selected for her. She had lost a great deal of weight and I supposed this was caused by her recent illness.

I curtseyed deeply to the Queen, Lady Hamilton and Countess Oldi, and helped Aunt Maude to lower herself as far as her poor old knees would allow.

'Pray be seated,' said the Queen. 'How kind of you both to welcome me! So, my Miss Barton is now Miss Langdon?'

'That is so, Your Majesty,' I said. 'I'm pleased to say I have found my father.'

'Is he what you expected?'

'I had no expectations at all, Ma'am,' I said, 'only hopes, so I'm happy he has welcomed me back into the bosom of my family.' I smiled at Aunt Maude. 'Miss Weston is my great- aunt,' I explained.

'How fortunate for you, Miss Weston, to have your great-niece returned to you.'

'I count myself truly blessed, Your Majesty,' replied Aunt Maude. 'It was a terrible thing when Emilia was taken from us as a child. I never expected to see her again.'

'I was sorry to hear that you had been indisposed, Ma'am,' I told the Queen, 'and were unable to travel when you had intended.'

She shook her head and sighed. 'So many delays.'

'I was pleased to read in the newspaper that your arrival was a triumph and that a crowd had gathered to welcome you.'

'It was a great relief to me.' Her blue eyes sparkled. 'We stayed at Canterbury where the cheering of the people kept me awake. It was so all the way to London, with people waving as we went. Men unhitched the horses from my carriage and pulled it themselves!'

'Eventually we requested them to desist,' said Lady Hamilton, 'since otherwise we should not have reached London before nightfall.'

'The rain stopped and the sun shone when we reached Deptford,' the Queen took up the story, clasping her hands to her bosom at the memory. 'We folded back the roof of the carriage so the crowd could see me. They shouted and cheered and said the sunshine was a good omen.'

Smiling, I said, 'I'm sure that it will be.'

'There was a great gathering at Blackheath,' said Lady Hamilton. 'You would have thought it was a midsummer fair. At Shooter's

Hill we could barely pass for the barouches and chaises filled with respectable people come to welcome Her Majesty. And then we progressed to Alderman Wood's house in South Audley Street with all those carriages in procession behind us.'

'I stood on his balcony so my subjects could see me,' said the Queen. 'I waved my handkerchief at the crowds and the cheers were deafening.' She sighed. 'It was wonderful. The King has fled now to Windsor, fearful the people will turn against him. Brougham and Thomas Denman, my Solicitor-General, will meet soon to discuss our strategy.'

There seemed nothing to add to this. Besides, I hoped to turn the conversation so as to ask about Alessandro. 'Was little Victorine well when you saw her last?' I enquired.

'She didn't want me to leave,' said the Queen. 'The Baron had to pull her, weeping, from my arms. It nearly broke my heart. She was sad, too, because her Signor Fiorelli had also left my household.'

'Signor Fiorelli has gone?' I was shocked, knowing how fond he was of Victorine.

The Queen shrugged. 'He is no longer in my employ and I hold you responsible for that, Miss Langdon.'

'Me? But why?'

'When you left my household he suffered. He was miserable and I missed his merry laughter. Why didn't you return to make him a happy man?' The Queen shook her head. 'Anyone could see that you loved each other.'

'I will return to Pesaro,' I said, 'but I wish to spend time with my rediscovered family first.'

'Are you enjoying your time here in London?' asked Lady Hamilton.

I hesitated. 'I promised my father I would do a season before returning to Italy. He wishes me to enjoy any opportunities that may present themselves.'

'And meanwhile you will wear pretty clothes and enjoy all the balls and parties?' said the Queen.

209

'Yes.' I must have sounded doubtful about that because she smiled.

'I do believe you are finding them tiresome already.'

'I am a little tired of dress-fittings and endless polite conversation with the same people. I miss the freedom I had in Pesaro. Can you imagine what my father might say if I told him I'd been sea-bathing, for instance?'

Lady Hamilton and Aunt Maude looked shocked, while the Queen threw back her head and laughed. 'It is the same for me. I know that as soon as I begin to enjoy myself someone will disapprove and it will probably be written about in the newspapers,' she said. 'Lady Hamilton tells me every day that I must take particular care to restrain myself.'

'Impropriety always comes home to roost in the end,' said Her Ladyship, in a forbidding tone.

'Indeed it does,' said Aunt Maude, looking at me. 'Society can be very unforgiving.'

Lady Hamilton rang the little bell on the table beside her.

'I have enjoyed seeing you again, Miss Langdon,' the Queen told me. 'Call again, won't you? And I haven't thanked you for visiting Mrs Webbe to choose dress materials for me. You have helped to make me look suitably respectable.' She gave me a conspiratorial smile and there was a mischievous glint in her eyes when she continued, 'Even though I might have preferred at least one gown with a low-cut bodice made out of transparent silver gauze.' She turned cordially to Aunt Maude. 'Goodbye, Miss Weston.'

The footman held the door open, waiting for our departure.

Aunt Maude and I both curtseyed and our audience was over.

We ascended the steps to the carriage in silence while I wondered where in Pesaro Alessandro was working now.

'Well!' said Aunt Maude as the wheels began to move. 'The Queen wasn't at all as I expected.'

'What did you expect?' I said.

'She was far more dignified than I could possibly have imagined from all the scandalous tales I've heard about her. And she has a knack of putting everyone she speaks to at ease. I can perfectly well see why the people like her. No wonder the King doesn't want her to return!'

'How do you mean?'

'She forms such a marked contrast with a monarch whose spend-thrift and immoral ways have made him justifiably unpopular,' my great-aunt commented. 'I can well imagine why the populace would wish her to take her rightful position as Queen. I suspect Whigs like Alderman Wood and their allies, the Radicals, will do their utmost to use her popularity as a means of bringing down the Tory government.'

'Why, Aunt Maude,' I said, 'I had no idea you knew so much about politics!'

'I may be an old lady no one much notices,' she replied in astringent tones, 'but that doesn't mean to say I don't see what is going on.'

'No,' I said, 'of course not, Aunt Maude.'

A few days later we were returning to Grosvenor Street after meeting Araminta and her brother for an ice at Gunter's. As our carriage rolled up outside, the front door was flung open. The footman pushed a smartly dressed young man out of the hall and onto the front steps.

'Oh, dear!' said Aunt Maude, looking out of the window as she gathered up her reticule and stick, ready to descend. 'An unwelcome caller.'

Protesting volubly, the young man shrugged his shoulders with palms turned upwards in an unmistakably Italian gesture. He gesticulated in the air and my heart nearly leaped out of my chest as I realised who it was. A burst of joy made me laugh aloud. Alessandro had come to England to find me! He must have realised at last how desperately important it had been for me to find my family and come to apologise.

211

Aunt Maude was blocking the carriage door as she descended one painful step at a time and I couldn't pass without knocking her over.

'Alessandro!' I shouted. Excitement and impatience to be with him again made me fidget as I waited behind Aunt Maude.

She turned to look at me, her mouth pursed reproachfully at my unladylike shout.

I peered between the plumes on her hat and saw Father rush out of the house and barge Alessandro with his shoulder. I gasped as Alessandro teetered on the steps, overbalanced and fell backwards. He landed hard, sprawling on the pavement.

Father threw a small bundle after him and then went inside, slamming the door.

'What a disgraceful scene!' said Aunt Maude.

'Why did Father do that?' I said. Shocked, I watched as Alessandro sprang to his feet, shook his fist at the front door and strode off down the street.

I wriggled past Aunt Maude and hurried after him but he was already a considerable way ahead. Dodging around strolling pedestrians, I ran along the pavement.

Hands tugged at my sleeve and a beggar in a tattered army uniform implored me for alms.

I prised his fingers from my arm. 'Alessandro, wait!' I shouted, but he was too far ahead to hear. I dashed after him, my pulse racing.

At the end of the street I stopped at the junction with Bond Street. Shoppers crowded the pavement and carriages and horses swished past. Frantically, I looked both ways but there was no sign of him. My shoulders drooped and I swallowed bitter disappointment. He'd been so close, almost within touching distance, and I'd lost him! I could only take comfort from the belief that he'd return.

I was nearly home when Father came marching towards me, a scowl on his face. 'Emilia!' He took my arm in a fierce grip. 'Don't ever go running off alone in the street like that again! What will people think?'

'You threw Alessandro down the steps!'

'I certainly did,' he said, his voice cold. 'He's a most objectionable young man.'

'Alessandro is never objectionable!'

'He came marching into my house demanding to see you. He didn't believe me when I said you weren't there. He bellowed your name and had the impudence to start opening doors, looking for you.' He tightened his grasp on my arm.

'You're hurting me!'

'Don't embarrass us both in the street, Emilia.' He spoke through gritted teeth. 'I thought you had acquired a little sophistication but I can see now it's only a thin veneer over your lowly upbringing.'

A red tide of rage rose up in me. 'To treat me so violently clearly demonstrates *your* lack of breeding!' I wrenched myself free from his grip and picked up from the pavement the bundle Father had thrown after Alessandro. A clean napkin tied with silk ribbon enclosed something soft. Untying the bow, I caught my breath when I saw the rag doll. Alessandro had returned my beloved Peggy.

Scarlet-faced with rage, Father snatched the doll from me and dragged me by my wrist until we were inside the front door. He shoved the doll into the footman's hands. 'Get rid of this,' he barked.

'No!' I shouted. I grabbed Peggy and held her tightly to my chest. 'You shan't take her from me. Peggy has been with me on all my travels ever since I was a little girl.' Alessandro knew how much my old doll meant to me and had brought her all this way to return her. I buried my face in Peggy's woollen hair, willing myself not to burst into tears.

Aunt Maude hovered in the entrance hall, her lower lip quivering. 'Thank goodness you're safe, Emilia!'

'No thanks to you,' snarled Father. 'Get out of my sight, old woman!'

Outraged, I stared at him open-mouthed.

Aunt Maude didn't say a word but went upstairs, leaning heavily on her stick.

'How *could* you be so cruel?' I asked.

Father made a visible effort to control himself. 'You were in her care and she failed in her duty. Who knows what might have happened to you had I not intervened?'

I took a calming breath. I wanted to go home to Italy with Alessandro but it would be awful to leave England on bad terms with my father. 'What did Alessandro say?' I asked.

Father rubbed his palm over his face. 'He's in London for a few days.'

'Where is he staying?'

'I didn't ask. He said he wanted to say goodbye.'

'Goodbye?'

Father shrugged. 'I'm going to my study and don't wish to be disturbed.'

I watched his retreating back and heard the study door slam. I didn't understand why Alessandro wanted to say goodbye. My certainty that he must have come to apologise to me suddenly wavered.

I withdrew to my bedroom and placed Peggy on the pillow next to Annabelle. Her embroidered smile looked coarse by comparison to Annabelle's exquisitely painted face but no less precious. Melancholy gripped me. Sarah had taken the trouble to make Peggy for me, no doubt to soothe my tears after my previous doll had been left behind, and I regretted the times I'd been impatient with her.

Meanwhile, poor Aunt Maude, distressed by my father's cruel words, had been banished to her room as a result of my actions.

A few moments later I tapped on her door.

She sat by the window, her knuckles white on the silver handle of her stick.

'I'm sorry for what Father said.' I wrapped my arms around her thin shoulders, upset to see how diminished she looked. 'I've seen a side of him today that I don't like.'

Aunt Maude patted my hand. 'I've endured worse over the years. He's always had a temper if he doesn't get his own way.'

'Shall I fetch my book of poetry to read to you?'

'Thank you, dear. That would be soothing.'

We read and chatted until Aunt Maude's feathers seemed less ruffled but all the time I was conscious that Alessandro was somewhere nearby and I couldn't go to him.

It wasn't until I woke up in a cold sweat during the night that I wondered if he had come to say goodbye because he'd given up waiting for me and found someone else to love.

Chapter 23

Alessandro didn't try to contact me again and after a month of waiting and hoping, I could only assume he'd returned home. I cried bitter tears into my pillow, whilst nursing resentment against Father for sending him away.

The summer passed in an interminable round of balls, routs and excursions and I became heartily tired of it all. In July I received a proposal from Mr Perry. In his usual jovial fashion, he didn't seem to mind when I refused, which inclined me to believe his heart wasn't deeply engaged. I saw a great deal of Dolly, usually accompanied by Mr Gregory, and was relieved he didn't pressure me to announce a betrothal between us.

In August, Queen Caroline was called before the House of Lords to answer a charge of adultery and it was a nasty, undignified affair. The newspapers were full of salacious and shameful accusations, apparently based on events witnessed by her ex-servants. Father gloatingly read some of the articles aloud to me, as if he hoped to shake my own good opinion of the Queen. Surprisingly, the scandalous behaviour of which she was accused didn't appear to shake the Queenites' good opinion of her. Day after day, cheering supporters from all walks of life lined the streets as she passed by on her way to and from the House of Lords.

In September there was a recess and Father took Aunt Maude and me to Langdon Hall for some country air before the case for the defence began in October.

One morning in early November I knocked on the door of Father's study.

'Look at this on the front page!' he said, shaking his newspaper at me. 'It says, *It's the third anniversary of the death of the late lamented Princess Charlotte, the daughter of our ill-fated Queen.* The newspapers only write in these terms to stir up the rabble,' he commented bitterly. 'The Whigs and the Radicals are behind it, of course. They're using the Queen to curry favour with the common people, to whom she has so aptly allied herself, so as to discredit the King and bring down the Tory government.' He dropped the crumpled newspaper on his desk. 'Was there something you wanted, Emilia?'

'Aunt Maude has woken up with a putrid sore throat,' I said, 'so I must write a note to Millicent Deveraux and cry off from her card party this afternoon. Dolly was to have accompanied us so I must write to him, too. May I send James to deliver the notes?'

Father pursed his lips. 'I think it perfectly proper for Dolly to escort you on this occasion. He is family, after all. Send him to see me before you go, will you?'

'Thank you, Father, and since we need not take the carriage for Aunt Maude's sake, Dolly and I shall be perfectly happy to walk.'

'Absolutely not ... I insist you take the carriage!' he said. 'I don't want you to be caught up in all the vulgar commotion on the streets. It's likely to be worse than ever after the Lords' final vote on the Queen's trial this afternoon.' He picked up the paper again. 'At least that should see an end to it, though the majority so far has been worryingly small.'

'Fifty-two days now! I can't believe it's gone on for so long,' I said.

'The poor King is completely ground down by worry.'

I refrained from mentioning that the Queen must be in a state of high anxiety, too. 'There was another thing I've been meaning to ask,' I said. 'Have you received any further information on the Infanta's miniatures?'

He shook his head. 'I've written dozens of letters to art dealers in the towns you visited. I haven't received replies from all of them but nothing has come of my enquiries so far. Perhaps you'll rack your brains for any other places Sarah might have sold them?' He sighed heavily. 'You are the only key to solving this puzzle, Emilia.'

'I'll think about it again,' I promised.

Later that afternoon Dolly arrived, immaculately dressed as usual, and went to speak to Father while I fetched my pelisse and bonnet. When I came downstairs I heard voices in the study, raised in argument. I waited in the hall until Dolly emerged. He took my arm with a tight little smile and hurried me out of the front door.

I caught my heel in the hem of my skirt as I tried to keep up with his long stride. I gasped as I teetered on the top step and grasped at his arm.

Dolly caught me and held me tightly against his chest until I regained my equilibrium. But he didn't release me. I looked up and found his gaze fixed on my face. He stared at me for a long moment with unfathomable dark blue eyes and, despite my discomfort, I found myself unable to look away. Then he swiftly kissed the tip of my nose. 'One day, Emilia, you'll make some man very happy,' he said, releasing his grip on me at last.

Flushed with embarrassment, I trotted along beside him to the waiting carriage.

'Your father is becoming extremely pressing on the matter of our engagement,' he said, once we had set off. 'He's determined his grandson will eventually inherit the estate. Perhaps we should bite the bullet?'

I looked at him, aghast. 'I thought you didn't want that, any more than I do?'

He shrugged. 'I'll have to marry someday and you're as congenial as any other girl of my acquaintance.'

'How very flattering!' I said.

He gave a wry smile. 'I apologise, Emilia. That was ungracious. You are a delightfully pretty girl, one whom any man would be delighted to marry. It's simply that I don't feel ready to tie myself down yet.'

'I'm not exactly sought after,' I said, 'since I've received only two proposals. I can't count Mr Fortescue's since he was inebriated at the time.'

'You haven't received more proposals because you don't flirt and flutter your eyelashes like the girls who are desperate to find a husband. That sends a message to those who are actively looking for a wife, rather than simply bent on enjoying female company.'

I sighed. 'Father won't be happy when I tell him I intend to return to Italy next spring.'

Millicent Deveraux, the vivacious daughter of a Whig Member of Parliament, had recently become engaged to the second son of an Earl. She was full of bright chatter about her wedding preparations as we drank tea and nibbled slices of cake.

'I simply can't decide whether to have the wedding next July, before the Coronation, or to wait until August when the fuss is over,' she said. She glanced at Dolly, who was smiling at a comment her mother had made. 'What about you? Have there been any interesting developments yet in that quarter? So many girls have tried and failed. He's very handsome, isn't he?'

'I'm enjoying the season,' I said, heat rising in my cheeks.

'It's nearly at an end,' said Millicent with a pitying smile. 'You must make haste to secure him. Though I did hear a rumour that he's in a little too deep at the gaming tables.'

I was saved further embarrassment when Millicent's mother clapped her hands and shepherded us into fours to play cards.

Two hours passed pleasantly and we were about to leave when Millicent's father rushed into the room. He hadn't removed his coat and his hair was windblown. 'I have an announcement,' he called out over the hum of conversation. His eyes shone and his smile was triumphant. 'The Queen is acquitted! She stood firm and has been vindicated!'

I laughed in relief, delighted that her troubles were at an end. A number of cheers went up and someone called out, 'Long live Queen Caroline!' but others were clearly unhappy about the Lords' decision. Everyone, even the young ladies whose fathers would have tried to divert them from the most sensational reporting as being unfit for their eyes, held vociferous opinions on whether justice had been done.

'Shall we go?' said Dolly over the commotion. 'The streets are bound to be crowded with revellers celebrating the Queen's victory.'

It was dark as we left the Deveraux' house but lights blazed in many of the windows and the streets were nearly as bright as day. The carriage was jostled and rocked from side to side as the hordes ran past, shouting until they were hoarse. Men carried banners painted with slogans such as 'Truth will Prevail', while others waved flaming torches and bottles of ale. There was an air of wild, feverish excitement. Men threw their hats in the air and couples danced to the discordant music of street musicians gathered into makeshift bands. Cannonfire boomed in the distance, women screamed, dogs barked, and all around was the crash of splintering glass.

Dolly remained silent but drummed his fingers on his knee as the carriage forced its way homeward through the press.

The clamour and delight of the crowd exhilarated me and I fervently hoped Queen Caroline was now relieved of her cares and happily celebrating her victory.

A few days later Aunt Maude still suffered from her throat infection and I, too, remained in bed. At noon I told Daisy that I was ill.

'Leave me to sleep until I come downstairs, will you?' I said. 'I don't wish to be disturbed. I'll ring if I need anything.'

Once the door closed behind her I threw back the bedclothes. Father was at the House of Commons and not expected back until late. I dressed warmly since it was foggy outside and locked the bedroom door behind me, placing the key in my reticule. I crept downstairs, heart thudding, and tip-toed across the deserted hall. Thankfully, the front door hinges were well oiled and I was able to slip outside without being noticed. Head down, I hurried away, knowing that I'd be concealed by the fog before I'd gone more than a few steps. I reached Bond Street and hailed a hackney carriage. Once inside, I was in a little world of my own since the fog didn't allow me to see any further than a yard or two ahead.

I'd read in the papers that Queen Caroline was staying in Brandenburgh House in Fulham, lent to her by the Margravine of Ansbach, and very much wished to visit her there to congratulate her on her victory.

By the time the hackney carriage drew up outside Brandenburgh House the breeze off the nearby Thames had dissipated the fog. From somewhere in the distance I could hear the noisy cries and shouts of merrymakers. 'Will you wait, please?' I asked the driver. 'I shan't be long.'

He pulled his scarf up over his ears and settled down.

Brandenburgh House was an elegant, classically styled mansion and a great deal more grand than the narrow-fronted house where I'd visited the Queen on the last occasion. I was pleased to discover she would receive me.

The drawing room was overheated and smelled unpleasantly foetid, an unwashed, greasy smell I recognised from the Queen's wardrobe in Pesaro.

'You have not forgotten me then?' she said, as I rose from my curtsey. Lady Hamilton sat beside the Queen at the fireside but this time there was no sign of the Countess Oldi.

'Of course not, Your Majesty,' I said. 'Since you kindly suggested I might visit you again, I wished to congratulate you on your recent victory.' I noticed that she had lost more weight and the skin on her face and neck sagged.

'I feel no joy,' she said, 'only a great weariness.' Her blue eyes were lacklustre and her hands trembled. She pulled a shawl more tightly around her shoulders and huddled into her chair. 'I am never warm in this miserable country.'

The tumult of noise outside rose to a crescendo and I glanced out of the window at the river. Boats crowded with sightseers waved bottles and handkerchiefs in the air as they called out greetings to Her Majesty. A man stood unsteadily in one of the small boats, singing.

'We have been inundated by the numerous parties that come to ogle Her Majesty every day,' said Lady Hamilton, her face pinched with disapproval. 'The rabble use Brandenburgh House as an opportunity for an excursion.'

'But no one really cares about me,' said the Queen, her chin quivering. 'The whole unpleasant business has been more of a political battle than the championing of a poor, forlorn woman. I have been unwell and am tired of it all ... so very tired.' She picked at a stain on her crumpled skirt.

'I'm sorry to hear that,' I said. I glanced enquiringly at Lady Hamilton, wondering if I should leave, but she gave a slight shake of her head.

'You remind me of happier times in my beloved Villa Vittoria,' the Queen said. 'How I long to return! Do you remember the sea breezes and the sunshine warm on your cheeks, Miss Barton?'

I didn't correct her but simply nodded. 'I miss them, too.'

The Queen sighed heavily. 'But it is not to be until the King has answered my demands. When will my name be restored to the Liturgy?' Her voice rose in agitation. 'Where is my town residence? I should have a palace of my own and a proper household. He cannot expect me to live in borrowed houses while I'm in London.'

'You will return to Pesaro later?' I asked.

'As soon as possible,' she said, closing her eyes. 'After my Coronation. Now that I am confirmed as Queen Caroline, even George cannot deny me that right. I miss my darling Victorine so. She will be bereft without me or Signor Fiorelli.'

'Have you any news of him?' I asked, hope flaring. 'I saw him in London from a distance but wasn't able to speak to him.'

'He wished to improve his English and took a position in London as tutor to two boys,' she said. 'He visited me during the trial recess last September. I always liked that young man.'

'Do you know the name of the family he works for?' I asked, my heart thudding.

The Queen pursed her lips and shook her head.

'It may have been Beacham,' said Lady Hamilton. 'And I believe he said he was staying in Great Marlborough Street.'

I gave a little gasp to realise that Alessandro had been living only a stone's throw from Father's house all that time. 'Thank you very much, Lady Hamilton.'

She surprised me by giving me a conspiratorial smile as she rang the little bell, signifying the audience was over.

The noise on the river increased as the voices swelled in raucous singing.

The Queen covered her eyes.

'I shall take my leave, Ma'am,' I said, 'with my best wishes for your imminent return to good health.'

'Always such a kind girl,' she murmured, 'just like my darling Charlotte.'

Chapter 24

November 1820

London

I crept back into Father's house without being caught. I raced up the staircase and was unlocking my bedroom door when Daisy appeared.

'Oh, miss,' she said, 'I was that worried about you!'

I opened the door and pulled her inside. 'Does anyone else know I went out?'

She shook her head. 'I was in the kitchen making you honey and lemon for your throat when I saw you walking past the area steps.'

'I had some business to do,' I said, taking off my bonnet, 'and since Aunt Maude has been ill these past few days ...'

'I would have come with you,' said Daisy. 'You shouldn't go out unaccompanied, not a young lady like you.'

'Well, no harm done,' I said. 'Daisy, will you do something for me?'

'Of course, miss.'

'I want you to deliver a note.'

'But that's James's job. I'm not sure Mrs Hope will let me ...'

'If she's not happy you can ask her to speak to me.' I took a pen out of my writing desk and lifted the lid of the inkwell. After a moment's thought I began to write.

Dear Alessandro

I was distressed when my father sent you away in such an unkind manner, especially since you had been so kind as to bring Peggy to me. Afterwards I assumed you had returned to Pesaro but I called upon Her Majesty this morning and Lady Hamilton mentioned you are currently employed in Great Marlborough Street, only a step away.

Will you meet me tomorrow at noon by the Cumberland Gate to Hyde Park?

In anticipation of seeing you very soon,

Emilia

I sealed the folded paper with a blob of red wax. 'Please take this to Great Marlborough Street, Daisy,' I said.

She took it from me and frowned at the name written on the front.

'It's an Italian name,' I said. 'Signor Fiorelli.'

She echoed the name and I repeated it for her until she said it correctly.

'I don't know which house it is in Great Marlborough Street,' I said, 'so you'll need to make enquiries at the kitchen doors. Signor Fiorelli is employed as a tutor to two small boys.' I fumbled in my reticule and pressed some coins in her hand. 'He's an old friend from when I lived in Italy,' I said, 'but please don't mention this to anyone.'

'No, miss,' said Daisy, giving me a knowing look as she tucked the coins into her bodice.

I sat with Aunt Maude for the rest of the afternoon, simmering with excitement at the thought of seeing Alessandro. Although we'd parted with hard words, in my heart I knew we loved each other.

225

The Queen said he'd suffered a great deal after my departure. The balls, the presents, the new clothes ... none of that mattered to me as much as Alessandro did. I'd grown to love dear Aunt Maude and was pleased to know, if not love, my father but the endless round of social occasions held no further fascination for me. I'd saved most of my allowance to pay for my passage and was more than ready now to go home to Italy. I hugged myself in pleasurable anticipation of Alessandro's joy when I told him so.

I didn't see Daisy until she came to undress me for bed.

'I had to ask at a great many houses before someone could tell me where Signor Fiorelli was staying,' she said. 'There was a governess at number 12 who knew of him but he wasn't home. I left the note with a maid.'

I sat before the mirror while Daisy combed out my hair, wondering what Alessandro had thought when he received my message. 'I expect to meet Signor Fiorelli tomorrow at noon,' I said. 'I'd like you to accompany me.'

In the morning my reflection was pale and I was full of nervous agitation. At breakfast I was relieved to discover that Father was out so I'd have no need to explain my absence.

When I went to see Aunt Maude, she sat in her shawl by the fireside. 'I'm pleased to see you out of bed,' I said.

'I shall be right as rain in a few days, dear.'

'I'm feeling cooped up and intend to take a walk in the park this morning. Don't worry,' I said, as I saw her expression of consternation, 'I'll take Daisy with me.'

'That's not ideal,' said Aunt Maude, 'but I'm not sufficiently recovered to accompany you. Don't let Daisy stray from your side and come to see me when you return.'

'In Italy I frequently walked alone. No harm ever came to me.'

'No one in London need know what happened in Italy,' said Aunt Maude. 'It's not so much that I fear physical harm, my dear, as long as you hold your reticule tightly ... it's more that I fear malicious gossip might harm your reputation. A young woman can't be too careful.'

'Yes, Aunt Maude.'

Daisy had laid out my clothes and suggested I use a little of my Pears' Liquid Blooms of Roses to brighten my cheeks. I dressed in my favourite walking dress with a matching blue velvet pelisse and plumed bonnet.

'You look a picture, miss,' said Daisy.

I smiled, eager to set off.

Once outside, I was happy that the sun shone, albeit in a pale November fashion. I was relieved it wasn't raining; rain had such a dispiriting effect upon the bonnet plumes. It was a relief, for a change, not to have to meander at Aunt Maude's pace but to be able to walk as fast as was ladylike.

We reached Cumberland Gate but, disappointingly, Alessandro wasn't there.

'We'll walk for a while, Daisy,' I said. I didn't want him to think I was too eager, even though it was hard to contain my excitement.

Ten minutes later, Alessandro still hadn't arrived. It was possible he hadn't received my note, I supposed, but I fervently hoped Father's mistreatment of him hadn't changed his former good opinion of me. Although we'd parted on unhappy terms there had been such easy affection between us before. I knew that some men were not good letter writers but it hurt me that he'd made no attempt to contact me.

'My feet are cold,' I said. 'Let us walk to Stanhope Gate in case he's mistaken the location.' My mood of happy expectancy began to dissipate.

We hurried towards the next gate and I sent Daisy to speak to the flower seller who had a stall there but she returned, shaking her head. I worried we might have missed Alessandro at Cumberland Gate and we dashed back but there was still no sign of him. There we waited a further quarter of an hour while disappointment and humiliation gnawed at me.

'I don't think he's coming, miss,' said Daisy. Her nose was cherry red with cold.

'No,' I said, leaden disappointment in my breast. 'I don't think he is.'

We'd only gone a little way down Park Lane when I heard running footsteps behind us. I whirled around and my spirits soared. Alessandro stood before me. His hair was neat and he wore a well-cut dark coat that could not hide the breadth of his shoulders but his usual smiling demeanour was startling by its absence and that discomfited me.

'I thought you weren't coming,' I said. Two boys stood beside him.

Alessandro made a small bow. 'I apologise,' he said. 'George couldn't find his shoes and then William became tired of walking. May I introduce you?'

The children, wooden boats under their arms, made their bows.

'We shall talk while my charges sail their boats,' said Alessandro, turning away from me.

Once we'd entered the park gates the boys ran ahead towards the Serpentine. Daisy walked a discreet step behind me but, in any case, Alessandro's expression was remote and he didn't speak or offer to take my arm. I hadn't expected him to be so unapproachable and it alarmed me. A bitter wind gusted across the park and pinched my cheeks.

We reached the lake and Alessandro helped George and William to launch their boats and found them each a long stick with which to guide their craft.

'Daisy,' I said, 'will you watch the children while I speak to Signor Fiorelli?'

She nodded and went to stand by the water's edge.

'Alessandro, I can only apologise for Father behaving so badly towards you when you called upon me at Grosvenor Street,' I said, slipping naturally into Italian. 'I ran after you but you disappeared into the crowds.'

'I wanted to return Peggy to you. The doll was on Victorine's bed when you left last year. I thought you might miss it.' His voice was curiously flat and there was no dancing light today in his brown eyes.

'Oh, I did,' I said. 'But what are you doing in London? I thought nothing would induce you to leave Italy and your family?' I knew I was gabbling but Alessandro barely looked at me, gazing over my shoulder at the boys playing with their boats.

'Only my great love for you could have persuaded me to do so,' he said in that same expressionless tone of voice. 'After you left, nothing had any meaning without you. Every day was a torment. And so I came to London to look for you.'

My spirits soared again. He did still love me! 'Why didn't you come and see me? Or at least write to me?'

'You know I tried to see you and I did write to you,' he said. 'It hurt me that you never replied to my letters but I came here to try again to persuade you to marry me. I was dying without you and I wanted to take you home.'

'I promised you I'd return, Alessandro,' I said. 'I know I've been away longer than I expected but ...'

'You've been away much longer than I expected! When you left you begged me to write to you but after your first letter saying you wished to spend more time with your father, you never wrote to me again,' he said, his voice rising. 'For a whole year you left me believing you still loved me, despite your insistence on staying in London. I hoped every day you would return to me. I was driven mad with misery and in the end I left my home and my work to come to you. But you didn't have the courtesy to tell me you'd become engaged to another.'

'But I haven't!' I said. 'And I didn't receive any letters from you.'

'Don't lie to me, Emilia!' His eyes blazed now.

I stepped back. 'How can you accuse me of that?'

'Your father told me you are engaged to his heir.' Alessandro shrugged. 'It wounded me here,' he pressed his clasped hands to his heart, 'but I understand. These things happen and the life you live now, this rich life, is a dream come true for you. I cannot compete with your future husband, who has everything to offer you.' Shaking his head, he continued, 'But I am deeply disappointed in you, Emilia, for not telling me the truth before I found it out for myself.'

'But I'm *not* engaged to Dolly!' I blazed with anger at Father. How could he have told Alessandro such a lie?

'Emilia, I saw you.'

'Saw me?' I was puzzled.

Alessandro buried his face in his hands for a moment. 'I often waited over the road,' he said, 'praying you'd come out of your father's house alone. I gave notes to the servants, hoping you might come to the window to speak to me. But then I saw you on the steps with your future husband. He held you close, so close, in his arms, and your sweet mouth was waiting for his kiss.'

I gasped. 'It wasn't like that.'

'I *know* what I saw, Emilia. For *you* I have spent months in misery away from my family in a country that is cold and mean-spirited. For *you* I must remain here until my year's contract is finished.' He drew a shuddering breath. 'Enough. I have come to my senses at last and I will not destroy myself any longer by loving a girl who doesn't want me. We shall not see each other again.'

I reached out for him. 'Alessandro! You must believe me!'

He shook off my hand and strode away without looking back.

'You're wrong, Alessandro!' I remained fixed to the spot, trembling with distress. I stared after him as he collected the two boys and set off along the footpath.

A moment later Daisy came and touched my arm. 'Are you all right, miss?'

All right? My heart had broken, not in two but into smithereens. Alessandro and his charges were fast dwindling into the distance. I swallowed. It was too hard for me to speak.

230

'Come along, Miss Langdon,' said Daisy. Her voice was soft as if she were cajoling a child. 'Let's get you home and I'll ask Cook to make you a nice pot of chocolate. You look fair froze to death.'

By the time Daisy and I reached home we were both chilled to the bone. Daisy brought me the pot of chocolate and I insisted she drank the second cup.

'If you're struck down with a chill, Daisy,' I said, 'it will be my fault.'

She brought me a shawl and rubbed my frozen toes. 'I'll fetch you a hot brick wrapped in flannel,' she said.

An hour later I was warm again though I still shivered each time I relived the terrible conversation I'd had with Alessandro. It made my chest so tight it was hard for me to breathe.

During the afternoon my misery turned to anger. No matter what lies Father had told, Alessandro should have believed me. The deciding factor for him had, of course, been his mistaken belief that he'd seen me about to kiss Dolly. If only I hadn't slipped on the steps!

I was still alternately distraught and seething with rage when the front door slammed and then Father's voice boomed out in the hall. Barely pausing to think, I hurried downstairs, rapped on his study door and went in without waiting for his answer.

'Why did you tell Alessandro I was engaged to Dolly?' I blurted out the question before I'd had a chance to take a calming breath. 'You know it was a lie. And what did you do with the letters and notes he sent to me? I never received any of them.'

The expression in his steel-grey eyes was cold and unflinching. 'I don't care for your tone, Emilia. Do I take it that you have been in contact with that unsuitable foreigner . . . an illicit meeting, in fact?'

'You lied to him!'

'Answer my question, Emilia. At once!' thundered Father. 'Have you been meeting him in secret?'

'Only this morning and I wouldn't have resorted to subterfuge if you'd allowed him to speak to me when he called here.' I was shaking with anger.

'How dare you question my judgement!' Spittle formed at the corners of his mouth. 'Did you think I was going to allow my daughter to throw herself away on a low-born foreigner?'

'You've *always* known I intended to return to Italy and marry Alessandro.'

'And yet you were happy enough to stay here for a year enjoying the benefits I could give you.' His voice was cold. 'What more could I have done for you, Emilia? Have you not been pleased with the ball I gave for you, the new clothes and jewellery and the opportunity to move in the most exalted circles? Why, the King himself came to your ball ...'

Heat flooded my face. 'You know I'm grateful to you, but my real reason for staying here was in order to get to know you and Aunt Maude.'

Father slumped down at his desk and buried his face in his hands. 'Can't you see, Emilia, I want only the best for you?'

'Alessandro *is* the best for me.' I tried to stop my voice from wavering. 'And you lied to him and now he doesn't trust me.'

My father sighed deeply. 'One day, when you have children of your own, you'll understand how much they can hurt you. You're still young, Emilia, but you will come to learn there is more to happiness than stolen kisses. You must have security.'

'With Dolly, you mean?'

'Be reasonable, Emilia!' He rubbed the bridge of his nose. 'Open your eyes to the advantages of being his wife. You're a beautiful girl and have had every opportunity of meeting a suitable husband during the past year. Many were titled, most were young and several had fortunes, but you gave no encouragement to any of them. It's unlikely you'll meet any suitable men more to your liking in a second season and by then there will be a plethora of younger girls seeking a husband. You may have missed your chance already.'

I shuddered. 'I don't want a second season.'

'A year is a long time to a young man,' said Father. 'Alessandro has probably found another girl by now.'

'He wouldn't!'

'And what then, Emilia,' said Father, 'if you return to Italy and this Alessandro doesn't want you? You could continue to scratch a living as a dressmaker to the bourgeoisie, of course. Dolly, meanwhile, will marry and you'll lose that opportunity. Eventually you'll find life alone in Italy too difficult and come creeping back to me. I'd give you a home, of course, just as I have to Aunt Maude, but she'll be the first to tell you how difficult it is for a spinster living on charity.'

I shivered at the disdain in his voice.

'If you've had a disagreement with Alessandro,' said Father, 'I can only say, however upset you are at present, that you've had a lucky escape. You've returned to the life you were born into and I suggest you reflect on your very good fortune. And remember, Dolly won't wait for you forever.'

Unable to listen to any more of this, I fled.

Chapter 25

December 1820

Langdon Hall

We arrived at Langdon Hall a week before Christmas. Father had planned a variety of diversions to entertain his house guests over the festive season and, to my dismay, I was expected to act as his hostess.

'I fear I shall say or do something wrong,' I confided to Aunt Maude. I sat listlessly by the fire in the small parlour, planning the guests' table placements for the various dinners.

'I remember your dear mother saying the same thing to me many years ago,' said Aunt Maude. 'She was afraid she'd forget to order the musicians or the flowers and worried about inviting guests who wouldn't find each other congenial.'

'Did she?' I didn't want to think about my traitorous mother, however high she stood in Aunt Maude's esteem. That only proved how double-faced she'd been.

Aunt Maude smiled. 'Dear me, yes! Rose was an anxious hostess as a new bride but soon she forgot her worries and if there was a difficulty she managed to laugh about it.'

I turned back to the scraps of paper, each inscribed with a guest's name, that I was arranging around the perimeter of a larger sheet representing the table. As host, Father had to sit at one end but what was the correct order of placement for the rest of us? There were so many traps for the unwary that could cause offence.

'Rose kept a notebook for entertaining,' said Aunt Maude. 'She included names of the guests, the food and wine served to them, on which date, and other useful information. I wonder if we still have it?'

'It would be terribly old-fashioned now,' I said, distracted by the difficulty of deciding which of two local landowners' wives was the most important.

'Good manners never go out of fashion, dear,' said Aunt Maude with a reproving smile. 'I'll see if I can find it.'

Five minutes later I pushed the placements aside with an expression of disgust and went to look out of the window. There was an area of muddy grass and shrubs below and then the moat. The water was deathly still and very dark today, almost black, reflecting the sullen sky above. A few leaves floated on the surface.

I wondered what my mother had thought about when she drowned herself and if she'd considered at all the needs of the little daughter she was leaving behind. I imagined her being swept along by the current and battered against the banks and bridges. Or perhaps she'd sunk straight down to the river bed and felt the mud squeezing between her toes as she watched the silvery bubbles of her last breath floating to the surface. I closed my eyes, picturing her struggling against the weight of her sodden clothing while her red hair floated around her face like waterweed.

Shivering, I returned to my chair by the morning-room fire. I'd been prone to black moods lately, made worse by succumbing to a feverish chill the previous month after waiting in the cold to meet Alessandro. I couldn't shake off the malaise that ailed me and had given up any hope of receiving an apologetic message from him. It hurt me deeply that he hadn't believed me when I told him I wasn't engaged to Dolly. But Father could be extremely persuasive when it suited his own ends. When I remonstrated with him I'd glimpsed an entirely different side to his character from that of the affectionate parent that he usually presented to me.

The door opened and Aunt Maude returned. 'Dolly has arrived,' she said. 'He's talking to your father but says he'll join us in a while.' Triumphantly, she waved a red morocco-bound notebook at me. 'It was in the library,' she said, 'still on the shelf where Rose kept it.'

I made an attempt to rouse myself from the apathy that gripped me and reached for the notebook with a forced smile. 'How interesting!'

In fact, it was interesting, filled as it was with my mother's bold writing covering all aspects of her life as hostess at both Grosvenor Street and Langdon Hall. There were sketches of flower arrangements, menus, notes on which guests felt an antipathy for each other and mustn't be invited at the same time, addresses of recommended purveyors of hams and cheeses, small orchestras available for hire . . .

I put the notebook down as Dolly opened the door. Since I'd been unwell, I hadn't seen him for more than a few minutes at a time over the past month. 'Dolly, how nice to see you!' I said, noticing his face was even paler than usual and there were deep shadows under his eyes. 'You're a most welcome relief from arranging table placements.'

'I should think so, too,' he said, bowing to Aunt Maude before sitting down beside me. 'Would you care for me to advise you?'

'The very thing! I'm tired of it all.'

The next hour passed pleasantly enough and I even found the energy to laugh at some of Dolly's more acerbic comments about the intended guests. I glanced up at him once or twice to see that he was staring at me with an oddly watchful expression.

Finally, I slipped my lists into the red notebook and closed it. 'Aunt Maude and I shall speak to Cook in the morning about the menus.'

Aunt Maude stood up. 'If you'll excuse me, I'm going to rest before dinner.'

After she'd gone Dolly rubbed his eyes and yawned.

'Tired?' I asked.

He smiled ruefully. 'I've had rather too many late nights recently. And perhaps a little too much wine.'

'You can go to bed early tonight,' I said. 'Straight after supper, if you wish, since there aren't any guests but you. I hope you won't find it too tedious.'

'Indeed not,' he said, 'since you're here to keep me amused.'

'I don't feel very amusing at present.'

He regarded me closely. 'Stand up!' he commanded.

I obliged and he looked me up and down.

'You've lost all your womanly curves.'

'That's not kind!' I sat down again.

'It suits you to be so slender,' he said. 'If I put a laurel wreath on your head and handed you a lyre, I could be looking at a young Apollo.'

I narrowed my eyes at him. 'While you look dissipated enough today to be Dionysus.'

'You surprise me, Emilia, by your knowledge of Greek mythology.'

'I'm not just a pretty face,' I said. 'I've enjoyed the educational benefits of travel. Now, stop appraising me as if I were a piece of horseflesh you were considering at Tattersalls! I've barely shaken off that chill I caught last month.'

'Since neither of us is on top form we shall have to remain cosy by the fireside together, playing cards like an old married couple, shan't we?'

'Which is exactly what Father wants.'

Dolly kept his gaze on his highly polished boots for a moment. Then he cleared his throat and looked at me. 'Perhaps it is time to make both your father and me the happiest of men, Emilia?'

I froze, the light-hearted moment between us gone in an instant.

He placed his long white fingers over mine. 'Neither of us were ready for marriage before. And now your father tells me your Italian lover hasn't come up to expectations.'

I flinched, pulling my hand away, and it was all I could do not to cry out at the memory of my last painful meeting with Alessandro.

'Am I so loathsome to you?' asked Dolly. The expression on his face was hurt.

'I'm sorry,' I said, my voice high and tight. 'Of course you're not loathsome! You're one of the handsomest men in London. All the girls' mothers are hoping to catch you for their daughters.'

He cleared his throat again. 'It's taken me time to be sure I'm ready to settle down,' he said, 'but now I wish, most wholeheartedly and ardently, to make you my wife, Emilia. I've grown exceedingly fond of you. More than fond. In fact, you fill my thoughts so entirely I cannot eat or sleep.'

Struck dumb, I could only stare at him. Was this a declaration of *love*? I noticed once more that tiny tic at the corner of his eye.

'Emilia, say something!' He lifted my hand and pressed it fervently to his mouth. 'Can you not see that I'm desperate for you?' There was a sheen of perspiration on his top lip.

I swallowed. 'I'd no idea you had feelings of that sort for me,' I said, at last.

'I didn't, at the beginning. And when I began to admit to myself that I'd fallen in love with you, I was concerned I'd frighten you away if I began to court you,' said Dolly. 'But now, I can conceal my passion no longer.' He slid off the sofa and onto his knees at my feet. 'Emilia, please will you be my wife?'

I wanted to be somewhere else, anywhere else. I'd become used to considering Dolly as an ally against my father's domineering plans for me. Discovering now that Dolly actually loved me caused such turbulent feelings within me I could not fathom them.

'Emilia?'

'Dolly …' My mouth was dry. 'You've taken me by surprise.' I forced a smile. 'You gave me no inkling of your feelings.' I closed my eyes briefly, recalling how I'd slipped on the steps and he'd clasped me against him while Alessandro watched us from the other side of the street.

'I know we could make a success of our marriage,' said Dolly, his voice urgent. 'Please, please, say yes.'

'Give me a little time.'

'Time!'

My eyes widened as he raised his voice.

'I apologise,' he said hastily, 'but you've had nearly a year to think about it.'

'Of course I haven't!' I looked down at my hands, twisted together in my lap. Dolly loved me and Alessandro never wanted to see me again. 'The situation is entirely different now.'

'Tomorrow then?'

I looked away from the intensity of his gaze while my heart fluttered against my ribs. 'Give me until Christmas Day, Dolly. There's so much for me to organise here and if you press me too hard, I shall simply say no.'

He let out his breath in a ragged sigh. 'Then I must be patient.'

It was awkward and uncomfortable to look at him and I felt I no longer knew how to speak to him lightly. 'I shall retire to my room for a while,' I said.

Dolly nodded. 'You need time to think. Perhaps I'll rest too.'

We went upstairs together in silence, stopping in the Long Gallery outside the guest room where he was to stay.

'I hope you'll be comfortable,' I said, in formal tones as befitted his hostess. 'Please ring should you require anything.'

'Only you, Emilia,' he murmured, before closing the door behind him.

I avoided being alone with Dolly over the next few days, staying firmly by Aunt Maude's side and busying myself with the forthcoming festivities. At night I lay awake, struggling to decide which course of action to take. The truth was, I didn't know what to do.

It had always been my intention to return to my beloved Italy. Used to a quiet life with Sarah, I'd been overwhelmed sometimes by Alessandro's family, but I knew now that I wanted nothing more than to be a part of it. The cool, polite manners of English society held little charm for me.

Now that Alessandro had cast me aside, there was little point in my returning to Pesaro and my life as an itinerant dressmaker. The time had come for me to decide if I'd be better off staying with my newfound family. Except, of course, that I'd be married to a man I didn't love. The surprising change in our situation was Dolly's unexpected declaration. There were practical advantages in marrying him but could I ever learn to love him?

On the morning of Christmas Eve, I went to supervise the servants while they brought in the Yule log and the festive greenery. The log had stopped smoking and was beginning to spit and crackle in the stone hearth of the Great Hall when Dolly came to find me.

'Shall I help with the decorating?' he offered.

A number of servants were bustling about nearby, bringing me scissors and twine and sweeping up clumps of mud and moss that had fallen off the Yule log so I didn't fear any awkward conversations. I eyed his exquisite coat with its shiny brass buttons. 'It would be a shame,' I said, 'to snag such fine wool with a sprig of holly.'

Five minutes later, Dolly sported one of the linen aprons the footmen usually wore while polishing the silver. 'Thankfully none of my fashionable London friends will see me dressed like this,' he said.

'And you won't upset your tailor by ruining your coat, either.'

He smiled at me. 'What a very understanding girl you are!'

He surprised me by climbing nimbly up a ladder to drape an ivy wreath along the minstrels' gallery and helped me make a kissing ball with the sprigs of mistletoe. We wound ivy and sprigs of holly around the candles on the vast iron light fittings and he stood beside me, watching as the footman hauled the swaying cartwheels of candles up towards the star-painted ceiling again.

'The decorations look splendid,' said Dolly. 'We're a good team, don't you think?' He smiled tentatively.

'Better than I might have imagined,' I said. He had a smudge of dust on his cheek and his cravat was crumpled. I liked him the better for it. To avoid his gaze, I gathered up a holly wreath, climbed onto a chair and placed it on one of the stags' heads. 'How does that look?' I asked.

'Beautiful.' Dolly held out his hand to help me from the chair and his grip was firm and warm as I stepped down. 'Beautiful,' he said again, looking straight into my eyes.

I noticed how long his black eyelashes were but there were little lines of worry etched around his dark blue eyes. He stood so close that his breath fanned my cheek and I smelled his sandalwood cologne. Now that Alessandro didn't want me, would it be so very dreadful to be married to Dolly? I'd be safe, with a home of my own and, in time, children to love.

His hand tightened around my fingers. 'Emilia?' he whispered.

'Yes, Dolly,' I said, suddenly calm as the decision was made. 'Yes, Dolly, I will marry you.'

'Thank God!' he said. He pulled me tight against his chest and pressed dry lips firmly to mine.

Chapter 26

July 1821

London

Millicent smiled complacently as the company raised their glasses to the bride and groom.

'She looks like the cat that got the cream, doesn't she?' murmured Araminta. 'As well she might, having secured the second son of an earl. Her grandfather was only a linen-draper, you know.'

'I hope they'll be happy,' I said.

Araminta opened her brown eyes very wide. 'How could she not be, with his fortune?'

I sipped my champagne. Happiness was a fleeting emotion. Once I'd accepted his proposal, seven months later Dolly's declared passion for me appeared to have waned with familiarity. Father, of course, had been delighted when we confirmed our engagement. Almost at once I'd felt as if I were on a runaway wagon careering down a mountainside as he made wedding plans. He decided the ceremony would take place in St Paul's Cathedral in June. I'd demurred, using the excuse that he'd be occupied working with the committee organising the Coronation. Finally, though I'd have preferred to delay even longer, I'd agreed to the end of August, after the London season finished. Dolly and I were to be married at St Bartholomew's in Upper Langdon.

'Your wedding next,' said Araminta, 'and mine in September.' She stretched out her hand and smiled at the diamond on her finger. 'Is your wedding dress finished?' she asked.

I avoided thinking about my wedding. 'Almost,' I said. 'Mrs Webbe was inundated with orders for gowns for the Coronation. I had to beg her to fit me in.' I'd offered to make my wedding dress myself but Father had reeled back in shock. I didn't tell him but it was only my connection with the Queen that finally persuaded Mrs Webbe to accept the commission.

'All the world is being fitted for outfits for the Coronation at present,' said Araminta. 'Oh, look, there's Anna! Excuse me, I must have a word with her.' She drifted away.

I went to find Dolly. He was talking to Francis Gregory, who seemed to appear everywhere we went. It wasn't that I wanted to be alone with my betrothed but I'd become irritated by Mr Gregory's high-pitched laughter and pointed remarks.

'Here comes your little shadow, Dolly,' he said. His smile didn't reach his eyes.

'I thought the boot quite on the other foot,' I replied tartly, 'wherever my fiancé and I go, there you are.'

Mr Gregory's naturally pink cheeks glowed just a little brighter than usual. 'Dolly and I have been friends since our schooldays.'

'And no doubt we'll still be toddling off to play cards together in our dotage, Francis,' murmured Dolly.

'I hear you've been to visit your future mother-in-law, Miss Langdon,' said Mr Gregory. 'Dolly says you were the best of friends by the time the second cup of tea was poured.'

I glanced at Dolly, who refused to meet my eyes and cleared his throat in that annoying way he did when he was nervous. 'It was very pleasant to meet her,' I said. In fact, Mrs Pemberton had such an insipid personality it had been difficult to have any kind of conversation with her.

'I'm so pleased,' said Mr Gregory. 'Warfare with your mother-in-law would be so dispiriting, don't you think?' His blue eyes were guileless. 'Especially when she's going to reside with you.'

I managed to prevent shock from showing in my face. 'That isn't yet decided,' I said evenly. 'Dolly, have you told Mr Gregory that Father is giving us the Dower House on the Langdon Estate?'

'Not yet,' said Dolly. 'But we must also have a place in town. I've no intention of living up to my knees in mud all year round.'

Mr Gregory pressed a hand to his heart as if the very idea pained him.

'I shall be pleased to spend more time in Hampshire,' I said. 'After a while, the social engagements in London all seem to blend into each other.' In fact, I'd begun to loathe them.

Dolly looked down his nose at me. 'You remember what Samuel Johnson said, my dear? "When a man is tired of London, he is tired of life."'

Mr Gregory laughed. 'The perfect solution presents itself! Miss Langdon, you shall live in Hampshire with the delightful Mrs Pemberton for company while Dolly will remain in Mayfair, close to his tailor and his club.'

'No doubt we shall divide our time between town and country,' I said. I had no intention of wasting my energy bickering with Mr Gregory.

'If he'd still been alive you might not have found Dolly's father so pleasant, of course,' continued Mr Gregory. He looked pensive for a moment. 'He had very strong opinions, didn't he, Dolly?'

Dolly shuddered. 'And tried to thrash them into me at every opportunity.'

'Died of an apoplexy while in a rage,' Mr Gregory told me with obvious relish.

I didn't feel it appropriate to comment.

Later the assembled party went outside to wave to the bride and groom as they set off for Scotland in a shiny new landau.

I was relieved when it was time to leave and Father came to find Dolly and me.

'I've been so occupied with the arrangements for the Coronation,' said Father, 'that we haven't yet talked about your honeymoon.'

'Perhaps we might go to Bath?' I said. 'It's very fashionable.' Wherever we went, I hoped there'd be plenty of diversions. The prospect of spending a great deal of time alone with Dolly was daunting.

'Bath is for milksops,' said Father in tones of disgust. 'You shall travel to Italy. You can show Dolly Pesaro and other towns where you stayed.'

'I like the idea of Bath,' said Dolly. 'Travel abroad is so exhausting and the beds are never properly aired.'

'I'd prefer not to return to Italy,' I said. The last place I wanted to go with Dolly was to where I'd been so happy with Alessandro and his family.

'Nonsense!' Father rubbed his hands together with satisfaction. 'It's a perfect idea. It'll give you the chance to retrace your steps and look for the Infanta's miniatures. Despite all my letters I've had no more contact . . . ' He broke off at sight of the expression on my face. 'What is it, Emilia?'

I glanced at Dolly, whose lips were pressed tightly together as he studied his boots.

'I have no secrets from Dolly!' said Father. 'After all, he's my heir as well as your fiancé. He knows all about the missing miniatures.'

'Still,' I said, 'I don't wish to go to Italy.' It would be far too painful to be reminded of what I had lost.

The smile faded from Father's face. 'I thought you were committed to the idea of returning the miniatures to their owner?'

'We need not make final decisions about a honeymoon yet,' said Dolly, clearing his throat again. 'We'll discuss it after the

Coronation. And how are the preparations proceeding, Sir Frederick? I heard that the King's red velvet Coronation robe is to be nine yards long, exquisitely embroidered with gold stars and lined with ermine.'

'Indeed,' said Father, easily deflected to his involvement with the Coronation arrangements. 'His Majesty will be most gloriously attired. A new crown has been made, too, encrusted with over twelve thousand diamonds.'

'And what of the Queen?' I asked.

'It's the King's prerogative,' said Father, 'to decide whether Caroline of Brunswick will be crowned and he'll never agree to it.' He laughed. 'She actually wrote to the Home Secretary declaring it was her right. Her mantua-maker is preparing splendid dresses for her but, mark my words, she'll never wear them in Westminster Abbey.'

'Can the King prevent her attendance?' asked Dolly.

'He won't have her anywhere near him,' said Father. 'He's worried she'll make a scene so he's hired prize-fighters to be dressed as pages. They'll stand by all the doors to the Abbey to stop her.'

Father and Dolly continued to discuss the Coronation while I looked out of the carriage window. I knew better than to defend the Queen in Father's hearing but it saddened me she was not to be crowned. Although declared innocent at the end of her trial, her reputation had been left in tatters. Now that the Radicals and the Whigs no longer found her useful in supporting their cause against the King, her popularity with the people had waned. I'd visited her in March and been shocked by how little care she was taking of her toilette. Unwashed and wrapped in a coarse shawl, she'd laughed about the popular belief that she'd taken to drink but I'd seen tears in her eyes even as she made a joke of it. The next time I went to visit her I was told she was indisposed.

The carriage come to a halt in Grosvenor Street.

'Dolly, there are some matters of estate business to discuss,' said Father. 'Come to my study, will you?'

Dolly handed me down from the carriage and I was pleased to escape upstairs to the solitude of my bedroom.

A few days later, after Aunt Maude had retired early and Father had gone out, I curled up on the chair by the open window in my bedroom and watched the sun setting behind the roofs opposite. I wrinkled my nose as the breeze wafted in the odour of horse dung and drains from the street below. I was bone tired but knew this was the physical manifestation of the sickness of the spirit that troubled me. All those years I'd travelled with Sarah I'd been desperate for a place to belong. Now that I'd returned to my family home, I realised it hadn't brought me fulfilment. I had everything a girl could possibly want but I wasn't happy.

There was a tap at the door and Daisy stood in the doorway, her fingers twisting together. 'Begging your pardon, miss, but may I have a word?' She glanced over her shoulder.

'Come in.' Her expression was so agitated I wondered if she'd come to confess a petty misdemeanour: a scorched lace collar or a snagged stocking.

'It's your Italian gentleman friend,' she whispered.

I sat bolt upright, my stomach twisting into knots. 'He's here?'

'He was in the area outside,' said Daisy. 'I didn't know what to do with him so I hid him in the coal store.'

Flustered, I stood up and smoothed my hair. I wanted so much to see Alessandro but this time I had to face him as Dolly's fiancé. 'Did he say what he wanted?'

Daisy shook her head. 'He was very excitable, miss, you know how foreigners are, and said you're to come at once.'

We hurried downstairs and Daisy led me into the scullery. The day had been hot and it smelled unpleasantly of rotting vegetables. The scullery maid, up to her elbows in greasy water, hastily averted her eyes when I smiled at her.

We stepped into the paved area and stood outside the door to the store room under the pavement.

'I'll go back,' Daisy whispered.

I fumbled with the latch and slipped inside the coal store. The air was heavy with dust and mould. I stood still, listening to the thudding of my heart, until my eyes grew accustomed to the gloom.

'Emilia?' Alessandro's voice was barely a whisper.

Light filtered through the crack around the coal-hole cover in the pavement above. In the dimness I saw him. My mouth was dry and I hardly knew what to say after the way we'd parted last time.

His shoes crunched over scattered coal. It was all I could do to stop myself from running into his arms. Immediately I saw him I knew I still loved him.

'I had to come,' he said in an undertone, 'to warn you.' He spoke in Italian but there was no warmth in his demeanour.

'Warn me?' I'd hoped he'd come to apologise for not believing me when I'd told him I hadn't received any letters from him and that I wasn't, at that time, engaged to Dolly.

'Listen to me.' His voice was urgent. 'You're in great danger.'

Whatever I might have expected, it wasn't that.

'I followed him,' said Alessandro, 'and then I realised who he was.'

'You're not making sense,' I said.

He grabbed me by my upper arms and shook me. 'Listen, will you! That man you're going to marry . . .'

'I know what you thought,' I said, 'but I *wasn't* going to marry him when we spoke last.' I had to make him believe me. 'I only became engaged to Dolly *after* you made it so clear you didn't want me.'

'You cannot marry him. He's a murderer.'

Nervous tension made me laugh. 'That's ridiculous!'

He released my arms and stepped back. 'I followed him again last night . . .'

'What do you mean, you followed him?'

'I've followed him on many nights,' said Alessandro, shrugging. 'He spends his evenings in gambling dens. *Of course* I wanted to know more about this blackguard who'd stolen the affections of the woman I once loved. But last night I was close enough to hear him cough and then I recalled where I'd seen him before. Do you remember I told you I'd seen a man looking in through your cottage window just before Sarah was murdered?'

'In Pesaro?'

'Exactly! I challenged him then,' said Alessandro, 'but I had Victorine with me and he loped off on those great long legs of his. Don't you understand, Emilia, *he's* the man who killed Sarah? I heard him make that strange cough at the time but thought no more about it.'

I remembered my own fear when a man had loomed up in the darkness in the passageway behind the cottage and almost knocked me over. 'But . . . Dolly has never been to Italy,' I said, bewildered.

'I *heard* him and I *saw* him, Emilia.'

I stared at Alessandro through the gloom. What could have made him imagine such a thing? 'You're jealous!' I said.

He spat on the ground. 'Jealous? I despise him. I tell you again, you must not marry that man.'

'You're jealous of him and you've made up this terrible lie.' My voice was cold. 'I thought better of you, Alessandro.'

'Why can I not make you see the truth?' he hissed, kicking at the coal. 'If you still insist on marrying a murderer, then I can do no more.' Roughly, he pushed past me. He snatched open the door and then he was gone.

I pressed my hands to my burning cheeks and fought back despair. I should have ignored our misunderstandings and made him listen to me. And now there was this dreadful accusation. Alessandro's words rolled around in my head as I fought to regain outward composure.

Eventually I felt calmer and opened the door into the area.

'Emilia?'

I went cold. Father was peering down at me over the railings. Had he seen Alessandro leave?

'What are you doing there?' he said.

I looked back at him, struggling to find an excuse for being in the coal store. Then it came to me. 'I heard a cat yowling,' I said, 'and came to see if it was hurt.'

'Did you find it?'

'It must have run away.'

'For goodness' sake, come up before anyone sees you! Your face is smudged with coal dust.'

'Yes, Father.' I hurried up the steps and followed him inside.

Chapter 27

Dolly and I had been invited to stay with the Perry family in Northumberland Gardens on the night before the Coronation. Daisy came to wake me at four in the morning, to dress me in my blue satin dress with an embroidered train. She arranged my hair in elaborate curls and topped them with white ostrich plumes. I made my way downstairs, with the feathers bobbing at every step, feeling more than a little self-conscious.

Mr Perry, Araminta, her fiancé Mr Carlton, and Dolly were already in the dining room, dressed in their finery.

'Isn't this exciting?' said Araminta, twirling around to show me her dress of apricot-coloured silk. 'You'd better have some coffee and bread since we don't know when we shall next eat.'

Sir Peter and Mrs Perry came to join us and after a hasty breakfast the ladies and Sir Peter climbed into the waiting carriage, while Mr Perry, Mr Carlton and Dolly set off on foot. We'd barely turned into Whitehall when we came to a stop. Carriages filled the road ahead, making it impassable.

'We'll have to walk,' said Sir Peter. 'If we're separated, go down

Parliament Street and turn left into Palace Yard. Our box is on the second tier, to the front of the first house.'

I held my train over one arm to prevent it being trampled on as we shuffled along in the press of the crowd. All was good-natured, however, with a palpable air of excitement. As we approached Bridge Street we saw the raised and canopied processional route snaking its way from the north door of Westminster Hall, turning down Bridge Street, into King's Road and thence to Westminster Abbey.

It took nearly an hour to walk the short distance to Palace Yard. Already the public had gathered at every window and even on roofs. Some must have camped there all night. Finally, we pushed our way to the tiered pavilions bolted to the front of the houses. An attendant took our tickets and we climbed the rickety steps to a narrow gangway leading to our box. It was disconcerting to look through the gaps between the boards to the ground below but, once seated behind a guard rail, I felt perfectly secure.

'We have a splendid view of Westminster Hall from here,' said Araminta. 'Father had to pull a few strings to secure our seats but it was well worth it, don't you think?'

'It certainly was,' I said. Our box afforded us not only a clear view to the front but also a limited view to our right where the raised walkway turned into Bridge Street.

'The procession will pass directly in front of us after it leaves Westminster Hall on its way to the Abbey,' said Dolly. 'There's nothing to do now but wait until ten o'clock when the King arrives.'

Araminta and I amused ourselves by looking at the ladies' gowns and arguing over which was the prettiest, while Sir Peter and Mrs Perry used their opera glasses to spy out friends and acquaintances. The sun was hot and I was thirsty. An orange seller came along the gangway behind us but we couldn't risk dripping juice on our gowns or staining our white gloves.

Dolly took a silver flask from his coat. 'Brandy?' he asked. I shook my head and he took a sip and put the flask away again.

I watched the crowd, my mind dwelling on the quarrel with Alessandro, wondering what I could have done to make him listen to me. And then there had been his dreadful accusation that Dolly had murdered Sarah ... I glanced sideways at my fiancé, who toyed languidly with his opera glasses, looking for someone of interest in the sea of faces. It was a ridiculous idea; I'd never seen anyone look less like a murderer than Dolly did. I rubbed my aching temples. Alessandro had never lied to me but in this he must be mistaken.

I was beginning to fidget on my uncomfortable seat when I heard a commotion in the crowd in Bridge Street. There was a series of whistles and then a shout, 'The Queen forever!' I craned my neck to see what was happening. A black carriage, closely followed by a yellow state coach drawn by six bays, forced its way through the crowd.

'Well, well! It seems the Queen has decided to attend the Coronation despite her lack of an invitation,' drawled Dolly as the carriages proceeded slowly down Margaret Street and past Westminster Hall.

I caught a glimpse of the Queen's white face and her feathered headdress at the carriage window. There were cheers and boos in equal measure as the two carriages turned towards the Abbey and disappeared from sight. I was afraid for her. It must have taken a great deal of courage to make that journey, especially since she'd received an uncertain welcome, so different from the ecstasy of the crowd when she was acquitted after her trial.

Nothing seemed to happen for a while but then the noise from the chattering crowd increased.

'Look!' said Mr Perry. He snatched the opera glasses from his mother's hand and trained them towards the Abbey. 'It's the Queen!'

In the distance two figures walked into view and stopped by the West Door of the Abbey. It wasn't possible to see more, even though we all took it in turns to strain our eyes with the opera glasses. Soon the carriages reappeared, stopped before the West Door and the Queen and her escort climbed back in. The carriages then trundled out of sight towards the Poets' Corner door, where the Royal Family were expected to enter the Abbey.

The crowd was full of speculation and word was passed from person to person that the Queen had been barred at both the West and East Doors of the Abbey.

The carriages came around the corner again and stopped outside Westminster Hall. The Queen descended with her escort but the guards shouted and some of the crowd hissed and yelled as she approached the door. Pages clad in scarlet livery and carrying battle-axes surrounded the party. Raised voices drifted towards us on the breeze. There were cries of 'Shame!' and 'Go back to Pergami!' as the guards closed ranks.

Defeated, the Queen climbed into her yellow carriage again and, as the bells of Westminster pealed out, she was driven away.

'That's the last we'll see of her!' said Araminta, unfolding her fan and fluttering it before her face.

'At least the spectacle kept us all amused until the main event of the day,' said Dolly, over the cacophony of the bells.

I watched the crowd in silence, noticing the sun glinting off brilliant jewels and feathers bobbing up and down as people chattered in excited anticipation, while the thought of the poor Queen's utter despair and humiliation almost brought me to tears. I hoped Lady Hamilton would comfort her.

The King was half an hour late. The crowd became restless as the sun grew hotter. Our box was in full sun and my bodice was too tight. Surreptitiously, I eased it under my arms, hoping my face wasn't too unattractively flushed from the heat.

Smart carriages came and went and, at last, the procession emerged from Westminster Hall to loud applause from the crowd. First came the heralds with a joyful burst of sound as they announced their King. Seven herb-women followed, all chosen for their beauty and dressed in flowing white muslin as they strewed lavender, rosemary and flower petals along the processional route.

Dolly nudged me. 'That's the Lord Great Chamberlain holding the mace,' he said, 'and here come the princes of the blood, the Lord Chancellor, the King's gentlemen and other officers of state.'

A collective gasp went up from the assembled company as the magnificent figure of the King appeared, nodding and bowing gracefully to his subjects. I was suffering from the heat but how much worse it must have been for the King in his ceremonial dress. Treading slowly and majestically, he wore a suit made of cloth of silver, lavishly trimmed with gold braid. His vast velvet train of scarlet and gold, trimmed with ermine, was carried by eight pages. He wore a black Spanish hat surmounted by sprays of ostrich feathers and a black heron's plume. Whatever my private opinion of him might be, he looked every inch a King.

A swelling wave of cheers and applause came from the crowd along the processional route.

'What a glorious show!' said Mrs Perry, her eyes shining as the procession finally disappeared from sight.

'And so it should be,' said Sir Peter. 'They say the King's clothes alone cost more than twenty-four thousand pounds!'

Araminta's eyes opened very wide.

'The King wanted his Coronation to be a grander affair than Napoleon's,' said Dolly, 'and I'd say he's achieved that, wouldn't you?'

The spectators settled down to wait while the Coronation took place out of sight inside the Abbey. Araminta and I joined the queue for the ladies' retiring room in the house behind our box and later Sir Peter bought us all a slice of pie. Another trader sold us glasses of negus. Mrs Perry, her nose shining in the relentless sun, complained the negus had been disgracefully watered down but I was grateful to quench my thirst.

After an interminable length of time a roar went up from the crowd as the news filtered out of the Abbey that the King had been crowned. Some threw their hats in the air. A little while later the procession left the Abbey and returned with all pomp and ceremony to Westminster Hall for the Coronation Banquet. Once the dignitaries had disappeared, the crowd began to disperse.

'I'm cramped from sitting so long,' said Araminta as we queued to descend to the street, 'but the celebrations aren't over yet.' The feathers in her headdress had wilted in the sun, giving her a rakish air. 'You will both come with us to the Coronation Fête in Hyde Park this evening, won't you? We'll return to Northumberland Gardens for dinner and then go on to the fête.'

'There's to be a balloon ascent and a pair of elephants pulling a golden carriage in the opening parade,' said Mr Perry.

'How could we miss such an opportunity?' said Dolly.

I gathered my crumpled train over my arm and we were jostled along with the happy horde. All around us was good humour and extravagant praise for the King. I clung to Dolly's arm and reflected soberly on how fickle people were. Only a few months ago there had been fervent support for the Queen but now, humiliated and reviled, she'd been forced to retreat to lick her wounds while the King, puffed up with self-importance, held court amongst his sycophants.

The following morning, I slept very late. I found Aunt Maude waiting for me as I came, yawning, down to breakfast.

'Your father is still abed,' she said.

'He wasn't home when I returned late last night.'

'I've seen the newspaper reports of the Coronation already,' said Aunt Maude, 'but I want to hear all about it from you.' She poured me a cup of strong coffee.

'It was a wonderful spectacle,' I said, 'though it saddened me to see the Queen turned away.'

'A shameful thing!' Aunt Maude shook her head sadly.

I sipped the hot coffee, feeling it revive me. 'I wish she hadn't tried to enter the Abbey. It was demeaning for her to be refused entry.'

'She always was impulsive and strong-willed,' said Aunt Maude. 'She must have known the King wouldn't allow her access and counted on her previous popularity, hoping the crowds would rally behind her. I expect she wanted to provoke him.'

'I imagine you're right.'

Some twenty minutes later I'd described all that I'd seen and Aunt Maude had exclaimed in wonder at it all.

'And then,' I said, 'there was the Coronation Fête in Hyde Park. I shall never forget the elephants in the opening parade. I'd never seen real ones before and I'd no idea they were so big. They wore gold headdresses and the most beautiful, brightly coloured blankets decorated with glittering sequins. And I do wish you could have been there to see the balloon ascent. It made me dizzy to see it rising so high in the air.'

'How wonderful to see the world from a bird's-eye point of view,' said Aunt Maude, 'though I should have been terrified to be so far off the ground.'

'There were Chinese lanterns in the trees,' I said, 'and an illuminated temple topped with a gold crown to commemorate the day. And at the end of the celebration there was a magnificent firework display that went on for at least twenty minutes. I daren't think how much it all cost.'

'I daresay the taxpayer will foot the bill,' said Aunt Maude.

I sipped my coffee. Now the excitement of the Coronation was over there was little to divert my thoughts from my latest distressing meeting with Alessandro. I was sure he was mistaken about Dolly but regretted that my refusal to believe it had prevented us from making up our differences. I sighed deeply, my heart aching for Alessandro.

'You look tired, dear,' said Aunt Maude. 'Shall we have a quiet day reading in the garden?'

'We must hold a ball,' said Father that evening after dinner, 'in continuing celebration of the King's Coronation. Will you arrange it as soon as possible, Emilia? Aunt Maude will assist you.' He smiled. 'And then the next big event will be your wedding, of course.'

My heart sank. 'Hasn't everyone had enough Coronation celebrations?' I said, hoping he'd change his mind. I glanced at Aunt Maude, sitting beside me on the sofa, but her expression remained inscrutable.

'Of course they haven't!' Father leaned back in his chair with a half-smile on his lips. 'The King is delighted that, at last, his people have recognised him for the great man he is. Thankfully Caroline of Brunswick has completely fallen from favour. Turning up at the Coronation, and all that undignified tramping about trying to push her way past the doorkeepers, made her lose any credibility she might once have had. The expectation is that she'll retreat to Italy and her lover with her tail between her legs.'

'She was shamefully treated,' I protested.

'Nonsense! No more than she deserved.' Father smirked. 'She had the gall to write to the King, demanding to be crowned on Monday. Monday! She'll be crowned on no day at all, as far as he is concerned. Anyhow, enough of that wretched woman! I shall inform the King that we're arranging a ball in his honour. He may even grace us with his presence again.'

'Is there a particular advantage to you if he attends the ball?' I asked. I was sure that there must be.

Father pursed his lips. 'He'll be pleased to hear that I continue to be a loyal supporter. And then, as you know, he's a great patron of the arts. He might be interested in my collection.'

I had an inkling of what was in Father's mind. 'And perhaps, if you were his agent, you might have the honour of procuring paintings or sculptures for his residences?'

'I have excellent contacts with art dealers both here and on the continent,' said Father, 'and many satisfied clients.' He smiled winningly. 'You have a good eye yourself, my dear. Should there be something in particular the King has in mind, you would be well placed, while on your honeymoon in Italy, to be my eyes and ears when you visit the dealers to make enquiries.'

'As I said before, Father, I'd prefer to visit Bath. Certainly Dolly doesn't want to go to Italy.' If Alessandro had known how much Dolly disliked foreign travel, he'd never have accused him of being in Pesaro when Sarah was murdered.

'I don't see why not,' said Father, sounding distinctly peevish. 'It's not as if he'll be paying for the honeymoon.'

'Will you give me your guest list for the ball?' I said, changing the subject to something less contentious. 'I'll talk to the printers and the musicians today and see how soon we can make arrangements.'

Father beamed. 'Good girl! Let me know tomorrow so I can be sure to hold it on an evening the King is free.' He stood up. 'I'm going to my club now so don't wait up.'

Aunt Maude sighed heavily after he'd left the room. 'He has no idea how much work is involved in organising a ball.'

Over the following days she and I were kept fully occupied. I threw myself into making the arrangements to divert my thoughts from Alessandro. We visited the printers to find out how soon they could produce the invitations, called on the florists to discuss extravagant arrangements of exotic flowers, hired chairs and ordered a magnificent sugar-paste centrepiece for the supper table from Gunter's. This was to be a Chinese temple, topped with a golden crown, similar to the one in Hyde Park at the Coronation Fête. There would be sugar models of elephants and spectators watching the balloon ascent and the whole arrangement would be set in a sugar-paste landscape representing the park.

Mrs Hope and Cook had discussed with us the elegant dishes to be provided for the supper and embarked upon a frenzied onslaught of additional cleaning and polishing. I interviewed and selected an opera singer to entertain us during the interval in the dancing and booked my dancing master to act as Master of Ceremonies.

At the end of a particularly busy day Aunt Maude and I drooped with exhaustion and could only pick at our supper.

'Whatever's the matter with you both?' said Father, spearing another slice of cold beef. 'Not sickening, I hope?'

I glanced at Aunt Maude's wan face and had an idea. 'We've run ourselves into the ground with preparations for the ball.' I said 'We'd like to visit Langdon Hall for some restorative country air.'

Father chewed contemplatively at his beef. 'Is everything organised? It must be perfect for the King.'

'We can do no more now until the last day or so,' I said. All at once I couldn't wait to escape, not only from the stifling heat in town but also from Father's overbearing ways. 'It would be *such* a pity if I were not well enough to act as your hostess.'

Father sighed. 'I suppose there's no real need for you to remain in town then,' he said.

I glanced at Aunt Maude, demurely contemplating her untouched supper. 'We shall return refreshed and ready to complete the final preparations for your ball.'

Chapter 28

Langdon Hall

The fountain in the centre of the knot garden splashed gently beside us as Aunt Maude and I drank our tea. Bees hummed on the lavender and the sun was warm on my arms. Langdon was a different world from London.

'Take care not to burn, dear,' said Aunt Maude. 'You don't want freckles for your wedding day, do you?'

I reached out and trailed my fingers in the cool water of the fountain. I didn't want to think of my wedding day. Meeting Alessandro again had thrown me into turmoil. I thought endlessly about the dreadful accusation he'd made. Despite our differences I trusted Alessandro, but I was sure he'd come to a mistaken conclusion about Dolly.

'You've been lost in thought for quite five minutes,' said Aunt Maude.

I withdrew my hand from the water. 'Am I making a terrible mistake in marrying Dolly?' I enquired.

She gave me a sharp glance. 'Do *you* think you're making a mistake?'

'I don't love him,' I said, 'but that's not unusual amongst my acquaintances. Father tells me how advantageous the marriage will be ...'

'But your heart isn't in it?'

I shook my head.

Aunt Maude put down her teacup and squeezed my wrist. 'You mustn't marry Dolly if you dislike him.'

I shrugged. 'He's presentable and well-mannered. I agreed to marry him because he said he loved me. But there's little sign now of the passion he showed for me at Christmas. It seems familiarity breeds complacency.'

'Love may grow once you're married,' said Aunt Maude, but her expression was full of doubt.

'I thought, if I married him, soon I'd have children to love.'

'What if there are no children?' said Aunt Maude.

I pictured Alessandro's big, noisy family and there was a hollow feeling in my heart. 'Then I should be very lonely,' I said.

She sighed. 'Do you still yearn for Alessandro?'

'He doesn't love me anymore,' I said, 'and he thinks I lied to him.'

'Emilia ...' Aunt Maude hesitated. 'An unhappy marriage is worse than no marriage at all, however difficult it is to be a spinster. Your parents' marriage was a disaster.'

'I know. He told me about Mother's affair.'

'Affair?' Her expression was outraged. 'There was no affair!'

'Perhaps she hid it from you so you didn't think ill of her?'

'Rose was as honest as the day,' said Aunt Maude, 'and utterly transparent.'

I didn't want to argue with an old lady but I'd seen Father's misery when he told me about my treacherous mother. While I didn't yet love him, his unhappiness had moved me.

A cloud passed over the sun and I shivered. 'Shall we walk?'

We ambled along the gravel paths, stopping to smell the flowers, while all the time I recalled with misery Alessandro's last words to me.

'I wish you remembered Rose,' said Aunt Maude. 'You'd know then how honourable she was.'

'I'm still hurt she abandoned me, a small child, to fend for myself in the world,' I said. 'If she'd really loved me she wouldn't have taken her own life.' My steps faltered as I remembered Alessandro saying, 'If you loved me you wouldn't leave me.'

'I don't know what happened,' said Aunt Maude, 'but I know she loved you above all else.'

Except for her lover. The pain of losing him had made her turn her back on my needs. 'All those years I thought Sarah was my mother,' I said, 'there was something missing. Perhaps I blotted out memories of Mother because they were too painful. Sarah tended to my physical needs but there was never any real connection between us, except that we were bound by our mutual need for survival.'

We walked silently through the avenue of clipped yews and rested on a bench beside the moat. The water level was lower than usual and it was green and turgid, giving off a foetid smell in the summer warmth.

'Frederick usually tells the gardener to open the sluices when the water is so low,' said Aunt Maude. 'The moat refills from the river.' She stared at the water, her brow furrowed.

'Rose kept a diary,' she said. 'I wonder what became of it?'

My interest quickened. Mother's diary might answer my questions, even if it made me unhappy. 'Might it be in the library, where you found her entertaining notebook?'

'Shall we go and see?' said Aunt Maude.

The diary wasn't in plain view in the library.

'She kept it private,' said Aunt Maude, 'and out of your father's way. She wrote in it when we were sitting together sometimes. She often concealed it in her sewing basket but that is long gone.'

We searched the library more thoroughly, taking down each book from the lower shelves in turn. Hours later we brushed dust from our hands and conceded defeat for the day.

The following morning Aunt Maude sat in the wing chair while I used the library steps to investigate the upper shelves. Now that I knew of the diary's existence it had become a matter of vital importance to me to find it.

At last I'd searched all the shelves, rummaged through the library tables, the cupboards and the desk. Frustrated, I came to the conclusion that the diary simply wasn't there.

'Where else might she have hidden it, Aunt Maude?' I asked.

'Your father has kept Rose's bedroom locked ever since she drowned.'

A tiny thrill of anticipation shivered down my back. 'If the room's been undisturbed since she died,' I said, 'then there's a chance it's there.'

'Frederick wouldn't like you going in there,' said Aunt Maude. There was a worried crease between her eyebrows. 'I really don't want to make him angry.'

'I shan't disturb anything.'

'I'd rather not know what you intend to do, in case he questions me. I shall take a turn around the garden.'

I rang for the footman and Aunt Maude left the library by the French windows.

'Robert,' I said, 'will you ask Mrs Bannister for the key to the locked bedroom?'

Five minutes later the housekeeper appeared, her stout figure neat in a black bombazine dress and white collar. 'Robert tells me you requested the key to Lady Langdon's bedroom?'

'I did,' I said.

'Sir Frederick gave express orders for that room to remain locked,' said the housekeeper. 'I'm permitted to enter only twice a year to dust.'

'I shall not require you to enter the room,' I said, 'only to unlock it.' I looked down my nose at her in my best imitation of Lady Hamilton's haughty expression.

After a moment, Mrs Bannister dropped her gaze. 'Very well, Miss Langdon, if that is your instruction.'

My breathing quickened at the thought of what I might discover as we walked upstairs together. Mother's diary might be the key to unlocking the family mysteries that troubled me.

In the Long Gallery the housekeeper stopped outside the locked room, selected a key from the chatelaine around her waist and opened the door.

'That will be all,' I said, outwardly calm. 'I'll send for you to lock it again later.' I stepped over the threshold and closed the door firmly behind me.

It was shadowy dark inside the room and I opened the faded silk curtains and folded back the shutters. Sunshine flooded in, illuminating delicate satinwood furniture, an Aubusson carpet and embroidered bed drapes in soft shades of green, rose pink and violet. The panelled walls were painted the same pale green as the curtains. Something about the room, the restful colour perhaps, was extraordinarily calming. It felt like a safe haven from dangers I didn't even know existed.

I sat on the bed, my fingers stroking the silky coverlet, and watched dust motes drifting lazily in the sunlight. Something teased my memory. Counting. Little hands ... my hands ... clapping. A clear voice singing. I closed my eyes, willing myself to remember as my fingertips caressed the roses and violets embroidered on the coverlet. I gasped as all at once I heard the song in my head.

Roses are red,
Violets are blue
Sugar is sweet
And so are you!

Mother's hair silky against my face as she snatched me into her arms and kissed me. The warm, sweet scent of her violet perfume. Giggling and squirming as her lips tickled my cheek. Begging her to sing me the nursery rhyme again. And then the memory was gone.

I reared to my feet but the happy echo from my past had disappeared, taking my mother with it. My pulse raced as I wondered if I'd been wrong about her. Perhaps she'd loved me after all.

Systematically, I began to search the room. The chest of drawers remained full of her clothes; lacy shifts, embroidered nightgowns and silk petticoats, still faintly perfumed with violets. Dresses hung in the wardrobe, too full-skirted for today's fashions but all exquisitely finished. Shoes were arranged in pairs and I slipped on a yellow silk dancing shoe decorated with a tulle rose. It cupped my foot as if it had been moulded to me. Shivering, I took it off and replaced it where it belonged.

I sat at the dressing table and opened the drawers to find a box of fine-milled powder and a half-used bottle of Olympian Dew. A chased silver cachou box held pink lip salve, shrunken and cracked now but still scented with Otto of Roses. I dipped my forefinger into the waxy compound and looked in the mirror while I rubbed the salve on my lips. It made me shiver, with pleasure rather than sadness this time, to think my mother would have been the last person to touch the salve.

I began to look for the diary in earnest. The back of the drawers yielded only a few hairpins and a handkerchief. I searched under the bed, feeling along the frame, I climbed on a chair to reach up to the top of the wardrobe, rolled back the carpet searching for a loose floorboard and, finally, felt inside the chimney.

I stood in the centre of the room. 'Mother,' I whispered. 'Tell me where to find your diary.'

Nothing.

Disappointed and inexpressibly sad, I closed the shutters and drew the curtains. The room was full of shadows again and I tip-toed to the door and left the ghosts to whisper in peace.

The following days passed in outward tranquillity. I retrieved Mother's portrait from where I'd concealed it in the back of my wardrobe and propped it up on the chest of drawers. Her eyes seemed to follow me wherever I went but now that didn't unnerve me. I gazed at her painted face for hours at a time, trying to read her expression. Sometimes I fancied she was trying to speak to me and I sat, motionless, listening for memories of her voice.

Aunt Maude and I visited the pretty Queen Anne dower house on the estate, which was to be my home after the wedding. As I walked through the echoing hall I thought I might be as happy there as anywhere. It had been closed up for years and I'd relish choosing new curtains and wallpaper to my own taste. Living in the house with Dolly as my husband was another prospect entirely and panic fluttered in my breast.

That night I paced up and down while dread made my chest constrict so tightly I could barely breathe. Again and again I wondered about Alessandro's accusation. Soon Dolly would be my husband and England my permanent home. For evermore I would have to forget about Italy and the man I still loved there, despite our difficulties.

In the light of day, I dismissed my night fears and simply avoided thinking about the wedding. Aunt Maude and I drove into the countryside and enjoyed a picnic on the banks of the River Test. I was happy to see her animated when we visited the local churches, explored the churchyards and the tea shops in the nearby towns. She appeared less frail when she was happy.

Mrs Digby, the wife of Father's solicitor, heard that we were staying at the Hall and called upon us. The weather was delightfully warm and we sat on the terrace overlooking the knot garden and the moat.

'It must be eighteen months since we first met, Miss Langdon,' said Mrs Digby. 'And here you are,' she said, 'happy in the bosom of your family and engaged to be married.'

'Two years ago I could never have imagined it,' I said. But then, two years ago I'd been in Italy, the country I loved, anticipating a happy future with Alessandro.

'I'm delighted for you,' said Mrs Digby. Her smile was sincere. 'And, if you won't think me presumptuous, may I say how proud of you your mother would have been?'

'Do you not think Emilia is so very like Rose?' said Aunt Maude.

Mrs Digby nodded. 'The picture of her.'

'I don't recall her,' I said. 'Although, here at Langdon Hall, I've experienced momentary flashes of childhood reminiscences.'

'I'm delighted to hear that, dear,' said Aunt Maude. She patted my wrist. 'I very much want you to remember Rose as she really was.'

'Sometimes I hear her singing a nursery rhyme,' I said. 'And I was standing on the bank of the moat the other day when I recalled her snatching my hand with a warning to be careful.'

'She was always anxious you'd fall in,' said Aunt Maude. 'The water smells dreadful in hot summers like this. Rose worried that if the river flooded, the moat would rise, too, and come into the house.'

'What an unpleasant thought!' I wrinkled my nose, imagining the stinking water seeping under the doors.

'Don't be concerned,' said Mrs Digby, 'the river hasn't flooded in fifty years. And, as far as I remember, Rose was more worried about the thefts of paintings from some of our friends and neighbours.'

'Father mentioned the art thefts to me.'

'We have no valuable paintings since Mr Digby has no interest at all in art.' Mrs Digby smiled. 'So I never had any anxiety that a thief would break in to take them. But Rose fretted that the thief might be someone we knew, someone who might steal Sir Frederick's collection from Langdon Hall. Thankfully, that never happened.'

Mrs Digby gathered up her reticule. 'I've enjoyed meeting you both again and hope I shall see more of you when you're living in the dower house, Miss Langdon.'

'I hope so, too,' I said.

After Mrs Digby had gone, Aunt Maude went inside to rest as was her habit in the afternoons. I wandered through the house, looking again for somewhere Mother might have hidden her diary. Of course, it was possible Father had destroyed it after she died. One place I hadn't searched was his study and I plucked up the courage to enter his private sanctum. I waited until the servants were elsewhere and slipped inside.

The shutters were closed and I dared to open them only a crack to admit some light. One wall was covered with built-in bookshelves but these contained only old ledgers and folios pertaining to estate business and his parliamentary affairs. The remaining walls displayed paintings and the desk was locked. I didn't dare to force it open. I would search the townhouse when I returned to London the next day, I decided. Dejected by my failure to find the diary, I closed the shutters again.

'That's everything packed, miss,' said Daisy. She closed my travelling bags and tightened the straps.

'Will you ask Edward to carry the luggage down?' I said.

'Very good, Miss Langdon.'

I dreaded returning to London. Father's ball was in a couple of days' time and afterwards I'd have to endure making the final arrangements for my impending wedding. Heavy-hearted, I went to look at my mother's portrait for the last time before we left. 'Where is your diary, Mother?' I whispered. I fancied she watched me as I left the room.

I went down to the little parlour to check I hadn't forgotten anything. Sun streamed in through the window and a wood pigeon cooed outside. Suddenly I was four years old again. I remembered kneeling on the window seat watching the pigeons billing and cooing on the lawn outside while Mother worked on her embroidery beside me.

That was it! I raced up the back staircase to the attics. Lighting the candle from the shelf outside the storage room where Father had kept Mother's portrait, I opened the door. Inside was a cradle and various trunks amongst dust-sheeted furniture. I heaved up the lid of the first trunk to find folded curtains and then another packed with children's clothing. I shook out a little muslin dress and there was something so familiar about the sprigs of yellow primroses and the pattern of the lace trimming that I could only believe I had once worn it myself. I fumbled hastily through layers of dresses, vests and tiny nightgowns until I was sure that the trunk contained only clothes.

Throwing back the lid of another trunk, I rummaged through ladies' shoes, a box of paints and a bundle of brushes. My heart nearly stopped when I found a leather book but it was a sketchbook of indifferent landscapes and not a diary at all. Delving deeper into the trunk my fingers scraped against something rough. My spirits soared when I saw it was a wicker basket.

I dragged it out of the trunk with trembling hands. Needle cases, scissors, pins and a small tape measure were arranged in the top tray. A second contained serried ranks of embroidery silks. Underneath that was an embroidery hoop containing a half-finished work of blue tits nestling amongst wildflowers. I burrowed beneath, amongst folded pieces of canvas, and then became very still as I felt smooth leather under my fingertips.

My mouth was dry as I extracted a green leather book with a brass clasp and the name 'Rose Langdon' embossed in gold on the cover. I hugged the book tightly against my breast.

I had found my mother's diary.

Chapter 29

London

I attempted to read Mother's diary in the carriage on our return to London but after a few tantalising pages the rolling motion of the coach made me feel so queasy I was forced to stop.

'My spectacles are packed,' said Aunt Maude, 'so we'll have to be patient.'

We arrived in Grosvenor Street in time for supper.

'I expected you to return before this,' said Father, his mouth pursed in disapproval. 'My ball is the day after tomorrow. I trust everything is in hand?'

'Absolutely,' I said, 'and I don't anticipate any difficulties.'

'I hope not,' he growled.

When he'd left the supper table for his club, I heaved a sigh of relief and soon I was sitting on the window seat in my bedroom opening Mother's diary. It was strange to read her private thoughts and after an hour or so I began to feel as if I knew her. It brought tears to my eyes to see her comments about me, her *pretty, clever little girl'*, and her hopes and dreams for me as I grew up. Even if she'd had a lover, it was clear that she'd loved me. She wrote also of her joy when she discovered that she was to have another child and hoped it would make Frederick happy:

I fear what he will say if I should bear another daughter. Although he is fond of little Harriet he makes sharp comments about me not doing my duty if I don't provide him with an heir.

I skimmed through the pages, taking little notice of the accounts of parties and social visits, except when she mentioned that Lord Cosgrove's house had been broken into and an important Russian icon stolen.

So many thefts! Not a month passes without another of our acquaintance being robbed by this impudent thief. There is a deal of speculation that the perpetrator may be one of our own set and that makes me look askance at our friends. The thief has a sense of humour since he leaves a pen-and-ink sketch of an empty picture frame in place of the work he's stolen.

Presumably, at that point, Mother had not been involved with the thief who later became her lover. I read on.

I cannot bear to envisage Frederick's rage if one of his paintings were to be stolen. His love for his collection borders on the obsessive and he certainly values it more than he loves his wife or child.

This distressed me but I could only assume she exaggerated. Then came the entry about Piers's birth.

Frederick is pleased with me and I am thankful that I have come through the ordeal with no more than the usual difficulties. My darling son, Piers Frederick George Langdon, made his appearance at dawn this morning, two weeks early. He is so tiny but already very dear to me. Sweet Harriet kissed his little cheek and offered to give him her precious Annabelle. In respect of my children I am the luckiest woman alive. They mean everything to me and make up for the rest.

My heart was very full as I read that entry. But what did she mean by 'the rest'? No matter what might have happened later, Mother had clearly loved her children. Nevertheless, something had happened to drive her into the depths of such despair that she had abandoned me when she drowned herself.

I read the next entries about my little brother's increasingly sickly constitution in the unhappy knowledge that it was to lead to tragedy.

The poor little mite suffers from colic and screams himself into sobs several times a day. Frederick wants to send him to a wet nurse but I'm determined to continue nursing him myself. I cannot bear to be parted from my poor babe. Bravely, I argued with Frederick. He was very harsh to me and left the house with much ill feeling between us. I am grateful to have dear Aunt Maude to comfort me.

It was apparent Mother hadn't taken her parental responsibilities lightly. My heart bled for her as I read about Piers's continual colds and his general failure to thrive, despite her best efforts. And then came the terrible day I'd expected to read about.

My angel has been taken from me. I'm ashamed because I slept well for the first time since his birth since I didn't hear him cry during the night. When I lifted him from his cradle in the morning I knew at once that he had gone. He was already cold and not my Piers anymore. Little Harriet doesn't understand and cries piteously for her baby brother, while Frederick rages and blames me for not sending his son to a wet nurse.

I touched my cheek and discovered it was wet with tears. The entries for the following months were infrequent but I read of Mother's continuing grief and of my parents' disintegrating marriage. Father coped with his sorrow by blaming her for their son's death. His temper flared at the slightest provocation and I was shocked when I read about the day he'd hit her, splitting open her lip. Two days later he hit her again.

The floodgates of his rage are opened. Frederick says I disgust him and he cannot bear me in his sight.

Horrified, I read on, holding the diary with fingers that shook with sorrow and rage.

I'm rarely able to leave the house since I usually have a black eye, a bruise or a cut cheek. Last night Aunt Maude tried to defend me and was

punched for her kindness. I cried and pleaded with him when he threatened
to put her out in the street, for she has no income and nowhere to go.

Sickened, I put the diary down. I couldn't bear to read any more until I'd considered what I'd learned. Father was irascible at times. I'd seen him push Alessandro down the steps but I hadn't imagined he was truly violent.

Confused, I allowed Daisy to undress me for bed, and then lay sleepless in the dark while I tried to make sense of it all.

In the morning, as soon as I was dressed, I reread some of the diary passages, trying to determine if Mother had really been mad or savagely mistreated instead. She appeared to be of sound mind but I'd seen Father's sorrow when he'd told me about their disintegrating marriage. I didn't know what to believe and read on. I gripped the diary tightly when I came to the entry about the theft of Lord Beaufort's miniatures.

At the Ashworths' rout this evening the assembled company were outraged to hear that the Picture Frame Thief has struck again. Three miniatures of the Infanta Isabella Clara Eugenia, daughter of King Philip II of Spain, have been stolen from Lord Beaufort. Only two weeks before Frederick and I, amongst others, were his house guests at Little Braxton Manor where he had proudly showed us the newly acquired works.

Puzzled, I rested the diary on my knee. The miniatures had been stolen not long before Mother had drowned. Since she wrote her innermost thoughts in a diary she kept hidden, why had she as yet made no mention of her lover, the Picture Frame Thief? I was still pondering on whether she'd had a lover at all when Aunt Maude tapped on my door.

'Are you ready to go to Gunter's?'

I'd completely forgotten our appointment to inspect the sugar-paste centrepiece we'd ordered for the supper table at the ball. Distractedly, I tucked the diary under my pillow and put on my bonnet.

In the carriage Aunt Maude said, 'Have you read the diary?'

I nodded. 'Not all of it. I'd like you to read it later and tell me if it marries with your recollections.'

The sunshine was hot when we arrived at Gunter's Tea Rooms, where a great number of vehicles were drawn up in the shade of the trees in Berkeley Square. Ladies sat in their carriages eating ices, while their escorts leaned against the railings nearby, chatting to other young bloods. Waiters dodged through the traffic, bringing the ices from the tea rooms to the carriages before they melted.

'I suggest you wait here, Aunt Maude,' I said. The heat didn't suit her and she looked weary. 'Once I've approved the centrepiece, we'll have an ice.'

'That will be delightful, dear.'

I crossed the road to the tea rooms but Mr Gunter was busy with another customer so I sat down to wait.

Two ladies were drinking tea and gossiping at the table beside me.

'My sister was at the Drury Lane Theatre last night,' said a lady in a yellow muslin dress. 'Mr Elliston was performing in a pageant of the Coronation and he impersonated the King so well it was like a portrait. And that wasn't the only interesting event of the evening. The Queen and her party arrived and a whisper went around that she became unwell during the performance.'

My ears pricked up at the mention of her.

'Sick with jealousy, I expect,' said the lady's companion, busy eating a macaroon.

'Still, she stayed to the end and Augusta said she rose and curt-seyed to the pit, galleries and boxes. "Positively haggard" was how my sister described her; a complete figure of fun with her wig crooked and her crumpled dress all anyhow.'

My heart bled for the Queen but I didn't overhear any more since Mr Gunter greeted me then. He led me to a workroom where the centrepiece was laid out on a clean cloth. 'As you see,' he said, 'we have yet to make the second elephant and the fountains are under construction.'

'I believe I mentioned that the King intends to honour us with his presence at our ball?'

'We'll work through the night to ensure the piece will be ready for tomorrow,' he assured me.

'It's exquisite,' I said.

Mr Gunter bowed.

'And now I shall purchase two of your excellent ices.'

I returned to the carriage followed by a waiter bringing a violet sorbet for Aunt Maude and a *neige aux pistaches* for me.

We gave our full attention to our ices for a moment. Then I said, 'Aunt Maude, did Father ever treat you violently?'

She paused in the act of catching a dribble of violet sorbet with her tongue. Her eyes filled with tears. 'I tried to stop him from hurting Rose. He was terribly angry and threw me to the ground and kicked and beat me.'

So Mother's account of that event, at least, was true. Softly, I touched my aunt's papery cheek while anger at my father burned inside me like a red-hot ember.

'It wasn't the first time,' she said, 'nor the last. He also threatened to put me in the workhouse.' Her chin quivered while she regained control of herself. 'I've never dared to flout his wishes again.'

'He's been kind to me,' I said, 'and given me so much.'

'Frederick rarely does anything unless it suits him.'

'Do you remember when Lord Beaufort's miniatures were stolen, before Mother died?'

'It was in the papers,' said Aunt Maude. 'There was a terrible furore.'

'Father told me that the so-called Picture Frame Thief was Mother's lover.'

Aunt Maude shook her head decisively. 'Ridiculous! Rose never had a lover.'

276

'Father and Sarah told conflicting stories. Father said Mother had hidden the miniatures in her luggage. Sarah said there was little of value among Mother's possessions. She ran away with me, taking the luggage, because she was expecting Mother to join her later.'

'I don't understand that at all.' Aunt Maude frowned. 'Rose would have told me what was happening if I'd been there. I'll always regret I wasn't at Grosvenor Street when she died.'

'Where were you?'

'Staying with my cousin's daughter. Her children, all eight of them, had measles, one after the other. She was utterly distracted and needed help to nurse them. Rose insisted I went and told me to stay away until Frederick's anger abated.' Tears spilled down her cheeks. 'When I returned, she was dead.'

Chapter 30

On the morning of Father's ball I awoke at dawn, propped uncomfortably against my pillows where I'd fallen asleep the previous night
still reading the diary. My dreams had been unbearable: visions
of Mother's distress at the continuing misery of her marriage and
frightening nightmares full of harsh voices and childhood memories
of being mistreated by Joe. I remembered being shaken so hard my
teeth rattled and then being shut in a cupboard.

I was tired and irritable, particularly as I knew the day would be
fully taken up with overseeing the final arrangements for the ball.
I groaned at the thought that the last guest probably wouldn't leave
until dawn the morning after. I decided to stay in bed for a little
longer. I picked up the diary from the pillow beside me and began
to read again.

*I must escape from the dread that overcomes me every time Frederick
comes home. I am taking Harriet with me to Langdon Hall for a respite.*

And then, three days later:

*I hardly know how to write this. My thoughts are utterly disordered
as I grapple with this terrible discovery. I cannot settle to anything for
worrying about what to do. I took Harriet out for a long walk to use up*

my nervous energy but on the way back her poor little legs couldn't carry her any further. I held her in my arms and our tears mingled. I love her so much and I'm very frightened of what I must do.

There was a tap on the door then and Daisy entered with my morning chocolate.

'Good morning, miss,' she said. 'I guessed you'd be awake early today. The servants have been up since before dawn, busy with the preparations, and the kitchen's already humming.'

Daisy returned downstairs and I scanned the diary as I sipped my chocolate, reading that Mrs Digby had called and, for a short while, Mother had enjoyed her cheerful company. There were accounts of supervising the turning out of the preserves cupboard, discussions with the housekeeper as to what new linen must be purchased from London and a host of other household trivia. But then I came to a passage that made me sit bolt upright.

I've tried not to think about what I found. I couldn't even write about it before, almost as if I thought it would go away if I pretended it had never happened. But I did find it and there are some things you cannot ignore, no matter what the consequences.

It was something Jane Digby mentioned to me that made me curious. One of my servants, a new scullery maid, had been found in a state of collapse after the others below stairs frightened her with tales of a ghostly priest walking the corridors of Langdon Hall at night, rattling his chains. They told her he'd been shut up in a hidden chapel and had died screaming, with no one to hear him. I told the poor girl there was no secret chapel and gave her the afternoon off.

When I related the tale to Jane, she shook her head. She said her brother had been Frederick's friend when they were boys and that they had discovered a hidden chapel at Langdon Hall. Frederick had made her brother swear never to reveal the secret but, years later, he had recounted their adventure to Jane.

A secret chapel! But Father had distinctly told me there was no chapel and the priest had escaped out of the window. Why would he wish to hide it? The days of illicit Catholic priests were long gone. Or had Jane's brother been spinning her a yarn? The answer had to be in the diary.

Curiosity, and a desire not to dwell on my miserable marriage, set me to the task of searching for the chapel. I poked around in all the obvious places, the attic and the cupboard under the stairs, and spent several hours examining the panelling, searching for a secret door. Then I had the idea of looking for the deeds of Langdon Hall, hoping there might be an old plan showing the chapel's location. Frederick kept folios of legal papers in his study and that was when I discovered his secret.

I looked up as Daisy brought in a ewer of hot water.

'May I help you dress now, miss?'

'Will you come back in ten minutes?' I said. I couldn't bear to stop reading when a secret was about to be revealed.

Daisy bit her lip. 'Mrs Hope asked me to be quick. She needs me to dust the ladies' retiring room for the ball tonight. And I believe you're supervising the footmen while they clear the drawing-room furniture? They'll start that any minute now.'

Reluctantly, I rose from my bed. 'I'll wear the yellow muslin today, Daisy.'

'Very good, miss. And your white satin ballgown is all ready for you for this evening.' She poured hot water into the wash bowl and laid out the soap and flannel. I barely listened to her chatter as she passed me a towel, stockings and shift while I wondered what it was Mother had found. Might it have been an ancient plan of Langdon Hall or could she have found the chapel itself? I started at a touch on my arm.

'Your shoes, miss.'

I smiled distractedly. 'Sorry, Daisy. I was daydreaming.'

I sat at the dressing table while she brushed my hair. Suppose Mother had discovered the priest's skeleton in the chapel? But although that would have been unpleasant, it wouldn't have inspired such fear.

'Will that be all, miss? Only Mrs Hope is waiting for me.'

I picked up the diary again. Perhaps there was time for another quick look ...

'Miss Langdon? The footmen will have started moving the furniture out of the drawing room by now.'

I sighed. 'I'll come down.' I hid the diary in the chest and followed her from the room.

Mr Gunter's deliverymen slipped on the freshly washed front steps as they delivered the fragile sugar-paste centrepiece. I nearly cried when I saw that one of the elephants' trunks had snapped, two of the trees had crumbled and the gold crown had toppled off the temple.

'We expect the King this evening,' I said, sounding calmer than I felt. 'Will you take the broken pieces back to your workshop for repair and return them here this afternoon?'

The deliverymen looked relieved I hadn't wept and railed at them, and retreated after promising to make all as good as new.

I had no time to fret since the florists were waiting to be told where to place the enormous urns of sweetly scented roses, lilies and peonies, and Cook wanted me to admire the jellies. I hoped they wouldn't melt in the heat.

I attempted to escape during the afternoon, desperate to read more of the diary and discover what Mother had found. I was half-way up the stairs when a footman called after me.

'The musicians are here, Miss Langdon. They want to discuss where they are to perform.'

I suppressed a sigh of irritation. 'Show them into the drawing room, James.'

'And the men from Gunter's are back and need you to approve the remedial works.'

Later, I was in the dining room, inspecting the glasses to be sure they were properly polished, when I heard Father's voice in the hall.

'The supper table is ready for you to see,' I told him.

Father surveyed the room, his critical gaze taking in the bounteous arrangements of fragrant flowers, the gleaming silverware and starched napery. A vast crystal bowl waited to be filled with punch on a side table and the chandelier, holding the best beeswax candles, was twined with wreaths of rosebuds. He stood silently before the sugar-craft construction representing Hyde Park, running down the length of the table.

'You have surpassed yourself, my clever girl.' He put an arm around my shoulders and hugged me, his eyes shining. 'This is truly a supper table fit for the King.'

It unnerved me that Mother's description of Father's violence was in such contrast to his benevolence to me. I rested awkwardly against his broad chest as he smiled down at me. What should have been comforting made me uneasy instead and I wanted to weep, knowing that either my mother or my father was not what they seemed.

'The King will enjoy the ball since he's in unusually good spirits,' said Father. 'The Queen grows sicker by the minute and he's extremely hopeful he'll be released from any awkwardness in that quarter before long.'

'That's a dreadful thing to say!' I pulled myself out of his arms, unable to bear his touch. The Queen's humiliation at the Coronation must have sent her into a spiral of despair and I pitied her. 'I heard she was taken ill at the theatre.'

'Apparently so,' said Father, rubbing his hands together.

His gloating smile sickened me. 'I'm going to rest now,' I said, 'before it's time to put on my finery.' When the ball was over, I decided I would visit the Queen to offer my commiserations.

I hurried upstairs to my bedroom and curled up on the window seat with the diary.

Searching the folios on Frederick's bookcase I found the secret staircase almost by mistake. It smelled dank and mouldy and was too dark to explore further without a light. Fortuitously, there was a candlestick on the bookshelves. Perhaps Frederick keeps it there for exactly this purpose? Harriet was resting so I lit the candle and descended the stairwell.

I gripped the diary tightly, impatient to read on.

I found myself in an underground chamber. Narrow shafts of daylight entered from above, illuminating a magnificent canvas hanging above an altar. I was drawn to it by the vivid colours and arresting composition.

As I passed one of the shafts of light I realised that the whitewashed walls displayed a great number of paintings and drawings. Candle sconces were fixed to the walls at frequent intervals and I lit several. The resulting flickering light illuminated a breathtaking array of works of art. I knew at once that Frederick must have created this secret art gallery hidden in the lost Papist chapel.

I stopped reading. So there *was* a hidden chapel! But why had Father kept it a secret? He was so proud of his art collection and loved to show it off.

I came to three tiny oval frames hanging in a row. Holding the candle closer, I saw images of a dark-haired young woman: full face and two opposing profiles. Her expression was grave but there was the smallest curve to her mouth, which made it look as if she were trying not to laugh. I realised with a jolt of recognition that I had seen the little portraits before. They were Lord Beaufort's stolen miniatures.

I closed my eyes in shock while my heart banged in my chest. I didn't want to believe it but if what Mother had written was the truth, rather than the result of an over-vivid or disordered imagination, the only and inescapable conclusion was that Father was the Picture Frame Thief.

Chapter 31

I forced myself to smile and greet our guests with equanimity and soon the house was full of chattering people. It was hot and the odour of perspiration mingled sickeningly with the powerfully sweet scent of the flower arrangements, like the stench of decay. I watched Father on the other side of the room, acting the genial host. How had he managed to conceal the fact that he was the Picture Frame Thief for all that time? And what must I do about it now that I knew?

Aunt Maude waved at me from the chaperones' corner. 'Are you quite well, dear?' she asked, her expression full of concern. 'You're very pale.'

I smiled brightly. 'Just a little tired. I can see Dolly has just arrived,' I said, 'and Mr Gregory is with him, as usual.'

'They're late,' said Aunt Maude. 'Dolly's usually so punctual. Indeed, that is one of his better points.'

When they appeared Dolly had a face like thunder and Mr Gregory's eyes were red-rimmed.

'Don't let me come between you two lovebirds,' said Mr Gregory in a waspish tone. 'I shall fetch myself a glass of punch while you bill and coo in a corner.' He marched off.

'Have I upset him?' I asked.

'Of course not,' said Dolly tersely. 'We had an argument. He lost more than he can afford at the gaming tables.'

'It's a shame he didn't stay at home then, instead of bringing his bad temper here.' I heard the vinegar in my voice but had matters of more importance to worry about.

Dolly's mouth tightened and he gave me a look of undisguised loathing before following his friend.

Anger washed over me. Why had I agreed to marry Dolly? Sometimes I didn't even like him, and I certainly didn't like his friend who stuck to Dolly's side like a burr. But, of course, the main reason I'd agreed to marry him was because it pleased Father and, in the present circumstances, that was the worst reason of all. I felt thoroughly out of temper with them both.

Mr Sandys clapped his hands and called out that the first dance would begin shortly.

Father and I were to open the ball and he came to lead me to the top of the set. I flinched momentarily from the touch of his hand and, unable to meet his eyes, looked steadfastly over his shoulder.

The first violin struck a chord and we stood, poised to begin. The music shrieked discordantly in my ears and I wanted nothing more than to escape, to be somewhere quiet far away. Somewhere I could walk along the beach listening to the soothing hiss of the sea. Somewhere far away, like Pesaro.

I moved through the dance like an automaton, bending, pirouetting and jumping, coming together with my father and receding again, while all the time I thought about what Mother had written and what Father had said and what I was to do about it.

We reached the end but there was no escape since I was promised to Dolly for the second dance. He appeared distracted, too, and his smile quite as fixed as my own. We exchanged barely a word and it struck me how joyless our relationship was. Could I stand to go through life with this man at my side? But, of course, if I accused

285

Father of being a thief, if I reported him to the authorities, Dolly wouldn't marry me after all. And then I would be alone in the world again, but this time penniless and branded the daughter of a thief.

After what felt like a lifetime, the dance ended and Dolly escorted me off the floor.

Almost immediately, one of Father's friends, a portly man whose name I'd forgotten, stood before me.

'Will you do me the honour of partnering me in the next dance?' he asked.

Since I was the hostess, I was obliged to accept.

Half an hour later my lips were fixed into a rictus smile as the dance finished. I lied to my partner for the eighth time that, of course, he hadn't hurt my toe when he stepped on my foot and that the tear in the hem of my ballgown could easily be mended.

'Always had two left feet,' he chortled, drips of sweat falling from his shining brow. 'Well, that was fun! Haven't danced with a pretty girl for ages. Last chance before you're married, eh? Shall we join the next set, too?'

'I've promised to sit with my aunt for a while,' I said in desperation.

Fanning my flushed face, I backed away and instructed a footman to open the windows wider. I went to the card room to collect two glasses of punch. A cluster of young men stood at one side of the room, laughing uproariously, and I noticed with surprise that Mr Gregory, very pink about the cheeks, was at the centre of the group. He was recounting some tale or other with vivacious hand movements while Dolly looked on with a sour expression.

Aunt Maude glanced up anxiously as I went to sit beside her in the chaperones' corner. 'I wish you'd tell me what has disturbed you so,' she murmured as she took the glass of punch from me.

'Not now,' I whispered, still fanning my overheated face. 'Tomorrow perhaps. Here comes Father.'

He hurried up to us. 'The King will be here imminently,' he said. 'You will be ready to greet him, won't you, Emilia?'

I nodded.

He laughed. 'Don't look so overwhelmed!'

I was more overwhelmed by the thought of what the King would say if I told him I believed my own father was the infamous Picture Frame Thief.

I was expected to take part in every dance and the music was shrill to my ears as I moved through the steps whilst an agonising band of apprehension tightened around my head like an iron maiden. Despite the open windows, the stench of overheated bodies packed closely together was unbearable. It was almost a relief when the King's arrival was announced. The music ceased, the dancing came to an abrupt halt and the assembled company bowed and curtseyed in silence.

'Excuse me,' I whispered to my partner. I hurried to join Father as he welcomed the King.

'Perhaps you remember my daughter, sir?'

I sank into a deep curtsey.

'Indeed I do,' said the King. 'Uncommonly pretty girl.'

The music began again and the dancers resumed their positions.

I rose and smiled at the King. Though dressed in the first stare of fashion with jewelled medals glittering upon his chest, I'd forgotten how very fat he was. Once, he might have been handsome. 'We shall shortly be going in to supper, Your Majesty,' I said. 'Perhaps you would care for some refreshment?'

His small pink mouth curved in a smile. 'Delighted,' he said, and offered me his arm.

Followed by Father and the King's equerries, we made a stately progress through the ballroom. The King stopped to bow stiffly, due to his corsets no doubt, and to exchange a word or two with selected guests. I noticed that sweat beaded his forehead and his nose shone greasily in the heat.

We entered the dining room and the footmen sprang to attention.

'I dare to hope you will like the centrepiece for our supper table, sir,' I said. 'Since the Coronation Fête in Hyde Park was such a success, I took the liberty of having the scene recreated in sugar as a tribute to the occasion.'

Amused, the King peered closely at the scene. 'Splendid!' he said, mopping his face with a handkerchief. 'The elephants are particularly fine.'

I held my breath, wondering if he'd notice where the trunk had been mended, but he'd already lost interest.

I stepped away as Father moved in to flatter and encourage our sovereign to taste some of the array of cold meats, soups and jellies. I was relieved to note that the jellies hadn't collapsed in the heat.

The guests began to arrive for their supper and a glimpse of the King. Before long the buzz of conversation and laughter was so loud it was hard to hear what was being said.

Dolly came to sit beside me to eat his supper but was so morose I didn't exchange more than two words with him. His gaze was directed over my shoulder to where Mr Gregory, clearly in his cups, was laughing with an elderly dandy.

After supper we returned to the ballroom where an Italian opera singer waited to entertain us. The King appeared to enjoy the performance, perhaps for the singer's voluptuous bosom quite as much as her musical skills. Whilst it was a pleasure for me to listen to the lyrical cadences of the Italian language again, the singer's high notes sliced into my head like a sharp nail scraped down glass.

The King took his leave after the singer had finished her rendition and the dancing began again. I was much in demand as a partner, not only as the hostess but because my guests were eager to know about my conversation with the King. Several told me how much they were looking forward to the wedding breakfast at Langdon Hall. The band of worry around my head grew even tighter and I counted the minutes until everyone would leave.

Two hours later I was exhausted, not only from the energetic country dances and the excessive heat but from smiling and remaining polite when all I wanted to do was lie down in a darkened room while I decided what to do about Father. At the end of the next set I slipped out of the ballroom and made my way downstairs and into the garden. I paused in the doorway until my eyes became accustomed to the dark. My kid slippers made little noise on the path as I walked past the apple tree to the bench under the rose arbour. Careful of my dress, I brushed leaves off the bench and sat down with a relieved sigh.

The air was still very warm but infinitely cooler than inside the house with the heat generated by sixty guests and hundreds of candles. Music, light and high-pitched laughter spilled from every window. I breathed deeply, inhaling the perfume of the roses that almost overpowered the usual summer reek of city drains.

As I was about to return to the ball, a shaft of light fell across the garden as the door opened. I heard male voices. I looked through the trelliswork of the arbour and saw two men silhouetted against the doorway. They spoke in an angry undertone, too low for me to hear but I realised it was Dolly and Francis continuing their argument.

Dolly placed a hand on his friend's shoulder.

Francis pressed his hands over his ears. 'No!' he said, and ran down the garden towards me.

Dolly called out, 'Francis!' and ran after him, catching him by his coat sleeve as they reached the apple tree not eight feet away from the arbour.

I shrank back in the darkness, peeping at them through the trellis.

Dolly gripped the shorter man by his upper arms and shook him. 'Stop this!' he said. 'It's no good. I don't have any choice.'

Francis muttered something and struggled to free himself.

'I've told you, it's the only way out,' said Dolly, his voice pleading. 'You know I haven't a feather to fly with and this marriage will change all that.'

'I hate her!'

'Don't. She's nothing to me.' Dolly wiped tears from Francis's eyes. He glanced around, then bent to kiss him.

I pressed my fist to my mouth to stifle a gasp. It was absolutely clear to me that this was a passionate kiss between lovers.

Francis wound his arms around Dolly's neck and they fell back against the trunk of the apple tree, their bodies locked together.

When they finally drew apart Dolly tenderly smoothed back a lock of Francis's hair. 'There was only ever you,' he said. 'Nothing and no one will change that. Later, when it's all over, we'll go away together. Just the two of us.'

Shivering with shock, I pulled my feet up onto the bench, accidentally knocking over a plant pot. It tipped and fell with a dull thud onto the path. I curled myself into a ball and my hair snagged painfully on the climbing rose.

'What was that?' said Francis.

I held my breath.

'Nothing of importance,' said Dolly after a moment. 'A fox or a cat, perhaps.'

Francis nodded and the two men kissed again and returned to the house.

Trembling, I untangled my hair from the prickly stem of the rose. So much was explained now. Of course Dolly didn't love me! He never had and never would. His taste lay in another direction entirely. I leaned back against the trellis feeling the tears seeping from beneath my eyelids. How could I bear this terrible discovery so soon after the other?

I don't remember how I endured the last hours of the ball. Dolly partnered me in the final dance and I flinched away from him when he touched my hair.

'Whatever is the matter, Emilia?' he said, frowning. 'You're not going to faint?'

290

'Of course not,' I said and forced a smile. 'I'm simply a little tired after all the preparation for the ball.'

He didn't speak after that while we danced, his thoughts clearly elsewhere.

I was relieved to be spared having to make polite conversation while I dwelled on what I'd seen in the garden.

Thankfully, the guests finally left. When it came to saying good-night to Dolly, I became rigid when he pecked my cheek.

At last only Father and Aunt Maude remained.

'You must go straight to bed,' I said to Aunt Maude. 'It's very late for you.'

'I will, dear,' she said. 'We'll talk in the morning,' she whispered. 'Goodnight, Frederick.' She leaned heavily on her stick and looked very frail as she slowly mounted the stairs.

'You will be pleased to hear,' said Father, rubbing his hands together in delight, 'that I managed to have a word with the King regarding my contacts in the art world. He said he'll call on me next time he's looking for a particular piece.'

'So the ball achieved its purpose,' I said, knowing that the King would never buy anything from my Father if I exposed him as a thief.

Benevolent in his triumph, he kissed my cheek. 'You've earned a day of rest tomorrow, my dear.'

I said goodnight and retreated to my bedroom.

Bone-weary, I allowed Daisy to undress me and slip a fresh night-gown over my head. I slid in between the sheets and once Daisy had closed the door behind her, I pinched out the candle. I couldn't bear any more heartache and reading the rest of Mother's diary would have to wait until the morning.

Confused and miserable, I felt under the pillow until my fingers found Peggy's woolly plaits. Hugging her against my chest, just as I had so many times as a child, I curled into a ball and shut out the world.

Chapter 32

Sleep had come quickly to me but I awoke before dawn and relived, over and over again, the passionate embrace between Dolly and Francis. As the sun rose, I tried to understand my disturbed feelings. Occasionally I'd overheard people talk of love affairs between men, in hushed and scandalised whispers, but I'd never seen any evidence of it before. Such a thing upset the natural order of life and bewildered me quite as much as if I'd discovered water flowing uphill.

One thing was certain now, though. I could not and would not marry Dolly. I had never deluded myself that I loved him, it was only his declaration of love that had allowed me to believe there was a chance of making a marriage between us successful. In the light of what I'd seen, Francis would always occupy the first place in his heart and Dolly and I could never have a true marriage.

I pulled myself up against the pillows, thinking about Alessandro's accusation that Dolly had caused Sarah's death. Supposing this was right, what possible reason could he have had? I rubbed my fists against my eyes, trying, and failing, to comprehend. Deep regret for the happiness Alessandro and I might have shared if I'd never left Pesaro nearly choked me.

I slid out of bed and opened the curtains before padding barefoot to the wardrobe to lift the muslin cover from my wedding dress. It was made of the finest ivory silk with a ravishing guipure lace bodice and train but I shuddered when I looked at it. I'd never wear it now. Closing the wardrobe door, I went to the writing desk and took out a fresh sheet of paper to write to Alessandro.

Fifteen minutes later I blotted the ink dry, folded the note and sealed it. Two sheets of crumpled paper lay by my feet, the ink smudged from my tears. I gathered them up and stuffed them into my reticule to dispose of later. I had no intention of allowing them to fall into Father's hands.

My eyes were gritty from lack of sleep and I rubbed them as I pondered again on what I was to do about Father. If he was the Picture Frame Thief and I made this known, disgrace and ruin would fall on us all. I wasn't sure if I was brave enough to face that. If I was, the future for Aunt Maude and myself appeared very bleak.

Sighing, I took Mother's diary out of the chest, hoping it would shed more light on the mystery.

I've barely slept for worrying about what to do. Harriet climbed onto my knee to kiss away my tears and brought me Annabelle to cuddle. I love my daughter beyond life itself. Whatever I do, I must keep her safe.

Mother's dilemma had been similar to my own. Her words didn't sound like those of a woman who was prepared to abandon her own child and there was still no indication she'd had a lover. If that were true, I couldn't understand why she had drowned herself.

Harriet and I return to Grosvenor Street today and I have made a momentous decision. I am going to ask Frederick to agree to a legal separation. He won't like it but he must see that we are both so unhappy this cannot go on. My very existence irritates him and he lashes out at the smallest thing. I rarely dare to initiate conversation and creep about the house trying not to attract his violent attentions. I have written to my old friend Anne-Marie in Paris. When she last came to London, after Piers died, she noticed my bruises and promised that

Harriet and I would always have a home with her if we needed it. And now we do.

I rested the diary on my knee. So Mother's friend in Paris wasn't a lover and Father had lied to me.

I have taken the miniatures. Frederick is unlikely to visit Langdon Hall for a while and won't know they are missing. I shall return them to Lord Beaufort on my way to Paris and leave it to him to decide what to do about Frederick.

Mother hadn't intended to steal the miniatures herself, then, but had packed them in the luggage that Sarah later conveyed to the inn at Dover. I turned back to the diary and saw that a week had passed before the next entry.

My mistake was to believe Frederick would ever be reasonable. He became a madman when I asked for a separation. Only now can I hold a pen again. He has locked me in my room. It would be too shaming for him if anyone saw my terrible bruises. The beating was severe and I heard my fingers and ribs crack. It's still hard for me to breathe and he will not let me see Harriet. We must escape.

Shocked, I reread the passage. My inclination was to believe Mother's account but I couldn't help remembering Father's distress when he'd told me of her apparent infidelity. I rested my head in my hands, wondering if he could have been so cold-bloodedly deceitful.

The diary was nearly at an end and I gripped it tightly as I read on. There were a few entries about Mother's anguish at not being allowed to see me and then, this final paragraph:

It will be tonight. Sarah will give Miss McCorquodale a sleeping draught and fetch Harriet to come with us. I pray that by this time tomorrow we will be free.

The remaining pages were blank. If what Father had told me was true, he'd caught her trying to escape and sat up with her all night. In the morning, after he'd left, she'd escaped and drowned herself. Despair must have driven her to take her own life, knowing Sarah would take me to safety abroad and that Father would never let her go. I ached with pity for my mother. Carefully, I wrapped the diary in a clean shift and hid it again at the bottom of my chest underneath Sarah's quilted petticoat.

Father had abandoned his newspaper on the breakfast table before going out. I read the latest account of the Queen's ill health and was sad to see that she was worse.

While I was reading, Aunt Maude came downstairs. 'What happened last night to upset you?' she asked.

I glanced over my shoulder as James carried in a fresh pot of coffee. 'I wondered if you'd like a ride in the country this morning. To Fulham perhaps?'

Aunt Maude gave me a sharp look. 'That would be very pleasant, dear.'

Half an hour later we were in the carriage. I had asked Dobson the coachman to stop in Great Marlborough Street at the house where Alessandro worked. The butler informed me that Signor Fiorelli was not at home but had taken the young masters out for their morning walk. Reluctantly, I entrusted my note for Alessandro to the butler and returned to the carriage.

'The Queen is very unwell,' I said to Aunt Maude as we set off for Fulham, 'and I want to offer my best wishes for her recovery.'

'I assumed that was the reason for this visit.'

I nodded. 'And I must tell you what I read in Mother's diary. I thought we wouldn't be overheard in the carriage.'

'Perhaps not,' she said, 'but Dobson may report back to your father where we go today.'

'Father has no reason to suspect I've read the diary so I don't believe he'll be spying on me,' I said, 'but I've discovered some terrible things and I don't know what action to take. If the Queen is going to return to Pesaro once she recovers, then I may need to ask her if she'll make room for me in her retinue.'

Aunt Maude pressed a hand to her mouth, her rheumy eyes wide and anxious. 'You're not leaving? But what about your wedding? It's only three weeks away.'

'My discoveries have changed everything,' I said. 'I cannot and will not marry Dolly now. And then there is what I've found out about Father.'

'I *knew* something had happened last night!'

Once I had recounted my story, Aunt Maude shook her head in dismay. I was relieved she'd understood the particular nature of the friendship between Dolly and Francis and I hadn't had to embarrass myself or her by being too explicit.

'You can't possibly marry him now,' she said, her mouth pinched with distaste, 'unless you believe you can use all your womanly wiles to make him suppress his unnatural impulses?'

'Aunt Maude, I saw how tender he was with Francis,' I said. 'I think he really loves him and, even if I wanted to, I don't imagine any woman could seduce Dolly.'

'That sort of behaviour is against the law,' she said, 'but I suppose it does explain why Dolly wasn't more in love with you. I couldn't understand it. You're so pretty and clever, any man should be proud to be your husband.'

'Dolly is very handsome but I didn't fall in love with *him*,' I pointed out.

'I'm bewildered as to why he proposed to you in the first place.'

I gave a wry smile at the thought that he most probably hadn't wanted this wedding either. 'Perhaps because society expects him to have a wife and then he'll be free to continue his association with Francis.'

'When will you break the news that the wedding is not to go ahead?' Aunt Maude asked. 'There will be terrible ructions. Your father ...'

'I daren't say anything yet,' I said. 'To be absolutely sure of the truth about Father, I must go to Langdon Hall and find the hidden gallery. If I call off the wedding now, after what I've read in Mother's diary, I don't trust Father not to imprison me in my room. Without proof that the chapel exists, I'm sure he would laugh off Mother's diary entry as the wanderings of a disturbed mind. Once I have proof, I can report it to the local magistrate.'

'And what will happen to us afterwards?' said Aunt Maude. Her lower lip trembled.

'I don't know,' I said. I felt as if a deep pit had opened at our feet. I was young and could work as a dressmaker; Aunt Maude had no such reserves to fall back on and I wasn't confident I could earn enough to keep us both. 'If the Queen doesn't take us with her, I suppose I might find someone to marry who would give us both a home.' I rubbed my eyes. 'Or, of course, I could blackmail Father.'

'Emilia!' said Aunt Maude, shocked. 'Although he's my nephew,' she said, 'and I've tried very hard, I cannot care for Frederick. At best, he's two-faced and self-serving.' She leaned towards me. 'It makes perfect sense to me that he is the person who stole all those pictures but, if you did blackmail him, I wouldn't trust him to keep any bargain that is not to his own advantage.'

'Do you believe that what Mother wrote in her diary was true?' I asked.

'I should like to read the diary, if I may, but I have no reason to doubt Rose's account.' My great-aunt looked close to tears. 'When you came to Grosvenor Street it was as if Rose had returned to me. I was so frightened for you and did everything I could to make you feel unwelcome. I wanted to drive you away.'

'I remember,' I said.

'It was to protect you. Frederick is unreliable, perhaps even dangerous if he doesn't get his own way. I believed ... still believe ... he wanted you back only to serve his own ends, whatever they may be.'

I thought about this as the carriage jogged through the streets. 'He had two reasons for encouraging me to stay,' I said. 'Firstly, I'm the most recent lead he has to the miniatures. I'd already guessed that but thought his reasons were altruistic and he wished to return them to Lord Beaufort. Having read Mother's diary, now I think he wants to keep them himself.'

'Surely, if they are found, he must know you would want them to be returned to their rightful owner?'

I shrugged. 'Perhaps he thinks he can tell me they have been returned but then keep them in his secret gallery. Or maybe, because he knows I'm interested in art, he believes he can persuade me to share his illicit pleasure in them.'

Aunt Maude sighed. 'And what do you think is his other reason for wanting you to stay?'

'He's never liked Dolly very much but, since it's not possible to change the entail, at least Langdon Hall would stay within his direct bloodline if I had children with Dolly.' I smiled briefly. 'Perhaps he hasn't realised that his heir might not care to give him a grandson since his proclivities lie elsewhere.'

Aunt Maude reached for my hand and we spoke no more until the carriage drew up outside Brandenburgh House.

The steward told us that the Queen was indisposed and I asked if we might speak instead to Lady Hamilton. A few moments later she came downstairs to receive us.

'We came to pay our respects to the Queen, Lady Hamilton,' I told her, 'but we understand that she is still unwell?'

'She is,' said Lady Hamilton. Her eyes were deeply shadowed and her fingers plucked anxiously at her skirt. 'Dr Holland is with her now. She has a great deal of pain in her stomach and, despite being bled and taking heavy doses of magnesia and laudanum, can find no relief.'

'I am sorry to hear that.'

'Her spirits are very low,' said Lady Hamilton, 'and I'm terribly afraid she has lost the will to recover.'

'I was outside Westminster Abbey when she was so shamefully turned away,' I said. 'I daresay that affected her greatly?'

Tears made Lady Hamilton's eyes glitter. 'She shut herself in her bedroom for four hours afterwards and would speak to no one. Then, at supper, she put on the semblance of unusual gaiety but, however hard she tried to hide her distress from her friends, she deceived only herself. Tears of anguish rolled down her face, even as she laughed and joked.' Lady Hamilton was unable to say more while she struggled to regain her customary control.

'She has a good friend in you, Lady Hamilton,' I said, 'and she'll be relieved that you are at her side to support her.'

'The Queen has made her will and I fear …' Lady Hamilton broke down again. 'I don't know how to ease her grief!'

'Please convey to her our sincere best wishes,' I said, at a loss for what else to say.

'Pray for her, won't you?'

'We will.'

Lady Hamilton nodded without saying more and Aunt Maude and I left.

The following days passed quietly. Aunt Maude and I sat in the morning room while she read Mother's diary. Frequently she would stop to wipe her eyes and we discussed particular passages in an undertone.

'Aunt Maude,' I said, 'I've been wondering about something.'

She closed the diary, marking the place with a piece of silk ribbon. 'What is it, my dear?'

'Something occurred to me and I can't get it out of my head.' I swallowed. 'Do you think it possible that Father drowned my mother?'

Aunt Maude bowed her head over the diary and then looked up at me, her expression bleak. 'I'm very much afraid I do.'

I nodded and returned to my confused and wretched thoughts. All the while I listened for the doorknocker, hoping there might be a response from Alessandro to my note. I sat by the morning-room window for hours at a time, in case he was outside, trying to catch my attention, but as the days passed without word from him, I finally lost hope of any reconciliation.

At breakfast one morning Father picked up the newspaper James had placed beside him. Then he banged his cup down on the table, slopping coffee onto the starched tablecloth, and laughed. 'At last!' he said.

I mopped the stain with my napkin. 'What is it, Father?'

'She's dead! The King is free at last!'

The jubilation in his expression made my stomach turn over. 'The Queen is dead?'

Aunt Maude gasped.

'Isn't that what I said? Listen to this!' Father rustled the paper and began to read aloud.

'The Queen had suffered terrible pain all the previous day. Dr Holland, who was attending her, felt her pulse at twenty-five minutes past ten at night and then closed her eyelids. He declared, "All is over."'

'Thank God,' said Father, his face wreathed in smiles. 'Now there'll be celebrations in certain quarters.'

'How can you be so cruel?' I said.

'For goodness' sake, Emilia!' He frowned at me and rose to his feet. 'It's time you saw the truth about that woman.'

I stood up, clenching my fists in fury. 'You don't know the first thing about her.'

He strode from the room and slammed the door behind him.

I shed tears for the Queen's turbulent and misunderstood life, reliving those moments when our paths had crossed in Pesaro. I remembered her kindness when Sarah died and how she'd taken a fancy to me when I'd comforted her after she spoke of her daughter's death. I remembered her romping on the floor with Victorine and that perfect, sunny day when Alessandro and I had joined her for a picnic on her yacht. She may have been anathema to her husband and much of society but I had seen another side of her character. All she'd wanted was to be loved for herself. I supposed that was no different from what most people wanted, myself included.

Chapter 33

On the morning of Queen Caroline's funeral a week later I looked out of the window to see grey skies and rain. I still hadn't heard anything from Alessandro. I'd hoped desperately we might have made a fresh start together and I tried not to think about how empty my life would be as the last vestiges of that dream faded.

Daisy came to help me dress and I defiantly chose to put on my old mourning gown as a mark of respect for the Queen, despite what Father would say.

'Mr Soames says half the shops and businesses will be shut today,' said Daisy as she buttoned my cuffs. 'And a crowd's already gathered at Hyde Park Corner, waiting in the rain to follow the funeral procession.'

'I understood the Prime Minister had insisted on sending the procession north of the city?'

'That's as may be,' said Daisy, 'but the people want to say goodbye before her body is returned to Brunswick. They won't put up with the procession being hurried out of sight.' She nodded with satisfaction. 'They'll block the road if Lord Liverpool tries to send the procession north.'

I reflected on how fickle the populace was. They had abandoned the Queen during the Coronation and, now she was dead, wanted to show their support again.

After my maid had gone, I sank down on the window seat and miserably watched raindrops running down the glass. Aunt Maude had finished reading Mother's diary and agreed with me that nothing could be done until we knew for sure that the secret gallery existed and that it contained stolen paintings. We would all travel to Langdon Hall the day after tomorrow since the wedding was set for ten days' time. It made me queasy with anxiety to contemplate not only calling that off but also telling the authorities about Father. And then what would Aunt Maude and I do? I had some money saved from my allowance but it wouldn't keep us for long.

One good thing had come out of the bad. I was now sure my mother had loved me. I took the diary from its hiding place under Sarah's quilted petticoat, to comfort myself by rereading Mother's loving words.

A while later, I tucked the diary under the petticoat again. I'd given the residue of the gold coins to Father to keep in his safe. I wondered how long Sarah had kept them concealed. If I knew that, I might be able to work out in which town she'd sold the miniatures and then be able to trace them. Of course, she might have sold them one by one as we had need of the money. Hurriedly I ran my fingers all over the petticoat, double checking each coin pocket. Nothing. Sighing, I replaced the petticoat in the chest and went downstairs.

Father was in the dining room finishing his breakfast. 'I shall be out until early evening, Emilia,' he said. 'I'm going to Kingston to view an auction of Dutch paintings. I expect to purchase an addition to my collection and we shall take it with us when we go to Langdon Hall.' He rubbed his hands together. 'And the happy day of your wedding is fast approaching now. You will have final arrangements to make.'

'I plan to do all that is necessary,' I said, non-committally.

302

'I must leave now if I'm not to be late. The roads are likely to be congested with that wretched woman's funeral procession.'

'My maid tells me that crowds have turned out to pay their respects to the Queen.'

'You see, she's still causing trouble even after her death,' said Father. 'Is that why you're all dressed up in black like a crow this morning?'

I lifted my chin and gave him a defiant look. 'She was kind to me,' I said.

He frowned. 'You know nothing about what she was really like.'

'On the contrary,' I said, 'I lived in her household and probably know her a great deal better than most, including you.'

Father pushed back his chair abruptly. 'I'm not going to argue with you and make myself late.'

I sighed in relief when the front door banged behind him. Since Aunt Maude hadn't come downstairs I went to tap on her bedroom door.

She lay back against the pillows with her white hair in a thin plait over one shoulder. 'Are you unwell?' I asked, distressed to see her like this.

She shrugged. 'I feel very old today,' she said. Her bony fingers plucked at the sheet. 'My heart flutters so.'

'May I bring you something?'

'I was thinking about dear Rose,' she said. 'I keep wondering if there was something I could have done to save her.'

'You cannot blame yourself for what happened.'

She turned towards me, her milky blue eyes full of anxiety. 'You must be careful, Emilia. Your father is unpredictable.'

I enfolded her trembling hand in mine. 'Having read Mother's diary I'm forewarned of how quickly his mood can turn,' I said. 'But I must find out the truth about the hidden gallery.'

'And what then?'

'Once I tell Father I have no intention of proceeding with the wedding I suspect he'll attempt to coerce me into marrying Dolly.

303

As for what action to take over the stolen paintings . . . ' I sighed. 'I don't know yet. Will you be well enough to travel to Langdon?'

Aunt Maude nodded.

'There's something I must do today,' I said. 'I shall pay my last respects to the Queen when her funeral procession passes on its way to Harwich. Her body is to be conveyed to Brunswick for burial.'

'You can't go out alone, Emilia!'

'Perhaps I'll take Daisy.' I had no intention of doing any such thing. 'I shouldn't be longer than an hour or two. In my ancient travelling cloak, no one will take me for a lady.'

'If you really must go, come and see me as soon as you return.'

'I will.' I kissed her forehead. 'Rest now.'

I went to my room to fetch my cloak. It was at the back of the wardrobe as I hadn't used it since Father had provided me with clothes suitable to my position as his daughter. My fingers brushed against my old travelling bag and something occurred to me. I dragged the bag out of the back of the wardrobe and then delved in it again to find Sarah's bag. One after the other I turned them inside out. I fetched the embroidery scissors from my work basket and ripped open the seams in the linings. Quickly, I searched between the lining and the scarred and worn leather of each bag, hoping there might be a hidden pocket for the miniatures, but there was nothing. Sighing, I returned them to the wardrobe.

As I was tying the ribbons of my cloak, I paused. Where else might Sarah have hidden the miniatures? It must have been in something we always carried with us, somewhere that no one would think of looking. Slowly, I turned to face the bed. Peggy, faithful companion of my childhood, lay on my pillow, her familiar woollen smile still slightly crooked. I squeezed her but she was so well stuffed that her body was hard. I unbuttoned her dress and reached for my scissors.

I hesitated, finding it difficult to cut open my old friend, then carefully snipped the stitches down her calico back. Pulling out the stuffing I recognised the shredded fabrics, each one reminding me of one of our commissions: Signora Donati's afternoon dress, Maria Lagorio's first Holy Communion dress, my own lawn shift, the Conti bride's wedding dress … I fingered the white silk gauze. I hadn't restuffed Peggy for years and the Conti wedding had been in Florence shortly before we arrived in Pesaro. Could Sarah have put those scraps inside Peggy more recently? I dug my fingers more deeply inside the cavity. And then I found it. A small silk bag. I teased apart the drawstring. Catching my breath, I extracted an exquisitely painted miniature portrait in an oval gold frame. The Spanish Infanta.

I stared at it in horrified fascination. Had I carried the priceless miniatures around with me everywhere I went? I remembered Sarah being sharp with me once or twice when I was a child when I'd nearly left Peggy behind. And, more recently, I'd forgotten all about the doll and left her with Victorine when I came to London. Sarah had used me, an innocent child, to conceal stolen goods. I could only assume she had sold the other two miniatures and that accounted for the gold coins in her petticoat. A bubble of hysteria welled up inside me and I hugged the remnants of the doll against me and laughed and laughed until I cried.

Once I'd recovered my equilibrium, I replaced the miniature, restuffed Peggy and sewed up the seam. I left the doll in her usual place on my pillow and went to see Aunt Maude again.

When I told her of my discovery, she pressed her fingers to her breast, her expression horrified.

'I wanted you to know where the miniature is hidden,' I said. 'It's a precautionary measure, to give you some proof to take to the authorities if anything should happen to me.'

Aunt Maude gripped my wrist. 'We cannot let it! I couldn't bear that.'

'Don't worry,' I said. 'I'm going to see the funeral procession now before it's too late but I shan't be very long.'

She nodded, her eyes wide and troubled.

I kissed her cheek and hurried downstairs.

The hall clock struck eleven. I waited until there were no servants in the hall and then let myself out of the front door. It was raining, that fine but persistent drizzle that always finds a way to trickle down your neck inside your collar. I pulled down the brim of my bonnet and scurried down Grosvenor Street towards Hyde Park.

A moment later I heard running footsteps from behind and then someone caught my sleeve. I gasped and whirled around, thinking it was a pickpocket. Shock made me stumble. 'Alessandro!'

He gripped hold of my hands. 'I didn't mean to frighten you.' The shoulders of his coat were dark, saturated with the rain, and his curly hair plastered to his head.

The flash of joy I'd felt on seeing him was mixed with disbelief. 'But what are you doing here?'

'You didn't answer my letter,' he said, 'and I've been loitering outside all morning hoping to catch you. I thought you might want to see the Queen's funeral procession.'

'I do.' I frowned. '*Your* letter? I wrote you a letter but you didn't reply.'

'Yes, I did.' His expression was grim. 'I gave it to your footman. It must have been intercepted. And it's not the first time, either.'

Anger seethed in my breast. 'My father must have taken them. He admitted he'd taken your earlier letters.'

A group of pedestrians jostled us as they hurried past.

'There's no time to talk now,' said Alessandro. 'Let's walk towards Hyde Park Corner, we should see the procession there.' He turned up his coat collar against the downpour, took my arm and set off at a brisk pace.

I splashed along beside him, my shoes sodden from the puddles.

He didn't slow his pace as we crossed Grosvenor Square and turned into Upper Grosvenor Street. Already we could hear the noisy crowd ahead.

'Hurry or we'll miss the procession. Afterwards we'll talk.'

As we neared Hyde Park the streets were crammed with pedestrians. We turned into Park Lane and Alessandro took a fierce grip on my wrist as we were swept along with the boisterous crowd making its way towards Hyde Park Corner.

People of all classes had turned out to follow the procession. Many wore mourning dress whilst others had tied on black armbands or waved batons with a flutter of black crepe at the tip. Men on horseback and numerous carts and carriages edged forwards amongst the horde, bringing howls of abuse from those who had their toes run over.

Wagons had been set across the street to form a barricade and the hubbub of the crowd echoed all around. The throng pressed so close around us I was fearful I'd lose my footing. I was relieved to have Alessandro hold my hand so firmly and didn't want ever to let him go. Ahead, men carried banners and shouted out repetitively but the hum of the multitude was too great for me to hear what they were chanting.

I turned to a man beside me, tightly pressed against my arm as we shuffled along. 'What's happening?' I asked. 'Is the funeral procession nearby?'

'It was stopped at Kensington about half past nine,' he said, wiping rain off his face. 'Lord Liverpool wanted it to go past the gravel pits and up northwards.' He grinned. 'But the people weren't having it and blockaded the road with wagons. Carts and carriages piled up behind and the procession couldn't go neither forward nor back.'

The horde ahead of us in the park began to chant, 'Through the city! Through the city!'

'Sounds as if the procession's on the move again,' said the man. 'There was talk last night of bolting the park gates so it couldn't cut through there and go up New Road.'

After a while we reached Hyde Park Corner and discovered a contingent of mounted Life Guards waiting there. Some of the mob shouted insults at them and an apple core sailed over their heads to resounding laughter from the spectators. All the while the Life Guards, resplendent in their scarlet and gold uniforms, stared straight ahead, ignoring the rain and the affronts to their dignity.

'I can't see that it's possible for the procession to make its way through so many people or the barricades,' said Alessandro.

By now we were near the gates to the park and pressed flat against the railings. 'The poor Queen!' I said. 'Even in death nothing is straightforward for her, but she would have been pleased the people turned out to support her at the end.'

A boy perched on his father's shoulders shouted, 'They're coming! They're coming along Knightsbridge.'

I peered along the road and through the haze of rain saw only the crush of people, men on horseback and a line of gigs and barouches along the side of the carriageway.

There was a muttering in the crowd and a few men climbed onto the gates for a better view. A ragged cheer rose, swelling to a roar as a dozen soldiers on horseback appeared, riding two by two, along Knightsbridge. All the while, rain continued to fall from the leaden sky.

The progress of the cavalcade was slow. At last the soldiers drew level with us and then passed, followed by three mourning coaches, each drawn by six black horses and interspersed with eight marshals riding in pairs, a troop of mounted soldiers and a dozen pages in black cloaks and headbands.

'Here comes the hearse,' said Alessandro. Like most men around us, he took off his hat and bowed his head.

The people fell silent as the Queen's hearse, decorated with the Royal Arms and drawn by eight matched horses with black plumes on their heads, trundled slowly forward, led by black-clad mutes.

Tears sprang to my eyes as I imagined the Queen inside her coffin, cold, lifeless and alone, wrapped in a shroud, hands folded across her breast. I preferred to picture her slightly crooked smile and the love in her eyes as she'd dandled Victorine on her knee.

A woman shouted out, 'God bless Queen Caroline!' and the cry was taken up by others until it became a resounding chorus. I joined in wholeheartedly, my tears mingling with the rain.

Alessandro reached for my hand and I grasped his as another four mourning coaches, a trumpeter blowing a mournful salute, various sodden dignitaries on foot and eighteen mounted soldiers passed by. I wasn't sure, but I believed I saw Lady Hamilton and Willy Austin at the window of one of the coaches.

'The Queen always faced her enemies so bravely,' said Alessandro, wiping his eyes. 'I shall miss her. Little Victorine will be inconsolable.'

The funeral procession jerked to a sudden halt. Angry shouts came from the front.

'What's happening?' I asked.

'I can't see,' said Alessandro as the muttering of the crowd grew louder.

A man balanced on top of the park gates yelled out, 'They're coming back!'

The cavalcade slowly turned around, carriage by carriage, and headed towards the gates again.

'Perhaps there were too many people for the procession to push through without injuring someone,' said Alessandro. He stood on tiptoe, peering ahead, while I glanced at the familiar lines of his firm jaw and high cheekbones. I longed to reach up and touch his face.

The crowd surged through the gates before the cavalcade reached it. There were yells as the press of people from behind propelled us forward and I struggled to stay upright, frightened we'd be crushed underfoot.

Alessandro's hand, wet with rain, slipped from mine as I was dragged away from him. A moment of pure panic washed over me when I was lifted up as if by a tidal wave. Just as suddenly I was deposited on the ground again as the crowd shoved through the park gates and we came out on the other side like a cork popping from a bottle. I hurried to a patch of open grass. Men and women ran past and a child shrieked without stopping. I looked wildly around for Alessandro.

'Emilia!'

I heard his shout and spun around to see him hurrying towards me.

He caught me to his chest, his face full of consternation. 'Are you hurt?'

I shook my head, showering him with raindrops from my bonnet.

'This country!' he said, making a face of disgust. 'Does it ever stop raining? Let's move out of the way until the crowd thins and then I'll escort you home.'

We stood back, seeking shelter from the rain under an oak tree, though I was already wet through to my shift. The procession moved slowly by, going north along the carriageway running parallel to Park Lane.

A mass of people ran past and a man on horseback cantered by, yelling, 'To Cumberland Gate! Stop the procession at Cumberland Gate!'

The rain abated a little and I pulled at Alessandro's hand. 'Let's see what's going on.' We walked briskly alongside the procession.

Hoarse shouts of, 'Through the city!' and 'Shut Cumberland Gate!' came from all sides as the seething multitude rushed towards the north side of the park.

The funeral cavalcade began to move faster and we ran to keep abreast as it proceeded at an unseemly pace towards Cumberland Gate.

The Guards galloped past, their horses' hooves kicking up clods of turf behind them and spattering the spectators with mud. In turn spectators threw stones at the soldiers' backs. A horse squealed and reared up, its forelegs flailing, terrifying those who couldn't move away fast enough.

With their feet slipping on the muddy ground, some men laboured to grip hold of the soldiers' mounts and wrestled with their bridles to make them halt. Others clung on to the Queen's hearse, knocking down the mutes and turning the terrified horses around yet again so that the cavalcade was facing in the direction of the city.

There was a crack of thunder and the heavens yawned. All around us bellowing men and soldiers brawled in the torrential rain. The mob rocked the mourning coaches and dragged the soldiers off their whinnying horses.

A shot rang out.

The crowd went silent for a fraction of a second and then roared in anger.

More soldiers galloped into the park from the nearby barracks, shouting, 'Clear the way!'

I caught my breath in fright as a great brute of a grey brushed my arm when it raced past. The smell of sweating horseflesh hung in the air after it had gone.

The soldiers let out another round of shots and Alessandro shouted, 'Let's go!'

Women screamed and then all descended into chaos. People ran in all directions, slipping and falling in the mud, desperate to get away as more shots echoed through the air. A man yelled and I was knocked down to the muddy grass and trampled in the rush.

Winded, I pulled myself into a sitting position as booted feet raced past. A horse pranced on the spot, inches away from my face. Terrified, I looked up at the underside of its belly while I heaved for breath. A deafening volley of shots rang out overhead. The horse galloped away and people all around me screamed and shrieked.

I crawled on all fours through the mud to find a place of safety but my cape and skirt were tangled around my legs. My bonnet was lost somewhere and my hair fell over my face in sodden strands. Yelling soldiers on horseback milled amongst the scattered crowd, carbines and pistols at the ready. I looked around for Alessandro amongst the confusion but couldn't see him.

Horrified, I saw a man on the ground thrashing about in agony as his companions attempted to staunch the blood gushing from his thigh. A little way off a woman sat on the ground comforting a fallen man. Blood ran from his head.

My breath was catching in my breast but fear gave me the strength to push myself to my feet. Shaking, I leaned against a tree and scanned the crowd in desperation while I prayed under my breath. And then I saw him.

'Alessandro!' I screamed. Pushing my way through the milling crowd, I fell to my knees at his side. He was slumped on the ground against the park railings, his eyes closed and his coat front scarlet. Sobbing, I cradled him in my arms while terror froze the blood in my veins.

Chapter 34

The kitchen in Great Marlborough Street was clean and dry and smelled of the comforting aroma of the apple pie cooling on the scrubbed pine table. The cook, a monstrously fat woman stuffed into a clean apron, stood watching me with her hands on her hips. 'He'll do,' she said, as I finished winding the bandage around Alessandro's upper arm and tied the end in a knot.

The wound would leave an ugly scar and it made me want to weep to see Alessandro's beautiful smooth skin damaged. But it might have been so much worse.

'It's only a graze,' he murmured, though his face was alarmingly white.

'A deep one,' I said.

Pain and blood loss had made him faint several times and it had taken over an hour for us to reach his employer's house. Now that he was safe, I trembled with the delayed shock.

'I've never heard of such a disgraceful thing, soldiers firing into the crowd like that,' said the cook. 'Sounds as if you got away lightly by all accounts, but you've both had a bad fright. I'm going to make you a nice pot of tea. And you, miss, can go in the scullery and have

313

a bit of a wash. Lizzie will bring you some hot water.' She looked me up and down. 'You could be one of them mudlarks after a day spent scavenging by the river.'

I looked down at my skirt but didn't see how 'a bit of a wash' could possibly make me look presentable. 'Thank you,' I said. 'Tea would be most welcome.'

'We need to get on with preparing the dinner and you'll be in our way here,' she said brusquely. 'You can have a sit in the kitchen office while you drink your tea.'

Ten minutes later I had mopped the front of my dress, washed my face and combed my tangled hair with my fingers. The cook, Mrs Bowker, had sat us down in her tiny office and the kitchen maid brought us a tea tray, leaving the door ajar behind her.

My hands shook so much the cup rattled in the saucer.

Alessandro took it from me with his left hand. 'Emilia,' he said, 'it's all right. We're both safe.'

'Will your employers be angry with you?'

He shook his head. 'Since I'd been in the Queen's employ they gave me the day off to observe the funeral procession. I must be fit to undertake my duties again tomorrow. What about you? Will your father be angry?' He smiled, and for a moment his face was lit by mischievous humour just as it used to be. 'Mrs Bowker was right – you do look like a mudlark.'

'Father is out of town today so I hope to return before he does.' I sipped the scalding tea and burned my tongue. 'Alessandro . . . '

He reached out and laid his hand on my wrist. 'I know. There are many things to discuss.'

Little shivers ran through me as he caressed the delicate skin with his thumb.

'You've grown so thin, Emilia,' he said. 'You look as fragile as a sparrow. Has finding your family not brought you the contentment you expected?'

'I wrote to tell you what I'd discovered about Dolly, though I still

314

cannot understand how he might have been the one who hurt Sarah. But there are worse things that I haven't told you,' I said. 'Things I've discovered about my father.'

'I don't understand – what things?'

My mouth trembled. 'Alessandro, I'm frightened!'

'Tell me.'

His sudden gentleness was more than I could bear and my face crumpled.

'Don't, Emilia! I can't bear to see you cry.' He stroked my cheek.

'I hardly know where to start,' I said. 'Of course I'll break off my engagement to Dolly ... you see, I found out that he loves someone else ... but before that I must go to Langdon Hall, my father's house in Hampshire.' The jumbled facts of what my mother had discovered came tumbling out and Alessandro patiently made me stop and asked me questions until he had the whole story straight.

'You're right to be afraid, Emilia,' he said at last, pulling me close. 'You cannot return to that house.'

'But I must! There's Aunt Maude, you see.' I leaned against his chest, inhaling the scent of his skin, my pulse skipping to feel him so close. 'And I have to know if the secret gallery exists. If it does, Father must be brought to justice.'

'And what kind of life will you have here once people know you are the daughter of a thief? Your father's actions will ruin you!' He paced away from me to look out of the small window at the teeming rain. 'I've been so unhappy in this city,' he said. 'I came here only to find you and make you come home. I never intended to stay. My contract is almost at an end and I shall return to my family gladly. But ...'

'But what, Alessandro?'

'My life has no meaning without you in it.' His voice was quiet and full of hurt. He sat down close beside me. 'I have regretted every day since you left me that I didn't let you go with my blessing.

315

It was selfish and wrong of me to try and stop you. I apologise unreservedly. Emilia, I shall ask you one more time and, if you refuse, I'll never mention it again.' He cupped my face in his hands so that I had to look at him.

The pupils of his amber eyes were very black and as I met his gaze it seemed that I looked deep into his soul. I yearned to tell him that I loved him, that I'd never stopped loving him, but I wasn't quite brave enough.

'Emilia,' he said, 'you have my heart in your hands.'

I sat very still, hardly breathing, while my own heart somersaulted under my ribs.

'You are as necessary to me as water and without your presence I die a little more each day,' he said. 'I want nothing more than for us to spend the rest of our lives together. Emilia, my dearest Emilia, please will you marry me?'

Alessandro still loved me, even after all that had happened between us. All my past fears that he would abandon me, as others had in my past, if I allowed myself to love him entirely, evaporated like mist in sunshine. I had no doubts now; we would put things right between us. I let out a sob of pure joy. 'Yes, Alessandro,' I whispered, 'yes, I will marry you.'

He released his breath on a long sigh and caught me against his chest before burying his face in my hair. Then his beautiful mouth was warm against my lips and his hungry kiss was so full of passion that I felt as if I was liquefying into a river of molten sunlight.

At last we drew apart and I was left trembling with wanting him.

'I cannot give you the life of privilege you have become used to,' he said, 'but I will do all in my power to bring you happiness.'

'I haven't been truly happy since I left Italy,' I said. 'I certainly haven't been happy since I left you. And as for my life of privilege: I came to London with nothing and I shall leave with nothing, but if I have your love I shall consider myself the richest girl in the world.'

'But I have such ambitions, Emilia!' His face glowed. 'I've had so much time to think lately and I want to set up a school to educate poor children. You know how Princess Caroline loved little children? I spoke to her about it on many occasions and she promised to provide funds to help me set it up, but now ... ' He sighed.

'Together, somehow, we shall find a way to build your school.'

He kissed me again, more gently this time.

As I slid my arms around his neck, the door creaked open.

'Ho! It's like that, is it?' said Mrs Bowker with a broad smile.

A scarlet flush rose in my cheeks.

'Mrs Bowker,' said Alessandro, 'may I introduce you to the future Signora Fiorelli?'

She gave a shout of laughter. 'Well then, congratulations are in order, I do believe.'

Alessandro kept a tight hold on my hand while we thanked her.

'I must go home,' I said.

'I shall walk you,' said Alessandro.

Mrs Bowker and I spoke in unison. 'Oh, no, you won't!'

'You must rest now, Alessandro.' I squeezed his hand.

'I'll send the second footman with you, miss,' said Mrs Bowker. 'I'll call him.' She winked at Alessandro and left us alone together.

'I expect to go to Hampshire the day after tomorrow,' I said. 'I'll look for the secret gallery and decide what to do about bringing Father to justice. And then I shall tell Dolly I have no intention of marrying him. All the guests will need to be informed that the wedding will not proceed ... ' I swallowed at the prospect of the fury and recriminations to come.

'Emilia, I'm worried for you,' said Alessandro. 'If you find the proof you're looking for, you must not challenge your father outright. If what your mother wrote in her diary is true, he may be violent. You must leave Langdon Hall and come straight to me and we'll speak to the authorities together. Will you promise to do that?'

317

I nodded, relieved I wouldn't have to face Father alone.

'I want to come with you but I'm bound to remain here until the end of the month.' He chewed his lip and looked at me with worry in his eyes.

'I shall be quite all right,' I said. 'Besides, you must rest and let your arm heal. I'll come to you as soon as I can.'

Footsteps sounded in the passage outside.

Alessandro kissed me swiftly. 'Take great care, *cara mia*.'

'*A presto, amore mio*,' I replied.

I entered the house by the area door, hoping to return to my room unobserved. The scullery maid, however, gasped at the sight of me and dropped a pan with a clatter.

'It's all right, Annie,' I said. 'I slipped over in the mud. Will you ask Daisy to attend me with some hot water?'

I crept past the kitchen door with my shoes squelching and hurried upstairs to my room. Glancing at my reflection in the mirror, I saw why I'd frightened Annie. My hair hung in dripping rat's tails, there was blood on my face and my sodden cloak and mourning dress were encrusted with mud. I laughed, thinking how much worse it would have been if I'd been wearing white muslin. I looked into the mirror again. My eyes shone and my cheeks were flushed. Despite my torn and filthy clothes, I hadn't looked so happy or pretty since I'd arrived in England. I hugged my arms around myself, hardly able to believe that Alessandro loved me and that, no matter what, soon we would be together.

Daisy entered with a jug of hot water and her eyes widened. 'Annie said you'd had a mishap in the mud, miss.'

'I'm afraid my clothes are beyond redemption, Daisy.'

'There's blood on your face. You're not hurt, miss?'

I shook my head. 'Though others were. I went to see the funeral procession and there was a riot. Soldiers fired on the trouble-makers.'

'I heard that,' said Daisy. 'If I'd known you were caught up in it I'd have been that worried . . . ' She shook her head. 'You'd better take everything off, miss.' She poured clean water into the basin and set out towels and soap.

Once I was clean I hurried to see Aunt Maude and found her sitting in a chair by her bedroom window.

'Thank goodness you're back!' she said. 'I was worried.' She looked me up and down. 'I saw your clothes were in a dreadful state when I spied you creeping in by the area door.'

I smiled. 'You don't miss anything, do you?'

Aunt Maude looked at me with her head on one side, like a robin. 'You seem surprisingly cheerful considering you've been to a funeral.'

'I have so much to tell you,' I said. 'The procession turned into a riot and I was caught up in it.'

She pressed a hand to her chest. 'You're not harmed?'

I shook my head. 'But Alessandro was with me and he was wounded . . . '

Aunt Maude gasped.

'Thankfully, it's not serious, though others were badly hurt. But then something wonderful happened.' My heart was nearly bursting with joy as I told her that Alessandro had proposed and I had accepted.

'My dear Emilia!' Aunt Maude reached for both my hands. 'I'm so very happy for you.'

'It makes me angry to think that if Father hadn't intercepted Alessandro's letters it might have happened before,' I said. 'This is a bitter-sweet day. I'm very sad I shan't see the Queen again.'

'Poor lady,' sighed Aunt Maude. 'And there will be difficult times ahead for you. Frederick will take the news of the cancellation of your wedding very badly, I fear.' She twisted the end of her plait round and round her fingers. 'You know, in the beginning he was passionately in love with Rose, or perhaps in love with the person he wanted her to be. It wasn't until she didn't conform to his ideal, when she voiced opinions that weren't the same as his own, that he changed so towards her.'

'And you fear his feelings towards me might change in a similar way?'

'Frederick is a formidable enemy,' she said, 'and you must be extremely careful, Emilia.'

Chapter 35

August 1821

Langdon Hall

Father, Aunt Maude and I travelled together to Langdon Hall, with our ladies' maids, Father's valet and the head footman following in the smaller carriage. The rain drummed down on the roof all the way, making our nerves taut as we jolted over muddy roads full of pot holes.

'I suggested that Dolly drive down in the carriage with us,' said Father, 'but it appears he has more important matters to attend to in town today. You'd have thought an appointment with his tailor or his wine merchant would be less pressing than the company of his fiancée and learning to run the estate that will one day be his.' He smiled in grim satisfaction. 'I gave him a piece of my mind ... and serve him right if he nearly drowns when he rides down on horse-back tomorrow.'

I shifted my feet, which were pressed uncomfortably against the box containing my wedding gown, with the canvas-wrapped painting

Father had bought at the auction tucked in behind. Daisy hadn't allowed Dobson to put the dress box with the other luggage on the roof, not even under a tarpaulin, in case the rain penetrated it and spoiled the silk. Perhaps I'd give the gown to her later. I certainly wouldn't wear it when I married Alessandro. I smiled to myself, imagining how wonderful that day would be, filled with happiness and laughter. I wouldn't care if I were dressed in rags so long as Alessandro loved me.

'What are you smiling about, Emilia?' asked Father. 'Dreaming of your wedding day?'

I laughed. 'Yes,' I said, 'I was.'

At last we arrived at Langdon Hall. It was raining still and as the carriage clattered over the drawbridge the water in the moat appeared black, reflecting the bruised sky. Dobson brought the carriage to a stop close to the front door and servants ran out with sheltering umbrellas before we dashed into the hall.

Soon we were drinking tea in the library, while the servants lit candles to dispel the gathering gloom.

Father unwrapped the new painting and propped it against the wall beneath his other Dutch interiors. 'Come and tell me what you think of this, Emilia,' he said. 'As soon as I saw it I thought how appropriate it was.'

The painting depicted a couple, holding hands and standing on a tiled floor in a darkly panelled room. Sunlight poured in through a large window with diamond-shaped leaded lights, illuminating the damask of the young woman's claret gown and the white linen of the man's shirt.

'It always strikes me how calm and peaceful these Dutch interiors are,' I said. 'There's a beautiful underwater quality to the light, similar to when sun falls onto a stream and you catch a flash of the secret world existing beneath.'

'It's called The Proposal,' said Father. 'It looks as if the portrait has captured the young woman just as she's about to speak.'

'It makes me curious,' I said, 'about whether she said yes.'

'Of course she did,' said Father. 'They would never have been painted together if she hadn't.'

'Well, I hope they had a happy marriage.' Sipping my tea, I wondered how soon I was going to have an opportunity to search his study for the staircase to the secret gallery.

The following morning, after breakfast, Father retired to his study. 'I have a considerable amount of estate business to attend to,' he said, 'and on no account wish to be disturbed.'

My heart sank since that meant he wouldn't be going out.

After he'd left the room, Aunt Maude said, 'Frederick will be expecting us to be making the final arrangements for the wedding.'

'That would be a waste of our time,' I said. My stomach knotted again at the prospect of breaking off the engagement. 'Instead, perhaps we should write to the guests to tell them it's cancelled? We can post the letters after I've broken the news.'

Aunt Maude bit her lip. 'Supposing Frederick were to find them?'

'Hide them in your work basket,' I said.

We sat in the library and worked steadily on the letters for the next hour until Samuel came to inform us that Mr Cole, the tenant of Little Langdon Farm, had called to speak to Father.

'Sir Frederick is in his study,' I said.

'I did knock,' said Samuel, 'but there was no response. I've looked everywhere for him since Mr Cole is so anxious to speak to him. I wondered if Sir Frederick might have gone out?'

I frowned. 'Not so far as I am aware. I shall speak to Mr Cole.'

He stood in the hall, as solid as an oak tree, with his hat grasped in his meaty hands. He wore a rough tweed coat and old-fashioned breeches on his sturdy legs. 'Ah, Miss Langdon! A pleasure to see you again but it's Sir Frederick I need to speak to on a matter of some importance.'

'Come into the little parlour, Mr Cole,' I said. 'Father is in his study and has asked the servants not to disturb him. I'll see if he'll come and speak to you for a moment.'

'That's kind of you, Miss Langdon.'

He perched his bulky frame incongruously on a delicately carved chair and I hurried across the hall to tap on the study door. There was no reply so I turned the handle. The door was locked and I returned to explain to Mr Cole that my father must have gone out after all.

Some two hours later Aunt Maude and I had finished the letters and stowed them away in her work basket ready for posting. I was sitting on the window seat watching the rain pock-mark the moat when Father appeared in the library with his newspaper rolled up under his arm.

'There you are!' I said. 'It's nearly time for dinner and I thought you'd gone out.'

'Not in this perpetual rain,' he said. 'Besides, I told you I was working.'

'So you did,' I said, 'but Mr Cole came to speak to you and I tapped on the door to no response.'

Father shrugged. 'Been there all morning. I didn't hear you. Probably concentrating too hard. What did Cole want?'

I looked at my father thoughtfully. 'He asked you to call on him at Little Langdon Farm. The rain is damaging the harvest and Lower Meadow is half flooded.'

'I'm not sure what he expects me to do about it,' grumbled Father.

'He asked if you'd visit him this afternoon. He's very anxious.'

Father sighed. 'I'll go after we've had our dinner. I need to talk to him about a rent increase anyway.' He opened up his newspaper and settled down to read about the shameful story of the people's rebellion during the funeral procession of the late Queen.

I made an excuse to slip away and hurried upstairs to my bed-room. Mother's diary was wrapped in a scarf and concealed behind the lining of my old travelling bag. I hastily reread the passage where she explained how she'd found the staircase to the gallery.

Searching the folios on Frederick's bookcase I found the secret staircase almost by mistake. It smelled dank and mouldy and was too dark to explore further without a light. Fortuitously, there was a candlestick on the bookshelves. Perhaps Frederick keeps it there for exactly this purpose? Harriet was resting so I lit the candle and descended the stairwell.

I closed my eyes and pictured Father's study in as much detail as I could remember. The folios were the clue. If Mother had been examining the folios when she found the access to the staircase, surely it must be behind the bookshelves? Father hadn't been in the study when I knocked on his door but I guessed he might have been out of earshot in his hidden gallery.

I hid the diary again and went downstairs as Robert announced dinner was ready.

I was in an agony of impatience as we ate and could hardly force down a morsel while Father had a second helping of beef pudding and seemed inclined to linger over his claret and cheese.

Aunt Maude watched me as I crumbled a piece of bread and tried to make light conversation about the continuing bad weather.

At last Father pushed back his chair. 'I suppose it's no use delaying any longer,' he said, glancing at the rain hammering against the window panes.

'Will you take the carriage?' asked Aunt Maude.

Father shook his head. 'Cole wants us to look at the Lower Meadow so I'll ride Shadow. Don't forget Dolly will probably arrive before I return.'

Aunt Maude and I retired to the library and a short while later I heard hooves clattering across the courtyard.

'This is my opportunity to look for the hidden chapel,' I said, 'before Father returns and Dolly arrives. Of course, even if I find it, the stolen paintings may no longer be there. Then I can't prove

Father is the Picture Frame Thief. You go and have your rest, Aunt Maude. Later, I'll come and tell you what I've found.'

I accompanied her to the bottom of the staircase and waited until she'd turned onto the first-floor landing. Glancing around the hall to make sure no servants were watching, I slipped inside Father's study.

I stood in the centre of the room, hearing only my own heartbeat. There was a faint smell of tobacco smoke. The leather desktop was clear except for a brass ink pot and a blotter. Five paintings hung on the walls and, as far as I could see, there was no concealed jib door. The bookcase, built in three sections across one entire wall, was stacked with buff leather-bound folios, books and a few artefacts: a Chinese vase, a small bronze figure of a boy throwing a discus, a candlestick and a stone urn full of marble chips.

I went to look more closely at the first bookcase, pulling at it to see if it would move forward, but it was firmly fixed to the wall. I tried the same with the middle section and then the final one. A flash of excitement left my pulse racing when it moved a fraction. Perhaps this was it? I pushed aside some of the folios on the shelves, not quite sure what I was looking for, and it wasn't until I reached the lowest shelf that I saw the brass hinges in its back corner.

I searched the shelves above more carefully until I found another set of hinges in the centre and the last set higher up. My fingers scrabbled behind the folios at the opposite end of the shelves and in only a moment I had located two small bolts. I lifted them up and hinged the bookcase out towards me. I drew in my breath as a door was revealed in the wall behind. Grasping the ring handle, I paused for a second and looked at my fingers, imagining my mother's hand in the same place all those years ago when she, too, had found this door.

It wouldn't open. There was a small keyhole under the handle but no key. Frustration boiled up in me and I could have screamed. I took a deep breath. Think! What was it Mother had written?

Fortuitously, there was a candlestick on the bookshelves. Or perhaps Frederick keeps it there for exactly this purpose?

I looked at the adjacent set of shelves and there was the candle-stick. A tinderbox and a used spill lay beside it. Where would Father keep the key? Somewhere nearby ... I rummaged through the marble chips in the stone urn without success and then my gaze fell on the Chinese vase. I tipped it towards me and heard a slight chink of metal against the porcelain. Peering inside, my heart leaped when I saw a key. My trembling fingers pushed it into the door lock and it turned with a satisfying click. I opened the door and shivered when I saw the rickety stairs disappearing down into blackness. The air smelled like that of a crypt.

It took me several attempts with the tinder box to light the candle but finally I stepped, dry-mouthed, onto a winding staircase. The sound of my footsteps was muffled as I felt my way down and my elbows brushed against the dusty, cobwebbed walls to either side. I tried not to think how suffocating the blackness would be if I dropped the candle. At the foot of the steps was a rusty gate with a key in the lock. I turned this and pushed the gate inwards.

Then I stepped through.

Chapter 36

The air was very still. It almost felt as if I was suspended in time in the cool, mould-scented gloom. Light filtered in through four narrow clerestory windows set high up along one wall, dimly illuminating a sizeable underground chamber. I had found the hidden chapel!

My eyes began to make out shapes in the shadows and I caught my breath at the sight of a group of people, all dressed in white, watching me. I froze until I realised they were marble statues, similar to those in the garden. I held my candle high to study the unseeing eyes in finely modelled faces and the sculpted drapes that barely concealed the perfect proportions of the figures. One of the women had a chipped nose but this did nothing to render her any less beautiful.

Reluctantly, I turned away from the statues. Four pews in the centre of the space were arranged back to back in a rectangle, facing the walls, and there were a number of marble plinths displaying artefacts such as an urn, a marble bust or stone figurine. Bronze sconces in the sinuous shapes of water serpents, each supporting half a dozen candles, were fixed to the walls at regular intervals. I lit them from my candlestick and the decorative mirror behind magnified the flames into brilliance. Only once the chapel was ablaze with candlelight did I allow myself to look properly at the paintings.

My eyes were immediately drawn to the glorious oil-painted panel of The Last Supper hanging above the altar. I lit the torchères to either side of it and the candlelight made the gold of the saints' haloes gleam and the rich colours on the canvas glow as if they were alive. The painting was in the style of Botticelli. Each of the apostles had a face so full of character that the artist must have modelled them on persons known to him. The central figure of Christ stared directly back at the viewer and there was something about his benign expression that made it almost impossible for me to look away. Enchanted, I stood in front of the painting for I knew not how long, wondering why it seemed familiar.

I had to find the proof I needed before Father returned. One by one I studied the other paintings, discovering that each was a treasure. I'd gleaned some knowledge of Italian art during my travels and was astonished by the number of religious works in the chapel that were beautiful enough to rival any I'd seen in Florence, Siena, Arezzo, and the many ancient hilltop churches and monasteries in the area surrounding them.

The religious paintings were hung at the altar end of the chapel but as I worked my way back towards the entrance I discovered secular subjects too, grouped together by type: portraits, landscapes, architecture, even some studies of exotic animals. Hurrying now, I glanced at the remaining pictures but wasn't sufficiently knowledgeable to recognise the artists.

Then I saw something that made me gasp. Two tiny portraits in oval gilt frames hung on the wall, spaced about a foot apart. Each showed the profile of a dark-haired girl, one facing to the left and one to the right. I knew without a shadow of doubt that the portrait that completed the trio was in my bedroom, safely sewn inside the rag doll I'd carried everywhere with me since I was a child. But how had these two miniatures come to be here? Father had told me he was still searching for them.

Confused, I returned to the altar, intending to blow out the candles on the torchères, but was seduced again by the beauty of The Last Supper. I sank down onto the pew placed in the perfect position to appreciate it and, for a moment longer, allowed the peace imparted by Christ's calm gaze to wash over me.

'It is magnificent, isn't it?' said my father's voice behind me.

Immobilised by shock, I was unable even to turn my head. Astonishingly, Father didn't sound angry and so I took my lead from him and behaved as if my presence here was nothing out of the ordinary. 'It has me utterly bewitched,' I said. That at least was true.

'I didn't know when I acquired it that it was by Sandro Botticelli,' said Father, 'but, like you, I fell in love with it as soon as I saw it. I knew immediately I had to have it.'

'Botticelli?' I said, shock making my knees weak. I tensed as Father sat down on the pew beside me.

'One of his early works from the time he was apprenticed to Fra Filippo Lippi. Imagine having such exceptional talent at only twenty years old!' Father sighed. 'It was this painting that made me abandon my own dreams of being an artist. I knew I could never achieve half of what he had, even if I spent every day of my life working at it.' He shook his head. 'That was when I decided to collect art instead and this was the first item in my collection.'

'It's an extraordinarily fine one,' I said. I glanced at the iron gate at the other end of the chapel. It stood open still and I took a calming breath and forced myself to smile at Father.

'I'm delighted you like it!' he said. 'It's clear you are the child of my blood, even if you didn't grow up at my side. This collection is infinitely precious to me and I've wanted so much to share the pleasure of it with the right person. Shall I show you the rest?'

I nodded and tried not to flinch as he slipped his arm under mine. Aunt Maude had said he was unpredictable and, if I ran, I might provoke him to violence. All I could do was humour him until it was safe for me to leave. It wasn't hard to look fascinated as he took me from one extraordinarily beautiful work of art to another. My mouth was dry and my mind whirled as he attributed works to Raphael, Titian, Donatello and Caravaggio as well as a number of other artists I hadn't heard of. Some were cartoons or sketches, others oil on canvas, but there was an indefinable magic about them all that left me in no doubt that they were priceless.

'What do you think of them?' asked Father.

He must have stolen them or he'd have exhibited them where he could boast about them. I couldn't begin to imagine how he had managed to steal so many treasures without being caught. 'I'm almost speechless,' I said at last. 'It's overwhelming.'

'Come and look at these,' he said, face glowing with excitement. 'Although the works of the Italian Renaissance are closest to my heart, I enjoy the best of every kind of art, be it Roman sculptures and artefacts or something more contemporary, like these exotic animal studies by Stubbs.'

I peered closer to look at paintings of a giraffe, a lion, a rhinoceros, a tiger and a monkey. Something teased my memory.

'The especially interesting thing about these,' said Father, 'is that Stubbs usually paints horses.'

Then I recalled a comment that Araminta Perry's brother had made to me. A Stubbs painting of a giraffe had been stolen and the thief had left behind a tiny sketch of an empty picture frame. A companion painting by the same artist had been stolen five years previously from the same owner. My stomach clenched. This was all the proof necessary to confirm Father was indeed the Picture Frame Thief.

'Fascinating,' I said.

'I brought Dolly down here,' Father said, 'but he wasn't interested in the paintings except to ask about their value. Philistine! He thinks they'll be part of his inheritance but I'm damned if he'll have them! You appreciate them properly and shall have them after I'm gone. I wish now that I'd shown you my collection before.'

'Why didn't you?' I asked. Would he admit to me that he'd stolen the paintings?

'This is my secret place,' he murmured. 'When the world treats me badly, this is where I come to drink in the beauty of some of the finest art mankind has to offer. It's a place of healing. After Piers and your mother died, whole days passed by without my noticing while I sat here.'

'And you didn't want to share it with anyone before?'

'It is a question of trust,' he said. 'I made an error of judgement when I showed it to Dolly.' He grasped me by my upper arms so that I had to face him. 'Now I've seen the way you look at these paintings with such awe, I believe I can trust you.' He looked straight into my eyes and it took a great effort of will for me not to recoil. 'I can trust you, can't I?' he said.

I met his eyes with a guileless gaze. 'I couldn't bear it if any harm came to these priceless pieces.' I was sincere about that, at least, but I had to persuade him to tell me more. 'Where did you find The Last Supper?' I asked, freeing myself from his grip to look at the painting again.

'Where else but Italy?' said Father, smiling. 'I was twenty-one and near the end of my Grand Tour, learning the language, painting and sketching the scenery and visiting the churches to see the frescoes. I stayed at a monastery in the hills of Tuscany. This magnificent panel was hanging in the refectory.'

I caught my breath. That was why it had seemed familiar!

'As soon as I saw it I was lost,' said Father. 'It made me angry that none of the monks appeared to appreciate its beauty.'

'So you took it?' I hoped he wouldn't notice the tremor in my voice. I had to convince him I condoned his thefts. If I didn't, well, I knew from Mother's diary how violent he could be.

He crowed with laughter. 'I was in that place for three weeks! The monks believed I was very devout, spending hours alone in my cell reading the Bible. During that time, I secretly painted a replica. As soon as it was finished I took down the original while the monks were at their prayers, replaced it with my copy and escaped into the night.'

I made an attempt to look surprised. 'That was you?'

'It made me smile when you mentioned you'd seen my painting,' he said, 'even though you were unkind enough to say it was poorly rendered.'

'But the panel is at least five feet long,' I said. 'However did you bring it home without damaging it?'

'With great difficulty! I wrapped it in a blanket and strapped it to the side of my horse. I travelled overnight. When I reached Florence I had a stout box made for it, wrapped the painting in muslin and packed it with straw. I hired a carriage and conveyed it to Livorno from whence I sailed for London.'

I felt sick to know he'd stolen something so precious from his hosts and now was boasting about his betrayal of their trust. 'A very clever move,' I said, unable to look at him.

He laughed again. 'Wasn't it? You cannot imagine my exultation when the boat sailed out of the harbour. The painting was mine!'

He had no sense of right and wrong at all. 'And I daresay,' I said, 'you'd have liked to see the monks' faces when they were eating their bean stew the next day and noticed their painting had been replaced by a copy?'

'I confess, I've often been amused by that thought.'

It made me want to cry that this man, who had appeared to be the affectionate father I'd wanted all my life, had turned out to be utterly despicable.

'Collecting became a compulsion for me,' he continued, voice bubbling with enthusiasm. 'Once I came into my inheritance, I made this hidden chapel into a gallery worthy of my growing collection. I returned to Italy as often as I could. These marble statues came from a site near the Colosseum in Rome.' He caressed the hair and cheek of the lovely girl with the chipped nose. 'Venus,' he said. 'Isn't she perfection? She reminded me of your mother before she became such a shrew. The bribe I paid to the guard was only a fraction of the value of the statues. It was surprising how often fine sketches and paintings were displayed in perfectly ordinary churches, with little to prevent me simply lifting them off the walls when the priest's back was turned.'

His elation as he described his vile trickery revolted me and I decided to change the subject. 'There's something else I wanted to ask you, Father,' I said, beckoning him towards the small oval frames. 'Are these the miniatures of the Spanish Infanta?'

'How sharp of you to guess.'

'Where did you find them? I've spent so much time thinking about where Sarah might have sold them.'

'Ah, well.' Father rubbed his nose. 'Perhaps I wasn't entirely straight with you about that but I hoped so much you'd lead me to the missing one. After your mother's maid stole you away I chased after her but lost the trail by the time I reached Lyons. I promised all the art dealers I knew a reward for information leading to the miniatures and, of course, to Sarah.'

It hurt that the miniatures appeared to have been of more importance to him than his own daughter was. 'You thought that was the best chance of finding me?' I asked.

He rubbed his nose again and his gaze slid away from me. 'Yes, of course. If Sarah sold one of the miniatures, I thought I'd be able to pick up her trail again and find the other two.'

'And me?' I asked, although by now I knew what his priority had always been.

He waved his hand dismissively. 'I thought it unlikely Sarah would sell all three at once because they'd be a good nest egg for her future. And then, a year or so later, I had a stroke of luck. Her husband, Joe Barton, came to London to find me. He and Sarah had separated and he sold me information about her whereabouts. I gave him half what he asked for, with the promise of the rest if the information was verified. He told me Sarah remained in Milan with the child.'

The child. Me. Shadowy images of those dark days returned along with memories of always being hungry and scared. 'What happened then?' I asked.

'I set off for Milan straight away. I put up reward notices and visited all the local art dealers. You can imagine my joy when I found one of the miniatures. I bought it and was able to glean enough information from the dealer to trace Sarah to Verona. But then the trail went cold again.'

'Hunger and desperation must have forced her to sell it,' I said. 'She was always frightened because she thought someone was searching for us but she didn't know if it was you or Joe. That's why we moved so often.'

'Very annoying it was, too,' said Father, a nerve twitching in his jaw. 'Since Barton knew her best of all, I paid him to find Sarah and discover what she'd done with the remaining miniatures. Several times he nearly caught up with her before she did a moonlight flit. It infuriated me that she kept getting away with it. Still, Barton has proved a useful employee over the years.'

'What do you mean?'

He shrugged. 'I don't like getting my hands dirty. I locate the paintings I wish to acquire and spy out the lie of the land. Barton then brings them to me for a consideration.'

'So I *wasn't* imagining it,' I said, 'when I thought I saw him leaving the house in Grosvenor Street?'

'I told him never to come to my house again,' said Father, scowling. 'Such careless disregard for my instructions could have caused untold trouble.'

'When did you find the second miniature?'

'Two years ago. I had a letter from a contact in Florence saying he'd bought a fine miniature from an Englishwoman. It was impossible for me to leave the country at that time as Parliament was sitting and I was involved in negotiations for several paintings for one of my clients.'

'So it wasn't you Sarah thought was chasing us?' I said.

He shook his head. 'Not recently. I decided it was time Dolly earned his inheritance.'

'Dolly?' Puzzled, I shook my head.

'He'd landed himself in severe debt with his gambling habit and his tailor was threatening to have him taken up and sent to debtors' prison. He went to Florence in my place. I said I'd settle his bills if he collected the second miniature, and promised him half the value of the third if he found Sarah and, shall we say, persuaded her to tell him where she'd hidden it. My patience had worn very thin by then.'

I pressed a hand to my mouth. So Alessandro *hadn't* been mistaken about Dolly being in Pesaro.

'Unfortunately,' said Father, his lips pursing in annoyance, 'when he found Sarah, she obdurately refused to tell him where she'd hidden the miniature and he was disturbed before he was able to beat the information out of her. Stupid fool lost his nerve, returned to England and said he'd never go back to Italy again.'

I stared at my father, stunned into silence. I remembered again how that man, a very tall man, in the alley behind the cottage had nearly knocked me over. It must have been Dolly, exactly as Alessandro had said. The true horror of it was that Father condoned, had even suggested, the beating Dolly had given to Sarah, the beating that caused her death. Would he also have condoned it if Dolly had beaten me, his own daughter, in search of the information he sought?

'Emilia?' Father was looking at me with a puzzled air.

There was something very wrong with him. He had no conscience at all. 'I'm surprised that Dolly found himself able to beat Sarah so severely that she died,' I said. 'He isn't usually so ...' I floundered.

'What?'

'What I mean is, I'd have expected him to be far too anxious that he might risk dirtying his coat.'

Father hooted with laughter. 'How true! The threat of debtors' prison, however, was a bit of a stiffener. He had little choice but to do as I told him.'

I had to know. 'When you decided you wanted me to marry Dolly, did you know he didn't like women?'

Father narrowed his eyes. 'What do you mean?'

'I mean,' I said, 'that Dolly prefers men. Do you care so little for me that you are prepared to condemn me to a hollow marriage, possibly without children?'

'Without children?' He frowned. 'You *must* have children, Emilia. A son is essential to maintain two centuries of the same bloodline at Langdon Hall.'

'Well, you're barking up the wrong tree if you believe it's a foregone conclusion that Dolly will be able to bring himself to give you a grandson,' I told him.

A dry cough came from behind us.

Father and I spun around to see Dolly emerging from the shadows at the foot of the stairs.

Chapter 37

Dolly's face was pale and strained as he confronted us. 'So I was right. I suspected you'd seen me with Francis in the garden.'

'How did you know?'

He gave a tight little smile. 'I was your partner in the next dance and you couldn't look at me. I'd heard a noise in the garden and there were rose petals in your hair.'

'Rose petals?' said Father.

'It was oppressively hot on the night of the ball and I had a headache,' I said. 'I went into the garden for some air. It was dark. The petals must have fallen on my hair when I hid in the arbour. I was so shocked when I saw Dolly and Francis together that I barely noticed my hair was tangled in the climbing rose.'

'Together?' said Father, frowning.

'Kissing,' I said. The expression of revulsion on Father's face was almost comical but at least it showed that, however else he'd tried to bend my will to further his own aspirations, he hadn't been aware of Dolly's particular inclinations.

Father pinched the bridge of his nose. 'I'm sure whatever Dolly may choose to do in his private life, Emilia, it won't prevent him from doing his family duty.'

White-hot rage rose up in me then and I threw caution to the winds. 'It's clear to me now, Father, how very little you've ever cared for my happiness. If you think I'm still going to marry him, you're quite mistaken.'

'Of course you'll marry him!' said Father through gritted teeth. 'You can't cry off so close to the wedding.'

Dolly coughed again. 'I rather think it's too late for that, Sir Frederick. You've told Emilia that I assaulted Sarah Barton, an assault that led to her death.' He shuddered. 'I still have nightmares about the sound of her skin splitting when I hit her. And now I'm sure that Emilia knows about my illegal relationship with Francis, I must take measures to protect us.' He took a step back. 'I will not risk my reputation and my inheritance, not to mention my liberty, should either of you decide to inform the authorities.' Spinning on his heel, he returned through the metal gate at the bottom of the stairs.

'It's hardly in my interest to denounce you,' Father called after him.

'Perhaps not,' said Dolly, his hand on the gate. 'But I believe Emilia is made of sterner moral fibre than you and that places me in a very difficult position.'

I realised with a jolt what he was about to do and launched myself at him.

Too late!

Dolly slammed the gate, turned the key and slipped it in his pocket.

'Don't be ridiculous, Dolly.' Father thrust his hand through the iron bars. 'Give me that key!'

'Let us out, Dolly.' My voice was calm but my fury was supplanted by fear. A flicker of panic at the thought of being locked in an underground chamber made my chest tighten.

Ignoring me, he said, 'As you may have noticed, it's raining in torrents.'

'What does that have to do with anything?' asked Father, rattling the gate.

'Have you noticed how high the river is?'

'Of course I have! I've been this very afternoon to see Cole at Little Langdon Farm. Lower Meadow is under water.'

'Opening the sluices to the moat will drain off some of the excess from the river.'

'You can't do that!' Father rattled the gate again. 'Idiot! The moat is already lapping over its banks. It'll overflow.'

'And when it does,' said Dolly, 'it will flood the cellars, including this chapel.'

I let out an involuntary moan.

'I'm afraid you've left me no other choice, Sir Frederick,' said Dolly. He rubbed his eyes as if he were deathly tired. 'I've grown quite fond of you, Emilia, and it grieves me that I'm forced to take this course of action.'

'Then don't,' I said.

He shook his head. 'I must. If I let you go now, even upon your solemn promise to say nothing, your conscience would eventually make you disclose who was responsible for Sarah's death.'

'Open this gate right now, Adolphus,' said Father, 'and we'll say no more about it.'

Dolly sighed. 'I'm sorry it had to be like this,' he said, 'but I understand drowning is quick and peaceful, Emilia, if you don't struggle.' His mouth twitched in a ghastly smile and he lifted his hand in farewell.

'Adolphus!' shouted Father. 'Come back at once and let me out! Don't you understand? If you flood the chapel, you'll destroy some of the finest art in Western civilisation.'

The sound of Dolly's footsteps faded as he climbed the staircase. And then the door to the study slammed shut.

I swallowed, my mouth suddenly dry. Whether the chapel flooded or not, we were incarcerated underground and I didn't like it. I didn't like it at all.

Father lost his temper. He bellowed and raged, calling down curses upon Dolly. He lifted an urn off one of the marble plinths and used this as a battering ram against the gate. Rusty or not, the gate stood firm. At last the paroxysm of rage dwindled and he sank down to the floor with his head in his hands, breathing heavily.

I started at the sound of a crash and then a large stone bounced into the chapel. Daggers of broken glass fell from one of the windows and skittered across the floor. A shadow moved across the casement.

Father looked up, his eyes red-rimmed. His usually smooth hair stood up in iron-grey tufts. 'Adolphus, let me out!' His voice was hoarse from shouting.

I winced as one by one the other three windows shattered, too. Tip-toeing over the broken glass, I sat down on one of the benches, my hands clenched together in my lap to stop them from shaking.

After a minute, Father pushed himself to his feet with a grunt and came to sit a few feet away.

'I always knew Dolly was a rotten egg,' he said. 'Just like his father. I can't bear to think of him getting his hands on Langdon Hall.'

I turned away from him. A damp draught drifted in through the windows and the torrential rain hissing down outside could now be clearly heard through the broken panes. My pulse began to skip as I studied the clerestory windows thoughtfully. At the top of the walls against the ceiling, beginning perhaps eight feet up, they were two feet wide and one foot high. The frames were set within the apertures, narrowing the access space to little more than an arrow slit turned sideways. Black depression descended upon me as I lost my last hope. I couldn't possibly wriggle through such a tiny gap.

341

A long time passed.

I wept a little as I pictured Alessandro's face. We'd come so close to being free to enjoy the rest of our lives together. I consoled myself by thinking that at least I'd die knowing he loved me.

'Emilia?' Father's voice breaking the silence made me jump. 'How did you find the chapel?'

We were going to drown anyway so what did it matter now if I told him? 'I found Mother's diary.'

He frowned at me. 'Where?' His voice sounded like a bark. 'I searched for it everywhere.'

I shrugged. 'In her work basket. It was in the attic with her portrait.'

'What else did you discover?'

'That you used to beat her so violently she was in fear for her life. That she wasn't unfaithful to you. And that you are the Picture Frame Thief.'

Father sighed. 'I loved her, you know. In the beginning anyway.'

'Did you drown her?' I asked. I had to know the truth.

He looked at me with bloodshot eyes. 'No,' he said.

I had no idea if I could believe him and still didn't understand why Mother might have drowned herself, however cruel he had been to her. 'You don't love anything other than yourself and your paintings,' I said. 'Or should I say, other people's paintings that you have stolen?' Then something caught my eye and icy fingers of fear ran down my spine. 'Look!' I said, staring at the wall in horror.

Water lapped through the broken window panes and trickled down the whitewashed wall, streaking it with muddy brown. Puddles grew on the floor and, as we watched, joined together into a pool.

Father moaned. 'I had those windows put in to air the chapel. I hid them behind bushes on the narrow strip of ground between the Hall and the moat. I was concerned damp might spoil the canvases.'

I laughed mirthlessly. 'Damp is certainly going to spoil them now,' I said. 'Did you never think about the moat flooding?'

'Of course I considered it!' he snapped. 'It hasn't flooded for generations. In any case, this is Dolly's fault for opening the sluices.' He gave me a baleful stare, his grey eyes as cold as slate. 'You sound just like Rose, always criticising and nagging at me. I couldn't bear the way she used to look at me with those great blue eyes of hers brimming with tears of disappointment.'

I didn't answer him. He clearly believed he was without fault and I wasn't going to waste my last breaths arguing with him.

The water began to flow faster. It gushed through the windows now in a stinking stream, filling the chapel with the reek of decay.

Father ran to the altar and snatched off the heavily embroidered cloth. He dragged a pew over to one of the windows and climbed onto it to stuff the cloth into the broken glass. The flow of water slowed to a dribble.

'There!' he said, jumping off the pew. 'We must find something to put in the other windows.'

'If we had a hammer and nails we could use some of the paintings to board them up.'

He gave me a look of outrage and at that moment the sodden altar cloth burst out of the windowframe and thumped to the floor. A great surge of water followed.

After a while, water eddied around my shins and I sat on a pew with my feet up. I was frightened to see how fast it was pouring in now that the level in the moat was higher than the windows. It made a terrible rushing noise and it was all I could do not to sob with terror.

Father sat on the altar with his arms wrapped around his knees and his gaze focused on The Last Supper.

Some of the candles had burned out, leaving nothing but drifts of acrid smoke. I splashed around the gallery and pinched out half of the remaining flames. I would relight them later when the others had burned down. I didn't want sit in the dark, waiting to drown, any longer than I had to.

It wasn't long before the water in the chapel was knee-high. My muslin skirt was sodden as it lapped over the seat of the pew and my panic was rising as fast as the water. I had to do something! Unable to sit still, I waded back and forth to try and keep warm as the cold began to seep into my bones. I looked up at one of the windows again and had an idea.

'Father!'

Slowly, he turned his head to look at me.

'Bring me that bronze urn,' I said. I climbed up onto the pew he'd left beneath the window and stood beside the cascading water.

He stared at me sullenly.

'Quickly!'

Moving as slowly as if he were walking through treacle, he brought me the urn. 'What are you going to do?'

I didn't answer but snatched the urn from him with both hands and raised it above my head. I brought it down to thump against the timber framework of the window. I gasped as my arms went into the torrent of cold water and it diverted a stream onto my face. I lifted the urn and held my breath as I crashed it into the frame again. Several minutes later I was wet to my skin but the windowframe had splintered.

'Don't just stand there watching!' I cried.

Father stepped up onto the pew and we began to prise away the broken wood. It wasn't easy since we couldn't see properly through the tumbling water.

Eventually I ran my fingers around the frame removing any remaining sharp fragments as best as I could.

'Now help me bring the altar,' I said.

We heaved the heavy table across the floor with the water swirling around our waists and placed it under the window. It took a great deal of grunting and swearing on Father's part and straining on mine, but we managed to lift the pew onto the altar table. I leaned against the wall to catch my breath.

'It's a waste of time,' said Father flatly. 'The window is too small.'

'I'd rather die trying to escape than by sitting here until I drown,' I said. 'You must shove me through as far as you can so I'm not forced back by the pressure of the water.'

Father chewed at his lip, water dripping from his hair. 'It's a pointless exercise but you're courageous to try.'

'Then put your back into lifting me up and pushing me out,' I said, not feeling brave at all. 'If I survive I'll fetch help. Then there's a chance we can save the paintings.'

'Save the paintings?' Hope lit up his eyes again. 'By God, we'll give it our best shot, Emilia.'

My teeth chattered as I hauled myself out of the swirling water onto the altar and then the pew.

Father clambered up beside me. The stinking waterfall poured down between us, carrying clumps of weed and twigs.

'Pray Dolly isn't outside watching,' I said, toeing off my shoes. I composed myself, taking several deep breaths and sending up a prayer of thanks that Alessandro had taught me how to swim. 'I'm ready,' I said. I took another breath, stepped into the cascade and gripped the window aperture. The powerful force of the water made me stagger.

Father grabbed me firmly around my thighs and hoisted me up.

I propelled myself through the window, coming to a painful halt as my hips wedged in the narrow opening. Water filled my ears and all sounds were muffled. Wriggling, I kicked my legs but it was hopeless.

Father was still thrusting me forwards and I fought frantically against him, trying to slide backwards. I was running out of breath and stars danced before my eyes. My hands flailed desperately in the muddy water and my hair wound itself around my face like tentacles.

If Father didn't pull me back, I'd drown. A furious rage rose up in me and gave me the strength to kick back at him, hoping that with my last breath at least I'd knock his teeth out. That last vicious kick twisted my wedged torso and at the same time Father gave me a violent shove.

There was a wrenching pain in my hip and I shot through the opening into the churning waters of the moat.

Chapter 38

My chest felt as if it would burst. I watched the bubbles of my last breath floating away as I drifted in the murky depths. Inside I was screaming *I don't want to die!* but at the very second I believed all hope had gone, I saw light above. I scissored my legs, all tangled up in my skirt, and then my face surfaced. A half-submerged shrub clawed at my cheek as I heaved in damp air.

I sank again. A current thrust me along and I thumped against something hard. Terror made me thrash my feet and I came, coughing, to the surface again. Langdon Hall loomed above and an expanse of black water lay ahead. The sky was darkening and still it poured with rain.

The water pushed me inexorably backwards and I grazed my heels on rough brickwork. The moat sucked me down and, when my foot disappeared into a void, I realised with horror that the current had carried me back to the very window I'd escaped from. I pushed against the wall with my feet, using the very last of my strength.

The water boomed and echoed in my ears as I bumped against the wall while muddy water swirled before my eyes. I was tired. So tired.

I floated face down. Something snagged painfully at my hair, jerking my head up. Water foamed around me and then I was on my back and rain pattered on my face. I breathed in great harsh gulps of air.

'Emilia!'

My eyes opened. I blinked at the rain-filled sky above as I was towed through the water by a pressure around my neck. Sleep ... I closed my eyes again.

My arms were hauled upwards and my legs slid along muddy ground.

'Emilia!'

Alessandro's face came into view above me. He smoothed the tangled hair off my face and covered my cheeks, my eyes, my nose with kisses while tears and rain dripped off his chin.

'Is it really you?' I whispered.

He scooped me up against his chest and buried his face in my neck. 'I thought I'd lost you!' His voice cracked as he rocked me against him.

I slid my arms around his shoulders.

Alessandro kissed my forehead again. 'I've been so angry with myself that I let you come here on your own.'

I leaned my forehead against his, my strength slowly seeping back. We were on the grass on the opposite bank of the moat. My hip ached. There was a long tear in my skirt and blood blossomed on the filthy muslin from a throbbing gash on my thigh.

'How did you come to be in the water, Emilia?'

I drew in my breath sharply. 'Father!' I tried to stand but Alessandro held me back.

'You must rest,' he said, 'and then I shall take you away from this place.'

I shook my head. 'You don't understand! Father will drown if we don't save him.'

Alessandro's shocked gaze never left my face until I finished recounting the story that tumbled out of me.

'So we must hurry and break through the gate into the chapel!'

'It's magnanimous of you to want to save your father after all he's done,' said Alessandro through gritted teeth.

'I must save the paintings,' I said, 'and Father must face justice.'

'What about Dolly?' Alessandro's lip curled contemptuously.

'I want him punished, too ... but we must send the gardener to close the sluices immediately.'

Alessandro pulled me to my feet and, hand in hand, we hurried off to seek assistance.

Mrs Bannister, after her first shocked reaction to us dripping on her polished floors, moved into action and set the scullery maid to boiling water in as many pans as would fit on the fire.

Mr Bannister sent for the gardener to turn off the sluices and Samuel and Robert went to fetch a crowbar to force open the gate to the chapel.

'Have you seen Mr Pemberton?' I asked Mr Bannister.

'Not since he arrived.'

'Will you find out where he is now? Take care, though. He may be dangerous.'

Mr Bannister sighed. 'A pretty pass that Sir Frederick's heir should conduct himself in such a fashion.'

I knew how shocked he'd be once he was appraised of the full extent of Father's perfidy.

'Go upstairs now, Miss Langdon,' said Mrs Bannister. 'Daisy will help you to wash and change and dress your wounds.'

'Later,' I said. 'Send for the parish constable, will you? Tell him to bring men with him. And take my aunt a message to say I'm perfectly all right and I'll come and see her when I can. We'll need candles to light the way.'

Robert reappeared, brandishing a crowbar.

Alessandro and I ran to the study with Samuel and Robert in tow. The door was locked.

'Look!' said Alessandro. He bent down and picked up a key from the floor.

'Dolly must have dropped it in his hurry to open the sluice gates,' I said.

Alessandro pushed the key into the lock. 'It's not the right one,' he said, examining the key and trying again. 'It's too small.'

There was no time to waste. 'Robert, force the door open!' I said.

His eyes widened.

'If you don't, I will.'

He grinned and forced the crowbar into the frame. The door swung open.

The bookcase was back in place and the three men stared blankly around the room.

I hurried to release the hidden bolts.

Alessandro drew in his breath as the bookcase hinged forward and exposed the door leading down to the chapel.

'Try the small key,' I said and smiled as the narrow door opened with a click. I started down the stairs. 'Father, we're coming!'

The river stench rose up to meet me and I gasped at the cold as I stepped into the chest-high water at the foot of the stairs.

Robert followed close behind, grimacing at the stink as the filthy water swirled around him. I held up my candle and he started to prise open the gate lock under the water.

I peered through the iron bars into the chapel. Several more of the candles had burned away.

Father waded through the water towards us holding a canvas above his head. 'Thank God!' he said. 'I thought you'd never come to let me out, Emilia.'

I noted he didn't profess any concern for me.

'Take this to safety,' he said, 'and I'll fetch the others.' He slid the painting through the bars into my hands.

'I'd have drowned if Alessandro hadn't pulled me out of the moat,' I told him.

'Never mind that now,' said Father. 'Get that gate open and help me!'

Robert forced open the lock with a cry of triumph.

Alessandro took the canvas from me.

'Careful!' said Father. 'It's a cartoon by Titian. Whatever you do, don't let it get wet.'

'Emilia, you've been in the water too long already,' said Alessandro. 'You'll catch a chill. Go upstairs now.'

'Don't you dare!' said Father. 'We need all hands.'

Alessandro balled his fists. 'Have you no care for your daughter? She nearly drowned!'

I caught Alessandro's sleeve and pulled him back. 'Later,' I said. I'd no intention of leaving until the precious paintings were safe but it warmed my heart to know that Alessandro, at least, cared for my health.

First of all came The Last Supper. Father and Alessandro carried it between them, resting it on their heads as they waded through the rising water. It was too heavy for me to handle safely on my own and Samuel helped me convey it upstairs. We propped it against the wall in the hall and Mrs Bannister stood by with clean muslin cloths to blot any wet fingerprints off the rest of the paintings as they arrived.

One by one, Alessandro and Father lifted the paintings off the walls, starting with the largest and the most valuable, and bringing them to me at the staircase. I carried them up to the doorway of the study and passed them to Mr Bannister. He carried them to the next person in the chain. All the while the water grew deeper in the chapel.

The candles began to flicker as they burned down. Soon there was so little light I feared for Alessandro and Father's safety. I called for more candles and waded into the chapel to replenish the sconces. Water lapped under my chin now and it was difficult for me to walk through it. Once the new candles were lit, I swam back to the stairs.

Alessandro handed me the Stubbs painting of a giraffe. 'The water is deep and your father and I are both tiring,' he said, wearily pushing a lock of hair from his eyes.

'Don't take any risks, Alessandro,' I said.

'Don't stop to talk!' shouted Father.

We brought out another five paintings but by then the water was so high that Alessandro and Father had to swim on their backs with the paintings held over their chests. The movement of the water as they splashed past the sconces extinguished yet more candles.

I shuddered as I peered into the increasing gloom of the chapel. The stinking water appeared black as Alessandro swam slowly back to me. I reached out to catch his collar and pulled him to the stairs. 'You're exhausted,' I said, noticing the wound on his shoulder was bleeding again. 'Come and rest.'

'Your father's bringing the last one,' he said, handing me the two miniatures of the Spanish Infanta.

I placed them on the stair above us as Alessandro dragged himself out of the water.

Several more of the candles flickered out and I squinted into the darkness to see Father swimming towards us. His breath came in rasping gasps as he clambered onto the stairs, his knees shaking.

I took the canvas from him. It was soaked.

Father collapsed in a half sitting, half lying position. 'That's the last of them.'

'Come upstairs,' I said. Now that the immediate crisis was over and the paintings were safe I was full of dread at what was to come next. I would have to ask the footmen to confine Father until the magistrate arrived.

'There are still the statues and the urns and the bronzes . . .'

I stared at him. 'But they're already underwater. They'll be safe until the flood goes down.'

'I'm not risking any harm coming to them!' He pushed himself off the steps and slid into the water.

'Father . . . come back!'

'No!' said Alessandro, gripping my wrist as I made to follow. 'It's too dangerous.'

Almost all the candles were submerged and the black water was only a foot below the ceiling. I shivered. Father didn't answer but I saw his dark head bobbing up and down like a seal's as he swam away.

At the far end of the chapel he disappeared under the water. A moment later I caught a glimpse of a white face coming towards us in the deepening gloom. The statue of Venus. There was a great deal of splashing as Father struggled to drag the marble statue along.

'He's lost his wits,' said Alessandro. 'It's far too heavy.'

As we watched, the statue slipped and sank. The surface of the water undulated and slapped against the walls. I waited for Father's head to reappear. It didn't.

'Where is he?' asked Alessandro, his voice tight.

My teeth chattered with cold and fear.

The water became still, all secrets hidden below its dark depths.

I couldn't bear it. I launched myself into the water and struck out towards the other end of the chapel. Alessandro's voice calling my name rang in my ears. I concentrated on reaching the place where I last saw my father. My head bumped against the ceiling and I couldn't touch the floor. And then I banged my knee on one of the statues and knew I must be in the right place. I took a breath and dived.

It was pitch black and I moved my hands before me. I touched several of the statues but each one was upright. I went to the surface to gulp another breath and dived again. This time I went deeper and my questing hands found Venus, lying on her side. Blindly, I ran my palms along the cold marble and paused as my fingers touched cloth. Scrabbling at it, I felt flesh underneath. Frantically, I tugged at the cloth but it was trapped under the statue. My chest was tight. I had to breathe!

Pushing myself upwards, I burst through the surface and gasped for air. I screamed and nearly choked when Alessandro swam into

353

me. He tried to pull me away but I fought him off. 'He's trapped! I have to go back.'

I dived again and felt Alessandro beside me in the black water. I found his hand and guided him back to where Father lay trapped. Together we heaved at the statue and rolled it to one side. We hauled at Father's clothing and towed him back towards the light.

Mr Bannister waded towards us and dragged Father out of the water.

I knew it was too late as, coughing and sobbing, I watched Mr Bannister and Alessandro pressing in vain on Father's chest.

At last Mr Bannister shook his head. 'I regret to say that life is extinct,' he murmured.

Alessandro carried me upstairs to the study. He placed me on Father's desk chair, chafed my hands and kissed me, murmuring words of endearment while I wept.

Chapter 39

It was still raining as the three of us stood by my father's open grave with the vicar. There were no other mourners. The story of Father's secret life as the Picture Frame Thief had spread faster than the plague and his neighbours and acquaintances had stayed away. I was glad of it since I didn't have to face them.

After Father drowned, once I'd stopped weeping from the shock, Alessandro took Shadow from the stables and galloped off after Dolly. From London he followed Dolly and Francis's trail as far as Dover, where he ascertained they'd taken the packet to France. Alessandro then returned to Langdon Hall to answer the magistrate's questions.

The vicar's voice droned on and Alessandro held my hand tightly as Father's coffin was lowered into the ground. Aunt Maude offered me a handkerchief. My tears were not for my father the man, but for the loss of my dream of having a parent to love and respect.

As soon as the service was over the vicar nodded to us without comment and took himself off, his duty done.

'Shall we go?' said Aunt Maude.

I took her arm and the three of us walked through the churchyard towards the waiting carriage.

Mr Digby, my father's lawyer, sat at his desk and sipped a glass of ratafia.

Gripping the arms of my chair, I waited for him to enlighten me on my financial situation.

He replaced the glass on the desk and smiled. 'My wife sends her good wishes and would be pleased if you and your aunt would call on her.'

A flush warmed my cheeks. Aunt Maude and I were tarnished by our connection with Father and there hadn't been a single caller at Langdon Hall since his death. 'Please tell her she is very kind,' I said. I liked Mrs Digby and was grateful to her for being prepared to support us but I wouldn't place her in an awkward position.

'On to matters of business,' said Mr Digby. 'In consultation with the magistrate, I employed an investigator, on behalf of the Langdon Hall Estate, to confirm Mr Fiorelli's account of events. Your father's heir, Mr Adolphus Pemberton, together with Mr Gregory, did indeed flee to France.'

'Did the investigator find them?' I asked.

Mr Digby shook his head. 'It can only be assumed Mr Pemberton intends to evade the justice that awaits him here. He would be extremely unwise to return.'

Dolly's actions had resulted in Sarah's and my father's deaths and he should pay the price. I pictured him squabbling with Francis as they were forced to lead an impoverished, vagabond life. That would be some small punishment but it angered me that, so far, he had escaped retribution. 'I have now been in communication with your father's second cousin, Mr Harvey,' continued Mr Digby. 'He's more than delighted to live at Langdon Hall and to manage the estate, an unthought of possibility for him. He is aware that he cannot inherit until seven years after Mr Pemberton's last sighting, when he can be declared legally dead. Mr Harvey intends to sell his trade premises and move his family here in two months' time.'

'I hope he'll be happy at Langdon Hall,' I said.

Mr Digby peered over his gold-rimmed glasses. 'I believe he and his wife and their eight children will find the Hall a considerable improvement on three rooms above a butcher's shop in Fetter Lane.'

'I'm sure they will,' I said, smiling slightly at the thought of Father turning in his grave.

'Mr Harvey asked me to send you his reassurances that if you and Miss Weston wish to remain at Langdon Hall or the townhouse in Grosvenor Street until you have finalised your plans, he will be pleased to allow it. He intends to retain the servants, too, should they wish to stay.'

I was relieved, knowing how much consternation there had been in the servants' hall. 'My aunt and I will be travelling to Italy with my fiancé as soon as I've finished sorting through my father's papers.'

Mr Digby nodded approvingly. 'And have you discovered any further information amongst Sir Frederick's effects regarding the origins of the stolen paintings?'

I shook my head. 'Not yet.' The paintings and sculptures had been removed to a place of safekeeping by the magistrate and the complicated job of returning them to their rightful owners had begun. I had personally undergone a humiliating meeting with Lord Beaufort to return all three miniatures.

'Your own situation is not entirely bleak,' said Mr Digby. 'Sir Frederick came to see me following your engagement ...' He paused. 'Perhaps I should say your *first* engagement. He made a new will, which still stands.'

'But the estate is subject to the entail?'

'Indeed. However, Sir Frederick's art collection ...' He coughed. 'That is, the collection he purchased *legally* over the years, with funds inherited from your grandmother and from his own dealings in art, was entirely his to gift to you.'

'I see.'

'The collection will be valued but, should you wish to sell it, there is likely to be sufficient to provide an income for the remainder of your life.'

I stared at him, dumbfounded.

'Furthermore,' said Mr Digby, leaning his elbows on the desk and steepling his fingers, 'there is your mother's jointure. This settlement was arranged on your mother's and father's marriage to provide an income for your mother, *or her surviving children*, should your father die first.' Mr Digby smiled. 'This sum, quite separate from the Langdon Hall Estate, is now due to you.'

A short while later Mr Digby ushered me out of his office.

Alessandro and Aunt Maude were laughing together as I joined them in the waiting room.

'There you are, dear,' said Aunt Maude with a smile. 'Your young man was telling me such an amusing story . . . ' She frowned. 'Is there something wrong?'

'No,' I said. 'Quite the contrary.'

Alessandro took my arm. 'Let's return to the carriage and you can tell us all about it.'

Dazed, I explained my good fortune as the carriage rolled away.

'It's no more than you deserve,' said Alessandro.

'But nothing will bring back your dear mother,' said Aunt Maude.

We sat in contemplative silence during the rest of the drive.

'I'm going to sort through Father's papers,' I said. 'I'm sick of the task and want to finish it today.'

'Let me help,' said Aunt Maude.

Alessandro settled down in the library to write a letter to his family and Aunt Maude and I went into the study. I opened the window to let out the smell of dank decay that still drifted up from below. The water had been pumped out of the chapel but it would take months to dry properly.

'Aunt Maude,' I enquired, while opening one of the desk drawers and lifting out a pile of loose papers, 'will you mind leaving England? Be honest now.'

'Mind?' She laughed. 'You cannot imagine how flattered I am that Alessandro has invited me to come to Pesaro with you. There's nothing for me here, without you.'

'Now I can afford to give you an income of your own,' I said. 'It won't be a great deal but enough for you to be independent. So if you don't want to go so far from home ...'

Her cheeks went bright pink and her mouth worked. 'Wherever you are *is* home to me, Emilia,' she said, her eyes glinting with unshed tears. 'But I thank you from the bottom of my heart.'

I hugged her, so grateful an aunt had come into my life. 'I suppose we'd better finish the task in hand.' I pushed a handful of papers towards her. 'We need to put unpaid bills in one pile, anything relating to paintings or art in another, and glance at the rest.'

An hour later I heard Aunt Maude take a gasping breath.

'What is it?'

Her face was bone white and she pressed a hand to her heart.

I sprang to my feet. 'Aunt Maude? Are you ill?'

She opened her mouth but didn't speak and then held out a paper to me with violently shaking fingers.

I took it from her and saw that it was a bill, dated July 1820. It read:

To the final quarterly sum for the continuing care and confinement of Rose Langdon.

To defraying the funeral costs of Rose Langdon.

I sank down on the desk chair and read it again while my pulse raced. 'I don't understand,' I said. 'My mother drowned herself ... Didn't she?'

'Frederick found her clothes by the river but her body was never found,' whispered Aunt Maude.

'But if she didn't drown herself ...' I crumpled the paper in my fist, suddenly breathless with rage. 'Father had her put away! He shut her up for *eighteen years* because she threatened to expose him as a thief. And he let me think she abandoned me because she didn't love me enough. If Father weren't already dead, I'd kill him with my bare hands.' Searing hatred for him ripped through me. He had lied to me, told me Mother was a thief and an adulteress, but far worse than that, he had deprived me of her love.

Alessandro pushed open the study door. 'I'm going to the post office ...' His voice trailed off when he saw me hunched over Father's desk. 'What is it, Emilia?'

I couldn't speak and Aunt Maude quickly explained what we had discovered.

Alessandro enfolded me in his arms with a muttered curse and I buried my face in his neck. He held me tightly and rubbed my back as I wept for the loss of my mother, knowing now for certain that she had always loved me.

Chapter 40

Italy

Alessandro and I waited in the *salone* of the Villa Vittoria. Late-September sunshine cast lozenges of light across the floor and I smiled, remembering my first visit here when I'd found Princess Caroline laughing uproariously while she played a boisterous game with Victorine. Even though she'd often been unhappy, the Princess always grasped life with both hands, taking small pleasures where she could find them.

Footsteps, light and quick, sounded in the hall and then the door burst open.

'Signor Fiorelli!' Victorine let go of Countess Oldi's hand and launched herself into Alessandro's arms, shrieking with delight as he whirled her around.

'I hope we find you well, Countess?' I enquired.

She shrugged. 'Life is very quiet at Villa Vittoria these days.'

Alessandro put Victorine down and bowed to the Countess.

'The Baron returned from hunting a moment ago,' she said, 'and wishes to speak to you, Signor Fiorelli.'

Victorine tugged at Alessandro's hand to gain his attention again.

'Look at you!' he said. 'You've grown up into a fine young lady since I saw you last.'

The child giggled. 'Why have you been away so long?'

'I went all the way to England to fetch Signorina Barton.'

'Mamma died in England,' said Victorine, her happy smile fading.

'We met her there,' I said, 'and she told me how much she missed you.'

'I miss her, too.' The corners of her mouth turned down.

Alessandro stroked her hair. 'But I have some happy news for you. Signorina Barton and I are to be married next week and we've brought you an invitation to our wedding.'

'We'd be delighted if you and the Baron would honour us with your presence also,' I said to Countess Oldi.

'I should like that. And will you be living in Pesaro?'

'I've been offered a position teaching at the University of Bologna but haven't yet decided to accept it,' Alessandro told her.

'Bologna is so far from your family!' the Countess exclaimed.

'I know,' he said unhappily.

The whole Fiorelli family had welcomed Aunt Maude and me with such warmth that it felt as if we were being wrapped in a soft blanket. I didn't want us to make our home too far away from them, either.

Footsteps rang out across the hall and the Baron strode in, carrying the pungent odour of hot horseflesh with him.

I'd forgotten how tall and handsome he was, with his glossy black hair and curled moustache, but he looked older and I fancied there were worry lines around his eyes.

'Papà!' cried Victorine. 'Signor Fiorelli and Signorina Barton are to be married and I'm invited to the wedding!'

'Then you shall have a new dress,' said the Baron. 'But now I wish to talk business to Signor Fiorelli. Go to the kitchen, my sweet. Faustina has baked almond cakes.'

After Victorine had pulled the Countess away with her, the Baron said, 'Congratulations on your engagement, Fiorelli.'

'Thank you,' said Alessandro, smiling at me.

'It's very strange to be here without the Princess,' I said.

A shadow passed over the Baron's face. 'At least her unhappiness is at an end,' he said. 'I heard you were back in Pesaro, Fiorelli, and I was going to ask you to come and see me.'

'Oh?' said Alessandro.

'I'm happy to tell you that Victorine's future is secure as she has inherited the Villa Vittoria.'

'The Princess loved her,' I said.

The Baron nodded. 'She always showed great compassion for children. Did you know that some years ago she adopted a number of orphans in London and had them trained in useful trades?'

'She spoke of that to me many times,' said Alessandro. 'She wanted to help the poor children of Pesaro, too.'

The Baron nodded. 'Although she made no provision in her will, I want her wishes to be honoured.'

I held my breath, hoping I'd correctly anticipated the drift of his conversation.

'As the Princess's steward,' the Baron continued, 'I managed her household finances. Her spending was sometimes impulsive. As a result of this I kept aside a sum for contingencies. I believe you, Signor Fiorelli, may be the right person to implement the Princess's wishes.'

'A school?' asked Alessandro breathlessly.

'Exactly!' said the Baron.

'She intended to give poor children a good education,' said Alessandro, his voice bubbling with enthusiasm, 'to help them make their way successfully in the world.'

'The sum available is enough to buy a house to convert into a school,' said the Baron, 'and to provide a home for the headmaster. The remaining funds, carefully invested, will allow salaries for two or three teachers. Is this project something you would be prepared to undertake?'

'Yes! Yes, it is!' Alessandro's eyes glowed. 'At least,' he glanced apologetically at me, 'I should like this very much if my fiancée is agreeable.'

I reached out to grasp his hand. 'It's a marvellous idea,' I said. 'But I have one proviso. The school must honour Princess Caroline's name.'

The Baron smiled. 'She would have liked that,' he said.

A week later afternoon sunshine bathed the wedding party in liquid gold. Mamma Fiorelli and her daughters had been cooking all week to prepare the sumptuous feast laid before us on tables decorated with wild flowers. There were vast platters of *frutti di mare*, chicken with lemon and garlic, bowls of glistening olives and salads, pyramids of crusty bread, and purple figs stuffed with mascarpone and drizzled with flower-scented honey.

We sat in the Fiorellis' garden listening to the happy chatter of the guests and I kept glancing at Alessandro, hardly able to believe my good fortune that he was now my husband. He squeezed my hand and light danced in his eyes as he gave me one of his infectious smiles.

Dear Aunt Maude sat beside me, her pinched, careworn expression replaced by a contented smile. All the people I loved were close by and I couldn't remember ever having felt so at peace.

Papà Fiorelli raised his wine glass for yet another toast. *'Per cent'anni!'* For a hundred years! The guests echoed him. 'If my son's marriage is only half as happy as mine,' he said, 'then he will be a very happy man indeed!'

I glimpsed Alessandro's mother, who was blushing like a bride herself.

Salvatore, one of my new brothers-in-law, called out, 'A kiss for the bride!'

My veil, lent by my mother-in-law, fluttered in the breeze and Alessandro laughed as it tickled his face. He kissed me and a roar of approval and clapping burst out around us.

'Hurrah for the newlyweds!'

Alessandro whispered in my ear, 'You're so beautiful you take my breath away.'

I touched Mother's pearls at my throat. I wore them with the lovely dress embroidered with roses that I'd worn for my first ball. How long ago it seemed!

'Let there be music!'

The musicians struck up on a mandolin and a violin.

'We must lead the dancing, Signora Fiorelli,' said Alessandro with a mischievous smile. He offered me his arm.

I touched Aunt Maude's cheek. 'Is it too noisy for you?'

Smiling, she shook her head. 'Music makes me feel alive again. Go and dance with your husband.'

Alessandro and I opened the dance and every touch of his hand on mine sent shivers up my spine.

'You must dance with every man who asks you,' he said, his gaze fixed on my mouth, 'and be aware they'll all kiss you to make me jealous.'

'I'll never give you cause to be jealous of another man,' I promised.

He smiled and kissed me slowly and thoroughly while the guests whistled.

Other couples joined us in the dance and the pace of the music quickened. Alessandro's father came to claim me and whirled me around as fast as a man half his age would have done.

The Baron took his place and was light on his feet as he moved expertly through the steps. 'How the Princess loved to dance!' he exclaimed.

I fancied there was a wistful tone to his voice. I glanced over his shoulder and missed a beat when I saw Aunt Maude dancing sedately with Papà Fiorelli. Her face was flushed and her eyes bright. Breathless, I danced with all Alessandro's brothers, even little Alfio, and then, one by one, the rest of the male guests.

Then Alessandro came to claim me again and we laughed as Victorine and Alfio spun in circles around us, showering us with rose petals.

The sun was slipping down behind the hills when, at last, we returned to the table, where Cosima sat with Aunt Maude, teaching her to speak Italian.

As it grew dark, Salvatore and Jacopo went around the garden with burning tapers and lit the myriad candles hanging from the trees in glass jars. The flickering flames reminded me of the fireflies that had enchanted us in the avenue of cypresses at Villa Vittoria so long ago.

Alessandro and I exchanged a few words with every guest, receiving their good wishes.

Later, as the garden became illuminated by moonlight, Mamma Fiorelli came to see us with her little grandson Enzo asleep on her shoulder. 'It's time for you to go,' she said. 'And don't worry, Emilia, I will look after your aunt. Tonight is for your husband.'

I hugged her. 'We'll come and take Aunt Maude home with us tomorrow.'

Mamma Fiorelli kissed Alessandro and he hugged her tightly.

The young men in the party began to whoop with exuberant high spirits.

Alessandro and I kissed Aunt Maude and said our goodbyes to the older guests.

A violinist, playing a lively jig, led the noisy procession out of the Fiorelli house and down the lane. Alessandro's friends sang at the tops of their voices, banging wooden spoons upon saucepans and setting off firecrackers as we danced along until we reached our temporary home on the cliff overlooking the sea.

Alessandro lifted me in his arms and carried me over the threshold to the accompaniment of loud cheers and whistles. Laughing, he pushed a group of revellers out of the door when they tried to follow us inside.

'Goodnight, my friends,' he said. 'Go back to the party and finish the wine.'

One by one they went off unsteadily down the lane, still singing. As the merry racket faded away, Alessandro closed the front door.

All at once it was quiet.

'Alone at last!' he said. Gently, he took me in his arms and rested his forehead against mine. 'Did I tell you how beautiful you are today?'

'Only about a hundred times.' I smiled into the dark.

'Not enough then,' he said, nuzzling my neck.

Shivers of desire and apprehension ran down my back.

He lifted off my wedding veil and pulled the pins from my hair, allowing my curls to tumble around my shoulders. 'My Botticelli angel.' His breath stirred against my cheek. Sliding his hands under my hair, he kissed me and when we drew apart, my heart was singing.

'Let's go upstairs,' he whispered.

We stopped to kiss again on the top stair, a long slow kiss that made me melt inside.

In the bedroom the shutters were open and the bed was bathed in a shaft of silvery moonlight. I hung back, excited but also a little afraid.

Alessandro sensed my nervousness. He drew me past the bed to the window and opened the casements. A fresh, salty breeze stirred my hair as we stood, hand in hand, listening to the soothing ebb and flow of the sea on the sand below.

'If it hadn't been for Princess Caroline, we might never have met,' said Alessandro quietly. 'And a year ago I thought I'd lost you. I've never been so miserable.' He pulled me closer to his side. 'But, tonight, here we are at the beginning of the rest of our lives together

367

and I'm filled with such joy and thankfulness I think my heart might burst.'

I watched him wipe away a tear and loved him all the more for his display of emotion. 'I loved you from the beginning,' I said. 'But it frightened me. I thought I'd been abandoned by those I loved and that perhaps I wasn't worthy of lasting love.'

'I promise to love you forever,' he said, cupping my face. 'Even when we argue, as married couples do, I'll never abandon you. Never, never!'

As I looked deep into his eyes something shifted inside me, as if a key had unlocked my heart. All tension drained away and I was filled with exultation. *This* was how it felt to trust and love another so absolutely. *This* was how it felt to be whole.

'Emilia?'

'Yes,' I said. I kissed him, gently at first, but then with rising passion. I slid my hands inside his shirt and shivered as I touched his firm, warm skin.

His lips were hot and urgent as he fumbled with my buttons and ribbons and finally freed me from my dress, shift and stockings. He lifted me in his arms and carried me to the bed.

Afterwards, Alessandro caressed my hair as we lay entwined together in the moonlight. 'My wife,' he murmured sleepily. 'Forever.'

'Forever,' I whispered.

He curled himself protectively around my back. And then he was asleep.

I nestled into the curve of his body, revelling in the silken touch of our naked skin. My husband's sleeping breaths echoed the peaceful murmur of the sea outside and very soon my own breathing rose and fell in the same rhythm.

Historical Note

Caroline of Brunswick 1768 – 1821

Whilst researching *The Dressmaker's Secret*, I went to Pesaro and walked up Monte San Bartolo to look for Villa Vittoria, visited the harbour, dipped my fingers in the fountain in the Piazza del Popolo and swam in the Baia Flaminia. All the while I had the feeling Caroline was looking over my shoulder and smiling at the places she had loved.

In 1794 Princess Caroline of Brunswick was twenty-six years old and longing for marriage and children. In London, George, the Prince of Wales, enjoyed an extravagant lifestyle that had plunged him into severe debt amounting to £630,000 (equivalent to fifty-nine million pounds today). His father, George III, urged the Prince to marry, since Parliament would then increase his annual allowance to £65,000. Reluctantly, he agreed. The King approved of the match to Caroline since she was not only his sister's daughter but also a Protestant.

The cousins had never met and Lord Malmesbury was sent to Brunswick as the Prince's envoy to arrange the marriage treaty. He reported that blonde and blue-eyed Caroline had *'a pretty face and tolerable teeth*'. Her short figure was '*not graceful*' though she had a '*good bust*'. Lord Malmesbury was, however, perturbed by her free and easy manner and over the following months made attempts to prepare her for the cool formality of the English court. It was a challenging task. The Princess was impulsive, lively and indiscreet, careless about her toilette, laughed too loudly and enjoyed, perhaps too much, the company of men.

The Prince of Wales appointed his current favourite mistress, Lady Jersey, as Caroline's lady-in-waiting. Lady Jersey was to meet her on her arrival in Greenwich but, in the first of many such snubs to the Princess, kept her waiting most of the day.

The Prince and Princess met for the first time on 5 April 1795, three days before their wedding. Caroline wore an unflattering dress that Lady Jersey provided for her, after persuading her that it was more suitable for the presentation than her own had been. Caroline knelt to the Prince, who then formally embraced her. He immediately recoiled and called for his equerry to bring him a glass of brandy. Without another word, he left the room. Caroline, affronted by the Prince's behaviour, commented that he was very fat and not as handsome as his picture. Later, it transpired that Lord Malmesbury's attempts to teach the Princess to be particular about her personal hygiene had failed.

The wedding was as disastrous as the first meeting. The Prince of Wales was agitated and almost unable, or unwilling, to utter his responses during the ceremony, and by the evening had consumed so much brandy he collapsed on the floor by the fireplace in the bridal chamber. Despite this, nine months later Caroline gave birth to Princess Charlotte.

The unhappy marriage was made worse by the malicious gossip spread by Lady Jersey, who poisoned the Royal Family against Caroline. Regardless of his own infidelities, the Prince was desperate to divorce his wife but the government wouldn't sanction it without proof of her adultery. Three days after Princess Charlotte's birth the

Prince drew up a will leaving all his property to Roman Catholic commoner Maria Fitzherbert, whom he had married illegally and without the essential royal permission ten years before. He referred to Maria as '*the wife of my heart and soul*', and to '*the woman who is call'd the Princess of Wales*', he bequeathed one shilling.

The humiliations continued and, deeply hurt, Caroline reacted with increasingly reckless behaviour. In 1796 the papers carried reports that Lady Jersey had intercepted and opened letters written by Caroline to her mother, in which she made rude comments about the Royal Family and referred to the Queen as '*Old Stuffy*'. The press took Caroline's side against the already unpopular Prince of Wales. They called for Lady Jersey's dismissal as lady-in-waiting and were critical of the Prince's spiteful attitude to his wife. The couple separated but the cruelties continued when Caroline was denied proper access to her daughter or an allowance or home suitable to her position.

Caroline rented a house in middle-class Blackheath, where she held some kind of a court of her own, encouraging politicians and society figures to visit. She hosted eccentric and sometimes wild parties, entertaining visitors while she sat on the ground eating raw onions or romped on her knees on the carpet with Princess Charlotte. She indulged in flirtations with a number of her guests, though her behaviour was somewhat sobered by the knowledge that adultery, in her case, was a treasonable offence. Her manner was extraordinarily open and confiding and she formed many intense, but often short-lived, friendships without regard for whether or not they were appropriate.

During the following years she became the protector of seven or eight orphan children, finding them good foster homes and supervising their education. Caroline's fondness for children and for irresponsible jokes led to a national scandal. She adopted a baby, William Austin, but teased her friend Lady Douglas by pretending that she had given birth to the boy herself. Later, in 1806 and following a quarrel between the two women, Lady Douglas spread vindictive rumours about the purportedly illegitimate baby. At once a secret committee was set up by the King, the so-called Delicate Investigation, but, to the Prince of Wales's chagrin, it was proved William Austin was not Caroline's natural child. She, however, was condemned for her 'loose behaviour with men' and left with a stain upon her character.

In 1814, with Napoleon apparently a spent force, a service of thanksgiving was held at St Paul's, followed by celebrations hosted by the Prince Regent and attended by royalty, peers of the realm and ministers of state. Caroline was incensed at being excluded and the press considered such treatment of her as shameful. The populace cheered her in the streets and at the opera. Exhausted by the continuing humiliations and political and financial wrangling of life in England, Caroline, now forty-six years old, decided to leave the country. She visited her family in Brunswick and thence travelled to Italy, appointing a lady's maid, Louise Demont, in Geneva on the way. Upon leaving Milan she hired a courier, thirty-year-old Bartolomeo Pergami. In Florence, in an attempt to assimilate the Italians, whom she had grown to love, Caroline bought a black wig and darkened her eyebrows.

Pergami became indispensable to her and was always attentively by her side. Following a sojourn at Villa d'Este by Lake Como, they set off on extensive travels. Caroline elevated Pergami to the position of chamberlain and purchased land and a title for him before they travelled back to Italy, eventually arriving in Pesaro in 1818. The facts of her life from 1819 to her death on 7 August 1821 are outlined in *The Dressmaker's Secret* except for her interactions with Emilia, whose fictional story is woven throughout.

Following her death, Caroline's body was conveyed to Brunswick Cathedral, where one hundred maidens carrying lighted candles lined the aisles. As her coffin was placed in its vault a prayer was said and then the maidens extinguished the candles.

Caroline was her own worst enemy and impossibly unsuited to life as a royal princess. Although her common touch was popular with the people, her sometimes outrageous behaviour made her a painful burr in the side of the Royal Family. Despite that, she was courageous and loving. She tried to live for the moment, squeezing as much joy as possible into a life led under difficult and often extremely unfair circumstances.

Further Reading

If you wish to find out more about Caroline of Brunswick, I suggest the following books:

The Unruly Queen by Flora Fraser
Rebel Queen by Jane Robins
Caroline by Thea Holme